WOVEN SOULS

Kris Leigh

ISBN: 979-8-9892514-0-7

For all who nourish the whimsy of the childlike soul.

CHAPTER ONE

My best friend had a dark secret, and it changed the shape of my life the day he was born.

"What are you doing?"

Startled, I relaxed my grip on the snow globe and dislodged my teeth from the groove they'd made in my bottom lip. Wow. Didn't even know I'd been biting it. Plus, where had he come from? "You scared me. Didn't hear you come in."

"That's obvious. What are you trying to do, exactly?" Jansen knelt in the cramped coat closet beside me, so his knees prodded against the cardboard box between us. Musty coats provided a low and swaying ceiling. "What is all this stuff?"

"My mom sent me in after that dish she has with the stars on it. Or is it stripes? Anyway, I couldn't find it, but look at what I did find. Do you remember this?" I handed him the snow globe.

"Sure, you got it for Christmas when we were, what, six? But why crush it?" His voice came out hushed, dampened by the small space. Creaky floorboards punctuated his sentences as he shifted.

I pulled my knees into my chest, rubbing them for warmth. The air vent right outside the closet door tickled the erect little hairs on my bare arms. "I wasn't crushing it. Just trying to get the snow to jump around the way *you* used to. I could sit for hours trying to make it dance like that. But I've never been able to work it."

With a slight hesitation, Jansen glanced toward the patio beyond our family room, where our families congregated for a Fourth of July celebration and my sixteenth birthday. Me being a proud holiday baby and all.

He grasped the globe by its glass dome, and within seconds, it glowed as red as hot coals in the diffused light beneath the coats. But how? Snow globes didn't work like that. Small bubbles formed at the bottom of the scene and then rose to the top, looking like the water boiled. But of course, that was impossible. The snow danced in a blizzard around the miniature cabin inside, the flakes whirling to hide the tiny Santa in his sleigh on the roof.

I stared, enchanted. "How do you do that?"

Before he could respond, I grabbed for the globe. Just as he'd always done when we were children, he held it overhead, out of reach.

"Aw, come on," I said. "Seriously, how do you do that?"

But he didn't listen. Instead, he grasped the base, hovering one hand over the sphere of the globe. "Wait, wait. One more trick, my impatient friend."

Impossibly, he made the glass glow a striking shade of blue that lit up the cozy space before tossing it back to me.

My heart kicked a warning as I caught the toy, but nothing happened. Not even after I shook it. Nothing. Maybe it was broken—but no, he'd just made it work. I shook it, and the snow swirled in a storm around the miniature cabin. What was wrong with this thing? I held it up to the light, angling it this way and that. Nothing. An ordinary snow globe.

Could it be the person who held it?

No, that was ridiculous. "Did you take up magic at some point, and never told me?"

He scoffed, but a shadow crossed his face, like an idea. "Just something I picked up from Uncle Fred."

Frustrated, I tossed it back into the box right on top of a worn-out baseball glove. Jansen pulled the container toward himself to sift through old, forgotten items with me: A Rubik's cube missing at least three bricks, a Walkman whose cassette tape had gotten jammed inside, Atari game cartridges, and a Magic 8-Ball whose messages didn't float quite flat.

The back patio door opened before we got very far. It was my mom, and the whoosh of her entry brought with her the smoky sweet smell of barbecue chicken from the grill, making my mouth water.

She got into the fridge and glanced my way. "What happened to you?" she asked as she pulled out her homemade potato salad. "Couldn't you find the dish?"

"The one with stripes on it, right?"

She kicked the refrigerator door closed using her bare foot. "Honestly, Ellie. It's blue with white stars. Jansen, maybe…"

"I'll help her find it, Miss Marie. I know the one you're talking about."

My mom slipped out the back, throwing a grateful glance at Jansen and a split-second glower at me.

Jansen stood with his familiar, remarkable grace. All the other boys who'd been sophomores last year had gone through awkward, lanky stages, but not him. Just getting off the ground was something he did with impressive agility. He did it in one swift movement, from sitting to standing, as effortless as his next breath.

Though he offered me a hand, it wouldn't help me crawl out of the closet. So I struggled to my feet and started toward the kitchen, but he gripped my elbow, pulling me to him.

"Wait, I have something for you. I wanted to give it to you before the others got here."

A present? I held my hands out with excitement. "What is it?"

Jansen's gifts were always unique and often exotic things

his uncle brought back from his travels around the world. I'd never met his Uncle Fred, but the man had a knack for finding rare items. The last gift had been hand-painted stacking dolls from Russia. Before that, he'd given me an intricate string art design of a baobab tree, hand strung in Africa.

Jansen shifted his weight to one foot and leaned against the wall. Just when I thought I'd have to wrestle him for it, he rooted through his pocket, pulling out a small box wrapped in light sky-colored paper tied with a delicate, not-quite-perfect little bow. With long, deft fingers, he tried to fix the bow, damaged from riding around in his pocket.

It wasn't the packaging that mattered. Not really. It was the excitement of the unknown, the anticipation of a never-before-seen treasure.

Before it found my hand, Jansen snarled, retracted the gift, and tucked it into his pocket again. I started to tell him to give it back, but the front door opened before the words were out.

"Andrew," I said instead, annoyed at our neighbor who had walked through the entrance. "Come on in."

Andrew had moved to our small Ohio town of about 20,000 residents when he and my brother, Tyler, were in the fourth grade. Since then, living next door to my family, with only a row of hydrangea bushes between us, they'd been together more by chance than choice. He was the yin to my brother's yang. Tyler loved fishing, hiking, canoeing, and generally getting dirty, whereas Andrew sneezed at the word "outside." Almost literally. Tyler was a closet slob. While he was well-kempt, thanks to our mom, his bedroom was just an extension of the county dump. Andrew's parents were minimalists, and he didn't seem to rebel at following in their footsteps.

Jansen slipped his sunglasses from their perch over his forehead to the bridge of his nose. "Ever hear of knocking?"

What was it with these two?

Andrew had been a long-time fixture in our home, and though they'd never hung out, he and Jansen used to be cordial. That had changed when my latest boyfriend, Carl, had graduated and we'd parted ways. For some reason, Andrew had found himself the target of Jansen's glares and bad humor ever since.

Never a fan of Carl's, Andrew had made sure to seek me out, making certain I had someone to come to about the breakup. When he called to talk to my brother, if I answered the phone first, he asked how I was doing before asking me to put Tyler on. Also, when he popped over, he looked for me in the basement or the pool to give a quick wave before dashing off to find Tyler. Though he seemed nice to me, Jansen had taken such an abrupt disliking to him that lately, Andrew had kept his distance when he was around.

Andrew twirled his own sunglasses in his long fingers and shifted his sea-blue eyes from me to the door and back again. "Oh, uh… sorry. It's just, well…"

"It's alright," I said. "We were expecting you. Tyler's in the back."

"Your brother. Right." He stood there a moment, shifting his weight from one foot to the other, his eyes on me. "Are you coming swimming?"

I inspected my attire. Yep, my navy, spaghetti-strapped bikini was still in place.

"That was the plan." How had he missed my scantily clad body? Was I just one of the guys around here?

He rubbed his chin, pink with razor burn, and winced. "Sorry. I'll just go out and see Tyler. Where did you say he was?"

"In the back," I repeated haltingly.

"Right. I'll see you two out there then?"

Jansen lifted his squared jaw, his face frozen, neither smiling nor frowning, his eyes locked on Andrew's.

Poor Andrew felt the heat, too. Must have the way he cleared his throat, not menacingly as Jansen had, but nervously. He tucked his sunglasses into his ash-brown hair, always finger-fluffed just so, and exited through the back door. Unfortunately, a kitchen chair had been left out, and he stumbled over it in his retreat. Andrew continued to bear the weight of Jansen's unrelenting scrutiny long after the door slid closed.

I waited for his attention to find me again, hands on hips, an icy glare waiting for him.

Instead of looking at me right away, he stared at the back door before at last pulling his hand from his pocket, clutching his gift. He'd seen me peripherally, though. Must have because he didn't even flinch when he said, "What?"

"That was rude."

"I wasn't trying to be." His shoulder shrug said otherwise. "Is he staying for fireworks?"

"Yes. Is that a problem?"

"No… It just seems like he's been here a lot lately."

"He *is* Tyler's closest friend."

Jansen brushed his free hand over my face, a sweet gesture he often did, the way one might tweak a nose or kiss a forehead. As often happened when he did that, it was as though he swept away my worries. "Are you going to accept my apology?"

Of course, he knew I would. So, I returned his little half-grin.

He raised his sunglasses to sit in his short, raven-black tresses. "Did you invite anyone?"

"Just you. Why? Was there someone you were hoping for? Clara, perhaps?"

Jansen snorted. "I hope you're joking."

"Maybe she won't be so bad this year."

He arched one eyebrow, a look that said "be serious" and "I can't stand her" at the same time.

"No, seriously." I laughed. "She's not so bad. It's just she was new last year."

"Yes, and?"

"And… I think she was trying too hard."

He chortled through his nose and sat on the armrest of the couch with an enviable air of confidence. "It wasn't because she was new. She just wanted to hook up with me."

"You didn't like her even a little bit?"

"She's not my type." He had an edge to his tone, his good humor slipping. In an obvious move to change the topic, he tucked his sunglasses into his pocket and tried to hand the gift to me.

"What about her isn't your type? Her long, wavy, blonde hair?" I fiddled with the bow as if one of Clara's curls. "Her perfect body? All the other guys are into her."

I'd gone too far. His eyes snapped to mine, locking me into the black depths of them. The room even heated a degree, like it always seemed to when he got angry.

"Her body is not perfect." He pushed the words out through his teeth.

"The other guys think it is. You're the only one I know who's immune to her charm."

Jansen said nothing but took my hand and placed the gift in it. "Open it."

Fine. I'd teased enough, so I pulled at the little bow. It came apart in my hand. The real difficulty was undoing the tape, which he'd gone overboard on, and I had to fight with it a little.

"Let me help," he said.

"No, it's my present."

After winning the great tape battle, I wadded the paper into a tight ball, held it in my fist, and lifted the box's tiny blue lid. What was it? I peeled back the thin white tissue—ah. There it was. A necklace unlike anything I'd ever seen.

"Oh." I drew out the sound like a musical note. It slipped from its box, and I weaved my fingers through its delicate, double chain. The gem was oval-shaped, with soft points on each end. A cat's eye. Its color was that of a blue sapphire. The horizontal white dividing line down its center gave the illusion of opening. A bright inner light trying to escape. "It looks like it's winking."

"It's called a Chrysoberyl Cat's Eye. That's the name of the gem. This one was found in a marketplace in Sri Lanka."

"It's beautiful."

"Thought you might like it. I asked Uncle Fred to pick up a necklace for you on his trip. Wanted something unique and beautiful."

"It's both. Thank you."

"I'll put it on you."

The moment he clasped its chain, a spark of energy zipped through me and something like champaign bubbles shimmied down my spine.

He tapped both my shoulders, nudging me to turn. "Here, let me see it." A smile spread as he lifted the Chrysoberyl to inspect, but jerked back as if startled.

"What's the matter?"

"How long have you had this?"

Had what? I followed his finger, crossing my eyes to do it, where he pointed out a small blemish I always thought looked like a starburst scattering freckles everywhere. I couldn't see it without tucking my chin tight. "What, this? It's a birthmark."

I'd had it my entire life. And barely dressed as I so often was with him around the pool, I was a little offended that he hadn't spotted it before now.

"What's a girl got to wear to be seen around here? First, Andrew doesn't notice me in a bikini—"

"He noticed," Jansen said with an edge.

I ignored him. "Now you're telling me you've never seen this gigantic birthmark?"

"I've seen it." He grimaced in that way men do when they think you're being ridiculous. "And it's not that big. Is it just me, or does it glow?"

"Glow? I think that's just you, bub. Bet giving Clara a necklace would make her glow."

"Clara? How'd you go from your birthmark to Clara?"

"Or is she more of a bracelet girl?"

Jansen's fingers slipped, and the Chrysoberyl dipped to rest colder than ice between my breasts, shooting a crazy, spine-tingling, hair-raising shudder to my core. Whoa. It's how I knew I had him, too, because Jansen never slipped.

I turned away from him to dig the pendant out. Gosh, I'd have to shorten this chain. "No, definitely a bracelet."

"What are you going on about?"

"She would never need to cover up her perfectly, unblemished chest."

He spun me around, and jeez, his bared chest was right at nose level. I didn't know if it was his earthy scent or if I grew dizzy from the spin, but a breath of charged air stalled between us.

"Would you stop?" He emphasized the admonishment with his hands clamped on his hips. The wrinkled brow, the darting eyes, the subtle twitching of not just his lips, but his chin as well… He wanted to say more, but held back.

Time to let him off the hook. I tousled the finger-length waves on his head, a higher stretch than it had been at the end of the previous school year. How much had he grown in two short months?

"What?" he asked darkly.

"Oh, nothing." I laughed as I darted out of Jansen's reach toward the back door just before calling over my shoulder, "Clara's going to love what the summer's done to you."

He didn't follow me out, which was good because I thought he'd wrestle me for that. And in my skimpy bikini? What was I thinking?

Hot air hugged me the instant I stepped outside, the humidity laying on me like a damp blanket; one I welcomed for the moment. Bikinis are designed for lounging in the sun, not air conditioning.

Under the shade of the covered patio, my dad worked over the grill, spreading barbecue sauce over chicken legs that sizzled when drips hit the burning coals. He wore khaki dad-shorts—too wide and too long—and held a barbecue brush in one hand, a beer in the other. It took rising high onto my tip-toes, but I kissed his cheek.

"Hey, baby girl. Happy birthday!"

I was so glad to see him. Yeah, he tried to arrange his calendar around important days like our birthdays, but it didn't always work out. He was a captain for a major airline and at the mercy of scheduling. Mom joked he was married to his job, and in some ways, that was true. It's just that when he was home, it was with his full, doting attention.

Outside of the shaded patio, our moms lounged in the sun on reclining chairs my mom had purchased the week before. Jansen had never known his father, but the two moms had been best friends since college. Miss Kate had come for the day, relaxing now with her fish-print beach towel rolled up beneath her neck.

When my shadow fell over her, she opened one eye from under her oversized hat. "Good afternoon, birthday girl."

"Back at'cha." Wait, that didn't work. I waved, brushing the silly retort away. "You look comfy."

"I am, thank you. It's a beautiful day for hanging around the pool."

I opened the cooler, picked out a soda, and popped open the can. "Any day is a beautiful day for hanging around the pool."

"True. Toss me one of those, would you?"

I plunged my hand back into the ice and tossed a can of lemonade to Miss Kate.

"Thanks, kid."

My mom blocked the sun with her hand and peered up from her lounge. "Please tell me you found the bowl."

"Oh, Mom, I'm sorry." I turned to head inside and ran smack into Jansen, who had come out so quietly I hadn't heard him.

"Here, Miss Marie," he said with a smirk, staring down at me. "I found it."

"Jansen, bless you!"

Miss Kate took the bowl from him and passed it to my mom. "How has your birthday been so far? Any presents yet?"

"Yes, in fact." I gave Jansen's warm hand a quick squeeze, a sort of thank you for the present. My other fingers fiddled with the pendant around my neck. "Jansen gave me this, but you probably already saw it. Uncle Fred picked it up on one of his excursions. Sri Lanka, wasn't it?"

Miss Kate grasped the jewelry for a better look, and her face turned as white as the vinyl fencing encircling the pool deck. Her glass tipped, spilling lemonade down the front of her cover-up.

"Are you alright?" I snatched the half-empty can and put it on the small glass table. When I dabbed at her with napkins, the familiar scent of lavender wafted over me. She didn't move to help, but sat statuesque in her lounge chair.

My mom stirred a crock of baked beans, eyeing us. "Why Kate, what is it?"

Miss Kate stopped me with a firm hand on my arm, and she fingered the pendant as gently as if it might crumple in her hands. "Where did you say you got this?"

"From me," Jansen said. "You know, from Uncle Fred."

"He thought this was an appropriate gift?"

She was blowing this out of proportion. Maybe she thought Uncle Fred had spent too much money. It couldn't be just because Jansen had given me jewelry. He'd done that before. In fact, I'd collected a butterfly pendant, an infinity bracelet, and a delicate ankle bracelet made of small hearts from him.

"Kate," Jansen said. He and Charlie both called their mom by her first name, unless they were really angry. Then she was "mother." "I think you're overreacting. You could rein it in a bit."

She grimaced and dropped the pendant on my chest. "Me, rein it in? You don't understand."

"Then perhaps you could explain it to me *later*." His words were like ice as he glowered at her.

Kate broke eye contact with her son, picked up her lemonade, took a swig, and rolled it around on her tongue before swallowing. Only the intermittent trill of a sparrow interrupted the awkward silence. She took another sip, and still nobody spoke.

"Ellie." She set her drink down with a clack of plastic on glass. "Who else is coming to this little party of yours?"

"No one." I shifted my weight from foot to foot, staring at my toes as if they were works of art worthy of great study. "I think we're all here."

Miss Kate fingered her jaw, deep in thought. "So, you've only invited Jansen?"

"And Andrew," I said.

"But *you* didn't invite him."

"No, Tyler did."

The concrete deck heated beneath my bare feet. I could empathize with the pieces of chicken on the grill. Enough already. Why was she grilling me?

"And there's no one else?"

"Charlie." I glanced at Jansen's brother who swam in the pool. As if he'd heard me from so far away, he inclined his head and returned my gaze. Though he couldn't have over the din of splashing and playful banter between Tyler and Andrew.

"So, you've invited two of your brother's friends to *your* birthday party."

"Kate," my mom said, "leave her be. These are the friends she feels most comfortable with."

"Besides," I said, "it isn't a birthday party. It's the Fourth of July."

"You should make some girlfriends." It wasn't a suggestion. In fact, it sounded very much like a command.

Charlie came, laying his enormous, cold, wet hand on my sun-ripened shoulder, which made me jump and belt out a peel of laughter. It was just so cold.

"Come on over and join us in the pool." He jabbed his mom on the arm and guided me toward the water. "It's awfully hot out here."

Before Charlie could lead me away, Miss Kate grabbed my arm. "Be wary."

What an odd thing to say. She could have said, "Be careful" or "Be good." Maybe, "Have fun." But no, she said, "Be wary." Guarded? Watchful? Is that what she meant?

Be wary.

CHAPTER TWO

It was a good idea Charlie had when he pulled me over to the pool. The water was cool and refreshing. Exactly what I needed. The sloshing, splashing water soothed my nerves and washed away Kate's ominous message.

Jansen and I hung off the edge while Charlie, Andrew, and Tyler shot baskets in the water. When the ball ricocheted toward me, I snatched it up.

"Charlie!" I yelled, simultaneously throwing it at the buckeye-brown curls covering the back of his head.

With no warning, and without looking, he reached up, palm facing me, and caught the ball from behind.

"Whoa," Andrew said, awestruck.

As if he hadn't just done the impossible, Charlie threw it to Andrew, who, jaw still at the bottom of the pool, fumbled it. After swallowing to regain his composure, he gripped it in both palms and commentated as he shot from mid-pool. "He shoots… He scores! The crowd goes wild!"

I cupped my hands around my mouth as an impromptu bullhorn. "Way to go, Andrew!"

The ball plopped into the water, floating toward Jansen, who palmed it with a thump. Not to be outdone by Charlie, he turned his back to the hoop, and made to shoot from behind, but I knocked it from his fingertips.

With barely a lift of his shoulders, not even a shrug, he leaned against the pool's edge, an easy indifference encasing him like smoke and mist. "What?"

"What do you mean 'what?'" I scolded. "Just let him have his moment."

He palmed the ball and tossed it toward Tyler. "Yeah, well, I could've made it."

"Could've? More like would've."

It was true enough, and he smirked as he resumed his casual wall-lean. "So long as you know."

"Gabriella." My mom's voice startled me so close to my ear. She squatted just behind us at the side of the pool, holding out a tube of sunblock. "Did you put any of this on?"

"Mom!" I said, with a hard to miss leave-me-alone whine.

"That's a 'no.' Honestly, everyone needs sunscreen, but with that hair of yours and that skin?"

She had a point, but I wrinkled my freckled nose, anyway. "I thought you liked my freckles."

"God got carried away with his stardust, pretty girl, and sun-roasted stardust turns into—"

"The devil's blisters. I know!"

My wavy, strawberry blonde hair came with about a million freckles. Heck, if you counted my neck, chest, and arms, I had at least three million. Not the darling little freckles that dot cute button noses, either. No, I had an all-out mud-splattering of them; or, as my mom called them, "stardust."

"Got it." Jansen took the bottle from her.

After he squeezed a dollop into my hand, I slathered it onto my cheeks and neck in ten seconds flat. "Done."

Jansen scrubbed his chin. "Were you going for white clown face?"

Rather than stick out my tongue, I squinted and pressed near him instead, inviting him to rub the greasy slop into my skin. Always attentive to the smallest of details, my friend rubbed both his thumbs along my cheekbones and then over my nose.

"Press your lips together." He spread it around my mouth, toward my ears, and finally, my neck.

Eyes closed, I heard the gloppy sound of shaking lotion

and then a squirt.

"Turn."

I did and pulled my hair forward, exposing more of my back, at which point he loosed a sharp breath. One that suggested he tried to power the sun.

"You okay?" I asked.

"Yeah, sure. Just…hungry, all of the sudden."

Hungry? Was that all? Because it sounded like—

Then I forgot the epic sigh as his hands glided over my shoulders. He used circular motions to spread it around and around, making certain he'd thoroughly rubbed it in before traveling between my shoulder blades. Down my arms, down my back, all with equal attention. How wonderfully warm. Unnaturally so, like his body magically heated the sunscreen.

"You're perfect," he said on a breath that seemed to stick in his throat. He cleared it and gestured to his own chest. "Though you might wanna…"

"Got it." I smiled, holding my hand out for a glob.

"You should get out and put this on the rest of you. You know, dry off a little."

While I rubbed the oily gunk into my chest, Charlie swam behind my legs undetected, and shot me into the air before I knew what happened. We'd done this hundreds of times, but since he'd caught me off guard, I landed in the water with a squeal. From the depths, I thrust off the bottom, resurfaced, and cried out in exhilaration.

Once I'd returned to Charlie, I readied myself to go again. "Higher this time."

He gripped my hips. "Can't," he said and tossed me.

What was that pathetic throw? As soon as I resurfaced, I made sure to tell him. "That was weak!"

Andrew wasn't having it and choked at the proclamation. Both hands on his hips, he scoffed. "Weak? You're not five years old anymore. That was an amazing throw."

For some, perhaps. Charlie knew what I meant—knew it was weak—and shrugged. "Mom's watching. Sorry."

"Yeah." Tyler swept wet hair from his brow. "What's up with that? Does she want something? Maybe you should go find out."

I glanced at Miss Kate, who was indeed watching. Studying me?

"No. She's just mad about the necklace Jansen gave me."

"Not mad, really," Jansen said. "More like, concerned."

With a wiggle of his finger, Charlie beckoned me to him. "Any idea why?"

"None." Jansen nudged his chin toward me. "And be careful with her, please."

"Super high," I whispered in Charlie's ear, but Jansen heard me all the same and shot Charlie a warning glare.

As if that could ever stop Charlie. "No worries." He tossed me into the air higher than before, but not as high as when the three of us were alone in the pool.

Once resurfaced, I slicked back my long, wet waves, wiping water from my lashes. "Anyway, it wasn't only the necklace. She seemed kind of mad that I didn't ask more people over today."

Tyler ducked as the ball he'd just thrown ricocheted off the rim, kicking back hard at him. "Like who?"

"Exactly," Jansen said as I swam up next to him. He weaved his fingers through my hair, arranging it behind my shoulders, then leaned close to my ear. "Aren't we all here?"

The wind blew, and I inhaled his scent of musk and sun-ripe wheat, something I had never noticed before. It made my heart race. Made heat spread from my cheeks down my neck.

That was new.

When we were younger, we balked at getting out of the pool for anything. We didn't mind storms, never got tired, no matter the hour, and our bellies never seemed to get hungry. There were even pictures of Jansen and me eating with our upper halves on the deck and our bottom halves submerged in the water while we ate hot dogs. However, we weren't kids anymore, and for the guys, nothing was as powerful as the dinner call. My mom waved an arm, and the four of them fled the pool as if it caught fire.

The scent of cooked barbecue had been making us drool for a tortuous half hour, so the boys and I helped ourselves to the chicken. Then we piled our plates high with potato salad, sweet summer watermelon, corn on the cob, deviled eggs, and baked beans sweetened with brown sugar.

We ate dinner as the sun set, rich with the colors of amethyst, lavender, tiger lilies, and sunflowers. The sun itself was a blinding red spot on the horizon, reflecting hot orange beams off the windows of the house. Dreamily, I had the thought that it shone like a spotlight on my family, both genetic and chosen.

Miss Kate made me uneasy, so I tried to ignore her while making small talk with Andrew. The heat of her gaze bore into me, though. So much so that even when my mom talked to her, her eyes remained riveted on me.

"Hello out there. Ellie?" Andrew broke my trance. Chuckling, he said, "I'm going to get more potato salad. Want anything?"

"Thanks, but I'm good."

No sooner had he left than Miss Kate was out of her seat, leaving my mom mid-sentence. She swooped into Andrew's empty chair and slid her untouched dinner beside mine. "Sun's in my eyes."

I doubted that. Though I was uncomfortable, a sick curiosity kept me rooted.

"Andrew's a nice guy," she said. "Is he here often?"

"Is that what this is about?" I slammed my can on the table harder than I'd meant, spilling some of it. "You think I'm interested in Andrew? He's my brother's friend. Not even mine. I only try to be nice."

I threw Jansen an icy glare across the patio, where he dug through the cooler for a drink, but he didn't look up. Just what had he told his mom about Andrew?

"What difference does it make, anyway?" I dabbed at the spill with my napkin. "It's not like—"

"No, it isn't that." She covered my hand to stop me from cleaning. "You should be nice to him. That's good." Her words turned higher in pitch, almost singsong-like. "I see how he looks at you."

In no mood to discuss my love life, I shifted in the chair, pulled my hand away, and scooted further from her. "He looks at me that way because he can't understand why I'm so close to Jansen, if you must know. He isn't exactly nice to Andrew."

"Yes, yes, I've noticed." Her attention narrowed on her youngest son, who turned around with a drink in hand, eyeing his mom almost as if he'd heard our conversation from such a distance.

Miss Kate leaned in near enough that her lips brushed my ear. "Love carefully, Ellie." Then she arose so quickly, I felt a cool breeze from her cover-up.

After she left, Jansen slid into her seat. "What was that about?"

"I have no idea."

Caught up in the festivities, we nibbled and conversed until the sky darkened, peppered with bright stars and two twinkling planets. Jansen pointed out which were Mars and Jupiter. Apparently, the moons of Jupiter were visible, too, but I couldn't see them.

After cleaning up a bit and taking leftovers inside, we prepped for fireworks. I looked forward to this the most. Not only did I get to view a fantastic display of fireworks, but also got a rare glimpse of pure joy on Jansen's face.

Charlie set the explosives out in the middle of the yard, as Jansen started toward the wick.

"Wait." Charlie fumbled in his pocket and handed Jansen a small box of matches. "Think you forgot these."

"Right. Matches. Got it."

The rest of us huddled as far back as possible, but Jansen

appeared fearless as he held the match to the wick, waiting patiently for it to light. He planted himself there for a time as the flame flickered and hissed before backing away. Even then, it was more because my father insisted than because he wanted to, folding his arms as he enjoyed the anticipation.

"Come on back now," my dad said. "That's still too close."

Jansen grimaced, but obeyed. You'd think he was fireproof.

The rocket exploded from its tubing. *Whizz! Bang!* What a grand sight. A detonation of glorious gold sparkles streamed from the sky like an umbrella of lights. Though the bang made me jump, Jansen stood solid as he looked on, his dark figure a shadow against the glittering backdrop.

He monopolized the lighting for much of the first half. Only when Charlie could no longer contain his own enthusiasm did Jansen hand over the matches and beckon me to follow him. He led me past our parents, who relaxed in chaise lounge chairs. Past Tyler and Andrew, who were opening a box of sparklers, to a spot in the grass where we could lay on our backs and gaze up at the dazzling display.

Was there anything better than this? The two of us soaking in the laughter of our families? Silently observing the beauty of the fireworks against a black velvety backdrop? The various tints took my breath away with bursts of emerald, ruby, and majestic gold. Best of all were the ones that sizzled and swirled toward the ground in glitzy spirals.

With my head close to his, I whispered, "I love to watch the colors change. I think my favorite is gold."

Jansen's face shimmered after the firecracker that had scarcely launched, and his smile spread, the flash reflecting off his sunglasses. He was sensitive to light and wore the glasses so often that he often left them on. Even at night. So, I removed them, folded them, and tucked the shades into the pocket of my loose cover-up.

His rich midnight eyes mirrored the colors in the sky as clearly as if they were glass. I fell so far into his glassy orbs that I swore I could see swirling, twisting firecrackers in varying shades of blue around a black core.

"Mmm," he hummed. "My favorite is blue." He winked as if telling me a joke I didn't understand.

Had there been any blue?

"Happy birthday, Ellie."

CHAPTER THREE

Late in August, days before school started again, Jansen asked if I'd help him with a melody he'd been writing, something we sometimes did together. He had a voice unmatched by any, and that wasn't my biased opinion. His voice wasn't merely nice to listen to. No, it seeped into the bloodstream and worked its way to the heart. Yet, it carried a haunting quality, leaving its listener aching for more. Men liked it, too, but when women, in particular, listened, they got a sense of other-worldliness. Honest to goodness, like the pied piper, he could lead a woman into Hell's fire with one sustained note.

Funny, he detested any mention of his voice. Ignored accolades and often needed prodding to say, "Thank you." The prodding was my job.

I'd asked him about it once when we drifted around my pool on flat, pillowy floats, both of us lying on our bellies. Our fingers tethering us.

"It isn't something to take pride in, really." I had protested, but he continued, "I'm proud of things I've worked hard for. I guess it's like having an arm. My voice is part of my genetics. You wouldn't feel good about being complimented for having an arm, would you?"

If it had been me, I might have compared it to hair or something I did take pride in. After that, I never praised him for his voice again.

I, on the other hand, had no singing talent. Maybe I could sing the right notes, but it fell short on quality. Tyler often said I "talked on pitch" when I sang. An accurate description.

So, I played the guitar instead, and was pretty good at it, too. What I lacked in talent, I made up for in theory. Rhythm, pitch, chord structure, and tonality came naturally.

"Oh, there it is." Jansen brushed an enormous banana tree leaf behind the music stand, one of many in his mom's tiny conservatory of a sitting room, and pointed at the sheet music. "That's the part I can't quite figure out. It goes something like this…"

He nabbed the guitar from my lap and finger-picked a couple of bars. His guitar-playing skills were enough to pluck out some chords and rhythms, and after a few notes, his raspy baritone broke into song. There was something about playing in his family room, with the ambiance of natural light through the plant-covered window, that made his singing soft and edgy. Maybe it was the subtle glow of candles on the coffee table, or the fact that he sang a song he'd written himself, but I couldn't help swaying a little to his music.

When he finished, I picked up the music sheet to study. "I think the rhythm's your problem. It's more like a pickup note here." I pointed. "That would give you more time for the lyrics you want."

"Why don't you sing it?" he said coyly. "It fits your voice far better than mine."

Yeah, right. "You've got to sit back and listen to me sing without your best-friend-ears on someday."

"You don't give yourself enough credit."

"Nice try, but you're not getting me to sing by myself." I pulled my guitar into my lap. "Can I ask you something?"

"You can ask me anything."

"Do you think we'll always be as close as we are now?"

"I hope so. Why do you ask?"

I formed a few chords on the fretboard and strummed absent-mindedly. Where was this coming from? I wasn't sure myself. Only, I'd noticed that my friendship with Andrew had changed, especially since Carl had left. At first, I thought he showed concern, but sometimes he seemed more upset about the breakup than me. He liked to rehash it, when in all reality, Carl and I had been near breaking up before he moved.

Then, Andrew started acting kinda jealous whenever Jansen's name came up, followed by quick subject changes. A new sense of nervousness wove itself into the air between us. Change seemed inevitable.

It was a crush, that's what, and I didn't like it. Didn't want something as stupid as that to come between Jansen and me.

However, I couldn't say that. "Oh, I don't know."

I'd strummed so absent-mindedly that I dropped the pick into the guitar.

Jansen took it from me and shook it, hole-side down, since he usually retrieved it faster.

I leaned back in my chair. "I don't ever want us to change."

Though school had started, summer hadn't yet faded into memory. Ohio's unpredictable weather gifted us four weeks of unbearably hot, humid days and stuffy, sticky nights. The ridiculously dense haze hung thick enough to wear. With weather this intense, it was hard to imagine fall would ever come.

I tuned into the weatherman, hoping this would be the day the weather broke, but was disappointed. As he droned on, I flicked the tube off, grabbed my backpack, and headed out the door to make my way to the bus stop at the corner.

Time to get this first day over with. Maybe stepping outside would relieve the nervous energy and eager anticipation that coiled around in my gut. I stepped out the door and clicked it closed as my thoughts drifted. The potted flowers embedded their scent in the humid air, smelling of something earthy and fresh. The moment fled when a nearby bird twittered like an honest-to-God car alarm, chirping through five unique sets of varied songs. Jansen had once told me that was a mockingbird. Pretty cool, if you asked me.

Out of nowhere, a dog howled and hurled himself against the privacy fence, the only thing that separated his vicious jowls from my flesh. My heart stopped and both my hands thumped over my chest as if to keep it from breaking out. I blinked several times.

From behind the fence, the neighbor bellowed at their dog. "Otis! No! Come here, boy."

Every dang morning!

The neighbors opposite Andrew had a huge, loud dog. I thought it was a rottweiler, but had never seen him. They called him Otis, or sometimes "Oattie," in the syrupy, sickening voice that did not match the Otis imprinted in my head. I also never saw the owners. No, I only heard them bark back at him now and then. He had his routine, which included peeing every morning when he heard me leave the house. He'd then snarl and attack their never-could-be-tall-enough privacy fence. And I was pretty sure he had an appetite for teenage girls, especially those with chocolaty sprinkles of freckles.

It's not that I hated dogs, not at all. I just liked the kind that didn't attack fences.

The bus arrived shortly after that, and I settled in behind the safety of its yellow metal frame. Stupid dog. It took the full ten-minute ride for my heart to slide down from my throat. By the time the bus pulled up to our small-town school, its squealing brakes put the scary brute far from mind. Beneath the overhang, Jansen leaned against the rusty support beam of the back loading dock, his hands stuffed into the pockets of his dark jeans, one leg crossed over the other. He looked like a bodyguard standing there with his sunglasses perched high on his nose. Or an aloof rockstar. I bent forward in my seat for a better view through the white film of the window.

Why did he look so stern? What did he think about? He'd get his license in a few days. Maybe that was it. Whatever it was, I could tell when he spotted me, because his lips cracked a smile. I peeled my bare thighs from the vinyl cushion to stand in the line of kids exiting the bus. Sweat already beaded my forehead, with the sun only barely over the horizon.

Jansen stood there, all casual, as the stuffy odor of sweaty teens and the noxious stench of diesel fumes filtered past. Yuck. It churned my stomach, yet he seemed unphased. Just threw his arm around my shoulder like sweat wasn't dripping down my back, then trickling between my cheeks. I'd have shrugged him off, but when he lifted that arm, I caught a whiff of his honey-wheat scent and, yeah. His arm could stay.

He gave my shoulders a gentle squeeze. "Only three more days. It can't come soon enough."

So I guessed correctly. Hey, score one for me. It had been a sore spot between us since I'd gotten my license first. Made no difference, not really. It's not like I had a car, license or not. Jansen, on the other hand, had inherited his brother's black four-door sedan with its boxy nose, which had been sitting in the driveway for several months now.

"I'll pick you up every day," he said, "and *you* won't have to bother with the bus anymore."

The emphasis on *you* caught my attention, but I didn't ask.

Ugh, this heat. I pulled my shirt away from my chest repeatedly, trying to circulate air between it and me.

When I swung my empty backpack over my shoulder, Jansen pulled back his arm. Might as well enjoy the light load now. It would be heavy by the end of the day.

Our high school boasted an unimpressive color that could best be described as drab. It perched on a hill overlooking its football stadium, which struck as more impressive than the school itself. Because of the hill, no one ever used the front entrance, with its unnecessary sidewalk connecting it to the back parking lot.

Since the building was built in 1958, it didn't have any air-conditioning, and in the summer months, the heat could be unbearable. It's how I learned the word "oppressive." The whirring of industrial-sized fans acted as background noise, a sound teachers had to shout over. Classrooms were kept dimly lit, shades drawn, and lights often remained off during the school day.

I fanned myself with my schedule as we walked. "What's your first class?"

"Beamer," Jansen groaned. "Figures I'd get the toughest teacher for math."

Yeah, like he'd have any problem with that. He'd only said it to make me feel better. Dude got straight A's, and I'd never seen him crack a book except to help me study.

"You'll do fine," I said.

We compared our schedules and noticed we had the same lunch period and then English together. That would be nice, English being my favorite subject, and all.

An arm slipped to encircle my waist, which caused me to stumble up against its owner, Aaron Long. He was a former, short-lived boyfriend of mine, and he lacked the natural gait that made walking with Jansen's arm around me easy. His finger-length, dusty-brown hair hung below his brow, so he often flicked his head to whip it back. And he appeared to have developed some stubble.

"Seen any freshmen nearby? I haven't had breakfast yet."

I scolded him with a slap to his shoulder, a higher reach than I'd remembered. Had all the boys in my class grown several inches over the summer?

"Hey, it's my junior year. I'd say I'm entitled." He combed his eyebrows using his fingernails and flipped his hair off his forehead. "Yo, Emily!" Then he disappeared as quickly as he'd arrived, which left my head spinning with the mixed scent of cologne and morning sweat.

Jansen took up Aaron's spot beside me, bending so low that his nose touched my ear, and I felt his whispered breath. "Never understood what you saw in him." He put his hand on my shoulder, and we walked down the hall toward the choir room.

Students arriving on early buses had about fifteen minutes to kill every morning before school started. Senior athletes gathered around the old mahogany bench near the unused front entrance. Most kids hung out in the empty space of the cafeteria. Choir geeks, an offensive name we alone were allowed to call ourselves, collected in the choir hall. There were no lockers in this hallway, so we each pulled up a spot against the wall and had a seat on the cheap laminate floor.

The hallway was dense with sticky air, the freshly waxed floor shiny and tacky beneath our feet. A few of our friends were already there and sat tight against the wall, chatting about the summer. I claimed a place and tucked my legs in, cross-legged.

It wasn't long before Gretta, a somewhat-friend of mine, strode down the hall, her ruby-red hair flying in her stride. Her sunburned cheeks matched the light delicate roses that blotted her sundress, appearing to wave in the wind as she sidled in next to me.

"Cute glasses." I took note of her oversized frames that complimented the same red coloring as her hair.

"Thanks." Her eyes flitted between Jansen and me before she leaned in close to whisper in my ear. "I see some things never change."

Please. Like I hadn't heard that before. I ignored the slam, and when I turned back toward Jansen to see if he'd heard, he stared straight ahead, right through the pair of legs that stood in front of him, one knee jutted out from her exaggerated hip tilt. Hers were two shapely calves that everyone else found hard to miss. Not Jansen, though. If it weren't for the dead-eye stare, I'd have thought he didn't see her. Seriously, was she invisible to him?

Clara flaunted a new mini skirt and cropped top that wasn't appropriate for school. It always amazed me the way she shelled out more money *not* covering herself than I did on clothes that covered all of me.

At Jansen's snub, she huffed an annoying little squeak from her nose and flipped her blonde hair extensions; I assumed they were extensions. I didn't know. If they weren't fake, she spent an awful lot of time in the mornings curling what I thought was likely pin-straight hair. After sliding down the wall, she sat demurely with her legs to her side.

Jansen's already tense pose stiffened as he flattened himself against the wall.

Unable to resist, I angled myself across Jansen and in a kindly, almost syrupy way, said, "Hello, Clara."

She ignored me. "Hi, Jansen. You look nice this morning. Something's different about you." She tapped her freshly polished nails on her lips, which were the same shade of dusty rose. "What is it?" *Tap, tap, tap.* "Oh, yes. You're quite a bit taller and have you been working out?" I wouldn't have believed it if I hadn't seen it, but she squeezed his bicep, a thing that prompted a snarl.

It made me take a second look at him. How odd I hadn't noticed it before. The way his once lean and boyish body had developed well-defined, toned muscles. I'd never known him to work out. He and his brother, Charlie, didn't own any weights. Just good genes, I guessed.

After an awkward silence, Clara's nose squeaked again.

Gretta ticked her head toward Tyler and Andrew, who strode our way. Andrew with a box of tissues in hand.

"Hey Clara," Gretta said with a distinct sneer. "Andrew's got some tissues if you need one. Sounds like you're getting a cold."

I stifled a laugh and tried hard not to look at Jansen, whose chest twitched. So, yeah, he got it, too.

Oh man, she fit the exact stereotype of a teenager that gives girls a bad name. She pouted and turned her attention to the schedule she held. The way Jansen had ignored her… well, it made me feel a little smug. So, yeah, it was rude of him to be standoffish, but I felt vindicated for how she'd flat-out ignored me.

Tyler and Andrew took seats across from us, narrowing the hallway even further.

A toothy grin lit Andrew's face just before sneezing into a tissue he held at the ready. "Hey there, Ellie. How's it goin'?"

"Okay."

"Me, too." Gretta kicked Andrew's sneakers. "Thanks for asking."

Andrew apologized by way of an awkward head nod and brief eye contact. "Ellie, I meant to tell you earlier, but forgot. I saw you waiting for the" —three sneezes in succession erupted before he continued— "bus this morning. Dang allergies always kick in on the first day of school. I swear I'm allergic to this place. Anyway, I'd be more than happy to take you to school tomorrow. And every day." Three sneezes followed. "Maybe even home today."

The thought of never enduring another day of hot, sticky bodies in the oppressive heat of the bus thrilled me to my core. "Jansen, do you mind?"

He lived on the opposite side of town from us and would have to ride the bus, so it left me feeling guilty.

Strange, he didn't appear to have heard me. I could see Andrew in the dark reflection of Jansen's glasses. The recipient of his unrelenting stare, which, of course, made Andrew gulp.

I'd opened my mouth to repeat the question when Jansen said, "Of course. That's fine, if that's what you want to do."

Andrew heaved a sigh of relief.

Then Jansen directed his words toward Andrew. "I'll be taking Ellie to school after Labor Day."

His tone surprised even me. I nudged him, and he apologized with a squeeze to my knee.

The bell rang, making several of us groan. A warning that we had four minutes to get to class. Jansen hopped up in one graceful motion, a thing I'd seen him do a thousand times over our lives. Yet, God, he was smooth. He caught me with my mouth agape as he extended his hand to pull me up, and we started toward my class.

Then, a syrupy, sweet voice interrupted our progress. "Help a girl up?" Clara presented her fingertips to Jansen, who wasn't even looking in her direction.

So, I prodded his foot. Hard. I think I got a sideways look from him—his glasses made it tough to tell—but he offered his assistance. She used her free hand to keep her short skirt in place as he pulled her to her feet. Ever so slightly, she kicked a high-heeled foot up. The shoes giving her height to match his. Dang if her fingers didn't linger.

Crap, they would have made a stunning couple. So movie-like. If he brought her hand to his lips, honest to God, it wouldn't have surprised me. He didn't. Instead, he took my backpack from me, carrying it by its handle, and guided me toward class, a palm on the small of my back. I glanced over my shoulder, pleased to see the pout I totally expected to find on Clara's face.

I brought myself around to the present and snatched Jansen's schedule from him. "Your class is on the other side of the building."

"Don't worry about me. Unless you'd rather walk alone?"

"No, no, I just don't want you to be late."

When we were out of earshot, he inclined his head and murmured, "Please be careful in the car with Andrew."

There was that scent again. What was it? Like tall grass, warm and inviting. Implausibly, it made my cheeks burn. I had to look away to hide it. "Why? He'll be the one driving."

"I realize that." His voice came out bitter. Angsty.

"What is it with the two of you? He's nice, and Tyler likes him. It isn't as though he's a stranger. Besides, it makes sense. He does live right next door."

"It's just a feeling I get."

A man's voice, an unfamiliar teacher, shouted over the bustle of students, "Lose the shades!"

Jansen lengthened his stride and threw back, "Prescription," taking my elbow to guide me through the crowd. "So. About Clara."

"It's so obvious! She has no shame. Are you going to ask her out?"

"Please."

"You might as well get it over with. I don't think she'll let it go."

"Drop it."

"You're the one who brought it up."

"I did. I wanted to ask for your help."

"You don't need any help, pal." I wiggled my pointer finger. "Beckon, and she'll be there."

"Are you done?"

"One little wink from you, and she's yours."

"Are you quite done?"

"Nearly. She probably already thinks you're a couple after this morning." That took it a step too far, and he groaned, so I said, "I think I'm finished now."

"Good. I hoped you might stop encouraging her."

"I don't encourage her."

"You remind me to be polite, and I need that, I realize. In this case, forcing me to be civil is the same as feeding the beast."

There were times I did feel like the puppet-master pulling his strings. It's just that I knew how incredibly wonderful he could be and it frustrated me knowing no one except me ever saw it. Well, Clara maybe. No. All she wanted was eye candy, like all the girls. She was merely brave enough to do something about it.

Even now, two freshmen girls strolled by, their sights locked on Jansen as if they'd never seen a good-looking guy before. It happened all the time. They whispered and snickered behind large yellow folders and didn't take their eyes off him, nor I them. My role entailed making them as uncomfortable as possible. Even after they passed, they stared and giggled, checking out his backside as well.

"Don't even bother," another girl said to her friend. "That's Jansen Wolff. Ellie monopolizes all of his time. You don't stand a chance."

Heat blazed in my cheeks and no doubt my face had turned a bright shade of scarlet.

"What?" Jansen asked, amused.

"It's nothing," I lied as yet another set of girls stared at him.

"Don't let them bother you. They're jealous, you know."

"Jealous? Of what?"

He scratched his head like he was uncomfortable. "Of you. Of us."

I stopped walking paces from my classroom to take in my friend, who stood close to the lockers. With his fingers running through his hair, he released that rich, earthy scent so wrong on this hot and humid morning. The way it washed over me and moved through—

"What are you looking at?" He rested a hand on the lockers and crossed one foot over the other, taking me quite off guard.

"I don't know." I stalled, trying to see what others saw in him.

With slow fingers, I grasped his glasses and lowered them to the tip of his nose. He surveyed the hallway before focusing on me. Oh, his eyes—piercing black, and so reflective. Of course, he was self-conscious about how unusual they were, but I found them captivating. My attention turned his lip up in an awkward smirk—

A couple of guys passed by and brushed my shoulder, knocking me off balance. *Typical*, I thought. Jansen snapped the glasses back into place and started after them.

"I'm fine." I touched his shoulder to turn him forward.

In no apparent rush, he leaned against the wall again.

So, I waved my hand. "See you at lunch." Hopefully my quick goodbye would encourage him to hurry off in the right direction.

He returned my wave, turned, and meandered toward his class, as if time were suspended.

I searched around the sea of faces and found Gretta already seated. She moved a book from the neighboring desktop and gestured to sit there.

It was a good seat. The fan that blew behind us rotated every twenty seconds or so, hitting the back of my neck. I pulled the hair tie from my wrist—I often wore it there for such an occasion—and tied my long, hot hair into a quick updo. The fan stirred the warm air, but at least it was something.

"Would someone turn that awful thing off?" Clara

complained, sitting in front of us. "It's messing up my hair."

Thank goodness no one answered. I sighed with relief and slumped back in my chair, enjoying the breeze.

When I opened them again, the boy to my left stared at me. Did I have something in my teeth? A booger in my nose? Matted, sweat-crazed hair?

"I'm Tim," he said, offering a hand and a shot of his perfect pearly whites. "Tim Bayer."

I took the offered hand. "Gabriella Wood."

"I'd rather be at the pool." He had the look of a swimmer. Bronzed skin, long, lean muscles, and short, sun-bleached hair. "I'm not ready to be back yet, especially in this heat."

Ah, the pool. Images flashed through my mind of my favorite reading spot on that top step where cool water bathed my hot, clammy feet. "That's where I'd rather be."

"What pool do you go to?"

"I have one at my house."

"Oh." He sounded disappointed. "I hoped you could recommend one. I'm new in town."

That explained why I hadn't seen him around. Our class consisted of about 350 students, and though I didn't know everyone, I usually recognized everyone's face.

"Was that your boyfriend?" he asked. "In the hallway earlier?"

"Jansen? No, only a close friend."

"Oh." He sat back in his seat and clasped his hands behind his head, arms out wide.

"What?"

"Nothing. I get it."

"I don't think you do. He really is just a friend."

This boy I'd barely met, who knew nothing about me, folded his arms and threw his legs out long in front of him, crossed at the ankles. His jaw jutted sideways, open-mouthed, as he studied me. "Sorry, but guys who walk girls to class want a little more than 'just a friend.'" His last words were a perfect mimic of me.

"Maybe that's true where you're from. Around here, Jansen and I are friends. We've known each other our entire lives."

"You'll get used to it." Clara snapped her compact mirror closed and smacked her freshly colored lips. "They're like brother and sister, only creepy."

Tim sat up straight and touched Clara's shoulder. Okay, so this guy was handsy. "Sisters don't stare into their brothers' eyes."

Clara flipped her phony-fake hair. "Like I said."

"I didn't—" Wait, I had, hadn't I? I'd stopped to see what others saw. I got caught up in his eyes. Who wouldn't? No, that wasn't staring. More like observing. This was stupid. "He's just a friend."

Tim rocked back in his chair. Its two front legs lifted off the ground, and I felt only a little guilty for wishing he'd tumble backward. His gaze burrowed through my skin, and I met it without blinking.

Finally, he shrugged. "Okay. You believe it anyway."

Obnoxious newbie. I whooshed a breath of hot air and turned to doodling stars and cat's eyes in my notebook.

"Honestly, Ellie." Clara leaned back to whisper, "I don't know how you expect to get any guy's attention if you react like that."

"React like what? We're nothing. Besides, I'm not looking for a boyfriend."

"Of course not. Why would you, with Jansen always ready at your heels? It's the beginning of the year. Every *normal* girl is wondering which guy is worthy of her heart." She leaned back. "And he's a pretty cute one."

"Leave her alone," Gretta said. "Not everyone is boy crazy."

Clara turned in her seat to face us. "I'm not boy crazy. Is it my fault the boys are crazy about me?"

Disgusted, Gretta threw up her hands, and I returned to doodling.

But Clara wasn't finished. "In fact, Mark Cassidy just asked me out."

"Mark?" Gretta and I parroted together.

Mark was a senior and a close friend of Andrew's. He

wasn't in the choir, but he broke ranks and joined us occasionally if Andrew was around. In the mornings, he usually hung out at the senior bench.

While tapping her pencil on her lip, Gretta sat forward. "I thought you liked Jansen."

Clara flipped her hair over her shoulder, letting out a small, impatient huff. "He waited too long, and Mark asked me on the way to class."

"That's great, Clara."

Maybe now she'd leave Jansen alone.

She turned around in her seat to face us head on, her expression serious. "We don't have school this Friday. It's a teacher workday or something, and with Labor Day on Monday, we have a four-day weekend."

And we care because? "What's your point?" I said instead.

"Well, Mark wants it to be a double date with Andrew. So, I thought maybe you could go?" She looked straight at me. "Please don't say 'no' right away."

Of course she'd want to double with Andrew, the one guy most likely to set Jansen off.

"But Andrew?"

"I see how he looks at you. He's awfully sweet. He likes you, but he'd never make a move because Jansen's always around."

Tim scratched the back of his head, drawing attention to himself. The morning wasn't going well for him. Clara wasn't interested, and neither was I.

"Is this Mark's way of setting us up?" I asked.

"So, what if it is? Come on." She drew out the word.

"Gee, Clara. That sounds like fun," I lied, with a slight drawl to my speech, giving me time to think up a plan.

Andrew? I knew he had a crush on me, and dating my brother's friend seemed weird. A wave of internal heat spread through me. Boy, didn't my pool sound nice about now? Cool water lapping at my ankles.

Then it dawned on me. My out. "See, I'm having a pool party at my house on Friday."

"Oh," they said together, both sounding hurt.

Of course they did, because they hadn't been invited to my fake party.

"It's an impromptu thing. Jansen and I barely talked about it this morning. His birthday is Friday, and he'll be getting his license on Saturday. I wanted to do something special for him. You'll both come, right?"

Clara gave a shoulder shrug, slightly mollified. "Of course."

Not Gretta, though. "Depends on how much homework I get." When she earned two looks of disgust from us, she amended her statement. "But I'll try."

Tim cleared his throat, reminding us of his presence. "Open invitation?"

"Sure, why not?" If I threw a fake party, I might as well make it big.

I tore a scrap of paper from my blue spiral notebook, and with a click of my pen, scribbled out my address for Tim. That made it official. No turning back now.

Jansen was going to kill me.

CHAPTER FOUR

I checked my watch for the twelfth time and then the hallway again. What had happened to Jansen? He always met me for lunch, usually right in front of my classroom. Earlier, we'd even compared schedules, so I knew we had lunch together. He was late.

Another wave of students hurried down the hall. My stomach growled, and I worried I wouldn't have time to eat if I didn't get in line. So, I fell in behind a couple who leaned into each other as though neither could walk without the other.

I grabbed a glass of watered-down lemonade, a hamburger with a dry bun, and a bruised apple that refused to stay upright on the old, yellowed fiberglass tray.

Where was he? I didn't like feeling all self-conscious, wondering if everyone looked at me as some kind of friendless has-been. There was something about always having a friend at your side. Someone to lean on. Someone to borrow confidence from.

Had he been in trouble for being late to class? A detention, maybe?

I scanned the lunchroom for my other friends and found Gretta seated beside Aaron, who busied himself combing his fingers through his eyebrows. To think, when we'd dated, I actually tried to get him to quit doing that. Their familiar faces steadied that unsettled feeling, and I headed toward them.

Still a few tables away, I slipped on overturned Jell-O. My stomach flipped in anticipation of a hard landing. Suddenly, a hand was at my elbow, the single thing that kept me from meeting the floor.

With relief, I scrambled to my feet. "Good timing, Jans—" When I turned around, it wasn't Jansen. It wouldn't have been the first time I'd been about to make a fool of myself, and Jansen appeared as if from nowhere.

Only if it wasn't Jansen, where was he?

"Tim. I thought—" I stopped myself, recalling our conversation from class. No need to give him more ammo about my relationship. "Never mind. Thanks."

"Not a problem." He flashed a row of perfectly straight teeth. "Thought you looked like you could use a hand."

"Yeah, that could have been embarrassing."

"Wanna join me for lunch?" He pointed to a nearby table.

"Thanks, but my friends are expecting me over there." I nodded toward my usual crowd.

Gretta caught my eye and motioned for me to hurry. So, I turned to leave, still thinking about Jansen. It wasn't like him to be so late. I didn't know why it bothered me, but Tim's earlier insistence that Jansen and I couldn't possibly be just friends had gotten under my skin, and here I was, proving him right.

So, I shook Jansen from my thoughts and focused on Tim. "Maybe you could eat with us?"

"No, thanks. I'm fine here. Come on, Gabriella. Join me."

Guess he didn't like my idea, because he tugged at my elbow. His penetrating, glassy blue eyes—the kind that looked like they were inlaid with diamonds—bore into me. If that weren't enough, he ducked his head and raised his brow, pleading, a face that was hard to refuse.

A smooth baritone sounded over my shoulder. "Ellie's eating with me." That voice could only belong to Jansen, and it made my heart flutter in relief.

"Ellie?" Tim questioned the name. "Ellie can do whatever the hell she wants. I'm talking to Gabriella."

Without a word, Jansen shifted his lunch tray to one hand, slipping the other into his pocket. He looked down his nose at Tim, and I knew behind his dark glasses he studied the space around Tim. An unnerving thing he sometimes did, his eyes seldom still.

Beads of sweat tickled my brow, and I wiped them away. "It's an old nickname. I told you... we're old friends."

How to end this exchange? And quickly, or I'd have explained the nickname then and there. Really, I should have. Might have humanized Jansen if Tim knew that when we were small, my mom insisted everyone call me by my full name. Jansen had called me "Gabri-ellie," and it eventually stuck.

"If you're just old friends," Tim said in a mocking tone, still laser-focused on Jansen, "then you won't mind if she joins me for lunch."

Jansen jerked his chin toward me. "I believe she told you she's eating with her friends. She offered for you to join her. I hope you choose not to. Either way, Ellie comes with me."

"Jansen—" I started to defend Tim.

Then he demonstrated how far from out of town he was.

Earlier, I'd thought perhaps Tim served as the "big dude" at his old school, accustomed to getting what he wanted. Perhaps he'd make a little small chat, and girls flocked to him. Maybe lunch invitations were not just rarely turned down, but never.

Whatever the reason, brimming with massive self-assurance, he took my hand and pulled me toward his table.

My heart lurched at the unwelcome touch of this guy I'd barely met. I jerked to release myself, but Tim's grip remained firm.

With alarming speed, Jansen seized Tim's wrist, giving him the full experience of his wrath. Tim growled in pain as his hand wrenched free of mine.

After letting go, though not without a good, hard thrust, Jansen simply folded his arms as Tim fell backward. Stumbled and collapsed right into the gray folding table, where he knocked over his lunch. The tray clattered to the floor. Corn and peas rained down around the hamburger and dented milk carton. A hush settled over the student body that clogged my ears with humiliation.

Mr. Bender, the gorgeous young Latin teacher on duty, strode toward us, the first three buttons of his shirt left undone. He was almost as tall as Jansen but narrower through the shoulders, his hair rumpled from the heat.

Jansen squatted to pick up what he could of Tim's lunch. Since he made it appear like an accident, Mr. Bender returned to scanning the lunchroom for actual trouble.

With a casual air, Jansen stood, tray in hand, and pulled his shoulders back in a smooth roll. "You don't want to mess with me." He slammed the tray on the table, took my elbow, and led me away.

The usual cafeteria chatter droned in earnest, louder than before. Everyone gossiped about whatever they thought had happened, probably wondering who the new guy was, and what had he done to irk Jansen? No one would believe Jansen hadn't done anything.

I gulped, tucked my chin, and hurried to sit with Gretta and Aaron. They'd been joined by Clara, Tyler, and Amelia, a girl I barely knew by name.

Of course, it wasn't that easy. As though amplified through a bullhorn that silenced tongues and turned heads, Tim said, "I think I'll join you after all."

We stopped dead in our tracks, our backs to Tim.

When he pulled himself up to his full height, Jansen stood over six feet. The corded muscles of his arms rippled. His biceps flexed, and the vein along his neck throbbed. Even the way he held my hand in his tight fist evoked a show of strength. I swallowed hard and winced, trying to tug my fingers free, as the hairs on the back of my neck rose.

Because Jansen did not turn around. Had never been tested before, that I recalled.

Oh, this couldn't be good. I pried myself from his grip and faced Tim to smother the smoke before the fire flared up in earnest.

"You're welcome to join us," I said as nonchalantly as

possible, swallowing the lump in my throat.

I scratched my fingernails along Jansen's back, encouraging him to retreat. Only he was as immovable as a quartzite statue. He breathed with an obviously controlled effort and concentration. So, I ran my hand down the length of his bare arm, teasing the coarse, shadowy hairs.

He shivered at my touch, but his expression didn't change.

Through the reflection of his glasses, I saw our friends, all of whom had stopped eating. Students around the lunchroom sat like wax figures, some with forks raised halfway to their gaping mouths. It didn't take long for Jansen's head to swivel, and his shades reflected Tim, who clenched and unclenched his fists.

When Jansen focused his attention on me, I found my reflection looking back. My mouth agape. So, I closed it and forced a smile. Prayed he'd realize that I didn't want them to fight.

Tim stood casually, one foot crossed over the other. His jaw jutted to the right, the portrait of confident arrogance.

Wall posters flapped from the whirring rotating fans. The single sound in the crowded cafeteria.

Ankles still crossed, Tim folded his arms over his chest, which trembled in wicked amusement.

All this, despite the palpable tension. Everyone knew—nobody messed with Jansen. Not ever.

Maybe Tim lacked any kind of instinct because that's when he did the unthinkable. Did he think this was a test? That he had to prove himself to his new school?

First, he lobbed an apple into the air a few times. Then, he retracted his arm and fired the bright red weapon at the back of Jansen's head.

Jansen spun in a blur of black jeans and white T-shirt to catch the apple squarely in his hand.

Without pause, the moment the apple smacked his palm, he drew his arm back, and threw that thing like a pro ballplayer.

The apple parted Tim's hair straight down the middle

and landed as mush against the cement wall, where creamy pulp slid to the ground.

Tim's eyes grew to the size of bushels as he absorbed the intensity of his foe's wrath.

Jansen issued a sharp growl and fixated on Tim. "Next time, I aim for your mouth." No one dared clap or even breathe. "And I never miss."

With that, he strode over to our table and stood back, giving me space to slide onto the bench-seat first. But what the hell, Jansen? It was the first day of school, and Tim was brand new. He didn't know the rules. Wait, what were the rules? Don't talk to Ellie?

But Jansen didn't gesture to hurry or flinch or do anything at all. Like if I wanted to go after Tim, I could. Maybe it was realizing I had a choice, but I swallowed hard and sat.

Gretta inclined her head. "What—I mean—seriously, what was that?"

"Nothing. Tim wanted me to eat with him."

"Is that all?" She clucked her tongue in Jansen's direction.

As for him, he said nothing.

I tugged on my earlobe, a nervous habit. "Tim wasn't taking "no" for an answer." Why was I defending him?

"Jansen, the hero." Clara tousled his hair, which made him recoil, though he managed a polite smile. More of a grimace.

Over my shoulder, I watched as Tim slunk away, with a funny hop to his step, like one leg grew a hair longer than the other.

Tyler shook my tray to get my attention. "Who was that?"

"Just some new kid. He's been in a few of my classes this morning."

Amelia opened her cardboard milk carton. "What's his name?"

"Tim. Bayer, I think."

An awkward pause followed. I'd never met Amelia, though I'd seen her around. She'd been the new girl last year, and we hadn't had any classes together. Like us, she was a junior, and had a unique sense of style. Today, it was a mustard-yellow, sleeveless turtleneck accentuating her ample bust, which she'd paired with a knee-length skirt the color of a chestnut. It looked cute, but the large rust-brown glasses and bucket hat really pulled it off.

Tyler moved closer to her and brushed her shoulder with his. "This is my little sister, Ellie."

"Sure," Amelia said. "I've seen you around. I'm Amelia. Your brother and I are in art class together. And you're Jansen, right?"

He surprised me by extending a hand to her. "That's right."

After wiping her fingers on a napkin, she shook it. "You're sweet." That was not an expression I'd ever heard associated with Jansen. "Like Charlie."

Jansen twisted the cap off his water bottle. "You've met Charlie?"

"Sure. From art class last year. He has a colorful soul."

Jansen choked on his water. Between violent coughs, he hacked out, "What?"

"You know. Very kind. He has the heart of an artist. Charlie knows his way around a pottery wheel."

"That he does." He took another sip of water to recover, pounding away the cough with his fist. "How did you know I was his brother?"

"Oh, honey." She popped a French fry into her mouth. "Everyone knows you."

CHAPTER FIVE

A drop of sweat started at my hairline and slid down my forehead, picked up momentum and tickled the bridge of my nose. Bored, I let it go rather than wiping it away. Instead, I concentrated on it, feeling its descent. The drop made a steady stream to the tip of my nose, fell off, and plopped onto my paper, leaving a salty wet spot. I ran my bare arm across my brow, but it did little more than smear it.

I turned backward in my chair to face the fan in the back of the room, hoping it might dry my underarms somewhat before the next class. Aaron grunted a commiserative laugh from behind and pulled his shirt out, letting the air flow between the cotton and his skin.

His lips formed the word ridiculous.

When the bell rang, chairs scraped across the floor, feet scuffled, and students bumped into one another, anxious to exit. I gathered my books and joined my classmates in the mass exodus to eighth period, the day's last class.

Casually waiting for me, Jansen leaned against the doorframe of my classroom.

"How do you do that?" I asked.

"Do what?"

"Get here so fast."

He shrugged. "It's a gift."

Beyond reason, he smelled of musk and fresh wheat. He wasn't so much as glistening, and here I stood, embarrassed to be near him, aware of my own body odor. Ridiculous indeed.

As if in response, he tilted his head, yet how could he have known? I didn't even feel the burn of my skin flushing.

Then he brushed his fingers down my face as if to wipe away a frown and lopped an arm around my shoulders. "Come on. I'll walk you to class."

The hallway filled with students who opened and slammed their metal lockers, slowing our pace. Jansen took my hand, not like a boyfriend does, but so he wouldn't lose me. Lucky, too, as he dodged traffic so much easier than me. Kids usually saw him coming and moved.

I bent forward, as close to his shoulder as possible, to holler over the noisy hallway. "By the way, where were you before lunch? I forgot to ask after the whole…incident." The veins in his neck popped, so I didn't wait for an answer. "Tim didn't mean anything. He's new here and didn't know we were such good friends."

"It wasn't about our friendship."

"Then what?"

He shook his head and pinched the bridge of his nose between his thumb and finger. "No one should ever tell you what to do."

"And no one has ever stood up to you before," I said, with perhaps a hint of antagonism.

Jansen sighed and stopped walking to lean a hand against the lockers. "It wasn't about me either."

"Then what was it about?"

"It's nothing. Maybe I misjudged him." He started forward again, a poor attempt at escape from our conversation.

He had a long stride, and I had to run a few steps to catch up. "Sometimes it's okay to let me defend myself. Sometimes, I don't even need defending."

Without slowing our pace, he lowered his glasses and assessed my body. I should have been used to it, but it unnerved me when he did it. What did he see? I couldn't figure out what about me captivated him. For that matter, it wasn't always clear what endeared him to me, either.

Plus, how dare he smell so good on such a humid—

"Who are you thinking about?" A note of concern touched his tone that I didn't understand.

"What?" Though I heard what he'd asked. Could I lie? I couldn't say "you."

"Who…are you thinking about?"

"Just now?" I stalled.

"Yes, just now. Who?"

Heat spread up the back of my neck like the morning sun on a hot summer day. Or a blaze through kindling. "No one," I lied.

He smiled. "That's what I thought." He turned into the choir room, leaving me dumbfounded in the hallway.

What just happened?

Gretta charged up behind me. "Come on, Ellie. You're gonna be late."

I entered the choir room feeling duped. How had he changed the subject so easily? Worse, I'd let him.

The choir room reflected one typical of most high schools. Cold, drab walls made of painted cement bricks, and like the entire school—no imagination: A drop ceiling, a set of never-used folding chairs in the corner, a trophy shelf for show choir, a baby grand piano on wheels, and enormous steps that served as risers.

Our choir director, Mrs. Harding, tried getting our attention, a challenging task with a space full of eighty teenagers who hadn't seen each other all summer break. So, Tim made an ear-splitting whistle between his fingers and teeth.

The room fell silent, and eighty heads turned to gawk at the bold newcomer. It seemed he was unaware of the unwritten code for newbies. This wasn't the way things worked around here. Aaron could have whistled. Tyler could have whistled. Heck, even I could have whistled if I had such a talent—which I did not. The new guy doesn't grab attention with a whistle to rival a shrieking banshee.

I couldn't help stealing a glance at Jansen, who was beside me for the moment. Soon, Mrs. Harding would move us. He stood tall; too tall for the front riser. Even long-legged Clara had to stand on her toes to see around him. His thumbs hooked into the belt loops of his dark jeans, his body motionless, expressionless. It surprised me that he had no interest after what had happened at lunch.

"Welcome back, choir." Mrs. Harding adjusted the music stand in front of her, its black metal feet scraping against the shiny linoleum floor with an ear-splitting squeal. She wouldn't have needed Tim's whistle if she'd just done that.

A kind, middle-aged woman, Mrs. Harding kept her hair in tight black curls which framed her face. Though some noticeable gray had begun to dull its sheen. "I hope you had a nice long summer because I have a lot planned for us. This year I've picked out some pieces that I think…" her attention narrowed on Jansen, "…will make use of our talent this year." She cleared her throat. "I'll be handing out solos later in the week."

"Mrs. Harding?"

"Yes…um?"

"Tim. Tim Bayer."

"Right. Yes, Tim?"

"How do you decide who gets a solo?"

Mrs. Harding visibly tripped over her thoughts as she pondered what was a simple answer. Jansen.

"Well… what we do is… we hold auditions." With that matter settled, she placed her baton at the bottom of the stand and opened one of the folders lying there.

Gretta leaned against my shoulder. "As if that's necessary."

"When are auditions?" Tim asked.

Mrs. Harding's fingers slipped on the folder, snapping it shut as she tittered to herself, caught off guard. The eyes behind her round glasses rolled upward, contemplating what to say.

"When are…auditions?" Her processing speed seemed a bit slow. "Auditions are…" Again, her thoughts were nearly visible. I could almost see the calendar that ran through her mind. "…going to be Friday."

Clara cleared her throat behind me. "There's no school Friday. Ellie's having a pool party."

I shot her a glare, but she shrugged as if to say, "What's the big deal?"

The guys around Tyler lobbed questions at him, and he responded with shoulder shrugs and a puzzled expression. Jansen, too, peeked at me. Of course, that was because I'd forgotten to tell him about it after the lunch debacle.

Mrs. Harding clapped her hands, bringing us back to attention. "Naturally, I mean next Friday. I'll pick Jans—I'll pick someone then." Her tawny brown skin reddened from the neck up.

Without skipping a beat, she proceeded to separate us into sections, but her slip of the tongue didn't go unnoticed. Jansen stood glowering, like he couldn't believe she'd done that. Yet, he can't have been surprised. It was no secret all the girls lusted after his voice, and that included Mrs. Harding. Or was he upset with me about the pool party?

Tim gawked, lips parted as he studied Jansen in utter disbelief. Then again, he'd never heard Jansen sing.

As for me and *my* voice, I sang in the alto section and liked it that way because it allowed me to hide. The choir was better off as long as no one heard me. Sometimes, honestly, I just mouthed along. As Mrs. Harding busied herself with other students, I remembered back to the seventh grade when my choir career started.

It had been Charlie's freshman year. After his fall concert, Jansen stumbled across a piece of music on the top riser and picked it up. When he began humming the tune, I had stepped closer to hear. It was rare he sang, and it stilled my heart every time.

Charlie had walked up behind him to sing harmony. Together, with their backs to the room, their voices swelled and melded. Everyone around stopped to listen. They didn't realize it, but as people nearby quieted, their circle of listeners grew. The room fell silent as they continued singing softly.

Mrs. Harding had been so impressed, she asked Charlie

who Jansen was and why wasn't he in choir at the junior high? She convinced him to join once she consented that I join as well. Since then, as long as I stayed in the choir, Jansen remained, and Mrs. Harding knew it.

She brought me back to the present when she grabbed my arm and deposited me beside Clara on the floor-level. With an awkward smile, she rethought her plan, but I didn't mind in the least. I sighed in relief as she put Gretta between us instead. Bumping me up next to the melody of the sopranos would be a train wreck, especially one as strong as Clara. Gretta could tune Clara's voice out, a talent I lacked.

The period passed quickly, if not chaotically, while Mrs. Harding positioned and re-positioned us according to height, range, and skill. Tim had made himself the center of attention between the lunch episode and asking about auditions. It was silly, but everyone gathered around him, and questioned in hushed tones, shooting furtive looks at Jansen—at me.

"Pool party?"

Startled by the voice so close to my ear that his breath tickled, I spun and bumped noses with Jansen. He smiled wickedly and lowered his glasses.

To recover a little personal space, I took half a step back. "Sorry." I rubbed my nose. "Are you mad?"

"Mad? No. Should I be?"

Mad had been an emotion I'd feared, yes. Of course, he didn't yet know it was a fake party. Or that I'd used his birthday as the excuse. Okay. Time to lay out the whole story from beginning to end.

Too bad all that came out was, "It's a party for Clara."

"Clara? You're throwing her a pool party?"

"Yes. I mean, no. It was her idea."

"Uh-huh. At your pool?"

"Well, she has this date with Mark…"

"Uh-huh."

"…and I have a pool."

Jansen released an amused hum.

What was wrong with me? "Mark asked Clara on a date

but wanted to double with me."

"You? What, are you chaperoning?"

"No, you don't understand. She wanted me to double with Andrew as my date."

"Andrew," he repeated under his breath.

"She wanted me to double with them…"

"At your pool?" He slipped his hands into his pockets. "I understand."

Wait, no. What? I pressed my fingers into my eyelids, trying to clear away the fog. "I'm having a pool party to get out of it."

"What?"

Nearby, Andrew rearranged things in his backpack, and I didn't want him to hear. So I gestured for Jansen to bend closer. "I don't want to go on a date with Andrew."

"You don't?" He sounded shocked.

Did he think… but he couldn't think I'd want to go. "To get out of the date, I said I needed to be with you."

That made his smile broaden and one eyebrow raise, a trick of his I found adorable.

"It's your birthday. So, I made up a pool party at my house because I needed something else to do instead."

My face burned. How red was I?

Mercifully, the bell rang, and Andrew slung his organized pack over his shoulder to saunter over to us. "Ready?"

I still reeled from the strange conversation. In taking a step back, distancing myself from Jansen, the fog seemed to lift and I could speak intelligently again. "Do you want to just come over?"

"No. You worry too much. Seriously. I'm glad you've got a ride."

Andrew drove his grandparent's ancient twenty-year-old gold Toyota Camry, the hood a shade lighter than the rest. So, what was I looking at here—sun damage or a bad paint job?

"It's a work in progress." He loosed an embarrassed chuckle. The guy had proven himself more than a little mechanically inclined and often tinkered with it. After retrieving a manila packet from his backpack, he tossed the pack into the trunk and gestured for me to do the same. "Hang on." He then climbed into the driver's seat and leaned over to open my door. "Handle's broken from the outside. That's next on my list."

There was no trace of clutter inside his car. No pop cans rolling around, tissues wadded in corners, or lost books. No stinky gym shoes, greasy takeout bags, or discarded banana peels; Tyler literally had a black banana peel in his car, unless he'd removed it the past month, which I highly doubted. Andrew moved a box of tissues from the front seat to the back, stowed an umbrella in the glove compartment, and the car looked brand new.

Andrew clicked his seat belt. "Why doesn't Tyler ever take you home?"

"My brother? Gosh, I don't know. For one, I don't like sitting in trash."

"Yeah. Can't say I blame you there."

"Tyler and I get along great and all, but he's still my brother."

"I guess." Andrew sniffled and handed me the manila packet. "Could you give that to Tyler for me? I picked it up at school today. Thought he might be interested."

"Sure. What is it?"

He waved a dismissive hand, but his face told a different story. That he was excited about whatever hid inside that envelope. "It's nothing. Well, he'll say it's nothing, but I want him to have it, anyway."

"Can I look?"

"If you really want to. I went to the guidance counselor's office today to ask about requirements for getting into the Air Force Academy." He gave me a sideways glance, checking my reaction. "It's kind of a lifelong dream of mine."

"No kidding? Have you ever talked to my dad about it?"

"Yeah, actually. He hooked me up with a flight instructor last week, and I'm going to get my pilot's license. Pretty cool, huh?"

"Very. What does this have to do with Tyler?"

He shrugged. "Nothing, I guess. I don't think he's ever been serious about it. It's just one of those things we've talked about doing since we were kids. You know, back when we used to want to do all the same things. It's silly, I suppose, but you get it. I'm sure you and Jansen have gone your separate ways here and there, being raised kind of like cousins, huh?"

"Cousin" didn't seem right. I had cousins on my dad's side, three of them. But they lived in upstate New York, a good ten hours away, and I really only knew two of them. The youngest I'd met once, shortly after he was born.

I fidgeted with my pendant. "Not like cousins. Brother fits better. Jansen's closer than a brother, though. More like my other half."

I wished the words back into my mouth as soon as they were out. That sounded charming and romantic, not the way I felt for Jansen…at all. Did I think of him as my other half? "I didn't mean it that way. It's just, we balance each other."

He reached behind himself for a tissue. "Has he ever been like a boyfriend to you?"

"No. Not at all. We're super close and always have been."

"He's protective of you. More so lately."

I hadn't put words to it, but yes, Jansen was protective of me. That's what friends did. I protected him too. Didn't I?

After the long silence, Andrew asked, "Would he let you go on a date?"

I furrowed my brow and stared at him for at least the length of a minute. In all that time, he said nothing. It wasn't that I tried to make him uncomfortable, but that I needed to think. He turned the corner of his lip up in an awkward grin, giving me the space to wrap my brain around my own spinning thoughts.

In some ways, I knew what he meant. To agree with him was to admit I depended on Jansen or wasn't a whole person by myself. It made my own statement true: he was indeed my other half. If I had complete autonomy, and nobody seemed to think I did, I didn't need his permission to do anything.

Finally, I formed the simple words burning on my tongue. "Let me?"

The wrinkles on his forehead smoothed, his pursed lips relaxed. "Well, he's pretty intense. There's not a guy out there who would cross him to get to you."

"Tim did."

"Oh right, Tim." He sounded annoyed. Or bitter? Jealous maybe? Andrew's crush seemed to rear its ugly head. Was this his way of fishing for whether I'd be willing to view him as more than my brother's friend?

No, that couldn't be it. "And yes, I have been out on dates. I went out with Aaron for a while. Plus, there was Carl."

He tapped his thumbs on the steering wheel as he remembered. "Of course. Guess I hadn't paid much attention to you before. You were always just Tyler's little sister."

"And what am I now?"

My directness seemed to catch him off guard, and he grew quiet. His focus fell on the pavement ahead, and he didn't even appear to notice the heat of my gaze. He passed a car, returned to the right lane, and finally relaxed. Only then did he turn to me to find I marked his every move, waiting for an answer.

He startled and glanced away. "Now, you're a friend. Someone I look out for. Guess I want to make sure Jansen doesn't hold you back."

"I assure you, he's hardly holding me back."

After pulling up in front of my house, he slipped the car into park.

"Oh, hey!" I suddenly remembered the fake party. "You heard that I'm having a birthday thing for him on Friday? I'm sure Tyler will ask, but do you want to come?"

"Will you be there?"

What kind of question was that? My head fell back in surprise and Andrew's cheeks glowed pink.

I pressed my lips together, trying not to let my smirk grow. "I'm thinking so. Charlie, too, of course. There'll be a couple of people you know."

"You should invite Amelia, too. I don't think Tyler has the courage to do it himself."

"Amelia? The girl we had lunch with today?"

"That's the one. He likes her, but he's afraid to ask her out."

"Okay. I'll invite her, too. Thanks for the ride."

"Any time. I'll wait for you here in the morning, okay?"

I grabbed the door handle, ready to step out, but Andrew touched my arm, grabbing my attention.

"Hey, I'm sorry I upset you. Sometimes what I think spills out. Jansen's a great guy…to you. I've never seen him treat *you* with anything but respect."

"You don't have to worry about me. Not with him."

"But can you be without him?"

I opened my mouth to respond. The words sitting there were, "Yes, of course." Then why did my tongue retract at them? Why did they get muddled in my head with doubt? Exactly what truth wanted to spill out?

CHAPTER SIX

How I managed to pull off an impromptu party, I'll never know, but I did. I pleaded with my parents, gathered supplies, and enlisted help.

Friday began with a morning rain shower and panic. It hadn't rained in three weeks, for crying out loud. Why now? Thankfully, around ten o'clock, the clouds cleared out, and the sun did its part by raising the temperature to a muggy ninety degrees.

We all got to work in earnest. The house came alive with the buzz of my father's weed-whacker and the steady hum of Tyler's mower, both father and son grumbling about the wet grass. I wiped down the patio furniture, spread out tablecloths, and carried out totes of snacks. By noon, I'd broken quite a sweat and skipped inside to start on the cookies—the break-n'-bake kind. Nothing fancy.

Once the cookies were in the oven, I set my laptop on the beige breakfast bar to check emails. Gretta wanted to know if she could bring anything to the party, so I shot her a quick response.

An ad for a free trip to Sri Lanka popped up in the corner of the screen, and my hand moved to the Chrysoberyl necklace. I'd have to meet Uncle Fred some day. He had a knack for gifts.

The timer rang, snapping me from my thoughts. I snatched the worn-out hot pads from the counter to pull the tray of browned cookies out of the oven. Before I got a firm grip on the baking sheet, Jansen appeared as if from nowhere, sitting on the countertop.

"Need any help?"

He caught me by such surprise that I jolted and burned my arm on the heating coil, making me yelp and drop the hot pads to the floor.

"What the heck!"

In a blur of limbs, he stood at my side and led me toward the sink. He turned on the cold water, ran it over the wound, then pulled my face into his chest where the words, "That was so stupid," rumbled low.

"You better be talking to yourself. Where did you even come from?"

He pressed his lips to the top of my crown. Not quite a kiss. "Of course I meant me. I came in too quietly, I guess. He nuzzled me with a squeeze before leaving my side to take the cookies out.

My vision blurred, mesmerized at the sight of the falling water, but I could still see him peripherally. I swore he reached into the oven without hot pads. I started to warn him, but he had already closed the door by the time I turned to get a look and the cookies lay on the counter.

What a ridiculous thought. Like he'd grabbed a hot tray barehanded and didn't scream?

Then I focused on the floor—where the hot pads were.

Before I could process that, he edged back to my side, his head hung low.

"Jansen, it's okay, really. I've had worse." Though inwardly, I cursed because I knew my arm would burn again as soon as I removed it from the water. What a way to ruin the party.

He scrounged through our cupboard, where we kept a variety of medicines, resurfacing with two Tylenol. What was he thinking? This was too painful.

"Just take them," he said.

Fine. I humored him and took the pills, but they wouldn't do any good.

After I swallowed, he blinked in approval and guided my arm out of the water. "Let me see it."

Though I didn't get a close look, a blister had formed, and it stung the moment I removed it from the water. I flinched at the light touch of his fingertips, but his hand felt surprisingly cool. In fact, it made my skin tingle, so I relaxed into it. He hesitated over the burn, and when he withdrew, all evidence had disappeared. How strange, I didn't feel it at all.

"Does it hurt?" he asked.

"No, actually."

He shrugged, and his lip ticked up the slightest bit. "Fast-acting Tylenol."

I sank into the corner of the counter to marvel at my arm a few seconds longer, flipping it up and then down. There *had* been a blister, I was sure of it. He brushed his long fingers over my face, a gesture he so often did, and as usual, whatever thoughts rolled around vanished, all worry gone. The branding already a distant memory.

Jansen picked the hot pads up off the floor and placed them in their drawer. "Charlie's out back with Tyler. We came to help set up."

"You didn't have to do that. It's your birthday party."

He slid his hands into his pockets. "It is not. It's to get you out of a date with Andrew."

Sure, it had started that way, but now, I'd invested a lot of effort and was excited. I knew he didn't want it, that he didn't want anything to "commemorate his birth," as he put it, but I could be happy for him. I had invited all of our—well, my—friends for the occasion, and they were all coming.

I wiped my hands on a dishtowel and walked out the sliding door to greet Charlie with Jansen at my back.

Under the shade of the patio, Charlie wound the leaf blower's neon-orange cord. "Was that a scream?"

Tyler looked up, too. "Yeah, we thought we heard you yelp. Sounded like a wounded puppy."

"Oh, it was nothing. Jansen startled me, and I burned my arm." I tossed the towel over my shoulder and waved my arm to show no harm had come of it.

Charlie set the blower down and sauntered over to look at it.

"See, nothing. Two Tylenol and I'm good as new."

I swore he glared at Jansen, who returned an apologetic expression, walked away, and left me to wonder.

We spent the afternoon setting up outside. The brothers made quick work of the setup. They set out large tables single-handedly and lugged around several chairs at once. At one point, Tyler stopped to watch Charlie carry a twelve-pack carton of two-liter bottles one handed over his shoulder. Tyler eyed them and rubbed his biceps. "I've got to get Mom and Dad to spring for a weight bench this Christmas."

After a while, we had nothing to do, and the guests weren't due to arrive for another half hour. Charlie and Tyler disappeared to the computer, and Jansen and I sat at the pool's edge to dip our feet in. The ripples mixed with the relaxing nature of the water to captivate us. I extended and retracted my foot, absorbing the feel of the cool water and the gentle resistance. With a flick of my ankle, I kicked out and watched as droplets flew, then descended to create rings on the reflective surface.

"Happy Birthday." I laid my head on Jansen's shoulder.

"Thanks. Just do me one favor?"

"Anything, of course."

"Put that big shirt on before anyone gets here."

Big shirt? "My cover-up?"

He stared straight ahead and wouldn't look at me but nodded slightly.

Ha! Such a big-brother move. In mock horror, I gasped and splashed him with my foot. He unleashed a breath as I returned my head to his shoulder.

"I already have one brother. Really, I don't need another."

"Brother, yes," he sighed. "Seriously, Ellie. That suit… and you invited the guys. They won't be able to keep their eyes off you."

It was the same bikini I'd worn all summer. Andrew had seen it enough, and I liked it. It covered me in all the right places; modest as far as bikinis went. Practically a sports bra…with spaghetti straps.

"It's a pool party," I said slowly for emphasis.

He grasped the cat's eye necklace he'd given me and tugged it higher on my neck, unveiling the freckled starburst beneath. Pretty sure he intended to draw attention *away* from my cleavage, but as soon as he let the pendant go, it plummeted. Low. Right between my breasts. He didn't seem to know whether to stare there or at the star.

It made me grin shamelessly. "What about you? Clara's gonna be here. Bet she won't be able to take her eyes off your bare chest."

"And? She's with Mark now, isn't she?"

"They're not together yet. Seems to me this pool party came about in place of their date."

"In place of *your* date." His black swimsuit and sun-bronzed skin brought out the rich inky velvet of his eyes as he flipped into brooding mode mid-sentence. "You invited Tim?" With that, he slid the sunglasses from his head to his nose.

Sure enough, there stood Tim, waving at us from the gate. How had Jansen heard him come up? It shouldn't have been a surprise, though. He always seemed to hear things before I did.

I returned the wave. "He was there when I asked Gretta and Clara."

As if on cue, she arrived at the side as well. Only she would wear bikini-matching stilettos to a casual pool party. Her hair was done up in a perfect French twist, one dainty curl left to dangle like a pet caterpillar. She had her hands full with a hefty gift, wrapped neatly and tied with a pristine, and rather large, gold bow. Her wide smile and attentive gaze were also only for Jansen, Mark being nowhere in sight. "Happy birthday!"

He responded with a mere slight nod.

"Oh!" she said. Then, like the perfectly reared diva at a garden social, "The yard looks lovely."

Moments later, Andrew's head surfaced over the fence.

"Hey, is it party time?"

I motioned him and several other guests in, ushering them toward the grill where Tyler and Charlie had appeared. When Tyler started the music, the backyard filled with the heavy bass of the stereo and the casual chatting of teens. Gretta and Clara gossiped about a couple of the girls at school. What they had worn on the first day. Who was seeing who, and, oh my, who'd broken up?

I couldn't have cared less.

Hot as it was, no one entered the pool. Who wanted to be first? So, half listening while dreaming about the water, I also watched for Amelia to come. Tyler didn't know I invited her, and I couldn't wait to see his reaction. He'd just picked up two drinks and stood near the fence with his back to it when she showed up. Her big floppy hat arrived first, and it took me a minute to realize who was under there. She said something to Mark and fumbled with the gate's lock.

When Tyler spotted her, his entire body tensed. The corners of his lips and brow lifted as one before saying something to her. Probably a polite "hello" or maybe, "I didn't know you were coming." He balanced both cups in one hand and managed the stubborn latch for her, swinging the gate wide. The gentlemanly gesture made her tilt her head sweetly as she walked through. Her flimsy cover skirt led the way in the breeze. It bore the same shade of sunshine yellow as her high-cut, plunging one-piece. That girl had enviable curves.

I'm pretty sure the cups in Tyler's hand weren't for her, but he handed her one anyway and casually shifted his weight, crossing one foot over the other.

In the distance, Jansen stayed in a huddle with Charlie and Andrew. What did they talk about? Something way more interesting than the effects of chlorine on hair. Jansen burst out laughing at whatever Charlie said. Was it possible he enjoyed himself? As if reading my mind, he winked and leaned back in his lounge chair, fingers laced behind his head, one ankle crossed over a knee.

Aaron came up from out of nowhere and startled me

from my trance. "Did you hear about what I did to my foot?"

"Huh?" I whipped around.

"My foot. Did you hear about it?"

"No." I scrutinized it with interest.

Clara clicked her tongue in disgust, but that didn't stop Aaron from removing the bandage.

"Ew!" Gretta looked away and held out her hands as a sort of protective shield. "We don't want to see it."

"What did you do?" I asked with something like a grim curiosity.

He smiled a toothy grin and flaunted his blackened toe with the nail hanging from it, nearly off. It was a gruesome sight.

Though repulsive and though it made my stomach churn, I put on a false bravado and leaned in for a closer look. "That's gotta hurt. What did you do?"

"Aw, it was nothin'." He wobbled on his good foot and, unable to pass up the chance to tease a couple of cute girls, waved the toe in the faces of horror-struck Gretta and Clara. Then he lost his balance and landed a heavy hand on my shoulder for support, his weight almost taking me down with him.

The scene made Jansen rise from his chair, where he stood motionless, intent on me. All joviality gone. Goodness, he could be over-protective. Even Tyler wasn't that worried about me—currently flirting rather loudly with Amelia.

I frowned at Jansen and helped Aaron steady himself.

Both feet on the ground again, Aaron slipped his shirt off and tossed it over his shoulder. "I was helping my dad roof the house and dropped a full pack of shingles on my foot."

"Wow." I shielded the sun with my hand. "It really took your nail off?"

"I was wearing sandals." He wiggled the nail, which resulted in squeals from the girls, much to his delight. "Think it's about to fall off."

Enough of that. Time to get him settled somewhere. So, I ducked beneath his arm and threw mine around his bare back. "Let's find you a chair."

He muttered something about gratitude and grasped my shoulders with sweaty fingers. It made me stumble under his weight, but I ignored Jansen's icy glare. He could just chill.

It wasn't ten seconds after settling Aaron into a lounge chair that Tim, from out of nowhere, scooped my legs from under me.

Seriously, where had he come from?

My initial screams gave way to laughter, and my feet thrashed. I'm sure it looked like I loved it, but seriously, I was practically naked and pressed against his chest. I thought he'd let me go once he got that squeal out of me. Isn't that why guys did such stupid things? For the reaction? Yet he didn't.

"Put me down!" I said, smacking his chest. What else could I do? I could flip myself from his arms if I had clothes on, but we weren't even in the grass. Also, if I wiggled too much, I'd wiggle myself right out of my darn bikini. I should have worn that dang cover-up.

Then, quite suddenly, he bent at the knees and launched us both straight into the pool.

I thought my chest would burst from the icy water.

His feet planted on the bottom, and he lifted me to the surface, where I sputtered, still cradled in his moronic arms.

I got goosebumps, making me super aware of his skin on mine.

Not Tim, though. He was oblivious. Unaware that I wasn't a giggly, adoring fan. "I thought this was a pool party!" he said, smiling a toothy invitation.

I pushed myself away and tried to swim to the side, where Jansen stood motionless beside Clara. I'd meant to pull him in—

But Tim caught me before I could get there. "No, ya don't."

I bantered and hit him playfully, but was only being polite. It's a thing girls do that men misinterpret. Seemed pretty obvious to me that I screamed to let me go. While I struggled to escape, he pulled me even closer, skin to skin, his hand high on my rib cage. Just under my breasts. It made me well aware of each delicate hair on my body rising to stand erect.

Jansen was over it. I knew it. Charlie, who readied himself in a battle stance aimed at his brother, knew it too, as he watched Jansen's hands curl into tight fists. Even Clara clicked her tongue in disgust, and Andrew stood as if to see us better with his sad eyes.

Tim really should have considered Jansen.

His toes gripped the side of the pool, readying to dive.

I tensed in Tim's arms—

With unnatural power, Jansen leapt straight at us.

I didn't have time to inhale before he knocked us into the water.

The world spun, and my heart hammered with a force that expelled what little air remained in my lungs. Tim's arms released as he flailed to stand himself up. I hadn't yet grasped that I sank before familiar arms wrapped around my waist, lifting me to the surface, where I gasped for much-needed air.

What the hell!

Tim glared over my head at Jansen, whose hand tightened into a fist in front of my belly. The veins of his forearm surged like venom-filled snakes. His chest swelled with heaving breaths. Tim had lit his fuse, its heat tangible.

The pool whirled on an axis, and no one else existed but me in the circle of Jansen's arm and Tim across from us. As though we'd gone through a tunnel and were on one side with the crushing silence of the crowd on the other, and everyone lobbied for a clear view of the show.

Charlie's timing was impeccable as he performed a cannonball, and Andrew was hot on his heels. Feet splayed wide, Charlie rose to his full height and gave Jansen a look of harsh reproach. Andrew gave Tim an unexpected high five, like congratulating him after a well-fought game, yet somehow also telling him to let it go. That it was over.

Fortunately, their antics were the diversion needed to evaporate the agitated energy that quieted even the birds. Tim skulked away, and I pivoted to thank Jansen.

That's what I intended, but I didn't end up thanking him.

Because when I turned to face him, he still glared at his retreating foe, and I started to think maybe Tim had been playing around. What, did he think I couldn't handle it on my own? He'd just embarrassed me in front of everyone, and Tim, too. Jansen had gone too far.

"What was that for?"

He gestured toward Tim with his chin. "He knows."

"Well, I don't. Will you ever let me have fun?"

Oh. Those were Andrew's words spilling from my mouth, weren't they?

He threw me a questioning stare. "You wanted that?" He shook his head as if I was a child, his kid sister. "You didn't want that."

How did he know what I did or didn't want? He didn't, and I wasn't about to give him the satisfaction of knowing he knew me that well. Because he did know me that well. But he didn't have the right to think it.

Then, all the boys cannon-balled into the pool one by one in quick succession, as each tried to outdo Charlie's splash. He stood so tall, there wasn't any competition, not really. When he rose, the glistening droplets highlighted his muscular frame, making him difficult to ignore. Like a look-at-me bronzed toner. Plus, the water tightened his brown ringlets, which drew more attention to his set jaw and the cleft in his angular chin. This was not a guy to be trifled with.

Charlie pulled me away from Jansen and threw me to the other end—a light toss coming from him, but still. It diffused any argument I might have got up.

While Tim didn't stop the flirting, he also didn't try to hold me anymore. Weird how he'd attempted to at all. Hadn't Jansen proven himself in the lunchroom?

Soon after, Jansen started up a round of water-basketball, so I swam over to the steps and sat where the waves lapped just over my legs. Mark got Gretta involved in the game by putting her on his shoulders. Surprisingly, that didn't even faze Clara. She was too busy watching Jansen from the edge of the pool and squealing whenever water splashed her. Jansen made sure that happened often, and it wasn't to flirt, either. He assured she wound up drenched each time.

To test the water, Amelia dipped a toe in. "Thanks for inviting me."

I blocked the sun with my hand to see her better. "No problem. I'm glad you could make it."

With a friendly wave to Charlie, who had spotted her, she then returned her attention to me. "Would you like my hat?"

"No, thanks, not if you sit by me. You know… so I don't have to look up."

It didn't take her long to sit on the edge, where she handed me a cup of juice. "Thought you might be thirsty." I thanked her, and she leaned in close to whisper, "The truth is, Tyler keeps bringing them to me, and I'm about to burst."

Charlie took about four strides to walk from the opposite end of the pool. "Mia, I didn't know you'd be here. Are you friends with our Ellie?"

"I am." Amelia winked, encouraging me not to mention we'd barely met. "And with Tyler, too."

Though Charlie looked at me, he tapped Amelia's knee. "I tried getting this one to join choir. Never had any luck."

"Mmm. The paintbrush is *my* instrument."

"Piano, too?" Charlie said, with a hint of questioning in his tone. "Didn't your mom teach you?"

"You remember. But, really…"

"Definitely the paintbrush." He waved Tyler over. "Hey, Ty! Amelia here was just saying she'd like to retouch a banner with Paintshop. You're our resident computer whisperer. Help her out, would you?"

"Computer?" Amelia choked. "Wait, I—oh." An idea touched her expression, and I swear she tracked it with her eyes. "You can do that?"

Tyler shrugged and tried to look casual, but he also wrinkled his nose and sniffed, licked his lips, tapped his cheekbone, and finally brushed imaginary lint from his bare shoulder, giving himself away. The boy was as bad as a batter stepping up to home plate. "A banner, huh?"

With that, Charlie took my hand and guided me to the center of the pool. My brother slid into my vacated spot.

I rubbed my earlobe between two fingers and glanced at Charlie with a touch of admiration. "That was smooth."

"I know. Tyler was kind of glowering in the corner."

"If you catch him alone," I said, "tell him to lay off the drinks."

We swam and ate snacks past the dinner hour and well into dusk. The sun set, taking with it the tension of the day. At last, one by one, our guests departed, leaving Charlie, Tyler, Jansen, and me alone again around the pool. The stars were out, and the moon cast a luminous sort of glow.

With muffled voices, Charlie and Tyler sat at one of the patio tables and chatted. The soft din of their conversation blended with the call of the crickets and the occasional hoot of nearby owls, performing the evening's soundtrack.

Too tired to talk, Jansen and I glided lazily in the pool now that we had it to ourselves.

I worked through a few breast strokes and took in the peaceful view. The moon cast shadows, all varying shades of black, onto the trees that framed the night sky. The limbs bowed to the wind in a dance, whispering to each other gently. Their serene exchange rose and fell with the din of the cicadas.

I flipped over in the water to float on its glassy surface, attempted to relax my neck, then stretched my arms out wide like wings. Half submerged, my soft breaths became a roar. The pool motor hummed, and the chlorine thickened in my nose. I held fast to the present and let the ripples lap over my thighs, my hips, my stomach, my breasts.

Jansen's fingers found mine, touching me just enough to keep us tethered. At his touch, my body went limp, and we floated side by side the way we used to do when we were small.

And ah! The feel of his skin.

My fingers slipped, and he squeezed the tips of them. Maybe it was the increased pressure or my heightened senses, but something triggered a shiver that spread outward from the center of me, taking me by surprise. All these years, he had always taken my hand, but tonight, it felt extraordinarily different.

I tamped down whatever that was and let the water bob us along. Stirred only by our beating hearts, the ripples lobbed us around the pool's edge. As we floated, warm blood flowed through my veins with a fizziness, the tingle of his hand still present. What was that?

It made me want to peek at Jansen, maybe open one eye to see if he felt it too. When I did, starlit eyes glittered back at me. For how long? Had he only just looked? Or could he have been as entranced with me as I was of him? Of us.

We let our feet drift downward, the water rippling as we found our balance. The motion of the water guided us to the side, where we propped our backs against the pool wall, shoulder to shoulder.

The silence was too exquisite to disturb, so I whispered, "It's beautiful, isn't it? Perfect."

He bent toward me as if to share a secret, only he lingered a moment, hesitating. No, not hesitating because he didn't seem nervous, but certain and purposeful. Like maybe his secret was how he wanted his breath to whisper over the shell of my ear. To reach through me where it curled my toes and spiraled my heart. "You have no idea."

I couldn't breathe. Why couldn't I breathe? When his fingers lifted from the water, droplets tinkled and I swallowed hard. Air came in short supply as his wet fingertip drew a line down my chin, and he guided me to look at him.

Whoa, this wasn't us. We didn't do this, had never crossed this line. Had never wanted to. But every tingling cell in my body told me to shut the hell up and step over that threshold.

Tyler belted out a laugh that shook the night from the sky. Really, the jolt that hit my insides lit as vivid as lightning, enough to make me glance toward the heavens in search of it. Damn him.

I cleared my throat and ducked my chin very near his

shoulder as goosebumps prickled along every inch of me, very aware of the way Jansen smelled of a nutty grain and chlorine and of how his heavy breathing fell over my ear.

"Ignore him," he said as a rumble from his chest. Then, I swore he said, "Please stay," but no breath came with it.

Whatever he did, or that I felt—or didn't feel—I jumped away. He released me and I swam about to face him.

"What did you say?"

He gaped at me with equal surprise. "I said, 'Ignore him.'"

"No, after that."

"After what?"

He held a hand out. "Come back to me," but his lips hadn't moved. His words—a voice without breath.

I blinked several times. "How are you doing that?"

When he pulled himself up to his full height, he looked at Charlie with eyes so wide they reflected the moonlight. At our commotion, Charlie rushed to the side of the pool at an impossible speed. He forced laughter and splattered water at Jansen. "High time we got home, little brother. I'm sure Tyler and Ellie have had enough for one day."

Jansen swallowed hard and swam to the pool stairs.

"Good night, Ellie… Tyler," Charlie said politely, and then they were gone.

Tyler looked at me with questioning alarm, but I could only shrug. I had no idea what had just happened.

CHAPTER SEVEN

Morning broke, and I hopped out of bed as soon as the sunlight touched my eyelids. Today, Jansen got his license. It wasn't that I couldn't already drive. I could. Only I had to beg my parents to borrow their cars.

When Tyler turned sixteen, our parents had bought themselves a new car, and he got their old one. Everyone assumed we'd share it when my turn came. Not sure what we were thinking. Tyler made such a dump out of the thing I held my nose I walked past it on the road. No way was I getting into that heap. Was it fair? Absolutely not. My parents should have forced him to clean it, but honestly, he'd trashed it so much, I didn't want it.

Truthfully, it didn't bother me. Jansen's birthday was a measly two months after mine, and anyway, we were attached at the hip; it wasn't like I ever went anywhere that didn't include him.

I put on my bathing suit, still a tad wet from the night before, and tied my hair up in a messy ponytail to keep it off my neck.

Where would we go first? The mall? I pictured us driving there, parking his sleek black car near the movie entrance, and maybe catching a matinee. Afterward, we'd grab lunch at the food court, maybe share an order of fries. He'd drink most of my Coke because I rarely finished it. Then we'd walk hand in hand back to the car—

Whoa, this sounded like a date.

I threw my cover-up over my head in case it was too chilly to get in the water this early.

Okay, miniature golf. That could be fun. He'd pick me up. We'd play golf as the sun set over the horizon, its light reflecting in his eyes so they glowed with hints of twilight, picking up echoes of peachy roses and amber. Maybe a hint of violet. I could feel his arms around me as he helped me figure out how to swing my club—

Wow, my brain was in overdrive. I darn well knew how to swing a club. Where was this coming from?

Before going downstairs, I grabbed the summer romance novel I'd been reading from my desk, and flipped the pages like a fan.

I figured I'd hear from Jansen around ten o'clock, so I headed out the sliding glass door to the pool.

My dad, also an early riser, drank his coffee under the overhang. He flicked his newspaper to fold it better and glanced up when he heard me. "Morning, El-Bell."

I kissed him on the cheek. "I didn't know you were home."

"Yeah, they dropped the last two legs of my trip, so I rode jump seat. Got in pretty late."

"Did you eat already?"

"Nah, only coffee. Wanna eat with me?"

"Maybe just an egg. I bet Jansen will want to go out for donuts or something."

"That's right. It's licensing day."

I grabbed a low beach chair, the kind where your butt brushes the ground, and set it in my favorite spot at the top of the pool stairs where I could dip my feet in. Birds in the nearby trees sang back and forth in short, sharp chirps, slightly louder than the soothing burbling of the filter.

Last evening played over in my memory on a loop. A deliriously pleasant loop. A wildly unexpected loop. The pads of his fingers had brushed mine, a mere whisper from his fingerprints to the nerve endings along my own. Whatever they whispered, I'd responded to it.

Also, what about that second tremor? Oh, and it had been a tremor, too. He must have felt it. His breath had ignited a spark against my ear, a jolt that shocked my body. My heart twisted over on itself, remembering. It had been that memorable.

A shadow fell over me, where my dad blocked the sun. "Whatcha thinking about?"

"Nothing at all. Just reading."

My dad did his best to hold back a chuckle. He took my book out of my hands, turned it around, and returned it to my outstretched fingers. "Eggs are waiting for you, Miss Nothing-At-All.'"

The day didn't get any shorter from there. What is it about waiting for someone that throws the whole schedule off? I spent some of the time plucking out a few tunes: a couple of ballads, some old campfire melodies, and my own rendition of *The Devil Went Down to Georgia*. Jansen always used vocals to mimic the banjo part, making me hoot with laughter. After grabbing a ham sandwich for lunch, I mulled over why he hadn't called.

Was it possible he failed his test? I'd driven with him while he had his permit, and he proved an excellent driver. Maybe it had something to do with the pool, like maybe he noticed the goosebumps.

I'd finished putting away a load of laundry when the phone rang. My heart leapt ahead of me, as if racing to answer first. "So, are you a licensed driver yet?"

"As a matter of fact, I have been since winter, yes."

The voice was not Jansen's.

"Oh. I thought you were…someone else."

"Jansen?"

"Yes. Is this Tim?"

"Yep. Nice party yesterday."

I glanced at the clock, which read 7:00, and sighed. Unless

it was Jansen, I didn't feel like talking on the phone.

At least Tim got straight to the point. "Listen, a few of us decided at your place to head to the movies tonight. Any chance you'd want to go with me?"

"Tonight? I don't know." I twirled the spiral phone cord around my index finger. "I haven't thought that far ahead yet. Plus, Jansen just got his license."

"When are you going to wake up? Either he's your boyfriend or not. Jeez, it's like you're married." A muffled growl sounded low over the phone, as if he'd covered the mouthpiece to let off steam. "Sorry. Call if you change your mind." *Click.*

Who did this guy think he was, accusing me of having anything but friendly affection for Jansen? He knew nothing about us.

Frustrated, I went to the kitchen to get a snack, where my mom sat at the table, flipping through a magazine. The child in me wanted her undivided attention. To fix me. So, I sighed and plopped down in front of her.

She peered over the pages without moving her head. "Was that Jansen?"

"No," I said with a pout. "I thought for sure he'd call."

"He will. Maybe things didn't go well, and he's embarrassed. Why don't you call him?"

"I don't know." That was true enough. I had no reason not to call. Just a feeling he didn't want me to.

"Who was on the phone then?"

I exhaled and my shoulders slumped. "That was Tim."

When I didn't say more, she stared at me before saying, "And?"

"He wanted me to go to the movies with him and some friends tonight."

"That sounds nice."

I stretched and yawned. "Yeah, but I don't want to go."

"It wouldn't hurt to get out with your other friends now and then." She touched my arm, which got my attention. "You two are getting older. Maybe it's best if you don't place all your eggs in one basket."

Ugh. When she started pulling out the idioms, it was time to end the conversation. So, with a grimace, I lay my head on my arm. "Mom, he's just my friend."

"If he is just your friend, he wouldn't mind if you went out with the others. I love him as much as you do, but you two have always been a little exclusive. I think it irritates your other friends."

It did irritate them. I knew that. And I didn't care.

By Sunday evening, I'd had enough of sulking around, waiting for word from Jansen. When I found Tyler playing solitaire in his bedroom, I challenged him instead to a round of two-handed Euchre. I asked if he'd taken a look at the packet Andrew gave him about the Air Force Academy, but he waved me off, saying he'd check it out later.

We played for a while before I launched into the real reason I challenged him to a game.

"Have you talked to Charlie recently?" With that, I took his ace.

"Yeah, I guess. Talked to him earlier. Dangit, I got a crappy hand."

"Oh?" Was that casual? I'd meant to sound casual.

Tyler bit his lip and managed to trump my last card, but I still won the round.

Once the pile was collected, he shuffled the cards. "Why? Something you wanted to know?"

"No." I sat forward, eager for more, but caught myself and reclined. If Tyler knew I cared, he'd tease, and I couldn't handle that just then. So, I picked at my fingernails to keep from making eye contact. "Did he say anything about the party?"

"Just that he'd had a good time, I guess. Nothing, really."

"Did he mention anything about Jansen's license?"

Tyler dealt the shuffled deck. "Why don't you call him and ask? Since when do you have to go through me?"

"I was only curious. They left so suddenly."

He looked up from his hand. "Yeah, they really did. You noticed that, too? One minute, Charlie and I were talking about Amelia. The next thing I knew, he was at the side of the pool. Got up muttering curses at Jansen. Came out of nowhere. What happened on your end?"

"Oh, pretty much the same. We were lounging in the water, and then Charlie told him it was time to go."

"Huh. Who knows? Don't worry about it, though. Charlie didn't say anything today. I'm sure he's just busy."

That had to be it. He was just busy. Too busy to call his closest friend.

"So, Amelia, huh?" I did my best to sound interested. Plus, I wanted to know how my matchmaking had gone.

Tyler tried to hide a smile that wouldn't quit. "You invited her, didn't you?"

With a tug on my ear, I nodded. "She's a nice girl."

"Thanks, El."

He beat me the next three rounds, and I gave up. My mind was no longer on the game. Worse, I didn't think Tyler's was, either, and he still walloped me. I had hoped he could distract me, but my thoughts would not be swayed.

The weekend dragged. By Tuesday morning, even though Jansen had made it quite clear that he, and only he, would be taking me to school from here on out, I had decided to ride the bus. I didn't want to beg Andrew for a lift. Either Jansen forgot his promise to pick me up or had failed the driver's test. Since he forgot nothing when it came to me, it was no doubt the latter.

I put my cereal bowl in the dishwasher, tugged on my shoes, grabbed my schoolbag, and hurried outside to catch the bus.

With one foot inside the car, Andrew stood at the driver's side and leaned over the door. He glared daggers as he blew his nose. When I followed his gaze, he stared at Charlie's second-hand black sedan, the windows all rolled down. Jansen sat with both hands on the steering wheel, deep in thought and staring straight ahead—

A snarl shattered time as Otis stormed the fence with claws that tore through wood.

God, would I ever remember to expect that? My heart thrashed. Whether from the beast or for Jansen, I couldn't say.

Fine. Then why hadn't he called? With conflicting feelings, I threw a quick wave to Andrew and let myself into Jansen's car.

He didn't greet me or even bother to look at me. I'd barely buckled myself in when he shoved the gear into drive, pulling away with such force, he slammed me into my seat. Well, this was a new, unwelcome Jansen. The engine revved as he switched gears in rapid succession, and the wind roared through the open window. I had to use my fist as a hair tie.

"So, you got your license!" I hollered over the wind, to which he lifted his chin. "Why didn't you call?"

"Didn't know I was supposed to."

Didn't know he was supposed to? Since when did I need to ask?

"What's wrong with you?" I demanded, pulling a long, stray hair from between my lips.

"It's nothing, Gabriella."

The sound of my full name from his lips slashed my heart and ripples of disappointment worked their way up my tight throat. I opened my mouth to say something, but unsure what would spill out, I closed it again. It was better to look out the window.

We sped past the elementary school. The park where we used to picnic whizzed by, as did the kayak rental shop and the old oak tree I'd once gotten stuck in. I just sat there in silence and wondered what I should say.

Something must have happened. Why else would he give me this freaking cold shoulder?

"Jansen, did—"

In one quick motion, he turned the radio on and up loud, drowning out any chance of conversation.

Tears stung but, too proud to let him see, I turned toward the window, the wind making it hard to breathe.

When we arrived at school, he drove the car around to the student drop-off point. I felt my face burn, and he knew because he wouldn't look at me. No, he stared off into the parking lot as if bored. Bored!

"What? You're dropping me off?" I choked back a sob and snatched my backpack.

Meanwhile, he said nothing. In fact, he seemed to find something interesting under his fingernail. So, I got out of the car and intended to slam the door. Before I could get any force behind it, he sped out of the drop-off lane. The door slammed itself shut, and the tires squealed as he made his way to the parking lot.

Steam swelled inside my head as my blood boiled. I stood there for half a minute, stealing large breaths.

How dare he? I had no other thought. How dare he? Tension built in my neck, squeezed my shoulders, bit down my arms. It prickled through my fingers until I had to do something—hit something. So, I swung the weight of my backpack around and crashed it into the metal support beam of the loading dock with all my might. The impact reverberated as a deafening ring, making the girl who stood next to it gasp and jump away.

My lip quivered, so I bit it into submission to walk by the polished mahogany bench where senior athletes gathered before morning classes. I walked past the water fountain and the library no one ever visited and the stark, drab walls with the broad scarlet stripe across the middle to my locker. Alone and rejected, I kept my head low and avoided all eye contact, withdrawing into myself. If I'd had a tail, it would be tucked between my legs.

My thoughts were so entirely on him that I didn't pay attention to collecting my things and grabbed my English book instead of science. Didn't realize it until halfway to class, and had to return to my stupid locker where my brother hovered over Jansen, several lockers away. He scowled, a pensive and foreign expression. Let him! I held back a huff, switched my books, and slammed my locker closed. With a spin on the heel of my shoe, I headed toward class again.

I wasn't out of earshot when Tyler said, "You've really hurt her."

That made Jansen snap. "Do you think I don't know that?"

So he knew? He did this on purpose? What had I done to make him act this way? I'd had breakups that didn't sting like this.

By lunchtime, my fury had become a volcano, its magma bubbling toward eruption. I hadn't seen Jansen since the morning and he wasn't waiting for me outside class, but I wasn't about to wait around for him. Not after the way he'd treated me. He would have to find me, I thought, as I huffed into the cafeteria.

There, Gretta sat between Tim and Amelia, cutting her salad into tiny pieces. Tyler busied himself scratching a pencil over his paper, probably finishing up some forgotten homework due next period.

Meanwhile, Aaron plopped his tray on the other end of the table. When he tossed a grape into the air, it missed his open mouth and bounced. Hopped onto the floor. Rolled under one table, then another. The green, oblong thing landed itself right under the foot of Mrs. Fushi. She stopped short and inspected the bottom of her shoe. Then she looked around the room for the culprit, at which point Aaron snatched up his milk carton, appearing to study it while raking his nails through his eyebrows.

"Where's Jansen?" I asked Gretta.

"Tim said he saw him talking to Clara by her locker. Did you two have a fight?"

"Of course not." Oof, that was hasty. It wasn't a lie. We couldn't very well fight if he wasn't speaking to me. But Clara? Of all people, I expected him to be with her the least.

Then I saw them. I didn't believe Gretta until I witnessed it for myself; Jansen walking…and laughing…with Clara. Each of them had their lunch tray as they strolled toward us, and I couldn't help but stare. Jansen wouldn't meet my gaze. Then they walked right by, passed us up, and aimed for a table beyond ours like we weren't there. I thought I caught a grimace on Jansen's expression as I turned, bewildered, back to Gretta. Even she looked shocked, a French fry poised halfway to her mouth. She dropped the fry and glanced at me as if I had any ideas.

"No." She extended the "o," and her face flashed from shock to amusement, then worry before touching my hand. "Oh gosh, are you okay?"

I yanked back and shrugged. "Of course, I'm okay." Ugh, too much happiness in my voice betrayed me. "It isn't as if Jansen and I are *together*." If that were true, why did it feel like my insides twisted and ripped apart?

What I wanted to do was slam my head on the table and be left alone. Instead, I rotted away in the middle of the crowded cafeteria, with more than a few pairs of eyes feasting on me. I had no choice but to put on a fake smile and somehow get through this lunch period.

I looked one more time to see if maybe I'd missed something.

Clara sat with her back to me, where her artificial blonde hair waved like a victory banner down to her waist. She leaned toward Jansen, her talons close to his hand. Something made him turn in my direction, but his face was as cold and expressionless as the glasses perched on his nose.

When he returned his full attention to Clara, I returned mine to the table. My elbows dug into its faux wood, the only things that kept me upright. I tucked my shoulders in tight.

The hundred-degree weather pressed in on me and squeezed my lungs. Beads of sweat slid down my forehead, yet I had chills, and had to wipe my clammy hands on my pink denim shorts. Andrew set his tray across from me as the smell of school pizza wafted my way.

My throat tightened to keep the scent from churning my nauseated belly.

"I'm not hungry." I got up to take my lunch to the conveyor belt, staring at my feet.

Gretta looked ready to follow, but I faked a dry heave, and she sat again.

"She okay?" I heard Andrew ask.

Without waiting for a response, I wandered through the shiny red double-door frame into the hall, my feet carrying me with no destination in mind. When I came upon a dead end, I turned the corner to another corridor. Natural light streamed through a doorway to the outside. Maybe a fresh breeze would clear my head.

Back straight, I walked out, where I sucked in the open air. Definitely not the reprieve I expected. A stifling stillness hung without the slightest wind to disturb it. Here the sun blazed on my neck and grass lay brown and dead, closer to straw than grass. Insects in the stiff blades buzzed, crackled, and clicked, giving the impression that the sun-ravaged land sizzled like tears in a hot oiled skillet.

I tried to shake it off and told myself it wasn't jealousy that plagued me, but the loss of someone I hadn't known I could lose. I wiped the sweat from my forehead at the thought. If he'd wanted to ask Clara out, he could have. Did he think I'd be mad? What, like I'd say "no?"

Clara. Long-legged, hair-flipping, tongue-clicking Clara. My go-to weapon of choice when I'd most felt like teasing him. Fingernail-tapping, gum-smacking, boundary-lacking Clara.

Again and again, I analyzed every angle, but things didn't add up. For that reason, I couldn't let it go.

With mere seconds to spare, I made it to English class. Jansen sat at his desk, absorbed in our assigned book, *Faust*. It was his favorite, and I knew he'd already read it twice. He still wore his sunglasses, and he usually removed them to read, the faker. So, I bit back the tears and sped by to sit at my desk, but knocked Tim's books to the floor.

"I'm sorry," I said, as we both bent over to pick them up.

"That's alright. You okay?"

I nodded and shoved the last book onto Tim's desk before glancing at Jansen. Did I glimpse a soft expression behind his dark glasses? It could have been anguish. Or maybe I read him all wrong because the next thing I knew, his nose was back in the book.

After class ended, he didn't bother waiting. In fact, no sooner had the bell rung than he was out of his seat, headed for the door.

Tim collected his books and tucked them into his sack. "What's with him?"

"I don't know."

"I saw him with Clara earlier."

Who hadn't?

He closed my notebook and handed it to me, since I froze. "Is that what this is about? If it is, he's being awfully cruel. That's what I think. I've never seen anyone flip so fast in my life."

"It's nothing," I lied, accepting the notebook and picking up my pencil pouch.

Maybe Clara had pressured him to ditch me. That made some sense.

Tim walked me to choir. Probably chatted with me, too, but I stayed buried beneath my thoughts. All through choir, I remained in my head, grateful Jansen didn't stand near me on the risers. I was so focused on him that I swore I felt the energy of his gaze on the back of my neck.

What did Clara think of all this? I leaned forward around Gretta to get a glimpse of her. She just stood there like a contestant who'd won the prize. Hands clasped behind her back, chest puffed, lips pursed and antagonizing. Her shoulders danced with a self-satisfied air.

Only I'd never even entered the contest.

Then, it came time for the solo, the one Jansen sang until tryouts, which was, of course, a joke. Andrew accompanied us on the piano for this piece, and even he glanced up to marvel at Jansen's voice.

In contrast to the hurt, when he sang, emotion overwhelmed me. Later, I'd wonder how my heart could be so fickle, but it melted in that moment.

It wasn't just me, either. It was the same for all the girls. His baritone touched us all, including Mrs. Harding. Her usual tense grip on her baton relaxed while he sang, and she appeared to forget the rest of us were even there.

In those moments when his singing drowned my sorrow, a sort of madness came over me. It could be nothing else. From his own lips, he sang the words in his voice. I heard him. But he also sang different words into my head and in harmony, no less. I seemed to hear dual voices; a musical duet with himself.

> *Be not anxious if I stray,*
> *Or fear you are not whole.*
> *Our hearts entwine eternally,*
> *You're woven in my soul.*

His silhouette reflected in the window of Mrs. Harding's office. Jansen sang, not watching Clara, not looking at his music, not following Mrs. Harding. His voice brimming with mournful tenderness, he serenaded the slumped shoulders of a girl with long strawberry-blonde hair and as many freckles as she had memories of him.

CHAPTER EIGHT

With my hand still on the doorknob, my heart sank. Jansen's black sedan sat in front of my house. But why? After the way he'd treated me yesterday?

The bacon I'd eaten for breakfast resurfaced, rising up my throat where it stuck in a knot.

I took a lungful of air and pressed forward, each step as if walking through mud. Could I get into his car and pretend nothing had happened? Maybe I'd yell at him. Or punch him. I'd ridden the bus home yesterday afternoon. I could do it again now. Maybe I should ignore him, like he'd done to me.

On the stoop railings, impatiens of pink, purple, and white waved as if saying goodbye. Their late-summer blossoms flowed low over their containers. My feet thumped over the gray-painted wood planks of the porch and dragged along to the brick steps. I dipped a foot down each cliff, like testing the water—my hand trailing the banister, delaying the inevitable. The stairs gave way to the flat plain of the sidewalk and I had no choice but to storm past his car.

Was he here to apologize? His conscience must have kicked in. Perhaps I misjudged, and he came to make things —

A growling bark cut through my thoughts as Otis slammed into the wood, and his claws scraped and dug.

My hands flew to my heart, guarding it. This morning, Otis shot out so fast that my lip quivered, and tears sprang. I muttered obscenities under my breath, more to myself for never remembering his routine. Because he was always freaking there.

That jolt to the heart lurched me past Jansen's car to the corner bus stop without giving him even a single sideways glance. My one thought? I hoped to look more composed than I felt inside, where my stomach twisted and churned.

I guess I expected him to chase me, maybe beg my forgiveness. Was it too much to ask him to at least lower the window and say "hello" in his smooth, melancholy voice? Instead, he revved his engine, making a real display of it, and when he sped away, it broke my heart.

Friendship should be safe. Who else pretended to enjoy princess movies or read Poe's haunting stories aloud in terrifying voices so he could watch my bottom lip tremble with delicious fear? Or knew my fingers ached even when the weather was only a little chilly or that I preferred fewer ice-cubes in my drinks? No one else knew my most secret desire: to experience a breathtaking, soul-ejecting kiss just once.

Focused on the bus stop, I didn't notice Andrew walk up the hill. When I flipped my hair off my forehead, there he stood, his lips a flat, sorrowful line.

"Come on." He took my pack and slung it over his shoulder, guiding me toward his car. "You're coming to school with me today."

To my surprise, when he pulled the broken handle on my side, the door opened. He shrugged, kind of shyly. "I fixed it," he said and stowed my backpack in the trunk.

I slunk into my seat and pulled the door closed. Once nestled against it, I rested my head on the window. When he slid behind the wheel, he patted my knee once, and then fell silent. He broke the tranquility only with a sniffle or a sneeze here and there.

Once we turned a corner, the early morning sun shone through the car to blind us both. Andrew flipped down a hidden compartment and took out his aviator sunglasses. My dad had the same pair. I should have asked him if he'd had his first flying lesson, but I didn't.

"Thanks for the ride!" I shouted over the raging battle in my mind.

At a red light, he brought us to a slow, gentle stop, so different from the way Jansen had sped off.

"Sure." He drummed his fingertips on the gearshift.

An uncomfortable pause followed. "I'm sorry," I said at last.

"It's not your fault. He's the one being a jerk."

"Is he?"

He tapped the gas pedal and guided the car into the school lot, where he eased over each speed bump. "You're too close to it." After pulling into a parking space, he turned to me. "Step back. Maybe take some time to be alone for a while, and then I think you'll see what's really happening."

"I don't understand."

Andrew twisted the keys and pulled them from the ignition. The car fell silent except for the cracking of the settling engine. Sometimes, silence is the loudest sound of all.

Uncomfortable in it, he tossed his keys repeatedly, playing with them. "Just take some time." He touched my knee lightly. "I'll wait for you."

"You'll wait for me?"

He chuckled softly and shook his head, gripping the steering wheel. With a deep inhale of air, he opened his door. "After choir, okay? Consider me your ride from here on out."

I was in computer class when the power failed. A certain excitement fills the student body when things like that happen. It's unexpected, the outcome unknown. What happened? When will it come back on? *Will* it come back on? Maybe we get to go home early. In any case, it was especially exciting in this particular class because there wasn't much we could do without electricity to run the computers.

At once, we all rushed to the window. It had been one of those stormy days, the kind where you lose track of time because the sun forgot to rise.

"Whoa," Gretta said in hushed awe.

I had to agree. The sky bore an ominous gray hue with a… What was that? The underside of an iceberg? And moving fast. The iceberg—or cloud—reflected bright white light from the sun, and its underside faded to a color darker than the sky.

Bested in his own classroom, Mr. Lawrence gave up trying to get his students back to their seats and joined us instead. He pushed his glasses up between his eyes and leaned in as close as he could to study it. When he saw what all the fuss was about, his nose crinkled and he stood with his mouth agape. "Huh. Would you look at that? Can anyone tell me what that is?"

"A UFO?" Bill asked. He was the kind of kid that relates everything to a singular topic, whether it made sense or not. Aliens were his favorite. Everyone snickered, but this time, he wasn't far off. Everybody thought it, even if nobody admitted it.

Mr. Lawrence seemed to agree, and in his nasal voice, he said, "Sure looks like one, doesn't it?"

"A wall cloud?" Gretta tried.

"Well, that is a sound guess." He pushed his glasses higher on his nose and scrunched his face further, clearly fascinated by what he saw. "Wall clouds make up the back of a storm and are usually smaller, though they can get quite big. No, that there's a shelf cloud. You find them at the leading edge of a storm. Believe it or not, I've seen bigger."

My heart bucked in my chest when the tornado siren blasted so loudly, I thought for a moment it came from within the classroom.

"Yep, yep, no surprise there. Quietly now, but hurry. Wait for me, please. Everyone know where to go? Follow me. Last person out, shut the door behind you."

The hallway turned dark. Barely a glimmer of light filtered through narrow windows from all the classroom doors. A couple of teachers had the sense to grab flashlights, and their jostling beams created an eerie effect.

We sped through the hallways and remained surprisingly quiet. Tornado drills weren't often serious, but this time, it wasn't a drill. It seemed as though everyone paused to hear when the windows broke and, barring that, they wanted to hear instructions. Mostly, students whispered and shushed each other.

We had to go down two flights of stairs, all pretty well-lit, with natural lighting from the windows. That is, until we hit the basement floor, where pitch darkness engulfed us. Only the occasional beam of a flashlight to show our way. Tim walked in front of me, and I touched a hand to his shoulder for guidance.

At first, he flinched, so I said, "It's just me."

His pat was as good as saying it was fine. We moved along like that for a bit, stopping and starting as we went. With my palm on his shoulder, his limp grew more noticeable, especially when we'd get going again after a pause.

"That's it!" Mr. Lawrence said. "Everyone against the wall. Hurry now and make room for more."

A jostling flashlight swiped twice across the wall ahead, revealing Jansen's dark sunglasses intent on me.

"What the hell?" Tim shouted.

I nudged him with my shoulder. "What's the matter?"

"How did he get to this side of the building? I know for a fact his class is on the other end, down the other set of stairs. There's no freaking way."

"He's always been fast."

"That's not fast. That's slippery. Like a snake." He hissed for extra emphasis.

"Shh. He can hear you."

"I don't care if Superboy hears me. And while we're at it, what's with the way he checks you out all the time? It's creepy."

Could he be any louder? Jansen sat feet away, right across from us. So, I leaned over and whispered as quietly as I could, "Stop it, okay? He's not checking me out."

Tim snorted. "Yeah, okay. You are so blind."

"He does that with everyone." Not sure why I felt the need

to defend him. Tim wasn't wrong, after all. And it *was* weird.

"It's creepy. What don't you get about that? It's why he has those stupid sunglasses, you know."

"What are you talking about?" I wanted him to shut up. Because if he kept going, all the things I didn't want to see would spin their ghostly dance in my mind.

He leaned over so close the heat of his breath whispered across my neck. "He wears them to check people out and thinks you can't tell."

"They're prescription."

"Then why wasn't he wearing them at your pool? He didn't put them on until he saw me. Seems to me it was bright out that day."

What could I say? It was true, wasn't it? He never wore those glasses alone with me. Everything he said was true. And worse, I knew it.

The basement grew eerily silent as the wind whistled outside in harmony with the soft drone of the siren.

"Do you think this is it?" I asked Tim. "A real tornado?"

He swallowed hard. "Nah, doubt it. I've never been that lucky."

Had this bravado act served him well in his old school? He seemed to have this need to prove something, but to who?

The siren stopped, and the principal appeared with a flashlight at the top of the stairs. "All clear," he called.

Before leaving, I hoped to get a reaction on Jansen's face. With everything Tim said, had we hurt his feelings? Only he wasn't there. I turned in a circle, peering into the dim hallway.

Jansen was nowhere in sight.

CHAPTER NINE

The storm brought a massive cold front that dropped the temperature a full thirty degrees in a matter of hours. With sweet relief, the cooling trend remained steady for over a week. I had a quiet Friday night ahead of me, too. Perfect for curling up with a good book. Of course, that also reminded me how very not normal I was. No doubt, all my friends had plans that included movies and food. Definitely human contact.

At least I could do the food part. I liked to cook even if no one else in my family appreciated my experiments. Scattered among the many items in the fridge, I gathered tomatoes, garlic, cabbage, and a few other vegetables. With chicken from the freezer, I figured I'd make a fair stir-fry.

The microwave whirred with the defrosting chicken when my dad walked in. He pulled up a stool and watched me dice carrots.

"You're cooking?" he said.

From my place at the bar, I glanced up, but refrained from answering the obvious.

"Do you want to talk about it, Tilly?" My dad and his nicknames; I don't think he ever called me the same thing twice.

"Talk about what?"

"Hmm, let's see. There's school. We could talk about that. Or, you could tell me what's going on with that boy who used to hang out here a lot. What was his name?"

"Dad."

"No, that's not it…"

I threw a piece of carrot at him, which he caught in his mouth with a grin.

"Dad!"

"Okay, okay. Where has Jansen been lately? He hasn't had dinner here in a long time. Hasn't been raiding our fridge after school. I'd started thinking about charging him for groceries."

"He has a girlfriend," I said.

"So? I seem to remember sitting through a meal or two with both Jansen and Carl. Not that I'd ever like to repeat that."

"It's different now."

"Why is it different? Who's he seeing?"

"Clara," I groaned.

"Clara Donnely? Oh…"

Yeah, "Oh." That's about how I summed it up, too. After scraping the carrot pieces into a bowl, I took a long, hard whack at the cabbage. It felt good.

"What about Andrew? He seems to have taken an interest in you."

"Dad!" I wailed, slicing the cabbage halves into quarters.

"I didn't mean anything by it. I'm just saying, if Jansen's seeing someone else, perhaps you should, too."

"I was never his girlfriend!"

"Oh, I know that, but you have to look at it from his point of view."

Not in the mood for any opinion but my own, with knife in hand, I took another mighty swing at the cabbage, and missed my thumb by a mere inch.

My dad snatched the weapon from me and held my hands in his. "Guys don't like to just be friends. That's hard for you because you've always connected better with the boys than any of the girls. See, you're getting older now and…"

My body tensed, and I looked away. Nope. Not having this discussion with my father.

"…the two of you will start drifting apart. That's only natural."

How best to end this conversation? Change the subject? "What are you and Mom doing tonight?"

"After dinner, we're going out with friends. I've got an early flight in the morning, though, so we won't be out late. How about you? Think you'll invite anyone over?"

That didn't get off the topic of my social life, so I sidestepped the question and tried again. "Andrew mentioned you set him up with a flight instructor."

"Right. He told you about that, huh?" He popped a cherry tomato into his mouth. "I'm heading out there with him next Friday to ride along in the back of the Cessna. Why don't you come, too?"

"I'm sure Tyler would love to go."

"Nah. He's not interested, but I bet Andrew would love—"

Nope. Didn't want to talk about Andrew either. "What's all the stuff I saw out in the garage? New project?"

His face lit up. Mission accomplished. "Oh, wait 'til you see it. I'm working on a fire pit for the backyard. Should be ready in time for some late-fall bonfires…"

He kept talking, but I no longer listened.

After dinner, I grabbed a throw blanket from the chest behind the couch and a mug of hot cider to curl up in the window seat with three books. My mom read everything and had never thrown a book away in her life, or so she told us. She had a wide variety, all arranged alphabetically by author, on shelves my dad had made. They were the standout feature of our family room. He'd designed them across an entire wall, ten shelves high. It even had an attached sliding ladder.

The first book I grabbed was a romance, which got tossed straight off. The second was a mystery. Promising. Until I read the first sentence. *I'd never been in love before…* That one, of course, got tossed, too. The third book was science fiction about a mute alien who traded his heart for a voice. Absurd. Who read science fiction? Still, at least the subject was benign.

Footsteps sounded in the kitchen, followed by the friendly back-and-forth banter between Tyler and his date. Tyler had worked up the courage to ask Amelia out, and they were returning from a movie.

Maybe they wouldn't notice me if I ignored the footfalls. I tried to focus on Alien Bob, who faced drinking orange juice for the first time. How exciting. I found myself re-reading the same paragraph five times. It wasn't long before Amelia's feet came into view beneath the spine of the drivel in my hand. Her shiny black high-soled boots thumped together at the heel, calling for my attention. Begrudgingly, I lowered the book to reveal first her black-wool beret, then her sun-kissed, auburn hair, dark chocolate brown eyes, and finally her soft smile.

"How's it going?" she asked.

"We didn't mean to break your concentration." Tyler craned his neck to read the title of my book, then released a soft chuckle. "Or maybe you want some company?"

"Thanks, but I'm good."

"We were heading to the basement to shoot some pool." Amelia rocked back on her heels. "You're sure you don't want to come?"

"I'm good."

With his hand gliding down Amelia's arm, and his feet heading toward the basement, Tyler asked me, "How about Monopoly or something?"

Part of me wanted to say "yes" just to see what he'd do. But only a small part. Most of me wanted to curl up in the window and go numb. For the tornado of thoughts in my brain to go silent. I *didn't* want to talk. Or have to pretend happiness. Air came in short supply, leaving my lungs compressed as the family room rounded to form an ever-closing tunnel.

So, I shook my head no, and swallowed a lump. "You guys go on. I'm fine. Just gonna read for a while."

"Okay." Tyler tugged on Amelia's hand. "You don't have to tell me twice."

Amelia said over her shoulder, "Holler, if you need us,

okay?"

I opened the book again and pretended to engross myself in it. At least until they retreated to the basement. When I couldn't sit still any longer, I threw the blanket off and ran barefoot out the front door.

My feet carried me from the porch to the driveway to the sidewalk, where I kept running, hair flying behind me. The pavement beat against my feet. I didn't even feel the pebbles beneath them, and I didn't care that the cool night air whipped hair around my face.

My lungs worked hard with each step, filling with cleansing breaths. I ran at a full sprint and didn't stop when the sidewalk ended. Sprinted across the road without caution. I dared any passing car to hit me.

It never occurred to me to slow down, and before long, I rounded the corner into the community park. The grass fell much kinder beneath my feet, soft and dewy between my toes.

Hardly stopping at a climbing spider gym, I scrambled to the top, each metal rung so cold it cramped the arch of my foot. From this vantage point, standing tall at the pinnacle, my neighborhood appeared bathed in bright lights. I gazed over the jagged rooftops and detached myself from that world to become a spectator. Not a part of it, but merely an onlooker, without the cares and worries and self-loathing. Lightning bugs twinkled their tiny orbs in rhythm with the crickets.

I was alone.

Jansen should have been with me. I'd have gasped at the fireflies, and he'd have understood without words. Would have pointed out the various constellations.

Then, rather suddenly, as I stood on top of that gym set, loneliness fled. Somehow it seemed someone—a strong presence—existed beside me and watched. The feeling grew so intense I extended my arm little by little into the empty air. Of course, there wasn't anything there—just me trying to fill a void.

So, why had the ache ceased? There was something—

something I couldn't explain, but something—next to me, in front of me, enshrouding me. Some peculiar force pieced me back together, and silently assured I was okay. I reached out again, faster—aching with the pure desperate need to touch it. To know I wasn't crazy.

This time, what I felt made my heart bang beneath my chest. Made me gasp and recoil.

A mist appeared, tangibly. I'd felt it. Felt the caress of the fine moisture against my skin. Tingles of solid moonlight. Like before, a sense of wholeness overcame me.

Then, as if he stood beside me, Jansen's voice, full of intensity, said, *"Stay there. Don't move."*

Every tiny hair on my body prickled. I willed myself to see through the black veil of night but saw nothing. My imagination had never played such cruel tricks.

"Where are you?" I called out.

Silence.

But I'd heard it. His timbre had sounded threatening. Even fearful, and I couldn't be sure which put me on edge more, the intensity of his voice or the words themselves. Or maybe it was simply him at all. It rang so clear, as if inside my head. The façade of peace cracked, and panic led me to descend, placing a shaky foot one rung below—

"Don't. Move."

The gravelly, assertive baritone resounded—a loudspeaker inside my mind, impossible to escape. For a second, I thought it could be the wind, but only for a second. It was nothing like the wind.

Thick clumps of trees lined the playground, and the air hung so motionless that the leaves didn't whisper. The moon oversaw the park, and between its glow and the streetlights, I could see enough to know that I was still alone.

Reality snapped into place, and not pleasantly. Of course, I dreamt him up in my head. Why, the madness of it! To think I was such a freak that I created his voice like some twisted imaginary friend. I'd never wandered outside at night by myself before. That's all this was. Jansen had always been with me.

Annoyed, I scoffed at the voice. What kind of delusional person could dream up such a convincing fantasy as all that?

With a newfound empowerment, I took the final step. One giant leap and the grass tickled my bare feet.

That's when I realized I wasn't alone after all. Off to my right, in the shadowy brush where I couldn't see anything—leaves stirred. Twigs snapped.

I froze. Whatever it was, if I didn't move, it wouldn't know I was there.

If I kept very still.

If I didn't blink.

If I didn't breathe.

A low snarl rumbled nearby, and I anticipated the *whack* of beast against wood, but here, there was no fence. Whatever it was, it knew I was here, knew nothing kept it from me, and knew my heart beat ten times too fast.

Dark clouds rolled across the moon, and it grew even harder to see. Still obscured, the limbs and leaves of the brush parted. A jet-black, enormous paw stepped forward.

Whatever beast let loose a savage growl that vibrated low in its throat; a cavernous, guttural warning.

I didn't whimper. Didn't make a sound. Didn't dare breathe.

One more step, and there he crouched. A black creature whose narrowed, jaundiced eyes glowed. Whose raised, alert ears tuned into my every breath. Could it hear the blood pump through my veins?

The thing, the creature, the beast... A giant canine, camouflaged by the black of night. A starved carnivore who bared its vicious teeth. My heart leapt, throwing me off balance, and I stumbled backward.

"Damn it, Ellie! Do not move."

Right. Don't move. My own voice told me that.

Yet, really? Don't move? Was that the best advice? Every ounce of me wanted to kick ass and run.

As fast as a computer, my brain ran through options. I could throw a shoe. No, I wasn't wearing any. A stick? A rock? Too dark—couldn't see any. Kick it?

I pictured the beast eating my foot, flesh tearing at the ankle, blood squirting—

"Control your breathing."

The monster growled the shallow rumble of an enraged predator. It vibrated low and long until the enraged beast needed air. Its jaw opened to lap in breath after breath with its lolling tongue.

It hunched into an attack position. Its enormous back claws gripped the earth. I knew that stance—

And prepared for the strike.

My pulse quickened, thumping, thumping, and in a total panic, I gasped, but the breath stuck. Couldn't get enough air. The sound enraged the beast. It gnashed its teeth and showed me exactly what it wanted to do with my tightening throat. The black hairs on the scruff of its neck stood erect.

"Tell yourself you're not afraid."

Yeah, right. My inner voice, the one that was not Jansen's, told me to flee, to scream, to cry.

"Keep eye contact."

I did try to listen. Tried to fill my lungs with air. But it got stuck in my throat, making me wheeze.

The brute crouched and, in less time than it took to inhale, it sprang from its back legs. Its massive front claws aimed at my shoulders, its teeth at my neck—

My head jerked into a rusty bolt on the gym set, tearing tender flesh to the right of my eyebrow—

Something grabbed the dog and lifted it from me. An invisible force that threw the beast to the ground, where it yelped, laying flat on its side. It snapped and growled at whatever had pinned him. An indentation appeared on its neck and another on its side as if someone held him. Then, implausibly, the dog turned away and lifted its leg in submission.

Submission to what?

"Go!" Jansen's voice growled in my mind.

He didn't need to tell me twice, and I clambered to my feet, slipped at first—a false start—then ran from the park. Never looked back to see if it chased me, but ran as if it did.

Once rounding the corner, I sprinted. Fear carried me over rocks, pebbles, and cold hard pavement, numbing my soles to pain. After the next bend, home came into sight.

Oh God, could my heart pound right out of my chest? At top speed, I dashed up my driveway, up my porch, and fumbled with the door. In no time, I threw it open, then slammed it closed behind me. Exhausted, I sank against it and inched my way to the floor.

Tyler and Amelia came running.

Through uncontrolled breaths, I managed to say, "Running…park…big dog."

Amelia fell at my side and rubbed my back, combing my hair away from my face with her long, slender fingers. "Oh, my God. You're bleeding."

Whatever Tyler saw, he took a step back and gasped. "A lot."

Instinctively, I grabbed the wound. Felt the warm, sticky blood from the bolt. Seemed like maybe it gushed.

Tyler disappeared into the kitchen and returned with a towel, which he pressed against my head. When he pulled it away to inspect the wound, blood saturated it. "It's superficial. Doesn't look that bad, but there's so much blood. We should take you to the hospital."

"No." I couldn't go to the doctor. What on earth would I say? "Head wounds bleed a lot."

Amelia tied back her sleek hair into a neat ponytail at the base of her neck. "He could have had Rabies."

"I'm fine," I said again with bite. "It didn't get me. I fell on a bolt."

Tyler handed me the towel, and I returned it to the cut, burying my face in my hands. The attack replayed in my mind. An endless loop that wouldn't shut off.

It wasn't the attack that made me cry, but the memory of the dog flying from me. The way it pressed so hard into the ground that I saw indentations in its body.

Also, I had to face whatever delusion led me to hear Jansen's voice that way. In my head. Not me thinking about his voice, but actually him, talking to me through my mind.

Like I was so reliant on him that my brain filled in the gap.

No, I didn't want to talk. I didn't want to tell them about any of it. Not about the ache in my heart. Not about the fit of anger that sent me running into the park. Not about the dog or the attack, and certainly not about the voice that carried me through it.

CHAPTER TEN

On Monday morning, I didn't need an alarm clock. My throbbing head roused me just fine. As if to squeeze the wound shut again, I pressed it hard. Why do people do that? It hurts more. We know this and yet we do it, anyway. The dang thing wasn't any better, which was strange, because I usually healed much faster than this.

I shuffled into the bathroom to check out the sore, which was kinda yellowish. How would I hide this now, and with too-small a Band-aid? It looked worse. Too bad my millions of freckles didn't camouflage the ugly thing.

Whatever. I'd just have to keep it hidden. So, I snatched the baseball cap I'd worn around my parents and gingerly placed it over the wound. This kept me out of the doctor's office, where I didn't want to explain why I had been out alone or that a dog attacked me.

I plodded into the dimly lit kitchen, where Tyler ate cereal at the bar. Mid-bite, he set his spoon down and lifted the bill of the hat. It made me wince, but I let him. When he dialed up the dimmer switch on the wall, turning the breakfast area into an interrogation room, he said, "That looks worse. I'm telling Mom tonight."

"It's fine." I pulled away. "I can't even feel it."

"Suit yourself." He reached for the milk to refill his cup. "I'm still telling Mom. Hey, where are you going?"

I grabbed my backpack and raced toward the door. "I

don't want Andrew to have to wait on me."

Unfortunately, he wasn't due to come out of his house for another eight minutes, but waiting for him on the porch suited me more than Tyler grilling me. To pass time, I counted the hanging ferns—four—the containers of impatiens—six—and the pots of geraniums that lined the stairs—four. If anyone ever asked, I could also tell them we had nineteen vertically laid bricks on each step, and it bothered me it wasn't an even number. Once satisfied that it was indeed nineteen bricks, I shivered from the crisp, early air, and Andrew's automatic locks beeped, announcing his arrival.

He tossed his backpack into the trunk of his car. "How's the head—?"

A bark and the sudden splintering of wood drowned out his question.

With false sincerity, Andrew rolled his eyes and said, "Morning, Otis."

The sound had scared me half out of my gourd, and my hands flew not to my heart but to my wound. As if they could protect me from the imagined attack. Stupid Otis buckled my knees, and I caught myself.

This happened every day. I had nothing to be afraid of. Just the moronic neighbor-dog.

Andrew rounded his car, hurtled toward me defensively, and yanked me into his chest with his hand behind my head.

It made me shutter, grateful for the hug. His arms were a place of refuge, smelling of a zesty cologne and breakfast syrup. How sweet he could calm my racing heart that way.

When I started breathing again, he pressed me back, assessing me. "Are you okay?"

"Dumb dog. I take it you know about that?"

"Tyler told me you cut yourself on a bolt running from some big dog loose in the neighborhood. Wondered if I knew who it belonged to. It wasn't Otis, was it?"

"I don't think so. I've never actually seen him before."

Andrew waved his hand as if to brush Otis under the rug. "He's harmless enough, just loud. He's got a funny way of greeting you, is all. So, the head? How is it?"

"Fine," I said, freeing myself from his arms.

He took my pack from me and lifted the bill of the hat. "Doesn't look fine."

Really should have searched harder for a larger Band-Aid. I let myself into the car and buckled the seatbelt. "My dad had a suggestion about the Air Force Academy. Did Tyler tell you?"

Andrew turned the engine over and clicked his seatbelt. "Tyler isn't just not interested. He's anti-interested. So, no. What did your dad say?"

"He thinks you should skip the academy."

Andrew's brow raised.

I waved my arms around, signaling the desire to erase my words. "Not forever. He says it's better to go the traditional college route. Thinks you should join the rotten-sea program at a university and get your degree first."

The way he smirked made me second guess some of that.

"Rotten-sea?"

I scratched my head, trying to remember what my dad had told me.

"What, like learning to fly sunken aircraft?" he asked. "Diving with rotten fish?"

"No, oh my gosh." I popped my hand over my mouth. "It was—"

"Piloting a ghost ship, right? Navigating the open oil spills?"

I buried my face in my hands, unable to help laughing at myself. At the quick wit and joyous cackles rolling out of him.

His laughter subsided to soft puffs of air. "Did he maybe say 'ROTC?'"

"Yes." I strung the word out and chanced a glance at him.

He gave me a reassuring wink, his gray eyes still sparking with leftover mischief. "Bet he said, 'Rot-C.' I wondered about that. Did he tell you he's going up with me during one of my lessons this weekend?"

"He did. Actually, he asked if I wanted to come." His eyes

lit up at the suggestion, so I jumped in with a mostly truthful excuse. "I get sick in those tiny planes."

"Afraid I'll crash it?"

"No," I scoffed.

It was true enough. Though now that he said that, I looked twice at him, tugging a bit at my earlobe.

He smirked. "No worries. Over the summer, your dad gave me a flight simulator game. My instructor's kinda impressed with what I already know, and your dad says it's because of the game. I don't want you flying with me until I have a few hundred landings under my belt, though."

"Oh, please. You'll fly around with the instructor and my dad, but you're afraid to kill me?"

"Well, would you look at that? Did I just convince you to fly with me?"

"No, that's not what I'm saying."

"Cuz, I think you just argued yourself into coming along this weekend."

"I did no such thing."

"I believe you said—"

"Are you providing the barf bags?"

We turned a corner and faced the blazing morning sun, where Andrew slipped on his Ray-bans. "You're not kidding about that, huh?"

"Not entirely."

"Tell you what. When I get my license, after I've smoothed out my landings, promise me you'll let me take you up when the weather is super clear. Just once. If it makes you sick, I'll never ask again."

"The last time my dad flew me in a Cessna, I threw up."

He rested his hand on the parking brake. "I'm not your dad. And you're not six."

There was something about the way he said it that made me hurt a little. Not that *he* hurt me. No, more like I just hurt. Like a thing inside me broke. A ligament, a heartstring, a connection to a piece of me I couldn't name. Because another part of me found it sweet and simple that he wanted to fly with me and that we could tease and be us.

I swallowed hard.

"Give it time," Andrew said with a grimace. It almost sounded as if he talked to himself.

After parking, we walked into the building together. No one paid us any attention the way they had when I entered with Jansen. Today, I was thankful for the shroud of the unremarkable. I wasn't entirely invisible, though. A teacher scowled, and I had to remove the hat, which violated some crummy dress code.

"Amelia wears hats," I muttered.

"Yeah, but not baseball caps." Andrew smirked. "Hers are high fashion statements. Or something like that."

I should have borrowed one of hers. Too late now.

We strolled past Jansen and Clara, who sat together in front of his locker. Not all that unusual, Jansen looked annoyed. Especially given he sat there with her. What surprised me was that he'd decided to be with her at all. Also strange was how he winced and held his forehead, as though he mocked me, but he hadn't even glanced my way.

Across the hall, Tim stood at the drinking fountain, wiping his mouth on his sleeve. Unlike Jansen, his attention landed entirely on me. In fact, he could have burned a hole through my wound with the intensity of his stare. I swallowed hard, trying to arrange my hair to cover my forehead, but it didn't work well, and I ran my fingernail over it. Ouch.

Jansen pulled his feet in when I walked by.

Her hand on his arm, Clara said, "Today, let's—"

Before she could finish her sentence, he rose to his feet in that graceful way he had. He came within inches of me and lowered his glasses. Peered at my forehead. "That looks bad."

Dang, I should have put the hat back on. I said nothing. These were the first words he'd spoken to me since my pool party, and I rather expected an apology; would have preferred it.

With a smack to her leg, jingling the multiple bracelets she wore on her wrist, Clara clucked her tongue. "Jansen, I was talking to you."

He didn't even turn to acknowledge her. His hand came so close I thought he would touch the wound. In his black velvet eyes, shadows of blue light danced. Perhaps because he caught me staring at them, he withdrew his arm and bit his lip while he scanned the space around me. It didn't escape me that he avoided my gaze, as his landed on my wound, his head cocked to the side. Then his arm twitched as if to reach up, but he didn't. Just a twitch.

Clara folded her arms across her chest. "Jansen," she whined.

A grimace shadowed his face, and I swore he tried to hide regret. He turned his face away as he touched the wound unexpectedly. It should have hurt, but his familiar touch tingled. Without meaning to, I kind of leaned into it, pressing into his fingers. I stood spellbound as he picked up the Chrysoberyl pendant and caressed it. A spark cracked between us—static electricity?—and he let it thump back onto my chest, over the birthmark.

With that final move, he retreated to sit with Clara.

"Sorry," he said, but I wasn't sure whether to her or me.

He'd barely sat when she closed the gap between them.

"Don't." He pushed her hands from his face. Away from his glasses.

"Why won't you take them off? You do it for *her*."

"No."

"So, you're sensitive to light, I get it. But you just took them off—"

"No."

She walked her fingers up his arm, the walk of a seductress. "Oh, come on. Please."

"Clara, I think I've been clear."

Her expression made my suffering worth it; the perfectly plucked eyebrows that came together as one, the caked-on foundation that cracked along her wrinkled nose, the too-pink lipstick that gaped around her overly whitened teeth. He'd shocked her, wholly and utterly dumbstruck by the rejection. A feeling she was very plainly unfamiliar with. Had I not been so hurt, I might have jumped in to tell him off for it. Instead, I stood idly by, amused.

"I—never—oh, never mind." She pouted, crossed her arms beneath her breasts, and stuck that lower, pink lip of hers out as far as it would go.

And Jansen? He opened his book.

"Jansen, why—"

"Drop it."

Her forehead wrinkled, her lips pressed tight in a thin line. "Honestly, what's the matter with you?"

He slammed his book shut and breathed deeply, in and out. I imagined he counted to ten, calming himself. After a lapse of about the predicted ten seconds, his shoulders lowered, his fists unclenched, and his jaw relaxed a hair.

I'd heard enough and whirled around to leave, only to find Tim blocked my path. His eyes pierced my forehead, and I covered it instinctively.

Not liking that, he pulled my hand away. "What the hell! What did he do to you?"

"He didn't do anything." I pushed him away, trying to sidestep him.

"Like hell, he didn't! It looked like you had a big old slash in your head." Tim rapped his knuckles into a locker. "It was so big I saw it across the hall!"

He made it sound as though it wasn't there anymore. My fingers massaged the mark nervously. It still ached, but nowhere near how it had before. Where my skin had been patchy and rough with infection that morning, it was now smooth. Maybe a little tender.

"What did he do?" Tim gestured wildly with his hands in a what-the-hell sort of way.

"That's what he does. He touches me and…" My brain caught up with my words. "…and then…" His touch always made me feel better. Tyler had run to Mom if he got hurt, but me? I'd gone to Jansen.

"There was never anything there," I said through clenched teeth. Why I lied, I couldn't say.

I pressed my books into my chest and moved to breeze past Tim, but he snagged my arm. He glanced at Jansen, and though I didn't look, Tim's quick release told me he'd received a stern warning.

"No one's that slick," he hissed close to my ear.

I jerked away and slipped into the bathroom to inspect my forehead. I slid my bangs to the side and marveled at how much it had indeed healed. It didn't hurt, and no longer had that yellowish tint of infection. A scratch remained, but even the bruising had faded. All I could think about were Tim's words.

What the hell?

CHAPTER ELEVEN

On Tuesday, after Otis' terrifying ritual greeting, I met Andrew by his Camry. The hood matched the shade of the rest of the car. When had that happened? I leaned closer to inspect it, touching its glossy sheen with my fingertips.

It made him smirk. "Like it?"

"Yeah. You painted it?"

"Yesterday afternoon. I'm surprised you didn't see me. Supplies were everywhere. All over the driveway."

While I'd been contemplating the supernatural— "You did that by yourself?"

"No, my dad got off work early. I took advantage of him."

"You guys did a nice job."

Andrew opened the trunk, and I tossed my backpack in next to his flight bag. Cute that he had added a Snoopy Red Baron sticker to the side of it. He'd left it unzipped with a black headset near the top, the cord neatly rolled up.

"So, okay," he said the moment we got situated in the car. "I've been pretty quiet about Jansen, right?"

"Right." I drew out the word. I hadn't even managed the buckle of my seatbelt yet, and his haste made me think this speech had been rolling around in his head for a while.

"Has he spoken to you at all since he and Clara started dating?"

"No." Wasn't it common knowledge I didn't like to talk about this?

"Doesn't it make you mad?"

I stared at him, expressionless, but he just concentrated on the road. Uncomfortable. "*You're* making me mad."

A deep V creased his forehead. "I mean, you seem sad, but never really mad. You should be mad."

"Oh, I have been."

"Feeling sad was fine at the beginning. Now it's almost as if you think it's your fault. Like you've done something wrong. Can't help it, but that makes *me* mad. If you were even a little bitter, I'd be okay."

"What good would that do?"

His head twitched backward. "Are you kidding? You do realize this isn't your fault, don't you?"

My fault? I hadn't fully processed what happened with him. My guess? He was pissed I noticed him at my pool, but I wasn't about to tell Andrew that.

"Not that it's any of your business, but I think Jansen just wanted to start seeing Clara and needed me out of the way."

"You're right, but don't you find that offensive?"

"Offensive? No. Disappointing, maybe."

"Disappointing," he said with notable disgust. "You're much nicer than he deserves. If you two were the friends you each claim to have been, why can't he date her and keep what you had, too? When I have a girlfriend…" he paused and glanced at me, "I don't suddenly exclude Tyler."

"I'm sure Clara's jealous. I can understand she'd want me to go away."

"Clara, yes. But Jansen? No. He should see that she holds nothing to you. If she's throwing a hissy, and I wouldn't doubt she is, he should tell her she takes him with you, or she doesn't get him at all. No, there's something else to the story."

"Something else?" I parroted.

"Wish I knew what." Andrew checked over his left shoulder to switch lanes as the signal clicked. "Jansen's not talking to anyone, though."

"I'm not surprised. Who would he tell?"

He grimaced. "He was only close to you, huh?"

How quickly that had changed.

The scenery zipped by outside my window. A billboard caught my notice, an advertisement for a hayride. "That reminds me. Tyler and I are having a few people over to watch movies in our basement for Halloween. Has he asked you yet?"

"Yeah, yesterday. Are you asking anyone?" He concentrated on the road as if it might disappear if he didn't.

"I think just Tim and Gretta. Gretta will bring Mark."

"You invited Tim?"

"He was there when I asked Gretta, so…"

"No problem. None of my business, anyway."

"What isn't?"

"Nothing. How do I get myself into these situations? Only, Ellie… Sometimes… you are truly very blind."

He put the car into park and stepped out.

The obnoxious buzz of the first-period bell rang, and I sat on the cold, hard laminate floor longer than I should have, dreading the start of a new day. With only a few minutes to spare, I dragged myself up. I was almost at my classroom when I remembered my folder back in the choir hall. I had virtually no chance of making it to class on time now. If I hurried, maybe.

What I saw when I rounded the corner chilled my heart and lungs in a way that light and sound spun, somehow, a disorienting effect.

In the spot I had just left, Jansen held my folder, contemplating it as if it were the picture of a lost loved one. He caressed its cover before raising it to his face. In all our sixteen years, I'd never seen him look this defeated.

He lowered the folder, and though I couldn't see his eyes behind the glasses, I knew he saw me. Because everything about him froze. An electric current coursed between us so strong it caused physical pain in the center of my being.

For that moment, time ceased. Students in a hurry scurried past. There might have been a few awkward stares. There may even have been a fire drill. I wouldn't have known. It was just us in a tunnel of swirling, unspoken grief.

Then my memory exploded. I remembered that one instant I stood shoulder to shoulder with him in my pool, and the next, he dropped me off in the car lane without a word. That because of Clara, he'd discarded me.

Andrew was right. It wasn't my fault. Never had been. For some unfathomable reason, he had chosen her over me. Clara, who'd grated on his nerves. Who still did. There had to be an explanation, and he owed it to me.

Tim's words resonated, too. More twisted questions arose than answers. Like his voice in my head, a sickness I couldn't explain.

It's unclear what kept me there, riveted to that spot in the hall. Whatever held me there, super glue or a magnetic pull wiser than me, it released, and I flew at him with weeks of pent-up frustration. I slammed my backpack on the floor. The crack still rang off the cold cement walls when I took a swing at his chest. It almost clipped an unsuspecting cheerleader who hurried past on her way to class. Of course, he blocked the punch with frustratingly quick reflexes and grabbed my hand in his. The girl gasped, her uniform skirt swaying like a bell.

Swiftly, he kicked my bag into the empty choir room, then dragged me in, my free arm flailing.

We were alone.

Our heavy breaths echoed inside the large, vacant space. One lonely fluorescent light hummed overhead, creating dark shadows to keep us company.

I pushed myself away so hard that I stumbled. "What is wrong with you?"

The way he examined his feet made it impossible to see his face. His listless body remained still as death, surrendering himself. I wanted fire to sear through his veins like it did through mine. Wanted him to lash out. To accuse me of whatever I must have done. This limp, defeated exterior only fueled the anger that roiled in my gut. The incessant tension in my neck, in my shoulders, in my head… it was more than I could bear.

I snatched his sunglasses before his quick reflexes could stop me and threw them so they clattered across the floor. Still, he did nothing. Hadn't even flinched. Behind those glasses, his downcast eyes made my throat burn with tempered rage.

"Look at me! I think you owe me that."

He hesitated, blinked, and looked at the ceiling before finally at me, the effort painful. As if he begged forgiveness. But he hadn't given me anything to forgive.

God, those eyes. They were different. No resemblance to the black onyx of the boy I once loved or any human I had ever seen. They swirled with shades of sapphire and charcoal and silver, like a misty midnight sky under glass. If I didn't know better, I might have thought he looked at me to fulfill a thirst.

I had to shake my head. Either that or fall prey to those wickedly absorbent eyes, where I'd lose myself. "Just tell me why. Why are you treating me this way? *Me*, Jansen. Why?"

"I'm sorry, Ellie."

"That's it? 'I'm sorry, Ellie?' I know I did something wrong at the pool, but I didn't even get to explain. How can you throw me away after everything we had?"

"What is it you think we ever had?"

I never knew words could wound so physically. Any hope I'd had rested in the core of our friendship. For him to negate it with one statement cut deep, unraveling me from the inside out.

Tears stung beneath my lashes, and my voice came out shaky, fighting them back. "Are you kidding me? You can't mean that. Tell me you did not just say that."

"You're the girl next door. You've said it yourself a thousand times. I'm your brother, right? Just a brother."

"You were more to me than my brother."

"We were together too much. That's all!"

"So, first you're attached at my hip, then you never want

to see me again?" He said nothing, and I paced. It didn't add up, these vile accusations. "No! I don't believe it."

"What do you find so difficult to believe? That I've decided you and I need space? Is it so hard for you to understand I could never have a girlfriend with you around? Did you even stop to think maybe Clara was the only girl who ever pursued me because there was always this—"

He paused, his neck throbbing, his teeth biting his bottom lip. For a second, I believed he'd thought better of what he was about to say. But no.

"There was always this little *leech* clinging to me."

I stumbled backward and clutched at the heart he'd stabbed. "Leech?" It felt like that, like he delivered a mortal wound. A sword strike might have healed faster. "I can't believe you said that. You've never even hinted that you—"

"You've never given me the chance."

"I wasn't done talking! What, *you* can attack, but I can't dish it back?" I stepped onto the first riser to better match his height. "You've never told me to back off. Not once, Jansen! I've dated boys, and it was you who got in the way. You were always there. *You* were the leech! That was you. Not me!"

"Well, maybe I wanted more. Maybe I didn't want a girlfriend with you constantly around."

"I could have given you more!" I popped my hand over my mouth. How could I let that slip out then? When fury burned inside me?

My head hung low and heavy as shame cloaked me in its dark shadow. The darkness squeezed my lungs but hid nothing. There lay my most secret desire, the one closest to my heart, exposed and bleeding on the cold choir room floor.

I couldn't take it back. Could never let it be unknown again.

Hadn't I known he'd reject me? And yet it left me with a lung crushing level of humiliation. I welcomed the anguish, wished it would squeeze harder, that it would stop my breathing and allow me to pass out. When it didn't, when I still lived despite myself, I waited for him to tell me how unworthy I'd become of him.

"You've got to let this go, Gabriella."

My full name, really? Yet his voice was so low and despondent I chanced a glance, surprised by what I found. His eyes met mine, and where I expected anger and fire, instead a haze of sky and mist swirled. Something akin to sorrow and remorse. My mouth hung open, my attention diverted.

With effort, I refocused. No, he couldn't make up for things that easily. How dare he? He'd stood there and told me I'd been like a leech—a parasite. That word sliced clean through, wounding something unmendable.

What right did he have? I might have had friends, if not for him. Maybe close ones. Hadn't he interfered in all my dates with Aaron? With Carl? He was the one who swooped in when Tim flirted with me in the pool. It was he who seethed with jealousy whenever Andrew was near.

Oh, I knew. I hadn't realized until then, but I knew how envy ruled him every time another guy noticed me. How it must have torn at his heart to watch as others adored me when I didn't return his feelings for me.

"You're jealous," I spat, seeing it all so clearly now. "All the times you lashed out at Andrew and that ludicrous display of macho idiocy at lunch with Tim. You are so jealous!"

"You're the one with this bizarre attachment to Tim." He advanced one small step and jabbed a finger toward me. "It's you leading Andrew around like a dog in heat."

I took a step backward, unprepared to deflect that line of attack. "You bastard." I clutched at the pain in my side.

"I didn't mean that."

"Like hell, you didn't." My mind spun in dizzying circles. The room collapsed around me, and I'm not sure what kept me on my feet. It wasn't just the words, but the person behind the weapon. When someone knows you the way he knew me: my triggers, my thoughts, my aspirations, my most inner self. Then to have that someone thrust his blade so deep—well. "I deserve better than this."

With deliberate stiffness, he straightened his back, an

abrupt change in demeanor. He had come to a resolve and was determined to make me see it, but the act was so blatant I saw it for the ruse it was.

He shrugged. "You're not getting it from me."

"I don't understand you."

"I know." Did he plead with me? What could he possibly want me to do? His actions and the truth revealed in those swirling pools of his onyx gaze were in complete contrast with—

"Hey, kids!" Charlie's voice from out of nowhere scared the hell out of me. "El Girl, shouldn't you be in class?"

Unbelievably, truly without plausibility, Charlie entered from behind, marched up to Jansen, and clapped him on the back.

"Shouldn't he?" I seethed. "And what are *you* doing here?"

"Yeah, about that. Jansen, remember our old buddy, Cronus? I *popped in…*" he emphasized, "*…*to tell you that, uh… he's thinking about you."

Jansen stiffened and pulled himself up to his full height, hands splayed at his sides. Fingers spread wide. He scanned the darkened room, and his lip curled into a scowl.

So that was strange, and I couldn't get past how untimely Charlie's interruption was. Infuriating, actually. "You had to come all the way to school to tell him *that*? What is wrong with the two of you? Have you both lost your minds?"

"It's kind of important. Cronus is sure to visit now." Directed entirely at Jansen, his speech was slow. "I'm thinking we need to prepare in earnest. That maybe Ellie should get to class."

Jansen's gaze darted around the room, resting on me intermittently. "But Ellie…" His words weren't directed at me, but rather about me.

"Yes," Charlie drawled. Deliberately. "Ellie needs to get to class. You know, stay out of trouble. *I'll* take her to the office and see her to class without complications. *You* make sure Cronus is"—his nostrils flared—"taken care of."

"When do we expect him?"

Charlie regarded me carefully, uncomfortable talking in

front of me, and I got more than a little impression that he marked his words cautiously. "At this point, I think Cronus is curious about how you're doing. From what I gather, he sensed some strong energy from you."

"Honestly," I said. "What *are* you two talking about? Why all the cryptic garbage? Jansen, you have a friend coming. What's the big deal? Charlie had to come all the way over here to tell you that? And your mom can't handle arrangements for your friend? What's his name? Cronus? Who names their kid that?"

Where Charlie had been scowling at Jansen, his demeanor took a sharp, light turn. Unmistakably forced. He straightened up and tousled my hair. "El, you know our mom works her tail off with us. This friend of his is a nuisance and we hate to bother her about it. No big deal, really, you're right. And you, missy, need to get to class."

I ran my fingers through my hair to fix the Charlie-tousling. With my finger up, I readied myself to tell him I wouldn't leave until they told me what was going on. No way Miss Kate couldn't handle things on her own.

His no-nonsense hand beneath my elbow encouraged me off the riser. "Come on, now."

I tried to resist, but he'd shifted to grip my shoulders, and I was no match for him. As I glanced back at Jansen, I shuffled my feet and fought against Charlie. That, of course, was futile. Jansen stood frozen in his battle-like state as he scanned the room, looking scary. Not a feeling I'd ever associated with him. Not me. He looked…monster-like.

"Charlie, I—"

"Nope, uh-uh." His voice rang light and chipper. "Any more lip from you and see if I lie to cover your butt."

I veered from the path he demanded I take to get my backpack, but he blocked me.

"On your way. Scoot."

"Charlie!" I stamped my foot and gestured toward my backpack.

His lips twisted up in that gee-I've-pushed-things-too-far way and bowed his head. "Sorry 'bout that. Guess we're not in that big a hurry."

He picked up my bag and slung it over his shoulder as the list I had made came to the forefront of my mind. Wasn't sure how to whittle it down to only a few words, but it definitely seemed list-worthy.

"So, here I am, back in the building I swore I'd never return to," he said, leading the way toward the office. "Hasn't changed much."

"It's only been half a year. Did you expect a shrine?"

That made him whistle a long, descending note. "Wow, remind me never to make you my enemy."

I ducked fast beneath his pressing hands, and came to an abrupt stop. "Well, what the hell? You interrupted an important conversation with all your cryptic crap, and you won't tell me what's going on."

His gaze darted around the hallway. "We told you… It's nothing. Just a friend."

"Whatever, Charlie. Maybe you two can gloss over me and pretend I'm not here, but I cannot—" My words hitched. Became instead unbridled tears.

He patted my head. "No, no, El Girl, not here. You can't do this now. Oh, jeez, yeah. Well, okay." He wrapped his massive arms around me and snatched me into his chest. "Guess a good cry's in order. Girls do that, right?"

"I…don't…under—understand," I said between sobs.

"I know, I know. Sure wish I could explain it to you. Listen, honey, you've got to understand. Jansen's in pain right now. He's hurting just as much as you."

"I highly doubt that." My words got mumbled into his rib cage, where he'd stuffed my face.

"Of course. I know. Aw crap, I don't know what to say. How 'bout them Mets, huh? No? Bought any new dresses lately? Uh…"

My tears intermingled with spurts of laughter, snorts really, as he fumbled his attempts to make me feel better. He thumped me on the head, then peeled me from his shirt to study my expression. His lips turned up in a questioning sort of smile, so I tried to put on a happier face.

I wiped a tear from my cheek and pivoted. "Let me just run into the girl's room and wash up."

When I pulled back to duck into the restroom, he stopped me.

"No!" he said too fast. "I mean, no, you look fine. No harm done. Can't tell you've been crying at all."

I wiped my nose on my sleeve and scoffed, trying once again to go into the bathroom.

His grip on me tightened, and he led me through the hall away from the girl's room. "You're gonna be in some big trouble if we don't get you to the office."

I tried to head the other direction, but he was too absurdly strong.

"Nope, uh-uh. I'm not sure my excuse'll work for you as it is. Come on now. You look fine, really."

He dragged me to the office, and before I could free myself, he pushed open the heavy pea-green door. Then walked me directly to Miss Simms' desk. She was an old lady who announced her retirement every year but appeared each September, more crotchety than the last.

"Ellie's late," he said for the entire staff to hear, and I smacked my forehead at the unintended innuendo. "No, that's not right. She… I mean, *we*…overslept."

A wrinkle-eyed Miss Simms looked from Charlie to me and back again.

His face flushed. "No, I mean to say *she* overslept, but it was my fault. I turned off her alarm."

Though he seemed proud of himself, his lie prompted her eyes to narrow, and I wanted to crawl under the desk.

"Miss Simms," I said, "I'm sorry I'm late. See, I overslept because last night Charlie and my brother figured it'd be funny to mess with my clock. I went to bed, and my alarm didn't go off."

Nope, she wasn't buying it. Not old Miss Simms. She opened her tiny lips to say something, and from the look of it, I could tell it would be nothing good.

Charlie scrutinized her, and I thought he said, *"Write her a pass,"* but he couldn't have because his lips hadn't moved.

The hair on the back of my neck stood erect. It was definitely possible I'd imagined it. Delusional thoughts weren't exactly new, what with Jansen's voice in my head. Only, I couldn't think how to rationalize Charlie's there, too.

Old Miss Simms still looked like she wanted to say something scathing. Yet she reached into her desk, pulled out the slips and, without looking at them, wrote out a pass, her eyes never leaving mine.

Her gaze grew uncomfortable, and I broke eye contact, but put my hand out to accept the pass.

It didn't come.

I shifted my weight from one foot to the other and then back again, yet the pass lay on its pad. Well, that made me feel stupid, thinking she'd give it to me. I retracted my hand and fidgeted through my pockets instead. There had to be something—anything—in there to fiddle with. When nothing fell under my fingers, I started reading the notices on the bulletin at her rear.

Charlie must have been uncomfortable, too, because he scratched behind his ear. "Oh, for goodness' sake." Then, in my head, *"Give her the pass."*

It could be she responded to his actual words as she tore the pass from its pad and handed it to me. It couldn't have been—wasn't possible that she, too, heard the unspoken message. Wasn't possible I'd heard it. Was it?

His hand gripped my elbow before I knew what happened, holding me up. He thanked Miss Simms and moved me toward the door.

"That was weird," I said.

"Weird," he agreed, but said no more.

I stopped walking to stare up at him. Had to crane my neck to do it. "Charlie, I—"

But what would I say? I can hear your voice in my head? I heard you command that woman to do something she didn't want to do? Is your brother a warlock? Are you?

Am I losing my mind?

"Ellie?" he said more tenderly than he'd ever spoken to me before.

"Yes?"

"Everything'll be okay." He tweaked my nose with his fingertip.

That afternoon, as soon as I got home, I ran down to the basement to reflect on all the unusual things I'd been tracking about Jansen. I sat at the makeshift desk under the stairs and flipped on the small lamp before pulling a crumpled sheet from my pocket, where I had jotted out a list.

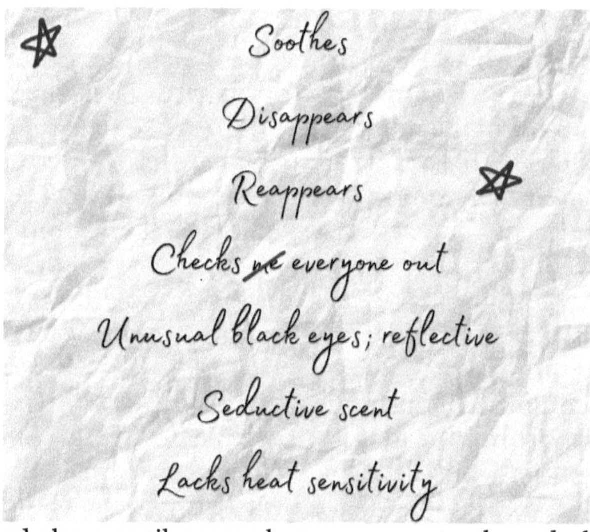

I placed the pencil eraser between my teeth and chewed on the tip as I considered writing another characteristic I'd recently noticed about him. The thought raised the delicate hairs on the back of my neck. I couldn't form it as a thought, let alone put it on paper.

I had heard his voice in my head, and not just once. At least in the pool, he'd been there, too. A ventriloquist-like trick. Still, what about at the park when he wasn't there? I couldn't explain that.

My pencil tapped over the first item as I considered it. What bothered me about soothing was how he—dare I even think it—*healed* me.

The disappearing and reappearing made sense. Both

brothers were unusually agile. Simple genetics. It only seemed as though they disappeared or appeared from nowhere. Not sure why I wrote that one down.

Next, I'd written how they both checked everybody out. Jansen was the worst about it, especially with me. It wasn't creepy, as Tim had suggested. He didn't stare *at* me, but more like around me, and he did it with everyone.

Anyway, the eyes explained why he needed prescription glasses. His iris was so black you couldn't find the pupil, as though dilated. No wonder he wore sunglasses; just not around me. Okay, so his eyes embarrassed him.

Human pheromones explained the seductive aroma. Unusually strong, perhaps, but I mean, Charlie had that alluring scent, too. But I didn't respond to him the way I did to Jansen. Still, other girls did, didn't they?

Footsteps overhead startled me and caused my heart to flip. I threw a notebook over my list so no one would find it. Muffled voices bantered, my mom likely asking Tyler about his day. When the footfalls retreated from the door, I relaxed, sliding the list back out.

Heat sensitivity. Huh. No explanation for that. Just my wild imagination. Somehow, those cookies got onto the countertop without oven mitts. Probably, he'd used a towel, and I hadn't noticed. Maybe he had used his shirt. On the other hand, what about when we'd been little, and he pulled my stuffed hippo out of the fire?

Could there be something supernatural going on?

I shuddered because no, this was ridiculous. It was Tim who had the problem, not Jansen. What was I thinking? Honestly, as if he was what? A werewolf? A vampire? A warlock?

After folding the piece of paper, I stuffed it into my pocket.

CHAPTER TWELVE

It was Friday, October 31st, and a euphoria had swept over the student body. Halloween was a battle of wits between teachers and students. Kids prepared their attire down to such details as fishnet stockings and cat ears. They equipped duffle bags with toilet paper and cartons of ripe eggs left to spoil in garages for at least a week. Meanwhile, the teachers planned homework, including five-page essays to be handed in the next day and extra pages of math problems that needed to be completed with work shown. Even the art teacher assigned a project for Beggar's Eve.

This year, Halloween fell on Friday, so teachers could give us as many assignments as they liked; it wouldn't keep students off the streets. We had two full days to toil on whatever the teachers doled out. Friday night, Halloween was ours.

Trick-or-treating ended in the sixth grade for me, but Halloween remained my favorite holiday. I enjoyed watching the little ones toddle up with outstretched hands, their parents prodding them to remember to say "trick-or-treat" and "thank you." Some children had store-bought plastic outfits, while others wore elaborate, homemade costumes, but each child proudly became someone else for the night.

For me, Halloween was just another tradition I used to do with Jansen. By that, I mean, every single year. This time, however, he wouldn't be sitting on my porch, pretending to be annoyed when I cooed at the babies who toddled up for a treat. Or to jump out of the shadows, making me throw full bowls of candy into the air. Wouldn't be there to crawl around on his hands and knees afterward to pick them all up, laughing all the while.

No, this year, he'd probably dress up as some silly counterpart to Clara and visit one of the many parties. I pictured him, likely uncomfortable, as a football player next to Clara, all decked out as a cheerleader. The thought made me laugh with a bitter edge.

While I pulled out snacks for the evening, my mom entered the kitchen dressed in a simple black dress with matching stockings and heels.

"That's not much of a costume."

"Hold on, I'm not done yet." She retrieved what looked like a headband from her bag. On it, she'd attached two triangles, passing as cat ears.

I grunted my amusement. "That's pathetic."

"Well, do you have any better ideas? I hate costume parties."

"You at least need whiskers and a tail. Got any black eyeliner?"

She searched her purse, pulled out a small, thin pencil, and handed it to me. "So, what are you kids doing tonight?"

"Horror flicks. First up is *The Exorcist.*"

My mom shivered. "Do you know I watched that movie the first time my parents ever left me home alone all night, and I ended up calling my brother to come over from his apartment to sleep in the house with me?"

"Of course. You tell that story whenever you hear the title."

She ignored me. "Who all's coming?"

With the thin black pencil in hand, I angled myself over the bar to fill in her nose. "Tim, Gretta, and Mark. I think Tyler asked Andrew and Amelia."

"And Charlie?"

I gave her my best give-me-a-break face. "Well, of course, Charlie. Stop wrinkling your nose."

"I can't help it. What about Jansen?"

"He has other plans." Had I growled? I hadn't meant to.

"I'm glad Charlie will be here. At least with him, you're not unsupervised."

I started working on whiskers. "We don't need a babysitter, Mom. We'll be fine."

"Maybe I should talk with Tyler about appropriate behavior with Amelia and what we expect."

That made me choke on a stifled laugh, and the last whisker I drew ended up past her ear. "Yeah, why don't you do that?"

"What? I don't like the idea of them being alone together in the house."

I wet a kitchen towel and wrapped it over my finger to erase the rogue whisker. "We won't be alone, and like you said… Charlie'll be here."

Though I hated to concede him as a babysitter, at least it got my mom to leave home once in a while.

"There, that's done. You look much better. Any ideas for a tail?"

"Yeah. We'll say it's hidden under my dress." She winked.

My dad clomped into the kitchen wearing heavy work boots, saggy-butt jeans, and a flannel shirt.

"And you are?" I asked, looking him up and down.

In response, he plopped an oversized cowboy hat onto his head.

Typical. I put the makeup back into its bag, rolling my eyes at him. "At least you're not going as a pilot again."

"But my pilot costume is the best one you'll ever find." He winked. "You gonna be okay tonight, Buttercup?"

"You guys have a great time. I'm sure Charlie will take excellent care of me." I added the last part for their benefit.

It worked, too, as my mom grabbed her purse from the bar and followed my dad out the door.

Charlie arrived about five o'clock to help set up and pass out candy. Everyone else should arrive in another hour. After dragging a cooler of ice and pop cans to the basement, I microwaved bags of popcorn, and he helped fill large bowls with it.

After the last bag was emptied, I wadded them up and threw them in the trash. "What's Jansen doing tonight?"

"Jansen,"—he smirked—"is going to a costume party with Clara. He's going as—"

"No, let me guess. He's a football player, and she's a cheerleader." I couldn't help flipping my hair as I said, "cheerleader."

His face blanched, and his mouth opened a bit in surprise. I burst out laughing, and in my fit of dramatic hysteria, dropped my bag of popcorn. Its buttery scent wafted around the kitchen. Charlie reached out so fast that I didn't even see his hand move, catching the popcorn before it hit the floor.

"I guessed right?" It's all I could say through the hollow laughter and tears streaming down my cheeks. My reaction was a tad over the top.

Plus, he knew it. "I'm really sorry."

"Sorry?" My laughter subsided to occasional spurts. "For what? I just think it's hysterical. She has him so tightly wound around her finger. It's absurd! That's not Jansen."

"Yeah, well… I think maybe you mean he wouldn't ever do that with you."

"No." I slammed the bowl onto the counter and stared into his keen black eyes. So like Jansen's. "He wouldn't do that with anyone. That's not who he is. Why are you defending him?"

Tyler ambled in, and interrupted our conversation, snagging a bowl and popping a handful of popcorn into his mouth. "What's so funny up here?"

"Nothing," Charlie and I said together.

At the sound of the doorbell, I broke the glare between us to answer it, grabbing the candy bowl as I went. Two children, a cowboy complete with a stick pony and the other a princess, greeted me with outstretched arms. I smiled and cooed, putting two pieces of candy into each of their small plastic pumpkins. The little girl looked at me, then into her pumpkin, and then back at me with a huge smile.

While I watched them toddle away, the wind blew in a frigid blast of air, so I slammed the door and shivered. Strange the way it carried with it a foul odor that lingered long after the door closed.

"Cute kids," Charlie said from the kitchen, where he'd been watching.

I wrinkled my nose at him—as well as at the stench. How could he take Jansen's side. I stepped around him and pulled a bottle of cranberry juice from the fridge. I'd just started pouring myself a glass when the doorbell rang again.

In two strides, Charlie lunged for the door. "Let me get it." He yanked it open and bellowed a throaty and terrifying laugh. "Bwa-ha-ha!"

Three boys about the age of seven sprang upward, so scared their poor little feet lifted off the porch boards as they screamed. One dressed as the devil, one the Grim Reaper, and the other Darth Vader. Of these villains, Charlie won for the scariest.

I whacked him on the shoulder and snatched the bowl of candy from him, deciding to hand it out myself.

As the children left, the Grim Reaper held up his treat to show his dad, and I thought I saw something squirm on the outside. Of course, that was ridiculous. Likely movement from the porch light over the reflective surface of the wrapper.

"More kids coming." Charlie pointed up the street. "Quick! Close the door."

"So, you can scare them again? No way!"

"Aw, you're no fun." He leaned on the doorframe, preparing to pounce.

A girl about two years old, dressed as a princess, waddled up the steps and held out her pumpkin. "Tricks!" she smiled.

"How about a treat instead?" I put a sucker into her outstretched hand.

When she brought it to her mouth, wrapper and all, before it touched her lips—what was that? Something moved on it—crawled. Or slithered, maybe? This time, it wasn't a trick of the light. I snatched the sucker before it went into her mouth, and the tiny princess wailed as her anxious mom started forward.

"I'm so sorry." I searched for a fresh sucker. "There was something—I don't know, something… Here, here's another. It's pink, same as your dress. You like pink?"

Her mom scowled, refused the sucker, and took her daughter's fist in her hand. She consoled the child as they walked along the drive.

Charlie nudged my shoulder with his elbow. "And you think I'm bad?"

Since I couldn't see well, I stepped out of the doorway and onto the porch below, where the light was still a bit too dim. The wind howled through the trees and blew my hair across my face, making it difficult to see. I set the bowl on the ground and crouched low to pick through it.

"There's something in here." I sifted through it.

"Like what?"

"Not sure, but it's coming off on the candy."

"Something sticky?" He towered over me, peering over my shoulder into the bowl. "Could be an unwrapped sucker or something."

"No, not like that. It's… I don't know what it is."

Something stuck to the bottom. I raked my hand through whatever it was, which felt like baked beans, all gooey and lumpy.

"Oh gross, what is this?"

I dragged the candy to the side for a better view, and—yuck! What was that?

Something small skittered across my hand. What the heck!

Reflexively, I shook my arm to brush off whatever it was. *Gross.* I pointed to the bottom of the bowl. "Can you tell what that is?"

"I don't see anything. It all looks fine to me."

I reached in and stood back a little, moving candies aside with my fingertips.

Whatever was in there latched onto one of my fingers, causing me to lurch and flick it away. *Disgusting*! Though I had no idea what it was, I stomped over nothing on the ground anyway—

Then I darted to the grass with the bowl—

The porch light blew out. Darkness leaked around us like ink. Prickly teeny feet skittered up my wrist—a whole freaking colony of them.

This couldn't be real. I dropped the bowl and flung my arm. Sent candy flying across the lawn. But I didn't care. It was all covered in maggots, spiders, parasites—I had no idea. My skin crawled with them. Eggs hatched and oozed onto me.

My knees gave out in the mud, and I bent low over the damp grass to gag and retch. "Get'em off. Get'em off!" I slapped and brushed, frantic to annihilate every last one.

Charlie gripped my arm, his hand hot against my flesh. "What is it?" He inspected it. Flipped it over and over again.

I couldn't answer. Didn't he hear that? I pulled out of his grip and dug my fingernails into my skin.

Not letting me go, Charlie took my shoulders and shook sense back into me. "Tell me what you see."

Only I couldn't respond—too busy swatting...gagging... retching.

Couldn't he see them? Hundreds, all hatched at one time.

He brushed at my body, joining my fight, but gently. "It's okay, it's okay," he said. "Nearly there, I got them." He sounded patronizing, like humoring a hallucination. "I think I got them all. Don't see anything else." He didn't say, "I never did."

Didn't have to.

His calm snapped me from the tendrils of my neurosis. The sharp pants of my breathing slowed as I took in the dark shadow of his face.

They weren't there. Whatever they were, they'd disappeared. I flipped my arms over. Tried to get a look at my elbows. Shook my whole self, just to be sure, but they were gone.

Because they were never there.

"I'm sorry," I said.

"None of that, now. Come on." He grasped my wrists and pulled me to my feet.

After helping me wash up, not allowing me to use the scalding water I wanted, he seated me at the kitchen table. I felt numb.

"How did they get in there?" It was more to myself than to him. I didn't expect a response.

"No idea." He swallowed and set his drink on the table.

"The candy's all over the yard."

"I'd say! You see a couple of bitty bugs and throw the whole loot out, bathwater, baby, and all." His words were light, but the merriment didn't meet his eyes. "What do you say we call it an early night? The porch light's already burned out, anyway. I doubt any more kids will knock on the door."

I stood and nodded as I moved to dump my glass of juice in the sink.

"You okay?" he asked, pausing on his way to the basement.

That was definitely the question of the night. The experience had been a glaring street sign that stared me in the face. It told me I'd been going in the wrong direction, heading along the wrong path, looking under the wrong stones. Because it wasn't Charlie or Jansen who were somehow otherworldly.

It was me, and I more than metaphorically lost my mind.

"I'm fine. Just a little creeped out."

A while later, I greeted Tim at the front entrance, who said a bit too enthusiastically, "So, horror flicks, huh? Can't wait."

Still rattled, I took the bottle of soda he offered, hugging it to my body like a teddy bear. "Charlie and Tyler are downstairs. Go on down."

He leaned a hand on the door frame so I couldn't close it. "You okay?"

In no mood for playful banter, and certainly not for flirting, I thought about leaving through the open door. "I'm fine."

He studied me in a rare moment of sincerity, like

appraising my temper.

"What?" I snapped and looked away. Did I have "psycho" written on my forehead? Could he possibly know?

"Seriously. Are you alright?"

Ugh. I'd have to try harder to hide this revelation or face questions. So, I pasted on a grin—okay, a grimace—and gestured toward the basement. Fortunately, he took the hint.

As I closed the door, I spotted Andrew walking up the path. With each step, his feet nearly bounded off the sidewalk, his hands clasped at his back. He sported a new brown leather bomber jacket that almost made me smile. Almost. I waited until he came up the porch steps and said, "Everyone's in the—"

Andrew pulled his hand out from behind himself—a bloodied stump.

I screamed. *Shit!* I screamed shrill, and I screamed loud.

But Andrew dissolved into laughter and gave me a one-armed hug.

Charlie appeared at my side so fast, it was as if he'd materialized from nowhere, scaring me as much as Andrew. Another scream tried to escape, but I stifled it behind my palm. It was on my tongue to yell at him, but instead of laughing at my overreaction, he bent in a defensive pose, and scanned the space around Andrew and me in the unnerving way he and Jansen so often did.

Only when his gaze landed on the fake bloody stump did he relax.

When he laughed too hard to stand up straight, Andrew threw his arm from around my shoulders to hold his stomach.

Charlie clapped him heartily on the back, knocking him off balance, and sighed a breath of relief. "That was pretty funny."

Curious about all the commotion, Tyler and Tim popped into the hallway. They were just leading a still-chuckling Andrew down toward the basement when Amelia poked her head around the open door.

Tyler left Tim to chuckle and snort with Andrew while he

greeted Amelia with a kiss. Dressed in all black, from her oversized button-down tunic to her ankle boots, fit snugly over skinny jeans, she looked every bit the smooth sax player, headed for a gig. He stood back an arms-length, studying her. "Well, look at you. You look…" He paused, and I thought to myself—beautiful, lovely, chic, charming. "…nice."

The boy needed a thesaurus, and I made a mental note to get him one for Christmas.

Amelia bent in a shallow curtsy and tipped her fedora in thanks, then handed me a large manila envelope. "I brought this for you. Open it when you have more than a minute to yourself. Definitely not now."

What could it be? Honestly, anything from magic spells to a collection of butterfly wings. My bets were on something thoughtful based on how she pressed my hand. She didn't wait for me to re-gather my wits, but glided away on Tyler's arm, leaving Charlie and me to stare after her.

"She does beat all," he said under his breath.

Prize in hand, I ran upstairs and deposited the envelope on my desk. I was terribly curious. Whatever it was, it called to me. My fingers traced the lip of the seal with burning curiosity, but she'd said I should open it when I had time. Which was not now.

CHAPTER THIRTEEN

When I joined everyone in the basement, Gretta and Mark had arrived and sat together in the faded yellow recliner. Mark flopped an arm over her shoulder, a simple gesture that took me by surprise. They'd started dating, and I hadn't even noticed.

How had I missed that? Was I that far removed from my friends? I had been so absorbed in my inner turmoil, I couldn't remember one instance where I'd asked a friend how they were instead of the other way around. How self-centered.

Another word to add to my list of psychoses.

As I pondered, I lay belly-down on the thin carpet and kicked my legs behind me, accidentally tapping Charlie's knee a few times. He shuffled his feet to get me to quit, but when I met his eyes, he was obviously kidding.

So I kicked him in earnest and stuck out my tongue.

The floor in the basement made me shiver, and sweet Andrew must have noticed because he tossed a blanket over me before he plopped down. His ever-present grin somehow charmed.

"Thanks," I said.

"No problem. It's chilly in here."

I held out a corner of the large throw. "Wanna share?"

His head cocked to the side, like deciphering my intent. *Please.* For that, I made a face and hoped he'd get my don't-be-ridiculous tone. He must have, because he scurried under the blanket and mimicked my pose, our chins propped on the heels of our hands.

"Start the movie already," Tim said from the couch, and I thought he threw a glare in Andrew's direction.

Tyler clicked the play button on the remote, starting the movie, which began a touch slow. Still, the tension in the room was palpable. The first time the girl in the film arrived on scene, Gretta jolted and launched her popcorn. Amelia snickered, but then Charlie sneezed a little too loud, which made her shriek.

Maybe everything that had happened already overwhelmed me, but my stomach felt sick. My hands still burned from washing them so many times in near-scalding water.

Gretta turned over her shoulder and switched out the lights, which highlighted the glow from the television. The wavering light flicked shadows across the walls. A startling sound erupted from Mark's throat when he cleared it, perfect for the eerie setting, and it made Andrew jump. From the titters around the room, he wasn't the only one.

It wasn't long after that Gretta said, "I'm scared."

The buttery popcorn smelled good, and I popped a handful into my mouth. When I went for more, I felt something soft tickle my arm. My heart hammered, and I jerked before realizing it was the hair on Andrew's hand.

He squeezed my forearm. "Sorry."

"I'm just jumpy."

"You've watched movies like this before. Didn't you pick it?"

"Yeah, it's nothing."

"Don't worry, Ellie. I'll protect—ow!"

"Oh, was that your foot?" Tim's voice dripped with sarcasm. "I had no idea."

"Shh," Gretta said. "I can't hear."

Good, I thought. Maybe that would get the guys to leave each other alone. Then her shushing didn't stop. A soft "shh" rang long after—a hollow whoosh. I tried to pop my ears, but it only grew, settling inside my mind.

No one else seemed to notice.

Andrew smiled when I looked at him, enjoying the extra attention.

It didn't seem to bother Tim, who glowered at Andrew with his arms folded across his chest. Charlie balanced a pop can on his forehead. Obviously, he wouldn't lose any sleep over whooshing sounds.

Man, was I keyed up or what? Must be the stress from earlier that messed with my inner ear. Sure wished it would stop, though. Instead, it grew into an increasing, rushing wail.

Andrew held the bowl up and offered me a bite. To look normal—trying to hide the crazy—and with the sound of screeching wind ever-present, I reached for another piece.

It crunched and squirted onto my tongue. *Ew!* Its taste bitter, I swallowed hard, and couldn't help making a face.

Andrew said something in reaction to my expression, but I couldn't hear him over the swooshing gusts.

"What?" I shouted.

With a finger at his lips, Andrew gestured for me to be quiet. His mouth formed the words, "Never mind," but the noise was too intense. I couldn't hear him.

Then, as quickly as it had started, it stopped.

Noiseless, dead air.

What the hell? Did they think this was some kind of joke? Someone had done it—played loud, windy sounds to mess with me. Who would do that? Amelia? Gretta? Not plausible. Andrew? No. They wouldn't have. None of them would.

Then it must be me.

I had to hide it and not let them know, couldn't let them see the descent into madness. Had to get through the night, the hour—hell, the next five minutes.

Had to fake it.

Though my hands trembled, I brought a kernel to my mouth and—Oh God, what was that? Some kind of liquid inside—inside of what?

I spat it into my hand where, there, in my shaking fingers, a brown spider writhed and pinched and drew into itself as it twitched to its end.

My throat spasmed, closing off. Making me gag. *This can't be real.* Hot tears burned as my tongue curled around itself. I labored to my feet, retched, and clutched my neck. In haste, I tripped over Andrew, then stumbled on all four limbs. I had to get to the bathroom.

Water…

The faucet turned in my grasp, but nothing came out. I turned and turned—off, on, off, on. But not one drop fell.

It was empty and dry. The same as my parched throat.

"What is it?" Tim rapped on the door.

It wasn't locked. I hadn't had time to do it. I turned the sink knobs left. Turned right. I gagged and heaved, desperate.

Tim knocked again, hard and demanding.

Come in… Go away… Didn't matter, because I couldn't flee the image of the spider. Couldn't shake its legs from my teeth. Couldn't wash my hands—my mouth.

Charlie burst through the door. Wood splintered everywhere, raining down around me in shreds.

Move! I pushed him out of my way. Stumbled to the coffee table, searching. Water, punch, anything. Didn't matter whose. The first cup I saw tumbled from my hasty grasp. I brought another to my lips. Swallowed a large gulp.

Not water.

Thick. Bitter, like acid.

The next cup wreaked of gasoline before I even got it to my lips.

Cup after cup, I smelled and discarded. Gas. *No, no, no!* All of it.

I grew desperate. My mouth dry, lips chapped, throat seizing. Like I hadn't had water for days.

The room spun.

I steadied myself on the nearest arm—Charlie's.

"Water," I croaked. "I just—water."

Stairs. Gotta get water.

Charlie pulled me back and handed me another cup of gasoline. "Drink mine."

"Gas." I swiped my mouth with my shirt. Wiped my tongue. "It's gas."

"What?" He sounded appalled. "No, Ellie, here. It's water. Come on, drink this."

"What's wrong with her?" Amelia whispered.

I turned toward her, but Charlie gripped the back of my head hard and put the cup to my lips. Sweet water trickled into my mouth. I drank feverishly after that.

"Jeez, El," Tyler breathed. "What was all that for?"

Charlie threw a warning glance at him, and he shrank into the growing and shifting shadows.

After setting the cup down, Charlie said, "You wanna tell me what happened?"

I wiped the water from my lips. Calmed now, I noticed everyone on their feet. Tim stood in the bathroom doorway, where the faucet rushed with flowing water. Andrew hovered over our spot on the blanket, the popcorn overturned around his shoes. Discarded plastic cups everywhere, stains on the carpet. The bathroom door shattered.

This wasn't happening. Couldn't be real. "It was nothing."

How had I dreamt up no running water and cups full of gas? All because I'd bitten into a spider? All the blood rushed to my face in my embarrassment, and a quick intake of air came out as a sob.

No one moved. The muted movie flickered, the cuckoo clock above the TV passed the time with its incessant *tick, tick, tick*. I couldn't handle the staring.

"Come on." I took a hesitant step down the stairs. "Just start the movie again. It was—it was nothing. Just, come on."

Weak-kneed, I plopped onto the blanket and picked up individual popcorn pieces. I took my time, picking them up one by one. Something to do other than look at anyone, but I could still feel the heat from all of their eyes. So I let my hair fall over my face as a welcomed veil. Andrew lowered himself beside me and helped gather the scattered kernels.

Someone, probably Tyler, restarted the movie, but I didn't glance up. Just studied the floor.

How could I act like that? The spider was one thing, but

the gas? No water? Wind in my head? It couldn't have been more clear, this gradual slip into madness.

As if my brain accepted my fate into mad darkness, a black mist settled over me, and I blinked and blinked, trying to see past it. Yet, the mist persisted. It lowered and encompassed all of me. My breathing labored, and my heart banged loudly in my ears, faster and faster. As if someone slowly turned up the dial on a metronome. Certain I'd lost my mind now, I pulled my knees in close and wrapped my arms around myself. I rocked and rocked.

The glow from the television flickered with a strobe light effect over the popcorn bowl between Andrew and me.

No, this was not happening. There was no spider. None of this was real. No way the eight-legged thing hitched a ride on the popcorn Andrew picked up. I wouldn't believe my lying eyes.

My thrashing heart stung inside my chest. I closed my eyes. *Don't knock it out of his hands. Let it go. There's nothing there.*

I peeked out of one eye, checking. Had he eaten it yet? Damn. He engrossed himself in the movie, hand hovered at his mouth.

My heart pounded…

It isn't there.

Th-thump. Th-thump. Faster…

No, Andrew, don't.

Th-thump. Th-thump. And faster.

Please, no!

The spider stretched a lanky leg toward his tongue.

I held my breath. *Not real, not real. No…*

I won't knock that popcorn from his hand.

He cringed at the television. Buried his face in his arm, but left the kernel untouched.

Thank God. I heaved a sigh of relief.

He took notice. "Scary, isn't it? This movie's always freaked me out. So realistic."

"You have no idea."

"Popcorn?" He held the bowl out toward me.

No! "I've had enough."

He shrugged and reached in again. Of course, like before, a spider hitchhiked on a kernel.

This was definitely a hallucination. Way too much for coincidence.

I forced myself to watch that spider…struggled to breathe…all the way to his mouth. God, how I wanted to smack his hand. But I didn't.

My fists clenched.

The spider rode to his lips.

He bit once, twice, three times, and then swallowed.

It was over.

If it had been a spider, he'd have spit it out. Would have known. You can't eat a spider and not know it.

I'd been staring at Andrew for so long that he noticed and smiled a toothy grin.

Spider legs clicked between his teeth. *Shit!* They thrashed their wriggling limbs.

I screamed.

Just screamed—

heads popping off, squishing onto his lips—

and screamed,

dripping with their blood—

and screamed.

Why is this happening!

I scrambled to my feet, kicked the bowl away, tripped, and fell over Andrew in my escape. Unable to speak, my voice now hoarse, I pointed a shaky finger at him.

With unnatural speed, Charlie flew from the recliner, grabbed my arms, and pulled me into him.

"What is it?"

I wanted to tell him, but I couldn't form the words. Then, the spiders appeared on my arm, where they pinched at me. I struggled against Charlie's chest—slapped at them and tried to flick them off, but they kept coming. Hatched as if from my skin.

The lights flipped on, and the spiders disappeared. Just like that, they vanished, leaving me with delusions and not a speck of evidence to prove to anyone, even myself, that I was not crazy. Andrew's teeth were clean, white, and normal, set between parted, horrified lips.

Charlie spun me to face him and squatted in front of me, fixing his eyes on mine. "What is it, Ellie? What did you see?"

How to focus on him when the world around me faded into itself? Spasms rolled through me, and I couldn't comprehend what he asked, unsure whether I dreamt or was even sane.

From behind me, Andrew said, "I don't see anything. There's nothing there."

Charlie's eyes pleaded with me, as if he knew something had been there. "What did you see?"

"N-n-nothing."

"I know you did. What was it?"

Quietly, so that he alone could hear, I asked, "Why do you believe me?"

I know he heard because he grimaced, but he only took my hand and led me to the place on the couch where Tyler had just been. Where he shooed Amelia from her spot so I could curl myself into Charlie.

"You saw them, right?"

He bit his lip and thumped at my hair, but did not answer my question.

"Charlie?" I pressed.

"I know they were there, yes."

I wanted to cry. I knew I was crazy—that nothing was there. Knew the laughter in my mind wasn't mine. Knew no one in that room laughed at me.

Yet that sinister cackle darkened. Deepened. It was so profoundly ingrained inside my head that it made my brain thump against my skull as it grew gleeful.

I knew it wasn't there because no one else winced. But I did. No one else covered their ears or pulled their knees in tight. But I did. No one rocked their bodies or had tears well up. But I did. On and on, that laugh rang.

Unable to free myself from the cackling, not able to hold it in any longer, I shrieked and hopped off the couch. Didn't matter that Tim and Andrew were there, or Mark or Gretta or Tyler or Charlie.

Charlie grabbed my wrists and bent low to whisper over my hysteria, but I couldn't hear him. His grip grew unnaturally strong. I struggled to free my fingers, but he wouldn't let go. With no effort, he held my tugging hands, and again, his lips moved, but I only heard mounting maniacal laughter. He shook me—lightly for him, but still rough—and his face showed immeasurable pain.

"Help me!" I cried. Likely screamed it.

Then he disappeared. Just like that, he ran up the steps, leaving me alone.

Black mist hovered ahead, so close it made me cross-eyed. It belonged to the cackling. No way it didn't. I stumbled toward the stairs—toward Charlie—but I couldn't breathe. No one moved as I sank to my knees, given over to whatever madness awaited.

The mist swirled around me. Up and up like a tornado.

Instead of one, two forms of that stony-gray, misty substance hovered. The laughter gave way to a roaring wind so loud I thought my ears would burst. Or my brain perhaps, because the sound was so manifestly in my head.

A warm hand on my shoulder startled me, and I opened one cautious eye, praying it was Charlie. But it wasn't. He'd left, hadn't he? The only one who saw through my madness had fled.

Andrew spread his arms, but I remained paralyzed. Couldn't relax one muscle to open my arms, and it didn't matter. Couldn't hear what he said, anyway.

Suddenly it—that form, that mist—settled over me, and Andrew disappeared.

All of it disappeared. My friends, the cuckoo clock, the basement, the stairs that supported me, all of it vanished. Everything stopped for that moment, that fraction of a second. Time, space, breath, everything.

I lay dying.

Then the mist was gone.

The wind in my mind stopped. My blood sped through my veins and rushed as if my heart pumped to make up for the second I had died. I dared not move. I dared not breathe.

Charlie flew down the stairs three at once, knocking Andrew out of the way to take his spot beside me. There, he lifted my rigid body until nearly seated and snuggled me into him. Stroked matted, tear-soaked strands of hair from my forehead, traced a line from my temple to my ear and then to the soft skin of my neck with his coarse fingertips. Gradually, one at a time, my muscles stopped spasming.

"You left me," I said, fists clenched tightly beneath my chin.

"I didn't." His voice crackled with anger.

It was a lie. I needed him viscerally, and he'd abandoned me there to die.

He took my chin between his finger and thumb, then forced me to look at him. I squeezed my eyes shut. Not even sure why. It could have been for any number of reasons. I was embarrassed. Knew he wanted to apologize, and didn't want to make it easy for him. Didn't want to look into the black onyx of his eyes, so like Jansen's, when he lied.

"Ellie, please." His voice carried the melancholy of a thousand tears. "I didn't leave you. I will never leave you."

"You ran away."

"Damn it." He breathed in, filling his massive lungs, and looked toward the ceiling. Probably counted to ten.

Tim stepped forward and opened his mouth to say something, but Charlie's palm told him not to take another step. "Ellie's not feeling well." He lifted me effortlessly. "I'm taking her up to bed. Feel free to stick around or leave, but we're done."

Charlie stayed with me that night, where he defied all laws of comfort by sleeping in my dad's straight-back chair with the awful vinyl cushions. It was a piece he'd brought to the marriage.

With his feet on my bed, Charlie laced his fingers behind his head. "Ah, comfy," he said with a wink.

"You don't have to stay." I whispered from beneath the four heavy blankets he had thrown over me to stop the shivering, afraid if I spoke any louder, he might mistake my politeness for truth.

"Just try and kick me out, El Girl."

Sleep did not come easily. The branches of the giant oak outside my window creaked and swayed like the gnashing snakes of Medusa's hair. Charlie squirmed in the stiff chair, but to me, it sounded like a vampire ground his fangs. A toilet flush sounded like the yowl of a werewolf, and even the whir of the digital flip clock on my bedside table became the fluttering wings of a dragon. Every nerve ending fired.

When I sensed light through my closed lids, I lurched. My heart raced, my lungs ached, and I shot straight up in bed.

"Sorry." Charlie took his cell phone away from his ear and snapped it shut. "Thought you were asleep."

I gulped back bile, drew air down to my toes, and concentrated on slowing my heart. With the covers up to my chin, I sank into the pillow. "Charlie, what's wrong with me?"

When he didn't answer, I panicked. I'd asked the question and expected a logical explanation. Instead, my pounding heartbeat crept into my throat and the ever-present whir of the clock that, somehow, I had never noticed before tonight, got louder. My breath came in gasping pants as darkness shuddered through me.

I buried my face in my pillow and prayed he wouldn't hear my sobs. It would have taken a miracle. They were the kind of cries that wrench all the air from the lungs until you're hollow inside. Until all the pain and suffering and heartache drain away, leaving a bottomless void of hopeless despair.

He flipped his phone. In a barely audible voice, he said, "Jansen, a dose. Now!"

"What?" I jerked my head up to confront him.

What I found took my breath away, and I was unable to make a sound. Jansen leaned over me, and before I could process how he was in my room without having heard the door open, he brushed his fingertips from my forehead to my chin gently.

The next thing I knew, the early morning sun broke through the slit between my shade and the windowsill.

CHAPTER FOURTEEN

I rubbed my eyelids, half expecting to find Charlie sitting in the ugly yellow chair. For that matter, I expected to see Jansen lingering over my bed, the gentle touch of his skin on mine still tickling my chin.

Yet somehow, they weren't there. They probably never had been.

My favorite coral sweatshirt, the one that felt like a warm hug, hung over my desk chair, so I slipped it on over the clothes I hadn't changed out of after Halloween.

I staggered into the bathroom, brushed my teeth, and tamed the mop on my head. The hair lay matted, framing my face where tears and sweat had dried. Knotted in places where I'd batted at it with abandon. Nothing but a full-on shower would tame it.

It didn't matter. I welcomed the delay, not particularly wanting to go downstairs, where I had some explaining to do.

Had Tyler said anything to our parents? My dad had to catch an early flight. Had to call in fatigued if he didn't get enough sleep. God, I hoped Tyler hadn't told him, at least. Unlikely, right? Wouldn't they be admitting me to a psych ward about now? Tyler knew, though. He'd give me the third degree for sure.

I shampooed and conditioned my hair, gave myself a good scrub, and breathed in the hot steam. With extra precision, I ran through all the routine motions: turned off the water, dried my body, inch by wet little inch, procrastinated with each brush of the towel. Now, what to wear? That decision should give me another fifteen minutes, right?

I was about to end the epic long delay and head downstairs to face the results of my worsening mental illness, but Amelia's manila envelope grabbed my attention. I turned on my desk lamp and opened it—then collapsed onto my chair.

Inside were two masterful pencil sketches that took my breath away. The first showed Jansen and me, a portrait drawn from the shoulders up. I caressed the images so as not to smudge them. As if I could absorb them in some way, and carry them with me forever.

She'd captured a pensive expression on my face, my gaze focused off to the left, but it was Jansen she had set to canvas perfectly. He gazed over my shoulder, eyes cast down, studying me with a serene smile. Each pencil stroke brought to life the essence of the guy I thought no one knew but me. She caught the air of mystery that surrounded him, the sensuality, the fierce loyalty. The way he cherished me.

Cherished. Past tense.

The other drawing depicted him alone, a close-up of his handsome face. My finger traced his soft eyebrows, his downcast eyes. It struck me how both drawings were of him looking down or away. She'd never seen behind the dark glasses. Yet somehow had captured acute sadness, an expression that made me want to wrap him in my arms.

A simple note accompanied the sketches. "He's lost without his friend—his heart."

Downstairs, it surprised me that Tyler lounged on the couch in his boxers and a T-shirt, eating a Poptart, TV remote in hand. How long had I slept?

I padded over to the fireplace and sat on the floor where

the flames made the ceramic tiles toasty warm.

"That was some movie last night, huh?" I said, attempting to appear casual.

"Mmm."

"What did people say after I left?"

"I don't know. Good night, I guess."

Did he try to insulate me, or was he that dense? Surely, our friends had a few things to say about the girl who screamed every half hour. Who made up imaginary spiders and insects crawling through her hair.

"No, I mean about me."

He snatched the remote from his lap and pressed the mute button. "I don't know. Why are you so worried about what people are saying about you?"

I'm sure my jaw dropped because this wasn't the way I thought this conversation would go. At all.

"No one said anything about the spiders? About the bugs?" I imitated myself, flinging my hair over my head.

With a wave of his hand, he brushed me off and resumed the sound of the newscast. "I don't know what you're talking about."

I got up, snatched the remote from the armrest, and muted the show. "Don't you remember me screaming about spiders last night?"

"Come on, Ellie. What are you playing at?"

"Bugs?" I pressed. "You had to keep stopping the movie. Charlie busted through the bathroom door to get me out. Then rushed me right to bed. Remember?"

"Give me the remote." He put his hand out, palm up. "Come on. You can tell me about your dream later."

My dream. Could it be? It had seemed so real.

I thought about the bathroom door in the basement. No way I dreamt that. The door was either splintered, shattered beyond repair—or it wasn't.

I started toward the cellar steps, but stopped at the refrigerator. There was something terrifying about returning to that dungeon. So, queen of procrastination that I was, I grabbed an apple and bit into it, letting its juice slide down nice and slow.

A broken door meant I hadn't dreamt it. Then what? Tyler lied? Protecting me from what? Myself?

Again, I walked toward the basement door, tucked away in the dark mudroom. The space smelled of wet grass and Tyler's foot funk from the old shoes he'd forgotten ages ago on the low shelf. Where we also kept backpacks and other items tossed there between trips from the car to the kitchen. The door creaked open, and I took a deep breath, but stopped short of going down, leaning on the handrail for support.

What if the door wasn't broken? Then I'd know… I was crazy.

Methodically, my feet advanced one carpeted step at a time, my hand pressing hard into the wood railing.

I made my way across the room, past the couch where Charlie had held me, past the comfy recliner, past the blanket Tyler had taken outside to shake free of spiders.

Incredibly, the door stood on its hinges, not a crack in its faux wood. I caressed the rough texture. Not even a dent. Everything appeared as if nothing had happened.

I turned on my heel to head back upstairs and mourn the loss of my sanity when something white made me look twice. Upon closer inspection, I found a small sticker on the door close to the doorknob. A barcode. I'd never noticed it before. Printed on it was the current year in tiny numerals.

But we'd had the basement finished six years ago—

When this door had been installed.

Weeks passed, and the weather turned colder. Winter arrived early, and the sky threatened to stay gray through all eternity. I pulled the sleeves of my sweatshirt down to the level of my first knuckles, allowing enough finger-wiggle room to strike the keyboard.

Tim popped his head over my computer monitor. "Hey,

Ellie."

Shoot! Where's that key? I searched frantically and erased the screen before he saw it.

He didn't seem to notice. "Some of us are going to hang out at my place after school. We're meeting around four if you want to come."

I hesitated. "I don't know."

"We're having pizza," his voice rang.

"Oh, well, as long as there's pizza."

"Great!" He missed the sarcasm, or perhaps ignored it. "See ya then."

I waited until the soft blond fuzz of his crown bounded away and out of sight before I clicked the key to return my screen to normal.

Enough of this crap. I figured it had to be one of three things: ghosts, mental illness, or a simulation glitch.

When I'd set out to research my growing hysteria, I hoped to find a little something here and there about visual hallucinations. Over the past half hour, I had discovered that ten percent of the population experienced them, probably higher than that. Who in their right mind would report it? Right mind, indeed. Most hallucinations stem from environmental factors, such as drugs or other inhalants. Still, wasn't there some logical explanation? Like my brother lacing the orange juice with something? Or maybe too much radon in the basement.

What I hadn't expected to find was the word *paracusia*. Basically, it meant auditory hallucinations. Jansen's voice, check. Charlie's voice, check. Tornado in the brain, check. Everything I found related to the topic showed a psychotic disorder.

I pulled out the crumpled list I'd made of things I'd noticed about Jansen. A few new items were added since Halloween.

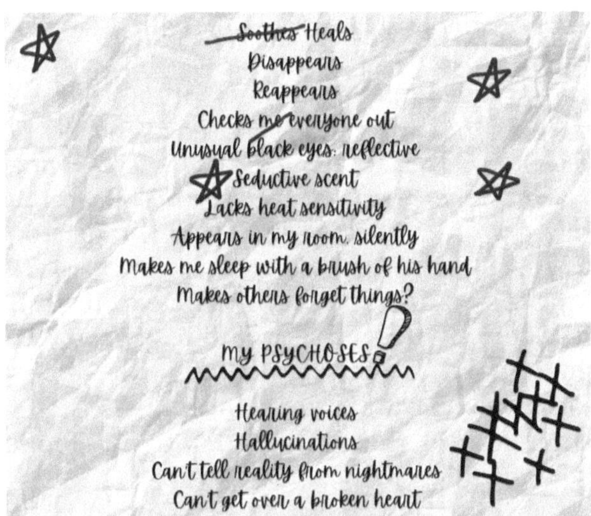

Either I'd had several psychotic episodes, yet had the sense to realize it, or the brothers were... Were what? I had no idea, but something beyond extraordinary.

Psychic, I could wrap my head around, but that had to do with ghosts. Paranormal stuff. I hadn't seen anything like that. Perhaps they were part of a cult—witches, or something. I'd heard witches were real. Only, more in the sense of religious practice than actual pointy-hatted women with crooked noses.

"Ellie, look."

I jumped and crumpled the paper, stuffing it into my pocket as Tim pointed out the window across the room.

Snow. Fluffy white flakes fell against a dusty backdrop of overcast clouds. I didn't care that it was ugly and gray outside. It snowed, and I lived for snow.

By the time school let out, I was a bundle of energy. I left the choir room ahead of everyone else, including Andrew, whose ride I needed.

About an inch of snow covered the sidewalk, and the crisp air stung my cheeks and lungs as I inhaled. Wet snowflakes dotted my lashes as I raised my face to the sky to taste winter's sweet tears. How light it fell as it clung to my coat and sprinkled my hair with its soft powder.

I extended my arms and marveled as the individual flakes attached themselves to my coat. This snow floated down lighter and fluffier than I'd ever seen. The weatherman had called it a dry snow, and as I studied it, I understood what he meant. It fell in tightly packed crystals.

Eyes closed, I turned in a slow circle to relish the sting of each speck on my warm face as if touched by fallen shards of starlight.

"God, you're beautiful."

I spun toward the voice and lost my footing. Jansen uprighted me.

"What did you say?" I breathed, certain I'd misunderstood.

"The snow." He twirled his sunglasses in his free hand. "It's beautiful."

He'd left his long black coat unbuttoned at the top, so his white-collared shirt poked through. The white contrasted against his sun-toasted skin, brown even in late fall.

Clara ran up from the rear and slipped in the snow, landing hard on the concrete.

"Are you okay?" I offered her my hand.

"I'm fine," she said, ignoring me and flipping her hair behind her shoulder. Slowly, she looked up at Jansen through caked-on mascara.

Jansen slid his sunglasses over his eyes and offered her his other hand, which she accepted eagerly. Just stared at him in a way like he'd offered her the moon instead of only a hand up.

She dusted herself off. "Are you ready, Jansen?"

"Ready." He slipped both hands into the pockets of his coat.

Andrew joined our awkward party, clad in his brown leather bomber jacket, buttoned to the collar. It fit as though tailored for him. Unbelievably, just as it always had, Jansen's face turned a brilliant shade of red. Behind his shades, I knew there were rich black flames.

Clara stuffed her hand into the narrow space between Jansen's elbow and rib cage. "Bye, Ellie," she sang.

Rooted to the snow, Jansen didn't move. His focus intent on Andrew, he said, "You're taking her to Tim's house, right?"

Andrew nodded.

"You should take her straight home. The roads are bad."

"We'll be fine."

"It's not you I'm concerned about."

Silence erupted, disturbed only by Clara's occasional huffs.

Jansen turned on his heel, dragging Clara with him, her arm wedged hard against his ribs, like he didn't want it there. Like he made it uncomfortable, so maybe she'd move it.

As they walked away, Clara slipped a few more times. "It *is* bad out. I bet the roads are slick." When he said nothing, Clara whined, "Won't you drive me home?"

"Fine." Clearly not, as he snarled the word.

I wished I could see her expression, but it couldn't compare to what I imagined.

As they were nearly out of hearing range, Andrew cupped his hands to his mouth, shouting, "I don't know why you put up with him, Clara!" Then, so quietly, I almost didn't hear him, he said, "Could he be any more transparent?"

"What do you mean?"

"He's so obviously in love with you."

Jansen came to an abrupt stop, as if, impossibly, he'd heard that, lurching Clara forward in her momentum.

"No," I said. "He can't be." I knew this with certainty. Felt it in my bones. Because if he was, if he felt about me as I did him, he couldn't physically deny it.

Jansen started walking again and his black leather coat flapped behind him, his feet steady even in the snow. He slung an arm around Clara's shoulder, stiff and robotic, but she melted.

Something inside me, something that had felt like a promise, like hope—died.

Tim's house wasn't far from the school, but it took us about twenty minutes to get there thanks to the snow. There wasn't a particular point to the gathering other than to kick back. Tim's mom provided snacks for us in the lower portion of the tri-level home, so we sat around eating chips and sipping hot chocolate. I opted for spiced cider and savored the explosion of flavor with every swallow.

This was the first time we'd all been together outside of class since Halloween. I prayed no one else would connect those dots. Then again, why would anyone bring it up? None of it had even happened, according to Tyler.

The conversation turned to casual school gossip after a while.

Aaron asked the group, "Does anybody have Fushi or Bender?"

A few of us mumbled we did.

Amelia perched in Tyler's lap on one scratchy couch cushion with a busy weave of brown, orange, and yellow. If she dropped the tortilla chip she nibbled, no one would ever notice. "Who's Bender?" she asked.

"Mr. Bender's my Latin teacher." Gretta sat forward in her matching chair with its sturdy, dark-wood frame. "He's absolutely gorgeous. I have the hardest time concentrating. It's terrible."

It was no coincidence that Mark then ripped open a fresh bag of chips with too much force, which sent a few flying over the rusty shag carpet.

Gretta jumped to help pick up the scattered snack. "Well, he is. All the girls think so."

"Anyway," Aaron said, "I heard that he and Fushi are seeing each other."

"No!" I added in shock. "That can't be. Mr. Bender's married."

As if they'd planned to tag-team the story, Mark said, "Exactly, but in the morning, before school starts, if you walk by Mr. Bender's room, she's always there. Honest, she's always there. I have first-period with Bender."

No way, because— "She's always in class when I get there."

"Well, sure." Tim sat peeling a piece of string cheese like a banana. "She runs down the hall to her classroom just before the first bell. You're usually still sitting outside the choir room."

Aaron took the reins back on his story, clapping his hands loudly. "One of the guys on the football team saw them having dinner together, way out in Wapak. He and the football team were there for an away game."

"Wapak," short for Wapakoneta, was a small Ohio town with fewer than 9,000 people, where hardly anyone ever traveled on purpose.

Aaron sat forward with enthusiasm, having captured his audience. "His grandparents live there, so his family went to eat afterward instead of going home on the bus. He said Bender and Fushi had dinner and held hands across the table."

A gasp rippled around the room, and I said again, "But he's married."

"Yes, we know." Tim smiled, almost a soft chuckle. "That's what makes it a good story. Otherwise, it would just be two consenting adults on a date." He mocked me with a wink.

"That's nothing." Mark squeezed in close to Gretta. "Clara told Suzy Meyer she wanted to break up with Jansen."

The burn in my cheeks struck fast and my hands moved over my heart. I didn't know if it was from hearing his name or the mention of Clara and him in the same sentence. Or maybe it was the flame of hope that burned.

Tim chucked a pillow at Mark. "Shut up. She did not."

Mark was too busy enjoying the attention to notice the mood in the room, even though the shift felt palpable. At least to me. He barreled on. "No, really, she did. The crazy thing is *why.*"

No one spoke for a while. Then Gretta said, "Okay, fine then, why hasn't she?"

"She didn't say. Only that she *can't.*"

The word hung in the air with all its tantalizing

possibilities.

Aaron asked, "Hey Ellie, why do you think?"

Good God, don't ask me. Most of the time, I tried not to think about Clara at all. I couldn't stop thinking about Jansen, but she never came to mind. Why couldn't she leave him? She'd fallen so in love with him that he was her drug? Or maybe he'd threatened to spill some secret, though that didn't sound like him at all. Fear of the unknown, fear of ever finding anyone that could compare to him. Could be she got lost in his eyes. That she sat up nights dreaming about his embrace and knew she couldn't give that up. She could be afraid of being alone. Maybe… but no. She couldn't be pregnant. Could she?

Tim jumped in before I could. "She doesn't know, you moron. It's not as if Clara's exactly confiding in her."

That made Aaron take offense, and he scowled. "I just figured she'd know what's up. They're such an odd couple."

With a snap of his jaw, Tyler accepted a chip from Amelia straight into his mouth. "I don't think he really likes her," he said with his mouth full. "I think she's got something on him."

Didn't look as though Mark thought so, as he shook his head. "Seems to me it's the other way around."

"Charlie says it's a relationship of convenience," Tyler said. "But he won't say anything more. Hey, anyone wanna order a pizza?"

Tyler's last sentence came with a wink. I mouthed "thank you" to him, grateful for the quick purge and dodge approach. I'd been enjoying myself for the first time in a while before the topic popped up.

Once pizzas were ordered, Tim slipped in a movie for everyone. It was a comedy I'd already watched.

So, I curled up on the plush carpet in front of the chunky couch where Tyler sat, and soon Andrew plopped down next to me.

We'd barely settled in when Tim walked up and loomed over us. "Ellie, you've seen this movie before, right?" I nodded. "Wanna come out on the porch? I'm gonna wait out there for the pizzas."

Sure, why not? While I got up off the floor, Tim extended a hand to Andrew. "Toss me that blanket, would you?"

Andrew scowled but didn't move a muscle toward the mustard throw.

Amelia tossed it to him and he winked as a way of thanks as I grabbed my coat on the way out the front door.

The blanket proved necessary against the bite of the storm as he led me to sit with him. Cold air tickled the delicate hairs inside my nose as the swing swayed.

"It's nice you came." He had his legs splayed wide, rocking from heel to toe.

"I'm glad you invited me."

"It's been great kicking back. I always thought you'd be someone I could chat with if I got the chance."

"What are you talking about? We see each other every day."

He reclined and rested his arm over the swing behind my shoulders. "Yeah, sure, but you're never alone. Doesn't feel like I've ever really gotten to talk to you."

Tim was nice enough, and I enjoyed the moments spent with him at school in my comfort zone. This was way-the-heck outside that zone.

"Look, I'm just gonna be straight. I'm not a bad guy."

"Well, no, I never thought you were."

He cracked each knuckle in his left hand, one at a time. Oh, what was on his mind? "Back at my old school, I was… well…you know…"

"Popular," I said.

"I mean, if you want to put it like that. I had a lot of friends, and I'd known them all my life. It was easy, ya know?"

I realized then that I knew next to nothing about Tim. "It must have been difficult."

"What, moving? Nah, that part was easy. It was the leaving that was hard." He returned to the slow knuckle cracking. "There was this girl."

"You had a girlfriend?"

"No, not a girlfriend. You might say she was my Jansen." He looked at me tentatively, gauging my reaction.

"That had to be tough to leave."

"It was." His voice grew distant, no longer with me.

A gust blew glittery snow from the porch railing and whipped it into an upward swirl of tiny, shining diamonds. Tim pulled the blanket higher on our laps and threw an arm around me.

"This wind," he said softly. "Is this okay? You know, for warmth?"

"Of course." Funny, it was okay, too. I rubbed my hands together against the cold. "Your friend. Did she have a name?"

"What? Oh, Anna, yes. Her name was Anna."

I didn't miss the past tense, and waited for him to continue. He didn't at first, instead playing absentmindedly with one of my curls. It might have made me pull away, put some distance between us, but when I glanced up, he wasn't with me, probably unaware he twisted and untwisted the curl around his index finger.

The wind picked up again, and he shivered as though to clear his head from thoughts of Anna. "There was a car accident. I don't like to talk about it." His voice had faded. He seemed to encourage himself to tell the story against his better instinct.

"It's okay." I pulled one of my hands out from under the blanket and laid it over his, a thing he didn't even seem to notice.

He sighed and turned his hand to engulf my fingertips, squeezing them lightly. "You don't want to hear this."

"Please," I said. "I do."

"It was last winter, about this time, come to think of it. She was so excited about auditioning for a local musical production. One of those county-wide things, so it was kind of a big deal. It's all she talked about for months."

Tim swiped at a tear, one he seemed to hope I wouldn't notice. Then, with a sniffle, disentangled himself from the blanket, and walked with a sedate, lazy limp to the other side of the porch. He turned away, facing that other world that existed in his memory.

"Sometimes, I'd go and hear her practice. I would wait in the hallway until I heard the rehearsal get up in earnest, so maybe she wouldn't notice if I snuck in. Then, I'd open the door. Sit in the back row where there wasn't any light. Her voice carried me to other places. Dug into me somehow, wrapping around some part of me. Ya know?"

Yes, I knew. How many times had I felt that myself? The way a voice could enter your bloodstream and pulse, penetrating that part of you that lives without the body.

"Like wrapping around your soul." I pulled the blanket across my shoulders.

He turned to face me and looked stunned to find me there. "Yeah," he said, awed at the suggestion. "She used to say my voice did that to her." With this, he hung his head. "We sang duets together sometimes and, I don't know, but our voices fit."

Snow had gathered in a drift from the gusts, and Tim sniffled and kicked at it. "Everyone there, at my old school… They thought I was a pretty good singer."

I'd never heard him sing, so I couldn't say we thought that, too, and I suspected I knew where this was going. He'd believed when he first came, he would be the star of all our shows, maybe win us over with his voice, but—

"Jansen doesn't actually want the attention he gets." For some reason, I wanted him to know that.

Tim scoffed, "Oh, okay."

"No, really. It annoys him if anyone mentions it. He knows he has this crazy, mesmerizing voice, but since he never trained it or put any work into it, it isn't praise-worthy. Not like what you or Anna…" My words trailed off. I wasn't sure which tense to end my sentence in, "have" or "had."

Tim bobbed his head in understanding. "Anna," he said, bringing himself back to her story. "Her parents couldn't take her to the audition, so she got a ride. It was so stupid. The guy had had his license for a month, and they were out on a night kinda like this. The light had turned green, so the guy stepped on the gas. Anyone would, right?"

I nodded in quick agreement.

"Yeah, well, the dude in the cross-traffic lane hadn't stopped. Hadn't even slowed down. Just pressed his foot on the gas and sped up to make that light. Only he didn't make it. He rammed into Anna, into her side of the car, crushing her into her driver. The accident knocked the driver unconscious and he had to have surgery on his leg but was… well, they say he was fine, but Anna…"

He didn't have to finish. I knew. Without trying to hide it, Tim swiped tears from his cheeks, and a small guttural sound escaped his mouth. "So anyway!" he said, a little too abrupt a mood shift to be natural, fighting to control it. "We moved here to this town God forgot about. My mom thought it would be good for me to get a clean start, make some new friends. Forget about the past. Forget about Anna."

He turned his back again and leaned all his weight on the porch rail. "And who was the first girl I should meet here? Do you know?"

Oh, I had a growing suspicion this was where I entered the story. Had I been the first? Even if I'd known that, I couldn't think why it was significant. Meekly, I got out the word, "Me?"

He gave a slow and deliberate nod. "Gabriella Wood. Soft red curls, kind eyes, unbelievably adorable freckles, heart-shaped mouth." He traced his lips as he spoke of mine. "You don't even wear makeup. The girl next door."

Gradually, one heel after the other, he walked back to the swing where I sat, mouth agape, enthralled with the direction the story had taken.

He fingered one of my curls. "Just…like…Anna."

"Oh." It wasn't a word so much as an involuntary sound.

"Yes, oh. That's why I acted so stupid at the beginning of the year."

"No, Tim. Don't—"

"Hang on. I'm almost finished, I promise. All that was just the windup." He sat beside me on the swing again, rubbing his hands together vigorously. "I behaved abominably when we first met. Abominably." He chuckled. "Do you know that's a very hard word to say? Try it."

"Abominably," I said, but not in one go. I stumbled over it and snorted at myself, which made both of us laugh harder.

"See? Oh, I don't know. I saw you, and instantly, you were supposed to be her replacement, I think. Only you didn't know that. How could you? And Jansen? Well, he sure wasn't having any of it."

He rocked us back and forth, but the stillness of the night rang awkwardly. "So, all that was a lame attempt at an apology in hopes you'd say 'yes' to a movie with me sometime." His voice sounded so sincere and sweet. The pure vulnerability of it took me by surprise.

"Ah, Tim, I don't know."

"Come on. You've got to let him go."

I thought I heard a growl, and my head twitched to the right, looking for a dog. Still skittish after the one in the park. There was nothing there but the wind stirring the bushes.

So, I turned my attention to a loose string on the blanket. "There isn't anything to let go of."

"Yes, there is. Whether you admit it or not, you guys have been a couple for a long time. You've broken up, and I don't even think you realize it."

The words stung because I knew there was truth in them. Tears started, but I held them back.

"It would be as friends, of course. Like I said before, I just want to get to know you better. What do you say? If you turn me down now, I'll never ask again."

I smirked, studying my hands folded in my lap. After a while, I grabbed a breath. "Sure, why not?"

"Really?"

"Friends, right?" I added quickly.

"Friends, of course."

The pizzas arrived, and Tim jumped up to pay for them. We took them inside to feed our hungry crowd, where Amelia hopped up first in the commotion, linking her arm in mine, taking me by surprise.

"So, what were you guys talking about?" she whispered.

"Nothing."

"You lie. He was grinning from ear to ear behind your back when you came in."

My cheeks burned, despite myself, and I hid my face. "We're going to the movies together, that's all. As friends!"

She squeezed my shoulders. "Good girl. It's about time."

Pizzas in hand, Tim walked into the kitchen with that funny, nearly imperceptible limp of his. He knew too many details about the accident that had taken Anna's life. It was only a suspicion, but a strong one, that it was he who had been behind the wheel that night. Of course, I would never ask, and he would never bring up the subject again.

CHAPTER FIFTEEN

My mom sat curled up on the couch in the family room. "Hold on, Ellie."

I stopped on the second step and faced toward her as she turned the volume up on the TV. The weatherman's voice blared.

My mom said, "The weather will be bad tonight. We're expecting a couple inches of snow and heavy winds."

"We'll be fine. It probably won't be all that bad until we're back, anyway. Isn't it supposed to start late?"

"Yes." She bit her lip. "But they're not always that accurate. Maybe you shouldn't go."

I even surprised myself when I protested. She'd handed me the perfect excuse to get out of this pseudo date. Yet I heard myself say, "Nothing's happening right now. Tell you what. Let me borrow your cell phone, and if the weather's bad when we come out of the movie, we'll call. Okay?"

"You really want to go, huh?"

Maybe I did. Perhaps buried deep, some part of me wanted to give Tim a fair chance.

So, I inhaled a breath all the way through to my toes, raised my eyes toward the ceiling, and started back up the stairs.

"Take your things!" she hollered after me.

Take my things, of course. Cardinal house rule number 101. I picked up the book, hair tie, and small pile of socks she'd collected on the steps and carried them to my room, where I tossed them all onto my desk. That done, I changed into a pair of jeans and a plunging V-neck blouse.

When I opened my jewelry box to pull out a topaz ring, a necklace sat inside that I hadn't worn in ages. It occurred to me it might be nice to wear. Its pendant dipped low on my chest and flattered the neckline of my blouse.

I caught my reflection in the mirror above my dresser as my fingers played with the Chrysoberyl. Its eye usually winked, but now stared at me, daring me to take it off.

The memory of the day Jansen had given it to me packed my heart tight, and it hurt to think of it. I felt again that strange sensation of a magnet drawing the necklace to it, and of something inside cracking open, pulling itself out of me. When I started toward the clasp, the pain mounted, so my hands found themselves wrapped around my middle, holding me together.

When would the missing him stop?

Okay, fine. I'd keep this piece of Jansen with me, even on my date. Instead of the topaz ring, I chose a blue sapphire to complement the Chrysoberyl.

When Tim arrived, I opened the door to find him wearing jeans, and—how sweet—a blue shirt I'd once told him brought out his eyes. On his feet, he wore a pair of brown leather shoes rather than his usual sneakers. He had neatly combed hair and smelled of fragrant cologne.

"Ready?" He held the door wide. "Hang on. You look lovely."

My blush was probably thanks enough, but I said it aloud, too.

"Be sure to call if you have trouble." My mom's voice boomed from behind, catching me off guard. She handed me her cell phone, and we were on our way.

Tim took me to the Mayflower Movie Theater to see *The Beautician and the Beast*, a romantic comedy. Though we purchased separate tickets, he politely held the door open as we entered the ancient, decrepit theater built before 1908 as a liquor store. It was in the heart of our small town's square and boasted just three viewing rooms. The bathrooms were spectacularly bad, located in the basement and rumored to be cleaned with a garden hose. I didn't doubt it.

"Do you want popcorn?" he asked, opening his wallet to pull out some cash.

"That sounds good. With butter?"

"Of course." I offered to help pay, but he insisted. "When my mom asks, I need to be able to say I paid for something."

Our movie aired in one of the two small viewing rooms, which seated only about forty-five. Realistically, though, it held about fifteen people if you like comfort. If you sat anywhere closer than the last few rows, you had to crane your neck to look up at the screen. A chill permeated the theater, as if the heater blew cool air. My coat lay between us, over the armrest, and it was tempting to put it back on.

I must have looked at it with longing, because Tim said, "Cold in here, isn't it?"

Would he try putting his arm around me? What would I do if he did?

"Here." He grasped my coat.

When he did, the armrest came with it, and we both had a good laugh over that. The building desperately needed repairs. He propped the armrest in its place, wrapped my coat over my shoulders like a shawl, and ended with a soft pat on my back.

A strange thing happened, something I hadn't expected. I found I half wished he'd put his arm around me. Instead, he shifted his weight away and leaned on the opposite armrest. Maybe all my worrying had been needless, and I'd been too hasty when I insisted on a night out as friends. Maybe—just maybe—I could move on.

Before the movie began, Tim figured we might as well make use of the removable armrest. He set it on the floor, and we sat with the bowl of popcorn between us. I can't lie and say I didn't find pleasure in the anticipation of what that could lead to. After a while, we stopped looking at the bowl as we put our hands in. When our knuckles bumped, a spark sizzled through me. But Tim simply smiled and retracted his hand.

At one point, I leaned toward him, testing whether he'd brush his arm or his shoulder against mine. He did not. Also, he had several opportunities to answer any of my questions about the plot, which could have left us nuzzled head-to-head. Yet, he always answered, then retreated to his corner.

When the movie ended, the wind had picked up, and snowflakes floated from the sky. We talked about the film's storyline and how unrealistic it was. When we got to the car, I had wrapped my coat around myself and zipped it to the neck.

As if to prove this wasn't a real date, Tim took his time. He fiddled with the keys, snickered, teased, and generally enjoyed my discomfort. I bounced on my side of the car, hand on the door handle, ready to yank the moment it unlatched.

"Please hurry," I said with a shudder.

Behind me, I swore something snarled, but when I pivoted, no one was there.

"Open the damn door."

That was Jansen's voice. No way it wasn't.

The lock clicked, but I didn't pull the lever. I was too busy looking around, searching for him. Streetlights lit the parking lot full of cars, all glistening in the falling snow. There were no trees, bushes, trashcans, nothing to hide behind but the cars. No way he'd hide anyway, not him. He'd confront us straight out.

"Jansen?" I called out softly.

A soft moan replied.

"Jansen!" I hissed as a wet snowflake landed on my eyelashes.

"You've got to be kidding," Tim said.

I regretted saying it as loudly as I had. As if he didn't already think I thought of nothing else.

With an impatient scoff, he pounded his fist into his forehead. "Well, aren't you getting in?"

I opened the door and slipped into the passenger seat. While trying to hide it, I searched the area for my deranged friend. He had to be there. This was getting ridiculous. I willed the dark veil of night to lift and reveal him to me, but he wasn't there—only snow and mist and shadow.

He wasn't there.

Just another phantom voice in my unhinged mind.

A chill scurried along my spine. Whether from worrying about Jansen or from the severe cold, I couldn't be sure. I rubbed at my arms, using friction to provide some amount of warmth, grateful the car at least sheltered us from the chilling wind.

At last, Tim put the keys into the ignition.

"Keep the car off."

No, no, no. Who's voice was that? I sat up, frozen in my seat. It wasn't Tim. Nor was it Jansen, and it was distinctly in my head.

Fingers on the car keys, Tim froze at the steering wheel. Jingled the extra keys on their chain. Only he didn't turn the engine over. Instead, he covered his face with his hands.

"You want to warm her."

My heart gave a sick lurch as if away from that voice. It was low, with a silkiness unlike any I knew, and it came from nowhere. I wanted to ask if he heard it, too, but I couldn't handle the mortification when he inevitably told me "no."

Unbidden, he leaned across the console and threw an arm around my shoulders and pulled me near. "You're cold." He'd come appallingly close to my ear. His pupils were so large I couldn't see the blue of his iris, and his skin flushed.

I froze from the inside out.

It wasn't real, I told myself. Just voices. The danger wasn't what the voices said. No, the threat was me. That I grew increasingly ill. That my dreaming brain melded with my conscious one. I'd soon have to face life in an institution.

Please don't try anything, I thought.

He brought himself closer...inch by inch. His eyes fixated on my mouth. When his lips touched mine, I could only picture a flabby, wet fish.

Maybe he'd get the hint if I gently pushed him away.

"She can't stop you. She's weak."

He didn't get the hint. He sought my lips with all the intensity of a crazed predator. And that voice. Tendrils of blackness that wormed their way through my mind and burrowed deep to take root.

Goosebumps prickled beneath my skin. I turned my head, so he kissed my neck instead. Inexplicably, he loosed a groan of pleasure.

"No, Tim, wait." I pushed hard against his forehead. "Tim!" That broke him from his trance. I forced myself into my door, molded up beside it, as far from him as I could get.

Gross, was that spittle on his lip? He wiped it away and sighed before directing his attention to the steering wheel. With shaky hands, he turned the key over, and the engine's purr sprung to life.

I shivered and shivered and shivered. My fingers went numb—my toes, my lips, my stomach—all numb.

In silence, he pulled out of the parking spot.

He'd become my friend. So how did we get here? This sudden assertiveness? These unwanted advances? Before, at the movie, I'd wanted him to brush my arm. Thought he might take my hand, maybe linger after whispering in my ear. Yet, he hadn't. Why skip that and go right to—whatever the hell this was? Why now?

Where was that voice coming from? What kind of delusional person created not one, not two, but three voices in their mind?

And this voice—like darkness trapped inside myself.

Tim turned the radio on low and rubbed the back of his neck, massaging it. "That was some homework assignment Clemmons gave out," he said, breaking the disquieting silence.

"I guess." Good, he changed the subject. I still shook, terrified of the voice and that made me doubt my sanity. "Did you get started yet?"

"Heck, no. I'll probably start it the day before it's due." He chortled and then turned serious. "Ellie, I'm sorry about back there. Not sure what came over me."

"That's okay." So very not okay, but relief spread through

my body, anyway.

"I just thought maybe you'd be ready to date."

"What are you talking about?" Exasperation thickened my voice. "I've dated before."

"I mean, now that your *husband* leaves you alone."

"Are you on that again? I don't want to go there."

"Oh, come on. Everyone knew you were off limits as long as Jansen was around. You were a different person on my porch. I just figured since he finally left you alone..." His words trailed off, and cold crept an ice trail along my spine.

The word "alone" made my mind spin. Is that why I created the voices? To keep from being alone? The snow fell in thick, heavy pellets, and I felt nauseous as I stared at them, so I bent over in the car with my head between my knees.

"Turn left."

There it was again, that low, gravelly, perverse tenor that penetrated my thoughts. Nourished my fears.

I sat up swiftly and hit my crown on the glove box. With a wince, I pressed my hand on the bump and swallowed hard. "Did you hear that?"

"Hear what?" He turned the car to the left as the voice had directed.

He was not taking me home.

When we turned onto a side street, the sign read "Horseshoe Bend." I knew this road. Tyler used to talk about it. Said it was notorious for its seclusion. There were no houses on this route, and the only farm sat across the enormous field. Woods, a deadly drop to a ravine, and a cornfield. Nothing more.

"Pull over."

Why would he do that? He wouldn't—but he did. Parked the car half in the grass, half in the shoulder. Then turned to leer as he obeyed my twisted mind. As if taking orders from it.

"She's all yours."

I scrubbed my eyes with fisted fingers and tried to dislodge the all-consuming illness. My pulse raced so fast, surely that alone would wake me up.

Too bad that didn't happen, and I shivered from the marrow of my bones.

"Ellie, come on. You and I have been friends for a while now."

Had we? I wasn't feeling friendly toward him. The heat from his hand spread across my leg. How was it so hot when I was so cold?

Goosebumps arose again, which he mistook for pleasure. He leaned in with a calculated pace, his warm breath on my cheek. If he didn't stop soon, I'd vomit in his mouth, and I did draw some satisfaction at the thought. My breath stuttered as my throat tightened.

With one fiery hand on my frigid leg, he tugged my head toward his.

"No, Tim, no," I said, but he wasn't listening.

"Take her."

Oh God, that voice! As though Tim listened to my sick, twisted thoughts. Yet, I knew—I *knew*—they were not my thoughts at all.

Before I could respond, his mouth crushed mine. I put my hands on his shoulders and pushed and pressed and shoved, but he dragged my face to him even harder. Jammed his eel-like tongue through the slit of my lips, then crept along each tooth as if counting his prey.

I rammed into him, but his strength overpowered me. Pulled a leg up. Braced myself against the dashboard.

He prowled toward me and slithered from his seat, never taking his lips from mine. He yanked my leg from the dashboard and straddled my body along the bench seat. Used his weight to make me lie across the middle, my head on the passenger's side, jammed against the door.

The wind picked up outside and rocked the car along with the contents of my stomach. The motion forced him on top of me and he pinned my arms to my sides, immobilizing me.

I couldn't lift a knee to drive into his groin, couldn't raise a fist to bloody his nose, couldn't use my thumb to gouge an eye. Too bad I hadn't chomped down on his tongue when I had the chance. Could almost taste the tang of the blood that would have drawn.

My head still pressed against the door, and at least it gave me leverage. With the muscles in my neck, I forced my body up and mashed myself as close to it as I could get.

So unlike him, his breath wreaked of decay as he slimed my face with wet lips. I could only turn my head and thrash to get away, his stubble chafing the tender skin of my cheek.

Then, I guess because I pushed so hard against the door, a miracle happened. Somehow, it opened. I fell and braced for the impact, but it never came. Instead, something warm stopped my fall. Something soft.

I stared at another set of wild eyes, and those black orbs fixed on Tim.

Who was this new predator? I didn't at first understand who arrived outside Tim's car on this deserted road. Didn't recognize the arms that pulled my feet from the car. Didn't fathom I could know the hands that stood me on the ground.

Without thinking, some internal signal in my limbs dropped me to the pavement. I pawed at the snow like a terrified animal, and I had only one thought.

Escape.

Before I could move, a firm hand strapped me to his body.

When I realized it was Jansen, I collapsed into him. Let him support all of my weight.

How could I have doubted him? It was always him, wasn't it? I sobbed, and as he pulled my face into his chest, his chin didn't rest on my crown. No, his attention wasn't on me.

I had to blink through blurry tears, but saw him stare hatred into the car at Tim. That's why he was there, why he held me now. Because of what Tim had done. Because of his groping hands, his snake-like tongue, his body that had pressed into mine. Because Tim listened to that voice in my head.

It was all too much. Never mind that Jansen held me as if I mattered. He had me trapped, caged, yet again. Trapped by

Tim, by Jansen. By madness.

Terror hit so extreme, I sobbed in huge choking breaths.

It wasn't even possible for Jansen to be there. How? Without a car. Without knowing where I was. How could he possibly have found me?

Unless he wasn't here at all and I fell captive to another hallucination—a dissociative episode. I'd read about it.

I cringed as I tried to make sense of it all, and Jansen tightened his already firm grip around my waist.

He was too strong and wouldn't let me go, and that feeling of entrapment made my blood run cold.

I couldn't shake how Tim had pinned me—the same way Jansen held me now, against my will.

Just like that, my mind returned to the car, and because I was so confused and so certain of my insanity, I knew I'd never left the car. That this whole Jansen-rescuing-me thing was an escape, a ruse, the mad conjurings of a sick head.

Let go! I choked on screams and fumbled with his fingers. Tim, Jansen—whoever the hell it was—he didn't seem to feel the fingernails that dug into his skin.

Madness.

The memory of Tim's claws on my face, my back, my hips—

Here was Jansen—or was it Tim—who pressed into me? Who ensnared me?

In one swift movement, I dropped to my knees, out of his grasp. Like a wild animal, I ran and slipped in the fresh snow. Staggered, screamed, and choked on sobs.

If it was Jansen, he'd chase me, so I listened for crunching footsteps in the snow... but the only sounds came from mine. If I outran him, and it sounded as if I had, then it had to be Tim who chased me.

I didn't look back. Told myself never to look back.

Behind me—oh, God. Someone breathed fast, like he tried to catch me.

If I kept running, eventually, I'd run into something, some sort of help. Or I could hide. Across the field, there had to be trees or shelter or a barn, anything—

Then, what the hell! From where? Jansen halted before me. How? Somehow, without footsteps, without even breath, he had passed me. I stumbled to a halt a foot in front of him.

"Ellie!" he shouted.

That got my attention. I swung at him and tried to run around him on the other side, but he blocked me too fast.

Get away. Run! Had to escape Tim and the voices and Jansen and my twisted insanity. I remained petrified of being in my own skin, and if I could have stepped out of myself, I would have.

"Ellie, stop!" Jansen's hands were on my shoulders but tentatively, barely touching me. "It's okay. I'm here. I've got you."

I stared and stopped struggling. "It's not okay," I said through clenched teeth. "You shouldn't be here."

"I've always been here."

"You left me."

"No, Ellie. I never did."

It was a lie. It was a delicious lie, the kind I wanted to believe. His eyes met mine. Held mine. If he lied, he was masterful.

Horrible laughter smothered the lie from my mind. Cackling so loud I couldn't form thoughts.

I cradled my head in my hands and squeezed my eyes shut tight. "The voices. I can't—can't make them stop."

He was still for such a long time that I looked up and found he looked at his shoes, wincing. Then he met my gaze and nodded. Nodded.

"It's okay," he said on a breath. "I can explain that."

He could explain? In my delusions, I'd created voices that comforted, protected, or harmed, and he could explain? What was wrong with him?

Over the laughter and out of anger, I yelled, "I hear three voices. Three distinct voices. You can explain that? Because one of them is yours."

Then, I got the expected reaction. Where before sorrow touched his mask, now he wore fright, as if he could see how truly insane I'd become. The black of his eyes altered, becoming white as they grew so wide they reflected only snow and moon and ice. A current ran between us as disgust seethed from his soul into mine.

Shame weighed so heavily that my chin dropped toward my chest.

His arms tensed at his sides. "You hear *three* voices?"

"Sometimes," I said, hugging myself tight.

"Tell me about them."

"There's you."

He nodded. Inexplicably, he nodded as I told him I heard his voice in my mind. "Go on."

"There's Charlie."

He rolled his eyes. Actually rolled his eyes. "And the third?"

"I don't know. It's hideous, a monster inside my head."

"Ellie, tell me more." Frustration added gravel to his voice.

"It wanted Tim to hurt me."

He snatched my hand. "We have to go."

My feet were clumsy in the wet, snow-laden grass, but he steadied me with abnormal strength. I tried to pull away, but his grip tightened. "Hurry," he said, but I couldn't keep up.

"I'm trying!"

He stopped fast and spun me around, facing me 180 degrees in the other direction. My back pressed into his front, and he gripped my upper arms, pinning them to my side. He leaned close and brushed his cheek against mine, as his breath mixed with the wind to rush over the arch of my ear. "Trust me?"

I melted, just like that. His scent, his touch, his old self buckled my knees.

"Don't look back." In an instant, his words fell not over my ear, but in my head. His hands released me, and he disappeared.

I knew on instinct that he was gone. No need to turn around. He no longer pressed into me. The breeze whipped at my coat, and that feeling I always got in my center that filled me when he was near left me empty and wanting.

Yet, of course, I turned and defied the voice. I don't know why I did.

Tim's car idled several feet away, and he stood outside his door. He had one foot in the car and the other on the ground as he leaned over the roof. As he watched me wistfully.

Then his demeanor took a sharp change. His body stiffened. He pulled himself straight, and still looking at me, got into his car. In a heartbeat, he had driven off.

Before I grasped Jansen had abandoned me, that I stood alone in a snowy field on a deserted road, he reappeared behind me, bent near my cheek like he'd never left.

"You looked," he said, a hint of pride in his voice I didn't understand.

"Of course." Who wouldn't? "I had to."

"No, actually. You proved the impossible wasn't."

The wind whipped itself into a fury. Inside my head, the maniacal cackles grew to a frenzied pitch.

Jansen's grip around me tightened, and he molded my body into his. "Don't be afraid."

Warmth spread outward. My eyes fell closed.

The wind stopped.

The laughter ceased.

Utter silence encased us.

"I'm sorry," I said at last.

"*You're* sorry?"

"I shouldn't have told you about the voices, and I shouldn't have put myself in that position. It was… I don't know what it was."

"You didn't do anything wrong."

The air was so quiet my ears tuned in to every syllable he uttered. I let his melodic voice reverberate like the final chord before the maestro lowers the baton. Allowed myself to linger over it as I put off what I knew I had to do.

"Ellie." He broke the silence.

"Yes?"

"Are your eyes closed, by any chance?"

A clock ticked.

"Yes."

A freezer turned over its tray of ice. *Thump.*

He hummed his amusement, a low rumble at the base of his throat, near my ear. "Open them."

Somewhere, a heater clicked on with a steady purr.

"I don't think so."

"Why not?"

"I'm…" I had so many phrases rattling around my brain, I couldn't pick one. I'm afraid. I'm insane. I'm not ready to face reality. I'm not sure what reality is. I'm at peace now, and if I open my eyes it will prove I've gone mad. I'm not ready to face the fact, because it was a fact I couldn't deny, that we had not moved one inch, and yet we no longer stood in the snow-covered field.

"It's okay," he said.

"It's really not."

He reached around me and made a slow trail from my hairline down my forehead. Grazed the bridge of my nose to its tip. His finger lingered over my lips. They parted, and my warm breath escaped across his skin, a thing that made him groan. The pleasure I drew from that throaty rumble opened my eyes wide.

"How did you do that?" I marveled at the calm effect the old gesture had on me. The tormenting voices slipped to a dull memory.

"*That's* your first question?"

Instead of snow, carpet lay beneath our feet. Where before, there had been open space outlined by trees, snow, and stars, now we stood in a small conservatory. Large trees and varying-sized plants garnished the room, candles flickered on the coffee table, and fairy lights lit along the ceiling. On the walls hung pictures of Kate, Charlie, and Jansen.

"I suppose I might ask how we got to your house."

"You might." He chuckled and seemed to assess the status of my knees, specifically their ability to hold me up, before he slowly released me.

When I proved myself steady, he gripped my coat's collar. His fingers grazed my neck as he dragged the garment down my shoulders. Slowly. My pulse quickened as he ignited every freckle, every hair, and every nerve ending.

Then, Charlie appeared where, before I had blinked, there had been no one there.

CHAPTER SIXTEEN

Charlie slouched in front of us, hands in his pockets. The look on his face mimicked one whose world had come crashing down upon him. "Jansen, what have you done?"

"We have to tell her. I had no choice."

I don't know why I thought it was over. When a black haze straight from my Halloween nightmare materialized, barely visible, I knew my chest would burst. A mist of empty blackness threatening to swallow us whole.

With a mournful look, Charlie shook his head slowly. "Her energy—the energy between the two of you—Jansen, it's ridiculous."

Jansen stood so close that when he swayed, his arm brushed mine, making my skin tingle along the goosebumps not from him, but from the Other. "Trust me, I'm aware."

Hey, guys… I raised my index finger, pointing, because words would not come, but they ignored it. Didn't notice what existed right in front of them.

Charlie gestured toward me. "Then you must also be aware he'll find her."

The laughter, God! That malicious mirth sliced through the air with a cruel edge. Was I seriously the only one who heard it?

Jansen said, "He won't look for her here."

"Oh." I found my voice. "I think he's here."

I knew the mist and the cackles belonged to the "he" they

spoke of. A fog so close I could taste his scent of rotting wood. The stink of a goat.

Jansen, Charlie, and that thing all snarled, and then Jansen spun me away from it. A scream ripped from my throat as I thought Charlie threw a ball of fire. That, of course, wasn't possible.

Kate appeared at their kitchen threshold, wiping her hands on a tea towel—

Jansen yelled, "Charlie, now!"

Charlie disappeared from his spot—

And reappeared quicker than a finger snap beside his mom. He strapped her to his body with an arm, and as quickly as we had gone from the field to the living room, we crouched in front of the gates of the local town cemetery.

The only reason I stood on both feet was Jansen's firm grip around my waist. Surely, I'd have a bruise there, but I didn't care. He loosened his clutch, and I slumped toward the ground. He shoved my coat into my arms and picked me up, carrying me faster and easier than was natural.

"We have to hurry," he said to Charlie and Kate. "Quickly, this way."

He carried me along the path, the gravel barely crunching beneath his effortless gait. At an unnatural speed, Charlie kept up with Jansen, but behind us, Miss Kate panted as her feet pounded the ground.

Then Charlie stopped running to swat at unseen things. His face twisted, and both hands clapped over his ears as he doubled over in apparent pain. But why? There was nothing to see. Nothing to hear but my heartbeat, too fast and too loud.

Then Jansen's arms cinched around my waist as he, too, fought something invisible. A thing I couldn't hear or sense or process. What was going on? His pressure tightened as he, too, bent forward, squeezing my organs.

"Jansen, you're scaring me."

Charlie removed a hand from his ear to swat at nothing. Pressed the exposed ear into his shoulder, protecting it from the nothing. From silence. From a noiseless, hushed lull.

All I could think was that I didn't know why. Couldn't make sense of it. Couldn't digest it or shoo it away. Couldn't flee.

In a low growl, Charlie said, "We're protect—protecting them!"

Jansen picked up one foot as if from hot tar and moved forward with effort.

"Boys, what's happening?" Miss Kate reached a hand toward Jansen.

"Don't touch me!" Jansen yelled, his eyes opened as mere slits.

My heart flipped as Miss Kate jumped backward. "Give her to me."

"No."

She clamped her lips together so hard they turned white. When her arms extended, I tried to lean into them, but Jansen's grip clenched even tighter.

Though I pressed and twisted and pushed against him, he dropped to his knees and buried his face in my chest but didn't let go. A guttural howl started low in his diaphragm, muffled only by my chest.

"Let her go!" Charlie growled.

It made Jansen tighten his grasp. "No!"

If I moved one muscle, my bones would break. There wasn't enough air.

Miss Kate stomped her foot. "You're hurting her!"

That did it. He released me, and I tumbled to the ground as he covered his ears. Curled into a tight ball.

Miss Kate helped me to my feet and pulled me away from him.

"What's wrong with them?" I asked between panting breaths.

"I don't know, but I think the spirits are angry."

Jansen removed one hand from his ear and gestured wildly toward the path we were on.

"Yes." Miss Kate shivered as she confirmed her suspicion. "Very angry. Put on your coat and come with me." She pulled me in the direction he had pointed.

No. I dug my heels into the ground and tugged away from her. "We can't leave them here."

With a snap, Charlie's back straightened as an unseen force yanked him up. His mouth opened as if to scream, but nothing came out.

Miss Kate stepped toward me and touched my chin, bringing it around so I would look at her instead of them.

"You have to relax. We'll explain all of it, but right now, your fear is hurting them."

"Me—?" I thumped my hand over my heart.

She nodded.

How could I conquer such terror? How, with them in pain and having twice now traveled miles in a fraction of a second and no explanation?

"I can fix her." Jansen struggled with every word.

"Not this time." Miss Kate led me away. "Come on. Walk with me. Take a deep breath. Come on. In through your nose. That's it, out through your mouth. Right. Now, do it again. In." She breathed with me. "And out. No, keep walking and put that coat on. Do you hear? They're getting quieter."

I choked and spun on my heel, but she caught me. "Are they dying?"

"Would I be so calm if my sons were dying?"

Okay, I could do this. Could focus on Miss Kate's voice, on her instructions. I started by slipping my arms into the coat.

"Jansen," Miss Kate said, but her tone cracked, and I knew then she was also afraid. "Where are we going?"

Distantly, for we had trod several paces, his weak voice rang out, "To the back—the old section."

Miss Kate took my hand and led me away toward the rear, looking over her shoulder a few times while I walked forward as if blind. Every step ripped at my gut, and I pressed my hands into my stomach.

When we reached a vast tree with so large a hole in it that an entire colony of bats could have moved in, Miss Kate told me to sit up against its trunk. That was the least frightful thing I'd been through. Somehow, it didn't matter that night devoured us, or that we were in the furthest section of a graveyard sitting against a giant oak that looked like a freaking screaming witch. Didn't matter that we huddled in an inch of fresh snow or that more snow fell as we sat. I reclined against the trunk. What happened next had to have been from pure exhaustion. Sleep swept in on a dark wind, onerous and dreamless.

When I came around, my head rested on the warm pillow of Jansen's thigh. His one hand pressed into my shoulder while his fingers toyed with my curls. I didn't let on that I was awake, not even to myself, afraid to re-enter the nightmare. Instead, I imagined myself sleeping, safe in his family room, on his couch. Just laying there, content to listen to the hushed, melodic cadence of their whispers.

Charlie said, "Will she be okay? She's been out a while."

Jansen traced patterns over my forehead. "Her pulse has slowed. I'm pretty sure she's sleeping now."

Miss Kate adjusted my coat and zipped it closer to my chin, her scent of lavender and cotton giving her away. "Why did you bring us here? Of all places?"

Charlie cleared his throat, a sound unique to him, throaty and rough, like a kitten who'd swallowed a lion. "Cronus can't get in here. You saw how the newer spirits turned on us back there, and most of them are used to us. What, with all their screeching and blinding bright lights. Jansen and I come here often enough. They trust us, and they still protected this place. It'd be impossible for him if *we* had difficulty getting past them."

"Jansen, what happened tonight?" she asked.

"It was my fault." His words came out hoarse, as though dragged through a tight throat. "She was on a date with Tim, and he—" His voice broke. Tension rippled through his arms. "He took advantage of her. I lost control and…"

"You rescued her." Miss Kate supplied the words he couldn't. "You've always been there for her. That was never going to change."

Something crackled, and I had the sensation of dancing light behind my closed lids. Did I feel the warmth of a fire?

"I don't think that's all, though," Jansen said. "I suspect Cronus tried to get to her through Tim. Pretty sure he projected to him, and apparently Ellie heard him."

"Heard him?" Miss Kate barked.

"Shh, yes."

I shuddered in his arms, the icy chill of their conversation lacing around my spine like frost.

"Ellie, are you awake?"

Was I? I hazarded a glance.

Jansen pressed harder into my shoulder, his chin tucked low.

"I'm fine." Yikes, my voice came out weak. "Just a little confused, I think."

Charlie cleared his throat and poked a stick at the fire.

"You must have a thousand questions." Jansen breathed out, releasing a breath for every question I might have. "I'll answer them, but I have to tell you something first. I never wanted you to know. Certainly not like this." Jansen spiraled one last curl before retreating, but his touch remained as a longed-for phantom.

Bile burned my throat, and I swallowed it down, hard. "You mean the voices?"

He blinked several times, a look that said, "yes." When it seemed he couldn't stand it, he looked away, then stood with such speed my head fell from his lap. But he didn't notice. He ran his fingers through his hair, and a husky growl escaped him as he paced.

"I don't know how to do this!" he roared. "How do I tell her? I can't."

This was something I'd thought about, so I pushed myself up to sit against the giant oak, my shaky knees pulled tightly into my chest. "I think I know."

Charlie slid in front of me, where he folded his legs, so his shins nearly touched mine. "Tell me."

My breath came in shallow pants, and my chin felt heavy, like I just couldn't raise it to meet his gaze. "I made a list."

"You made a what? A list?"

"I've been thinking lately. About things that don't make

sense. I know he can disappear and appear again." Did I dare say more? On a whisper, maybe. "I know you can, too."

"You know all that, do you?"

He took this well. If he could kneel there, this attentive to me, I could be brave. "I know he can speak in my head, and there was that voice that told Tim—well, told Tim to do—"

"Vile things, yes."

Jansen muttered to himself as he paced. Behind him, a moon-struck granite angel spread her wings, monitoring.

Nerves quivered through my fingers as I fiddled with my zipper. "And I know you threw fire."

Charlie took my face between his palms, getting me to look at him. "You're very observant."

"I figured it out."

"We're not the same as Cronus."

"No?"

"No."

"Is there a word for—for what you are?"

Despite the tension, he smiled, and there was an undeniable twinkle in his eye. "Did your list include possibilities?"

"Sort of."

"Care to share?"

I gulped back the lump in my throat. "Top of the list lately has been a list of psychiatric facilities to check myself into."

"Nix those, El girl. You're not going anywhere. Next?"

"Warlock?"

"Uh-uh"

"Vampire?"

Jansen threw a stick so hard I heard it whir. "Get on with it!" His outburst rumbled off the granite and sandstone markers. Birds fled from their perches in the skeletal trees.

Waving him off, Charlie said, "Not a vampire. Too dark. Terrible sense of humor. Next?"

"I thought perhaps werewolf?"

"Demon." The word slid off Charlie's tongue. Both

innocent and deadly.

"You?"

He nodded, the curls on his forehead bobbling along with him in the brisk breeze.

My bottom lip ached from biting it, so I tugged on my ear, instead. "And…and…Jansen?"

Again, he nodded.

I hitched a thumb toward Miss Kate. "Her too?"

His mouth pulled at the corners, thoroughly enjoying himself, and his head twitched, *no.* "Ready for all of it?"

I inhaled enough to overflow my lungs and on an exhale, breathed, "Yes."

"There isn't time!" Jansen bellowed from across the fire, an owl hooting in response.

"There's plenty of time. Cronus can't get her here. She needs to know."

Almost as if the flame had swallowed him, Jansen disappeared. I craned my neck to see better, and then he was inches from my nose. The shock knocked my head into the tree.

"Sorry." He winced. "I wasn't thinking, but you know now. Still… I scared you."

"I'll get used to it."

He swept his hand over my face, and then I didn't care. Just forgot that quickly about how he disappeared and reappeared. About how he and Charlie were demons. About Cronus cackling in my mind. However, this time, I saw the magic for the deception it was.

"What did you just do?"

Jansen sat beside me to form a triangle between Charlie, him, and me. "It's called riddling, a word that means "pass through." We can disappear from one place and reappear anywhere we want, passing through space."

"No, not that. I mean, when you brushed my face. When you do that, it changes my mood."

It sounded so crazy. I put my face in my hands and scrubbed at my eyes, but Jansen touched a finger beneath my chin. *Wow!* A spark erupted in my belly, like the embers from the crackling flames.

He lifted my gaze to his. "You're not crazy."

"Nah, El girl," Charlie said. "Not crazy. Your friends are just demons."

To my surprise, Jansen threw a dull ball of fire at Charlie, but Charlie unexpectedly laughed. "That was a weak one." His words aimed more at me than Jansen.

"A warning shot." Jansen studied his palms. "My hands throw energy that looks like a fireball. That one had low energy. It didn't cost me much, and it didn't hurt him."

"What do you mean, didn't cost you much?"

"We don't have unlimited ability there." Charlie formed a tiny fireball and positioned it at a twig's tip. When it flared, he pitched it into the fire. "We've never tested it, but the more we throw, the more we deplete our energy. Makes us tired."

Jansen held up his right hand, which glowed a pale shade of blue, barely perceptible. "My hands heal both the body and the mind. I do that often with you. More than I should."

Charlie thumped Jansen's shoulder. "Healing is one of his special talents. Not all demons can do it. We think there's a sort of hierarchy, and each has unique gifts, the way humans do. This guy here can heal."

"My forehead?" I gasped, and my hand fluttered to the old wound. "And my arm at the pool party when I burned it? And the splinter when I was a little girl?"

A gush of memories sped by, one on top of another.

"Yes, and thousands of other times besides."

"Just now, you made me relax?"

He packed a snowball. "Yes." Then, a small flame glowed in his hand, and the snowball vanished, dripping between his fingers.

With a tap on Jansen's knee, Charlie signaled him to take it easy. "Let her breathe."

These three faces that I'd loved my entire life stared back at me. Jansen and Charlie were demons. Yet, I didn't have the feeling I dreamt. Instead of my world crumbling as it should, every memory I had made sense. I felt alive.

"So, you have powers?" I grimaced at how crazy I

sounded, saying the words aloud.

An owl hooted, and the wind blew. It felt as though nature herself laughed at the absurdity of it. The three of them joined in, Charlie with hilarity, but it was kind, too. Like they huffed out relief.

Jansen said, "We like to call them 'talents,' but yeah, I guess we do."

"At my party, when I burned my arm—"

"When *I* burned your arm. I riddled without thinking and scared you."

"You pulled the cookies out with bare hands."

That made him scratch his head, a rare show of nerves. "Yes. I didn't know you saw that. Sometimes, I forget."

Charlie shifted his feet beneath himself. "Do you remember Halloween night?"

Every muscle tensed. "That didn't happen. That was a nightmare."

"It wasn't a nightmare. Jansen used that magic hand of his to help everyone forget what happened. We can't risk anyone knowing our secret. You get that, right?"

"But you're telling me?"

"Well, it's become a need-to-know sort of situation. You've heard us talk about Cronus? He's one of our father's henchmen, and he's been toying with you. Nothing you saw was real, but I knew to you it was. That's an evil trick demons play, forming vivid hallucinations."

The shiver of that reminder wove shadows around my spine.

"I stayed with you all that night. Called for Jansen to come, and I'm pretty sure you saw him, didn't you?"

I massaged my weary forehead. "I thought it was a dream."

"Did you, though?"

"No. I knew, but..." I threw my head back dramatically on the rough tree bark, and Jansen winced as if he felt it more than me. "No, I didn't know. I didn't."

Miss Kate played with my hair, pulling it away from my face. The strokes calmed, and I rubbed the back of my throbbing head.

Jansen placed his cool fingers where it throbbed. "I wish I'd been there. Could have taken it from you, the fear."

So many questions surfaced. All the times I'd believed I was crazy. I wasn't entirely sure I wasn't. "Do you know why I've been hearing voices…you know…in my mind?"

"More demonic traits, I'm afraid," Jansen said. "Demons can cast thoughts on their victims. Can project a sort of mental image for a man or a woman to kill. The victim perceives it, but it's just a musing, if you will. Humans can't distinguish between the demon and their own inner voice. It didn't occur to me until you told me earlier about the voices. You could hear mine, but I didn't know about the others."

The last words were more of a growl, casting a disgruntled look Charlie's way. "I think Cronus projected to Tim, who may have been an innocent victim in all this."

The memory of the ill-fated date made me shudder. The way it had ended. I remembered that horrifying voice in my head telling Tim what to do. "Innocent? You just said it's only a thought. I can *think* about slamming a door in someone's face, but I don't have to actually do it."

"No, he can't have helped it. Unless he's an unusually strong person, and I mean unnaturally so, he must obey. He *could* choose to ignore it, but first, he'd have to understand it as something to be ignored. It enters the mind as if one's thought. Then, even if he recognizes it, it creates an inner battle between his known truth and what he hears. It's far less torturous to follow than to fight."

I couldn't fathom thoughts that weren't my own. It was a convenient excuse to give Tim, but it wasn't like Jansen to be quite so forgiving. If Cronus had projected to Tim, and if Tim couldn't ignore the directives, the oddities of the evening did line up.

Jansen cocked his head, and a small smile spread as he waited for me to process everything.

"But not me?" Was it possible he was proud of me?

"No, not you. You seem immune to projections. You're kind of a wonder."

"Not kind of," Kate said.

"I tested her tonight," he told his mom. "I projected that she shouldn't turn around. It was for her safety." He tapped the tip of my nose. "I didn't want her to catch me riddling, but had no other option. Cronus was close, and I had to get rid of Tim."

"Get rid of him?" I bellowed.

"Sorry, poor choice of words. Send him away. How's that? I projected that he should leave. Anyway, I didn't want you to see all the hocus pocus, so I instructed you *not* to turn around."

"But I did."

"Oh yes, you did."

Miss Kate's breath stuck in her throat. "That's—"

"Impossible?" He finished for her. "Yes, I know."

"But is it?" Charlie dropped a log into the fire. Its bark snapped and popped as the flame sparked. "We already knew she could hear you."

Jansen sniffed. "Yeah, well, she also said something about hearing your voice."

"I suspected that."

"What?" Just like that, Jansen's mood shifted. "When? Why didn't you tell me?"

Charlie threw a snowball. "I don't know! I wasn't sure, maybe? It was that time the two of you had it out in the choir room. I needed to get Ellie to class without complications, but crotchety ol' Miss Simms wasn't having it. So, I used a little projection. When Ellie didn't say anything, I didn't either."

Miss Kate said, "Knock it off, you two. You're getting far from the point, which is that she shouldn't be able to resist."

After picking up a stone, Charlie tossed it so that it ricocheted off a nearby headstone. "Yes, we know. That's Jansen's point."

"No, I mean, she really shouldn't."

CHAPTER SEVENTEEN

The wind picked up. It howled in spirals, whipped the falling snow across our faces, and stole our breath. White flakes tinkled through the naked tree branches and clinked on the frozen blades of grass as some of it changed over to ice. Tiny crystals frosted Charlie's curls and dotted Jansen's lashes.

Kate brought herself nearer to the fire, where she warmed her hands, tightening our small circle. "Ellie, are you warm enough?"

With the roaring blaze Charlie stoked, yes. It couldn't warm the bite of the brothers' unveiled secret, however.

Kate tugged at my coat sleeve to get me to move closer to the flame and to her. "Humans have always been able to communicate with demons, but not easily. Sometimes they try to talk to deceased loved ones or other specters and accidentally end up with a demon instead. Or they try to contact demons on purpose using special stones and candles. It rarely works, but if it does, they might hear a demon's voice."

"Then why are you all so concerned that I can?"

"Because you aren't just hearing their voices," Jansen said. "You hear projections. Not only projections aimed at you, either." He glanced between his mom and Charlie. "Like I told you earlier, she caught what I projected to Tim tonight. I knew she could discern what I projected to her, but she's actually aware of messages not meant for her, too."

Jansen tickled the outline of my hand, not quite taking it. "People can't detect projections. Charlie and I have three kinds of voices. Everyone hears us when we're in our human form because we're...well...human. Full demons don't have human forms. When Charlie and I riddle, we take on our spirit forms, giving us a spirit voice."

With a wink that felt like a mother's hug, Kate used her shoulder to nudge my mine. "That's the voice some people can perceive if they concentrate."

Jansen traced designs over the freckles of my hand with a whisper-touch. Didn't seem like he knew he did it. "You shouldn't be able to pick that up, but we're not shocked you can. We can also project thoughts. Though we don't usually use it. Both of us feel it's one of our more demonic talents. Do you remember the first time you heard me in your head?"

"Yes." How could I forget? "It was at my pool. You told me to stay, and then to come back into your arms. You did say that!"

"Yes, but you shouldn't have picked up my voice as if I spoke to you." I thought he blushed. "I only meant to put the notion in your mind."

"How can I hear you, then?"

"We don't know. Maybe because our connection is so strong. Demons are immune to the projections of others of our kind. Even I can't pick them up."

He paused, letting the alternating sighs and gusts of the storm settle his words.

"Why do I hear Cronus?" They could explain all night, and I still wouldn't understand. "Or Charlie, for that matter? I've never lit candles or summoned demons."

"No." Kate scrunched her nose as a biting wind blew icy pellets in our faces. "Cronus came looking for you."

"Me? But why?"

"Again, we just don't know," Jansen said. "There's something unique about you that we don't understand. It's dangerous for a demon to have a relationship with a human because it attracts other demons. We've always known that, but it's never been a problem before. I allowed us to get too close, and I'm so sorry. I should have known better. To protect you, I had to somehow distance myself from you, while also being nearby in case you needed me. The only option that made sense was to make you angry. That way, you'd hate me instead of... well, instead of whatever you started feeling for me." His eyes shifted as he sputtered out the words. "It worked, too. Although, every second was torture."

"For me, too," Charlie and Kate said in unison.

Jansen snorted. "I haven't been much fun to be with, I guess. Oh, Ellie, what's wrong?"

The muscles on my face twisted—a mix of crying and laughing. The magic fog he'd wrapped around my brain lifted, and I remembered the past long months. How the one person I loved most in the world had abandoned me. "You mean, you don't hate me?"

"Hate you? I could never hate you."

"You've been so horrible. You left me!" Some pent-up fury churned in my stomach, whipping up a strength that shook me from the stupor he'd put me in. That other me, the girl who'd flown at him in the choir room, re-emerged, and sat up to stare blankly at him. "You cut me out of your life! You liked me well enough for a while, but you needed a more mature toy."

"What? You mean Clara? More mature?" Jansen rarely sputtered, and in that moment, I was glad for it.

"You snatched her up and did away with me. As if I meant nothing to you! You replaced me."

"El, calm down." His voice was too controlled as he started to brush my face, and I knocked his hand away.

"No!" The roaring wind mixed with my blood and pounded in my ears. "Not this time. You told me I was like a leech. You made me feel so alone!"

"I know. It was unforgivable. It hurt me more than you can know. Please understand. Those were lies. All lies."

Charlie shook his head like a dog, dislodging snow flakes to scatter in the breeze. "He's a demon. He's kind of good at it."

That got Jansen to snarl, but otherwise continued as if Charlie hadn't said anything. "I needed you to hate me so Cronus wouldn't suspect." He knelt so we were eye level with each other, and he let his hands swing between his knees. "You keep saying I left you. It hurts to know you thought that."

While adding sticks to the fire, Charlie hummed a sound of agreement. "She did that with me, too, once. It's a swift kick to the gut, El."

Jansen pulled at his bottom lip. "There's more to tell."

"This better be good," I said through clenched teeth.

As if the sky held the answer, he glanced heavenward and blinked rapidly as snowflakes evaded his lashes. At last, he locked me into his gaze. "I think you'll understand everything if you let me explain. You don't know the pain this has caused me. You have no idea what it was like, knowing the agony you were in, knowing it was because of me."

I raised a finger to throw out further accusations, but he took its tip, brought it to his lips, and kissed it. I'm pretty sure my heart skipped two beats. It definitely swelled and tightened my chest. His lips lingered, and the warmth melted the ice around it. He slid his thumb under my clenched fingers, opening them to plant a kiss in my palm.

Holy what-was-that. He'd never done that before.

Movement coaxed my attention away. Charlie and his mom had left us to walk down the winding cemetery path, its edges blurred by the fresh falling snow. They meandered as they read each headstone. The moon light reflected off each crystal, hiding the graves beneath the glimmer of shattered glass.

"Cronus has some kind of plan for you." As Jansen spoke, branches cracked overhead from their heavy, ice laden burden. "He expects to see strong feelings between us, and that's very strange. Demons don't form bonds with humans because they don't know any kind of love. The fact that you have formed such a bond with us is unusual. We are such close friends." He lingered over the word. "Do you understand?"

I nodded, and he smirked. Of course, I didn't understand and was merely overwhelmed.

"I'm afraid I've put you in danger, and I'm not sure how to undo it. Obviously, leaving you didn't work, but we can't be more than we are right now."

Did he know how much I loved him? Or how that love had grown? Had he known all this time?

He seemed to plead with me as he bent to place his forehead on mine. "We were getting too close. I don't presume you felt anything for me, but... We will never be anything but what we've always been."

The pain that had become a living reality rushed in. Nothing had changed, then. I would go home no different from when I'd come.

"Are you going to be mean again?" Unwelcome tears loomed, and I choked back the start of a sob.

"No, nothing will change. We can be friends, like always. It's me I have to control. Nothing at all to do with you."

"Friends." Sure. Same as before. Then—the brushes over my skin, the kiss he'd left in my palm, all of it the gesture of a loving *friend*. "Clara won't like that."

He sat back and adjusted himself, so he hugged his knees. His attention fell entirely to his tapping thumbs. "Clara. She has become a complication."

My heart, so fluttery with anticipation before, now curled up like a weighted porcupine and dove toward my toes. "She's pregnant, isn't she?"

He winced. "No."

That's it. Just "no." He let the word hover awhile, carried off on a wind gust. I tried to read the tone of that "no." He said it so softly, without an ounce of hostility. It was the softness, the concern that made me think, perhaps—

"I'll take care of Clara." He was awfully intent on his thumbs.

That was it then. Whatever strange relationship he had with Clara, it was real.

Friend.

My friend.

Every time I'd said he was only that hung like a weight—a thousand weights—tugging on my heart.

His hand twitched toward my face, but he stopped himself. "I wish I knew what you were thinking."

"Nothing, really. Only that we're friends."

"That makes you sad?" He gazed into my eyes, taking me in and letting me fall into the depths of his. There lay that beautiful cerulean spark. Hazier this time. Brilliant shards of sapphire hid behind a midnight fog.

A soft sound purred at the base of my throat, and I asked, "Why do your eyes change color?"

His nose crinkled. "I don't know what you mean."

"Never mind. You'll think I'm crazy."

He smirked and threw his head back, a little of our old easiness returning. "Yes, because this whole evening has been about how very normal I am. You can tell me anything. Forever and always."

Mmm. Then I should tell him I didn't want to be his friend anymore. "Your eyes. They swirl with color. They're usually black, but sometimes it's like they're mirrors reflecting something invisible."

"Reflecting what? Can you describe it?"

Yes, easily, with my own eyes closed. Only, I didn't close them. Instead, something lured me closer; so close a shadow couldn't fit between the tips of our noses.

When I described them, his eyes grew so wide that all the stars in the sky could have fit inside of them, and the ocean-lit sparks danced.

His voice, soft and reverent, he called for Charlie to come. He called too quietly for a human to hear, but Charlie wasn't exactly human.

Charlie raced to his brother's side. "What is it?"

"Stand next to Ellie and look into my eyes."

I fell so deeply into Jansen's, myself, that my insides tickled. Almost as if a blanket wrapped itself around my bones.

"I don't see anything," Charlie said.

"Ellie, tell him what you see. Describe it."

Only I couldn't breathe. It had been such a long time since we'd been close like this. The woody fragrance of the fire mingled with his own earthy scent, and I don't think he knew its effect on me. He swallowed hard, narrowing my focus to his lips. His face drew closer, his breath sweet on my tongue. Wasn't this stealing? A moment that should have belonged to Clara? Still, it was my moment, and I savored it.

"Describe it." His lips hovered inches from mine. They rested softly. Parted expectantly.

Charlie's hands grasped each of our shoulders to separate us. "Sorry, Dude. If you want me to see what she sees, you need space between you."

Jansen cleared his throat, pulled away, and broke the magnetic force between us. But his eyes never left mine. "Describe it."

In the short time we'd talked, they'd morphed into something altogether different. "I see lights. There's a sort of bulb of many lights and flowing tentacles of colors."

"What colors do you see?" Charlie asked.

"When he almost—" I stopped short. He hadn't almost kissed me, had he? "I mean, when he was so close"—so close I tasted his breath—"the colors were only blue."

"And now?" His grip on my shoulder tightened, and Jansen's breathing grew erratic, like he couldn't believe what I said. Like I'd given him a gift.

"Now?"

"Yes, describe what you see right now." Even Charlie's pitch had grown feverish.

"I still see blue."

"Yes, and?"

"Swirling color in a gray haze."

Charlie sucked in an audible breath. "Oh, wow. She sees your colors. She can read you."

Jansen's breath staggered as he fought to maintain it.

"Look at her colors." Charlie's voice fell as a reverent whisper. "I've never seen them more pure. Not a trace of red."

Jansen gave a warm smile and his eyes lit with something like suppressed joy.

"What is it?" I asked.

Apparently, this question was the one thing he wasn't willing to share.

The smile he fought to control eventually lost, and his brow furrowed. He landed firm hands on my shoulders and pressed me back to the present. "I'll tell you part of it. You know I wear sunglasses most of the time, right?"

"You're sensitive to light."

"Yes, but I'm not. Or at least not in that way, not to light. My eyes are sensitive to energy. Every creature has an energy force around them."

"An aura?"

"Yes, so you've heard of that. Some humans are sensitive to them as well, but you may have noticed my eyes, and Charlie's, too, aren't quite human. We see energies without trying. Basically, we read auras the same way you read body language. I know just by looking if someone is happy, sad, jealous—you name it."

"Is it a reflection of my aura in your eyes?" I asked.

"Not exactly."

"Is it yours?"

He flushed. "Sort of."

"Well, why couldn't you just tell me that?"

"Because there's more to it." He scratched his cheek, a rough, sandpapery sound, and beckoned to his mom to come over. "It's time to get you home."

"You're not going to tell me?"

He winked, shuttering the storm of color for that instant. "Another time. Telling you that... Well, I've risked too much already."

With hands that I knew, now, really were unnaturally warm, Charlie helped me to my feet. "Wait a minute there, little brother. I want to talk to El about something first. Kate and I worked out a bit of a plan over there. Ellie, I propose one or the other of us sleep in your room at night so you feel safe."

I had always loved his devilish grin, and now I had a good reason to consider it "devilish."

"Oh, that's hardly necessary!" Given my immodest sleeping habits, that was a hard no.

He flashed his teeth again, the same color as the snow. "You won't even know we're there. Wear decent pajamas and don't eat beans before bed."

My face burned in earnest, and he received a swift punch in the arm from Jansen.

"Okay, okay. Ow! Then—will you let me finish, please?" Miss Kate had joined in abusing Charlie as well. "Then... I will accompany you to classes in the morning, and Jansen will get you in the afternoons, as always."

Wait. Back it up. What? "As always?"

Jansen wore that guilty look. That I've-been-caught look. "We've made sure you're never alone since the day Cronus started hanging around. The dog...your date... I've been with you, making sure you're safe. When I wasn't there, Charlie was. If Cronus is anywhere near, we should know about it."

"You can't possibly—" I protested, but Charlie interrupted.

"Really, Ellie, he's right. We're only adding class time. Someone's watched you every night for a long time."

A squeaky gasp of shock and embarrassment chirped out of me.

Jansen punched Charlie in the shoulder, hard. "You weren't supposed to tell her that! She doesn't need to know that."

"What's the big deal? El Girl, you haven't exactly been alone much. Jansen's been with you everywhere you go. You just get to know about it now."

"Cronus." The reason dawned on me. "You expected him."

Charlie ducked when a tree dropped a snowball on his shoulder, then brushed away the flakes. "Anytime sparks fly between the two of you, there's Cronus. He does enjoy good fireworks."

With a guilty expression, Jansen gave a head to the shoulder kinda shrug.

Miss Kate threw an arm around my shoulder. "It'll be okay. My boys have been taking care of me for a long time."

My heart danced when Jansen took my hand and caressed it absentmindedly. But then dropped it again as we began to walk the path out of the cemetery. Friend. I wanted to hold on to his hand forever, but he was just a friend.

"Her colors are good," Charlie said. "Mostly good. What's going on with you?"

Miss Kate linked her arm through his. "Leave her alone. She's had a lot to take in tonight."

"But her colors—"

"Are hers to manage. Private."

He grimaced by way of apology. "Anyway, our exit should be more pleasant than our entrance."

The wind blew another wintry gust, spraying my face with snow. I pulled my coat tight around me. "What was all that about when we got here?"

Jansen kicked at the collected snow along the path. "Cemeteries are inhabited by many ghosts. Some are very old, and know us. They leave us alone. It's the new ones that give us trouble. The spirits know we're demons, and assume we're hurting you. That's why we brought you here. There's no way Cronus could get past them. They're great guards, honestly."

"Why didn't you just riddle straight into the old section?"

Charlie adjusted his sleeves lower over his wrists. "Because then the old ones would attack us before realizing it was us, which is way worse than what the new ones do. We've worked our way in here, but they like to see us coming. Once we've made ourselves known, they don't mind if we riddle around like Jansen did when you guessed what our secret was. If we had surprised them by riddling in before they saw us coming, who boy!"

"You just need to be calm," Jansen said. "When we entered, you were terrified. Your aura needs to project calm, or the spirits will scream again. It's not something you can hear. Be thankful for that."

We arrived at the entrance too soon for all the questions I

still had. They'd have to wait, as he took my hand and turned me, pressing my back firmly into his chest. It didn't feel particularly friend-like, that feeling of charged excitement.

"I'm going to take you home now." His lips came close to my ear.

"Okay." That was a dumb thing to say, but I couldn't think around his scent.

Jansen's chest shook against my back. "I've done this with you already, but you weren't prepared for it then. I'll pull you in tight." Wasn't I already? "Close your eyes." His lips were still at my ear, and his breath awakened shivers along my spine. "There will be a pulling sensation, and when your eyes open again, we'll be standing in front of your house. Are you ready?"

"Yes," I whispered, because I wasn't.

The muscles in his arms tensed as he molded me to his body. "You fit up against me like this. Like a puzzle piece." His nose tickled my hair as he inhaled, then sighed. A sensation tugged in my stomach, like something tried to turn me inside out. It didn't hurt, but it was a strange sensation.

"Open your eyes." He relaxed his grip.

We stood in front of my house, now covered in about an inch of snow. The flakes glistened under the moon and twinkled in the lamplight.

"It's beautiful."

"Mmm," he said, with his nose in my hair.

Caught up in ecstasy, enjoying the closeness again, I turned to face him. Wasn't even really sure what I wanted him to do. Or what I thought I would do. I just needed to look into his eyes. As I did, he closed them with a heavy sigh and a step backward.

"This is going to be so much harder than I thought. Let's get you inside. Your mom's probably wondering where you are."

"My mom." Wow. I'd forgotten I had parents. "I promised I'd call her if it started snowing."

A knowing smile slid up his face. "I know. I was there."

We opened the door, and my mom flew off the couch to

embrace me, hard. Nearly knocked me over. "Where have you been? I've been so worried!"

"I'm sorry, Mom."

"You should have called!"

"It was my fault," Jansen said. "I was at the movie with Clara and noticed Tim didn't seem to be feeling well, so I offered to bring Ellie home."

My mom shook her head and gave a hand motion that said she didn't care about the details. "You had my phone. Why didn't you call?"

Again, he said, "She left the phone in Tim's car."

My mom sighed and released me from her grip. "That doesn't explain why you're so late." She folded her arms. "Where were you?"

I waited for his next lie, and he delivered. "I got a flat tire on the way home. The weather was so bad we had to focus on what we were doing. We lost track of time, and I'm really very sorry."

My mom was still unsatisfied.

He glanced at me and bit his lip. *"You're just glad she's home."*

My mom stared at me with unfocused eyes, then embraced me again. "I was worried. But you're home now, and that's all that matters. I'm going to bed so I can call your father."

"Oh, don't wake him," I said.

"He'll want to know, trust me. I told him earlier I didn't know where you were. He won't sleep until I tell him you're okay."

When I was sure she was out of earshot, I asked, "Projection?"

"Yes." His voice had a guilty quality to it, unsteady and tight. "She wasn't buying the story. I didn't want you to be in trouble because of me."

"Hey, don't worry about it. I think I'm going to like your superpowers."

He chuckled and tousled my hair. "Talents, Ellie. Talents."

CHAPTER EIGHTEEN

The rest of the weekend passed as though a cloud had descended on me.

On Saturday morning, the scraping of a shovel awakened me as one of my neighbors cleared his driveway of the four inches of snow that had fallen overnight. At first, I thought it had all been a dream, but remembered it wasn't when Jansen sat at the foot of my bed reading a travel magazine. Before I registered what happened, his fingers found my face.

Though I didn't see him, he never left my side. He was there to swipe away my worries when a movie reminded me of Cronus, and at dinner when my dad yelled, "What the Devil!" at Tyler when he dared answer the phone during the meal. That was one of his more obnoxious rules.

By Monday, the fog had lifted, and I needed less of Jansen's healing each time a memory slipped through his filter. I was genuinely okay knowing my lifelong best friend was a demon.

I opened the front door with my pack thrown over my back. One foot over the other, Jansen stood against his car, arms crossed, his head bobbing. I marveled at him. What was different? Could it be that I now saw the demon? Or was it his bright smile I hadn't seen in so long? The dark and brooding days seemed so far away, a distant memory—

Without warning, Otis barked and crashed into the fence. It rattled at its base as he pawed to dig beneath. My hands flew to my heart, and just as quickly, he appeared by my side.

"You okay?"

"Yes. Will I ever remember he's there?"

He took my hand and walked toward the fence, but I pulled back.

"What? No! I don't want to greet that monster."

He loomed over me. "For the past several months, my hidden spirit-self had to watch that mutt torment you. I can solve that. Trust me?"

My sigh would have to serve as consent because I still didn't move.

So, Jansen tugged on my hand. "Trust me."

With our hands clasped, not entwined, we approached the tall fence. Large paws stomped, and his muzzle snorted. Claws pawed at the bottom of the gate, rattling it loose at its base. It all made me recoil.

"He's happy to see you, but that's not what's coming across." He placed my palm over a hole between two slats. A wet nose sniffed, and then he added a lick, which tickled. Jansen moved my fingers and hovered his hand, glowing the colors of a cloud-touched sky, over the hole. "There. Now, if he knows it's you, he'll associate you with calm, not excitement. He won't attack the fence anymore."

"Thank you," I said.

"I wish I had known about this sooner. You know, before I tried to distance myself. It's killed me more every day watching you endure that."

I'd missed this side of him so intensely that I stared at him in disbelief. In wonder of all that he was. I even watched him as I slid into the car and buckled my seat belt. Now I knew it wasn't a mere genetic fluke that he exuded grace. Goodness, he was easy to look at, right down to the way his arm muscle rounded as he closed my door. His hair lifted in the breeze and his scent filled the car.

So focused on the joy of being near him again, it took a while to notice that Andrew's car wasn't parked out front. My heart leapt, and I swallowed hard. I'd forgotten to mention that I wouldn't need him anymore.

"Where's Andrew?" I asked as Jansen's door shut.

"I told him to go ahead. That I would take you to school today." He clicked the seatbelt. "And every day."

"I forgot to tell him."

"Like I said, I took care of it."

Before I could ask how the conversation came off, he began talking fast. "Cronus is still out there, looking for a way in. Now, we doubt he'll attack you at school because it's such a public place, but there's no guarantee."

"I'm not worried about Cronus."

He looked as though I'd killed his favorite cat. "You should be. Have you forgotten Friday night already?"

A noise I couldn't control escaped my lips. Something between a snort and an outcry. "Very nearly. You've had me in such a stupor, I'm surprised I know my own name."

"I can't apologize for that. *You* angry at me I can handle, but I can't…" he gripped the steering wheel until his knuckles turned white, "…I couldn't deal with it if…"

After a pause, I said, "If what?"

"If you were…you know…scared of me."

"I'm not scared of you. How could I ever be?"

"No, because I removed the anxiety. I can do that. Though, I see now by keeping you in a… What did you call it? A stupor? I've taken away your fear of Cronus, too."

"I have two demons guarding me. There's only one of him."

"You shouldn't take this so lightly. Thanks for the vote of confidence, but I don't think you understand the gravity of the situation. While I want you to be cautious, we do have a plan, and it's a good one. Charlie will be with you in the mornings—"

"I get this was Charlie's idea, but doesn't he have classes?"

He pulled the car up to a stop sign, hitting the brake a touch too hard. "Be serious, please."

"His grades shouldn't slip because of me."

"He'd do anything for you, El, you know that." The horn blared from the car behind us, and Jansen moved forward again. "You're a little more important than classes. Besides"—he tweaked my nose—"his classes are in Paris. It's a slightly different time zone."

"Paris? But how?"

"It's all in the transportation."

"He doesn't even speak French."

"Les démons parlent toutes les langues." He turned the volume on the radio down. "Demons speak all languages. We also have photographic memories, not to mention our talent for projecting to teachers. So school isn't a huge priority."

"But—wait, how—" At last, I finished sputtering. "You never have to study?"

"You're adorable when you do that."

"Oh, the fun I can have with you."

I gripped Jansen's hand when the voice entered my mind and slowly glanced his way. It had not been him.

"What?" He scanned the inside of the car.

"A voice…in my head."

His face turned ghostly white. "Ellie, that wasn't me."

Without warning, where once there had been nothing, Charlie leaned on the seat that separated us. "Man, you two are jumpy."

Jansen swung at him, but Charlie, whose reflexes were every bit as good as Jansen's, if not better, dodged him so fast—had he riddled out and back again as quickly as I'd blinked?

So I took a swing. Hard.

Charlie furrowed his brow and pressed his lips together. "Was that supposed to hurt?"

I could only stare incredulously.

One corner of his mouth twitched. "That was supposed to hurt, wasn't it?" He grabbed his arm. "Oh… Ow."

I glared and gritted my teeth. "Wrong arm."

"Oops." He snatched at the other arm where I'd landed the punch for real and rubbed it, making faces as if he were in pain.

"That was a hard hit!"

"Very hard."

I faced forward again and crossed my arms over my chest. "Well, it was."

"Tremendously."

Jansen shifted gears, forcing me back into my seat, and passed two cars. It pleased me more than a little when Charlie was also thrown off balance.

As the engine revved once more, Jansen asked, "How long have you been sitting there? I thought the plan was to meet her in first period."

"What, and miss the chance to scare the livin' daylights out'a the two of you?" He leaned back in his seat, his fingers interlaced behind his head. Elbows wide. Might have looked comfortable if not for the knees pulled into his chest.

"So how 'bout it, El? You'll be my girl in the morning. His in the afternoon?"

An uncontrollable burn crept up my neck and spread across my face. Jansen studied the space around me and snarled as Charlie roared with laughter.

Charlie composed himself and leaned forward again, so his head rested on the shoulder of my seat. "Seriously though, I'll be with you in the mornings, invisible. I'm glad you hear projections. You do beat all."

"Me?"

"Yeah! You heard a demon in your head and never let on."

"I thought I lost my mind!"

Jansen stretched his arm across the space between us toward my face, but I grabbed his hand.

"No." Was that a firm voice? I hoped so.

Charlie asked, "You really believed that, didn't you?"

"Well, yeah. It was either that or you guys were superheroes or something."

"Nah. Just demons. We're only now starting to figure out what powers of ours have rubbed off on you."

"I don't have any powers." I felt like a preschooler talking about superpowers as we chatted up a plan to foil our supernatural villain.

Jansen adjusted the rear-view mirror. "Well, we know you can hear our projections. A rare gift, El. That's not surprising, though, as you're spiritually connected to me, I'm afraid." A shade of pink colored his cheeks, something I rarely saw.

"Would you like me to leave?" Charlie patted us each on the shoulder in mock seriousness.

"If you don't mind," Jansen said.

Without another word, he was gone, and though I knew he had riddled out, I couldn't help myself from peering over the seat.

Jansen chortled. "What are you doing?"

"Just checking. It's a little unnerving."

"To be honest, I'm surprised you've never noticed it before."

He pulled into a parking spot and came to an abrupt stop. "Ready?"

I pivoted to face him, and started to say, "Yep," but he disappeared before the word was out. So, I whipped my head to the right, and there he stood, a wicked grin gracing his lips, as he opened the door for me.

When we walked into school together again, heads turned. I'd almost forgotten what it was like to be with him and, therefore, always the center of attention. They gawked at his height, his dark coloring, his undeniable confidence. Honestly, so did I. Like seeing him now, as if for the first time, wanting him the same way all the girls did. They didn't know darkness lurked, trapped inside of him. Or that what they saw on the outside was the lit candle, made all the more brilliant because of the storm clouds within.

He looked at nobody. Crowds separated to allow him to walk at a steady clip. His nearly black hair sprang with each step. As one crowd parted, Clara stood unmoving in the center of the hall, eyebrows at the level of the ceiling, jaw dropped. She took a step back and stumbled in her kitten-heels.

"Oh, crap."

He came to such an abrupt halt that Aaron, who had come up behind us, ran into him.

"Dude!" he shouted. Then, seeing it was Jansen, "My fault entirely."

"Clara," Jansen said, as if Aaron hadn't interrupted at all. *"I haven't exactly..."*

Here I drew the line. I couldn't sit with him like we were just old friends. The image of him flanked by Clara on one side and me on the other was more than I could stomach, especially after the way she couldn't drag her eyes from him. So I started to walk away.

He grabbed my elbow and swung me around. "What is it?"

"It's fine. Just go be with her. So long as you're cordial to me at school, I don't care."

He stuffed his hands into his pockets. "I've made a mess of things, haven't I?" His focus remained on his shoes. When he spoke, it was so low only I could hear him. "Did you think I would stay with her? After everything this weekend?"

"We're just friends." My words were nothing but hollowed-out shadows in the dark. Meaningless and removed. I heard them for the lie they were. The lie they had always been.

I couldn't take them back. Not when Clara stood right there, staring daggers at us.

He winced. "Forgive me for this. It's something I have to do."

She glowered at him with every step he took, crossing the long hallway to face her wrath. Her arms folded across her chest, and her painted fingernails drummed one elbow.

When he got near enough, he placed a hand over her fidgety fingers and drew her nearer, sharing intimate space he avoided with me. As if I were her, I could feel those same warm hands on my skin and breathe in his intoxicating scent. Because I knew what that felt like; to be so close to him, he stole your every thought.

It felt as if he gave her a small part of himself, something I coveted. That was as certain as if etched onto my soul.

Though I remained too far away to hear the specifics, Clara's body language left little to the imagination. As he turned to leave her, Clara looked at me with disgust, anger seeping from her pores.

"Phew!" He wiped his brow.

"What'd she say?"

"Oh, you know. How dare you and a couple of vile names I'd rather not repeat. She did get in a few good points, though."

"Good points, huh? Like what?"

"She called me a monster. I told her, 'Not quite.'"

"Jansen!"

"In the end, she made it pretty easy. She gave me an ultimatum. Her or you. I said I choose you every time. She said I'd been using her and—"

His manner shifted. Became less casual. More alert. He became shadow and marble and sorrow, igniting a shiver down my spine.

What did he see that I couldn't? Cronus?

I followed the line of his gaze to Tim, standing ten feet away. The urge to flee rippled through my bones, and I wiped my cold, clammy hands on my jeans. Wiggled my frozen toes.

"He's embarrassed." Jansen maintained remarkable control over his tone. *"It wasn't his fault. He remembers what he did but has no idea why, and he's terrified of himself. Can you talk to him?"*

When I inhaled a gallon of air, he started to brush my face, but I grabbed his wrist.

"No," I said, his skin warm against my cold flesh. "I need to feel this."

I dropped his arm, and his fingers grasped at mine. For a moment, I thought he might interlace them and make the journey with me, but he only trailed them. And left me to walk up to my attacker alone. To stand directly before him, so close I had to tilt my head up to meet his eyes.

"Ellie, I… I'm so sorry."

"I know."

"I don't know what… I didn't… It was like it wasn't… wasn't me."

"Of course, it wasn't."

"I don't think… I can't think anything would have happened." A tear formed and fell to his cheek.

I touched his arm, which made him whimper as he fought back the tears.

"I… There was something, I don't know what, but something telling me you wanted me to do those things. I know it was wrong, but at the time… I…"

"Shh." To think this hadn't been his fault. And I couldn't tell him why. "It's okay, honest. Believe it or not, I do understand. You would have stopped, but Jansen got there first. I know that."

I felt the nausea he must have felt as he folded his arms, which hid his trembling hands. "How can you believe that?"

"Because I know you. Because you're a good person. Because you'll *never* do that to anyone again."

"No, no." He seemed bent on reassuring himself more than me.

"It's okay."

Jansen had crept behind me in that air and mist way of his. One hand in his pocket, he offered Tim the other, and they shook. "It's okay, man."

"No." Tim glanced at the floor. "It's not, but I appreciate the gesture. How were you even there?"

Jansen ran his hand over his mouth. "Would you believe I followed you?"

"In what? I didn't see a car."

"My car was right behind yours."

Tim shook his head, probably "remembering" the situation differently now. "Yeah, never mind. It's all such a blur."

The bell rang, which jarred me back to the present. We each nodded an awkward goodbye, and Jansen gripped my elbow, guiding me toward class.

"You handled that well," he said.

My knees gave out, and he caught me, his hand still on my elbow.

"Hmm, you almost handled that well. May I?" He offered his healing palm.

I jerked away, a new impulse, now that I knew what he did. "I'll be okay. Sometimes, you have to let me feel what I feel."

"You have no idea what you ask, but I'll try."

When we reached my first-period class, he said, "This is where I leave you. I'll be waiting for you after gym."

It was too much. I rubbed the thoughts from my mind with the fingertips of my free hand.

Between two fingers, I caught sight of Gretta. What was it about her that made me want to turn and flee? The straight back? The folded, demure hands? No, that was typical Gretta. Perhaps the way her feet jiggled beneath her desk, as if all her nervous energy could escape through her toes. No, not nervous energy. Glee—uncontainable glee, and that which couldn't escape from her toes, dripped through the tiny spaces visible between each and every tooth.

"How was your weekend?" She nearly bounced off her seat.

"Okay, I guess," I said, sliding into my chair beside her, thankful Tim hadn't arrived yet.

"Just found out my best friend's a demon, don't 'cha know?"

At the sound of Charlie's folksy input, so loud it was as if he sat in my ear, I jumped. Knocked my book straight to the floor, too. Half the class turned to gawk and I swear their stares felt like a hot, sweaty sock on the back of my neck.

I bent to pick up the dropped book. "Just caught up on some homework."

"Demon Hunting 101. Got some personal attention from the teacher."

It was a good thing I couldn't see more than barely-there mist surrounding Charlie because I'd have kicked him. What stares would I get then?

"And?" she inquired in a pitch I thought only dogs could hear.

"And…" Was there any way around this?

"Oh, come on. The last thing I knew, you had this date with Tim. Now you're walking into school with Jansen. What happened?"

"Jansen and I…"

"I can't wait to hear this."

"Jansen and you *what?*" Clara slammed her books onto my desk before folding her arms over her chest. Just stood back on her heels, the embodiment of fire and spite.

As I registered her outburst, I felt that strange mist I'd come across at the park the day the canine attacked. It moved past me and in front of me, all hoarfrost and disquiet, settling in the space between Clara and me.

Thrown into a panic, I processed several things at once. The sheer terror of the dog-memory caused me to raise my hands to the old wound, but I also had a sudden revelation about the haze. I hadn't connected it before, but the mist in the park and in my bedroom had been Jansen, a demon. The brothers had said Cronus likely wouldn't come to me in a public place, and Charlie's whole purpose here was to protect me. So, it must still be Charlie, then—an angry Charlie.

"Well?" she said impatiently when I didn't respond.

"Clara, I didn't—"

"God, you are so full of yourself. You couldn't stand that he was with me. That he might actually care about me."

"He was never with *you."* I felt Charlie's anger so strong it could have been my own. *"He* pitied *you."*

Soft, sinister laughter rang in my ears and rippled with doom. Was it Charlie echoing his disdain for Clara? Had to be, but the darkness of it blanketed me. Clara shivered, almost as if she heard it, too. Then, I couldn't be sure, but I thought her eyes rolled up into the back of her head before her lids squeeze shut over them. She leaned in close, encroaching on my personal space so that I molded my spine to the rear of my chair, yet couldn't escape her.

"He's using you," she hissed. "When the time is right, he will reclaim what is his."

Like a magician does with a quarter, she snapped her fingers and pulled a cockroach from my ear. *Crap!* She dropped the wiggling scavenger on my desk and I sprang from my seat, leaving my heart behind.

Disgusted, Clara retracted and clicked her tongue as

though nothing out of the ordinary had happened.

"What is it?"

"What is it?"

The voices of both Charlie and Gretta echoed in stereo inside and outside my mind in dizzying unison. Gretta tugged on the sleeve of my cardigan. "Ellie, what's wrong?"

Didn't they see it with its creepy legs and beady eyes? Honestly, I didn't see it now, either. Tim had arrived while I'd been off in my head, and I saw him. Just not any cockroach. I bent over and squinted to look under my chair. Nope. Not a thing there. When I smoothed out my jeans, I half expected it to fly from my legs, but it did not.

"What are you doing? What did you see?" Charlie's voice sounded panicky.

Maybe I was going crazy. It was entirely possible that without Jansen's healing hand, I overreacted, letting my imagination run wild. If I didn't collect myself soon, Charlie would probably appear in person and blow their secret, and for what? A silly girl afraid of a bug?

"It's nothing," I said to Gretta, but also to Charlie. I tried to laugh, but it came out as more of a squeak. "Thought I saw a spider, but it's gone now."

I sat at my desk, feeling stupid and exposed. How had no one else seen Clara whisper in my ear? Plus, what nonsense was she talking about? What child?

"Class!" Mrs. Fushi stepped to the front of the room. Thank heavens. "Today, we're taking a break from our normal routine…"

"Translation: I need some time to myself."

"…to watch a movie about the circle of life…"

"So I can grade the papers I didn't get to last night because Mr. Bender stopped by. Oh, he just sets my heart a' quiverin.'"

"…I hope you enjoy this film as much as I did."

"No one's buying it, Fushi. You made the same speech when I was in eleventh grade. Not the sharpest knife in the drawer, this one."

If I'd had a thought of my own, I'd have wondered how it was possible, without pause, that I forgot about Clara. Yet, my thoughts were Charlie's. I was his captive audience as he talked at length, endlessly, about nothing in particular. As though he had taken over half of my brain. I may control my own muscles, but his words in my head mingled with mine and became my thoughts.

"This is kinda cool. Wish I'd known I had this effect on you sooner. I have your undivided attention. Answer mammals. Mammals, El. SAY MAMMALS!"

I shouted it. Chairs scraped the floor as students flinched and jerked at my unexpected outburst. Heat built in my cheeks, and I covered my eyes as if I could blot out the other students. Someone in the back snickered, and Clara clicked her tongue; I'd recognize her tongue clicking anywhere.

"Correct, but no need to shout." Mrs. Fushi restarted the movie.

"Huh. Apparently, you don't pay attention when I talk in your head. Gotta stop doing that. So, as I was saying…"

I pressed my fingers to my temples. Would he ever shut up? There had to be some way to ditch my babysitter, but all his inane chatter left no room for thoughts of my own.

I needed answers. What had Clara meant? I focused on her, forming a picture of her in my mind, trying to block out Charlie's words. All I could think about was baseball or pigeon hockey—whatever that was. He talked about the Adder stone and the Mortal Soul Cleaver. That, I learned, was a sword that slays demons. On and on he went.

Each class unfolded the same. The teacher stood to give initial instructions, and Charlie was there to comment on Mr. Lawrence's fish tie or the way Miss Clemmons' lazy eye fixed on the students while the other studied the chalkboard. Then he translated what the teachers said into what they had, in fact, meant while I sat poker-faced. He had to feed me answers because I couldn't catch any of the questions.

By the time lunch rolled around, I was mentally exhausted. Jansen met me to walk through the cafeteria line.

"How was your morning?" He indicated to the air beside me that Charlie's invisible presence was no longer needed.

"Terrible," I groaned. "Your brother is impossible. He

wouldn't shut up! Just babbled constant, never-ending drivel about ridiculous nonsense the entire morning. There was no way to shut him up or tune him out!"

Jansen stood the apple up that rolled around on his tray. "Sorry about that. I told him to behave himself."

"Don't be mad at him." Huh. Not the thing I thought I'd say. "And I don't need a babysitter."

"He's not babysitting." He removed his glasses, showing me he was quite serious, and finished his musings in my head. *If Cronus comes again, we need to be there.*

The name made me shiver. With all of Charlie's nonsense, I'd almost forgotten why he was there. Then it dawned on me. Dang him, it was to stifle my thoughts. He didn't want me to think about Cronus or the danger they'd put me in. That's why Charlie prattled on and on.

Jansen scanned me and then brushed my face before I had time to react. He drew his fingertips down my forehead. Over the bridge of my nose, where his middle finger slipped into the groove over my lip. Finally, he rested on my bottom lip for the shortest of moments. The fear may have dimmed, but damn, his eyes. I knew now that I'd more than metaphorically lost myself to his soul. It made the hairs stand on my arm, and my every breath was of him.

When he withdrew, he closed his eyes, which had the effect of shutting down whatever that had been. "Oh, Ellie. I'm so sorry."

I couldn't guess why he was sorry, and didn't care.

With his chin tucked, he walked toward the lunch table, where everyone welcomed him back. All except Andrew. He scowled something fierce, so that if I hadn't known better, I might have thought *him* the demon.

Jansen belted out a joyous greeting, gloating more than a little.

Exactly as Jansen had so often done, Andrew returned it with a simple chin lift, then turned his attention to me. "So that's it? You're just taking him back?"

Whoa. That caught me off guard. I expected Jansen to snarl, but he didn't. Instead, he looked at me. Like to see what I'd say.

"There's nothing to take back."

Andrew picked up his burger and turned away from us.

Amelia's eyes met mine, giving me a soft, understanding grin. "It's okay," she mouthed. Then, to Jansen, "It's nice you get to join us."

Jansen managed a humble expression, and I expected him to give me his old, quick one-arm hug. Instead, he winked. He didn't touch me. Didn't take my hand. No, he kept at a friendly distance.

A frustratingly friendly distance.

Subdued and definitely repentant, Tim joined the table and sat beside Aaron, but avoided any glance my way. Maybe it hadn't been his fault, but it was still hard to believe a demonic force had made him do those things. Even if I accepted that, it didn't erase the mental image of his body pressed against mine. Didn't undo the memory of being unable to defend myself.

"What is it?" Jansen asked.

I leaned over. "Can't you wipe this away for him like you do with me?"

After a gentle forehead bump to mine, he used his fork to pick apart his pork. *"Doesn't work that way. For one thing, everyone would think it was weird if I reached across the table to brush Tim's face. Second, that kind of healing is temporary. It wears off when a new worry or fear arises. I could give him a powerful dose, but he'd be somewhat out of it if I did that. Anyway, his fears would return tomorrow. No, this sort of wound takes a long time to heal. Amelia. Ellie, Amelia. Say 'no!'"*

"Huh? Uh… no!" I jumped and gazed at her.

Perhaps offended, she looked puzzled. "Um, okay."

Jansen covered for me. "It's just that I already offered to take her home. Thanks for the offer, though."

All that I could do was smile apologetically.

"You really don't pay attention to anything when you hear voices, do you?" He laughed in projection.

No kidding! I put my head on the table and groaned as he patted my back, laughing aloud with uncharacteristic exuberance. Heads turned curiously.

I lifted my chin to pin his eyes. "This gives new meaning to the phrase 'inside joke.'" This was met with more uproarious laughter.

CHAPTER NINETEEN

One evening, Jansen and I sat on my front porch together. We could see our breath and needed a blanket over our laps on the swing. But that just made stargazing underneath the canopy of my porch cozier, at least if we put our heads back far enough. From there, our view switched between sky and ceiling, back and forth. If I leaned my head against the swing as it reached its farthest point, I had an unobstructed sight of the moon and stars against the dark weave of the world.

I got lost in thought, but was hyper-aware of Jansen beside me, his body heat its own presence. He'd joined us for dinner for the first time since he'd broken up with Clara. Since he'd reignited our status as comrades, buddies, pals, cousins—I didn't know.

My mom had been a little frigid at first, though she warmed to his charm by the end of the meal and sent us outside, insisting she and Tyler would clean up. Time by ourselves was great, and all, but it made me nervous, too.

He'd been frustratingly friendly all evening. On the one hand, I knew he kept his distance in some warped way to protect me. It was just that I hadn't realized my feelings for him before, and being so close ached.

When alone, I dreamt about him. About what it would be like to be in his arms. About hearing him call me his girlfriend. About what I foresaw as a soul-ejecting kiss, the type I'd never experienced before. When we were with one another, I pretended not to notice his muscled torso, his sculpted chest, or the elegant planes of his face…

The scent of his skin…

The feelings he aroused in me that made me need to press my knees together, hard—

"Where are you?" he asked.

I shivered and pulled the blanket higher on my lap, saying dreamily, "Lost in thought, I guess."

A rumble of delight rippled through his chest. "I should say so. Thought I might have to project to talk with you."

"Oh, did you say something?" I sat up to give him my full attention.

"I was just telling you it was nice…having dinner here again. When did your dad start collecting cell phones?"

My dad kept a basket on the kitchen counter where anyone eating dinner here had to deposit their devices. "No phones at the dinner table," he'd said.

"He came up with that one a few weeks ago, and my mom's started enforcing it when he's not here."

"I see. I was thinking—"

But I had stopped listening again. From somewhere close, like next to my ear, or in it, someone sighed a raspy stream of breath—

And beside me there arose a grave and ghostly haze.

"Is Charlie here?" I interrupted him mid-sentence.

"No, he's catching up on some coursework. He's in Paris, I'm pretty sure."

That wasn't the answer I hoped for.

"Ellie, what is it? Your colors—they're all wrong."

I stared at the doom-flecked mist, backing myself into his chest where he wrapped me into his arms.

Then disembodied laughter swelled inside my head. *"So, you see me, too. How interesting."*

"What do you want?" My chest constricted as I gulped in a breath.

Jansen's grip tightened, but I barely noticed. "What is it, Ellie?"

The voice that resided in me laughed again. *"Very interesting indeed. You hear me. You see me. But* he *cannot. One more experiment, if you'll allow… Kiss him."*

I knew Jansen spoke to me, but demonic projections pushed him out. While listening to Charlie and Jansen was easy, hearing Cronus in my mind, as if he were literally in my thoughts, made my blood run cold and the hairs on my arms stand erect.

"Ah, she can ignore me." Cronus said with a jubilance, like Dr. Frankenstein, proud of his monster. *"You are amazing. And you are still human. Yes?"*

Again, I refused to answer. Was that even a question?

Then Jansen's voice resounded inside me, too. *"What is it? Damn it, Ellie! Answer me."*

I choked on my breath and breathed out, "Cronus." With a start, I felt the pull of Jansen's riddle—

At the same time, Cronus entered my mind. The combination was a dizzying spin of daylight and dusk, of brilliance and murk. My insides stretched. My head pounded.

Jansen's body morphed into a ghoulish figure, his face skeletal, eyes bulging. The once beautiful, thick hair grew long, and turned thin and ink-black. It balded in patches of gray tissue.

What the actual hell! He kissed me with putrid breath and rotted teeth. Talons grabbed my stomach and dug into the skin.

I couldn't scream. The scream fused to my throat; a voiceless, living beast that choked me. I felt the pain as it tore flesh and felt the tickle of blood that trickled down my stomach. Yet, couldn't do anything.

His fist thrust inside of me. It clawed through skin and tissue and organs deep within. My mouth went dry. I couldn't swallow. His taloned claw seized the back of my neck and pulled me backward even as the pain folded me in half.

Jansen sneered. He hissed and snarled and licked his lip with a snake-like tongue then lowered me to the ground. My ears rang with a high pitched clang as he lifted one foot and jammed it into my flesh. His knees disappeared, his torso, his shoulders, until all that remained on the outside was his head, the eyes barely contained in their sockets.

He would kill me.

Then, it laughed—that Jansen, not-Jansen thing, that ghoul—and disappeared into my body.

I clutched at my expanded belly; the wound squished between my fingers. Blood oozed down my arm, hot and sticky.

Strong cramps gripped my insides and I grasped at the air, needing to cling to something. I felt a primal urge to crawl up something solid, but there was only air. The same primal instincts forced me to bear down, and when I did, a creature was born.

The world spun and my heart thrashed away from this nightmare of horrors. I crab-walked backward, retreating from the monstrosity, and slipped in a pool of my blood.

Before I could run, the thing had grown to the size of a toddler. It grew taller and taller until I thought it might never stop. Unfolded itself into a lanky, human-like shape. A humanoid monster with mucus instead of skin. It stood taller than me by six feet and stretched and raised its hands to the heavens and bellowed, "I am the Dark Ruler!"

The vision ended, and my mom knelt beside me on the cold, hard floor of our porch. She held me tight against her chest, where she squeezed my shoulders, rocking, and murmuring my name.

My legs twitched, and I couldn't control the convulsions in my arms or the wave of nausea.

"Jansen." I hardly had any voice.

"He's right here."

I eyed Jansen suspiciously as he stood by the front door, his fingers caught in his hair. His expression held more pain than I'd ever seen, but it was *his* face. *His* fingers that pulled at his full head of soft hair and his own dark eyes that looked helplessly back.

"It's okay," my mom said. "You had some sort of seizure. You're lucky I came out when I did."

"Lucky," I said.

With my face in her lap, I let her comb her fingers through my hair, the familiar touch of her cold fingertips returning me to reality a little more.

She motioned for Jansen to come closer. "Let's get her inside where it's warm."

His arms lifted me, and I stiffened, jerking myself away. I couldn't shake that vision. Maybe I'd said I could never be afraid of him, but I was wrong.

"I'll walk."

They helped me into the family room, where I curled myself into a ball on the sofa.

"I'm going to go make a phone call." My mom covered me with the fuzzy blanket we kept over the couch in winter. "I'll be in the kitchen if you need me."

Jansen crouched on the Persian rug between me and the coffee table but didn't try to touch me. "My God, Ellie. What was that?"

No, I couldn't relive it, and could only shiver. Couldn't tell the story even if I wanted to. The thought of it made my lips curl. "It was nothing."

"Like hell."

Yes, something quite like that. "I can't, Jansen. I just can't."

My emotions took over outside of my control, and I scrubbed at my eyes, heaving air in and out of my lungs.

What could I do? My only hope was to talk about it. How exactly was I to tell my friend I would bear his evil spawn? How did I then mention I saw it in gory detail? No, I couldn't say anything to him, but—

"Call Charlie." I wiped my nose on my sleeve and threw the blanket from my lap.

The kitchen phone clicked onto its base, and my mom entered the room. "Ellie, baby, get your coat. Dr. Hall wants you to be seen at the ER."

I shook my head at Jansen. "I need to talk to Charlie. Please. Get him."

My mom rushed me toward the coat closet.

"He's not here," Jansen said. "Miss Marie, I'm coming with

you."

"Yeah, that's fine. Frankly, I'd like the company, and you can explain what happened better than I can."

He climbed into the car even faster than he usually did. My mom held onto my arm while I got in, trying to help, but her efforts were futile.

I needed Charlie.

An idea occurred to me, so I dug into Jansen's coat pocket to pull out his cell phone. "Call him."

He dialed the number and waited a few seconds, frowning when it became obvious Charlie wasn't going to answer. "Charlie, it's about Ellie. Call as soon as you get this." He snapped the phone closed. Quietly, so my mom wouldn't hear, he said, "Tell me what you heard, please."

"I can't." Tears threatened to fall. "It was Cronus. He was there, and you couldn't see or hear him."

His muscles tensed, and the veins popped out in his hands. Those smooth, wiry-haired, non-taloned hands. "I'm so sorry."

"What on earth for?"

"Jeez, El. I can't even keep you safe. How can I when he isn't visible? When I can't even hear him?"

Boy, he really had no idea what had just happened. He thought I was upset because he couldn't protect me—

"Ellie."

The voice inside me made me jump nearly out of my skin, putting Jansen on high alert.

"What is it?" He was loud enough that my mom heard, too.

She looked at us from the rearview mirror. "Everything okay back there? Gabriella, you doing okay?"

"Fine, Mom." I gripped his hand before he could riddle and reveal his secret.

"It's just me."

Yes, just a demon talking in my head. The reason for our trip to the hospital.

I had to speak in code and trust both brothers to break it. "I hope Charlie meets us at the hospital. I know he got our message by now."

"Hospital? What happened?"

"Yeah." Better get a handle on this before he did anything stupid. "Sure hope he'll meet us there, where we can explain everything to him."

Jansen winked. Messages received.

Once we got there, a long time passed before Charlie could appear. We waited three hours in the waiting area, and my mom wouldn't leave my side, even to go to the bathroom. When they finally brought us back, we found a bed partitioned from the others by a hanging sheet on either side, with enough room for Jansen and my mom if they both stood. They whisked me away for an MRI almost immediately.

After another forty-five minutes, the doctor called my mom out of the room, and Charlie materialized in her absence.

"This place is insane," he said. "What's going on?"

"Jansen." I squeezed the hand that held tight to mine. "Would you go find my mom, please?"

"I'm not leaving your side. You think your mom is bad? You haven't seen anything yet."

"It's okay. I need to talk to Charlie alone."

"I got this." Charlie patted his brother on the shoulder. "Pop home for a few. Go on."

"You don't understand. You weren't there."

I picked at the hem of the hospital gown. "I don't have much time before my mom comes back. Please. This is important."

"Why can't you tell me?"

I couldn't answer. Couldn't even think of a good, distracting lie. And talking to him wasn't an option.

"Go home, little brother," Charlie said. "I'm here now. We'll talk later."

With a wounded grimace, Jansen directed his eyes toward the floor, riddled, and was gone.

Charlie sat on the bed beside me and I checked to make sure the gown covered my back end. Stupid, unnecessary, wide-open monstrosity.

Once satisfied, I shifted to my side, giving him more room on the tiny squeaky bed. "It was awful. I don't know what to do. Cronus came to see me tonight."

"To see you, as in personally?"

"He spoke to me in projections. I heard him, but Jansen couldn't. I saw him."

"Oh, that's not good. What do you mean, you saw him?"

"I can see you and Jansen, too, when you're in your spirit forms. Like a sort of gray, misty matter. Jansen's more of a blue-gray, actually. It's kind of like your body, but mist."

"Damn!"

"Damn!"

One awed "damn" reverberated along the walls. The other angry "damn" gave me a headache the way it ricocheted around my mind like shards of shrapnel.

"Jansen." I said it through gritted teeth as I spotted him trying to hide near the ceiling.

"Jansen?"

I pointed to my head and grimaced.

With obvious understanding, Charlie held up an index finger. "Hold that thought."

He disappeared, and by the time I finished assuring myself my gown still covered my back end, he reappeared. "Sorry 'bout that. Had to perform a mini exorcism. Go on."

"Is he okay?"

"Course not." He sat too hard on the bed and shifted it an inch. "But I'll explain it to him later. You were saying you see misty gray and blue stuff."

"Yes, and you and Jansen appear like misty bodies."

"Does Cronus appear that way, too?"

"Kinda, only his form is more of a blob and almost black."

He poured himself a cup of water from my bedside table. "I'm sorry, El Girl, but I have to say it again. Damn!"

It was said with such admiration that I couldn't help but smile and kick my dangling legs with a bit of joy.

"You've got some talents—no, your word's better. You've got some superpowers even we don't have."

"You can't see the misty blobs?"

He thought about it while he took a couple of sips from the cup. "It's hard to say because I think we're talking about the same thing, but we don't see them the way you describe. I don't know what they look like to a human. What am I saying? Humans can't see them. Jansen and I can only see spirit forms, or the form of Cronus, as the case may be, if we're also in our spirit forms. That's why I had to riddle out to see Jansen. We don't look like mist, though. Do you remember describing what you see in Jansen's eyes?"

Frequently, so I nodded.

He handed me a cup of water. "That's his soul. That's what we look like."

Mid-sip, I spilled some water from my mouth and popped my hand over it to stop the leak.

"Yeah," he said. "Don't tell him I told you that. Now, back to what you described. I believe you see us as a person-like shape because we're part human and spend most of our time in our human forms, our bodies. Cronus' spirit has never taken on a physical form."

"Your spirits used to be harder to make out, but lately, it's been easier to see all of you."

"Sounds like your abilities are growing."

Someone started to open the privacy curtain but then didn't. Footsteps grew fainter as they walked down the hall. It reminded us we didn't have much time.

"What did Cronus say?" he asked.

"That's the terrifying part." I nervously tapped my fingers on my lips. "Charlie, it was awful."

I cried again from remembering, and hated myself for it. The piercing beeps on the heart rate monitor sped up.

"That'll get the nurses in here. You've got to relax. Take a few deep breaths."

I clenched my teeth. "That isn't going to help. It's not so much what he said as what he showed me."

As I explained the nightmare to him, he listened as if

dumbfounded, struck mute. I bet he didn't blink once throughout the story. When I finished, we stared at each other, neither of us able to speak. The vision sat like a whisper of darkness between us.

"And you haven't told any of this to Jansen?"

"No, of course not."

"I don't think it means anything." He smoothed a stray hair off my forehead. "He was trying to scare you the way he did at Halloween."

"It wasn't the same. Kinda like looking through a window into my future."

"Just demon tricks. He's awfully good at it."

"No!" I yelled. "Don't you see? That's why he's so interested in me. He wants me for some sick plan of his."

"Okay, okay. Look, I have to tell Jansen about this."

"No! You can't. Promise me you won't tell him. He doesn't need to know that."

"He'll want to know. We have no secrets, the two of us. Trust me, this one's small."

"You can't tell him," I said, my voice shaking. "I came to you because I don't want him to know. This will destroy him, Charlie. One way or another, it would, and you know it. He'll either go after Cronus or get himself hurt or worse, something drastic to save me. You can't tell him."

"I'm afraid of what this means, El Girl. It may be that Cronus is looking for how to get to your soul."

"What makes you say that?"

"Because he isn't trying to kill you. I thought he was, but he could do that so easily and he hasn't. See, when a human is near death, the soul often lifts from the body and can be intercepted. When he sent you that vision… I think that's what he wants."

Death or intercepting my soul, did it matter? It sounded the same to me. "Would knowing that change anything? Could Jansen protect me any better just by knowing?"

He thought it over and eventually shook his head. "Probably not, but we need to step up our game. You two have to squash these feelings. It's what draws Cronus. That bond between you is much deeper than you understand. Jansen wants you to find someone else. Do you think you can?"

"There's no one else. It's not like I *have* to have a boyfriend."

"Have you ever thought about Andrew?"

"Andrew?"

"Yes, Andrew. I've seen the way you look at him. He's nice, and he likes you. Has for some time. Jansen's always known you'd end up with him, eventually. I think if our demonic powers weren't so dominant, maybe you'd like him, too."

"He's just a boy."

"Yes, Ellie, just a boy. Not a demon, a boy. When we first told you what we are, I was kinda shocked by your reaction —or your lack of one."

"How should I have reacted?"

"Gee, I don't know. Shocked. Horrified. Scared. Any of those."

"Well, you have a brother who won't let me feel those things. He's so quick with that hand of his."

"True. I forget about that. He never uses it on me."

"Have you ever needed him to?"

He thought about that for a bit. "No, guess not."

At that moment, my mom slid the curtain aside, startling us.

"Why, Charlie! When did you get here?"

"A few minutes ago. I sent Jansen home. He looked pretty tired." Then he projected, *"El, did he drive here?"*

I shook my head slightly.

To my mom, he said, "Do you mind giving me a ride? I let Jansen take my car."

"Yes, of course." She sighed and trailed her fingers down the side of my face. "It's been a rather long night. Ellie, honey, the doctor couldn't find anything wrong with you. I guess that's a good thing, but we're puzzled about what happened. From what I described, he admitted it sounded like you had a seizure, but the brain scan didn't show anything unusual. He said you could go home for now but that we need to keep an eye on you."

You have no idea, I thought. All the human eyes in the world couldn't keep me safe.

CHAPTER TWENTY

In the morning, I yawned through breakfast.

"You don't have to go." My mom poured me a second glass of orange juice. "In fact, I wish you wouldn't."

"I'm"—I yawned—"fine."

"Clearly. What's so important that you just have to go?"

Nothing in particular, but if I had the choice to stay home and read or watch TV versus spend the day with friends and demons, well…

I stepped outside early to wait for Jansen. An invisible Charlie assured me he'd be here soon. On the stairs, I found Andrew, who didn't turn to look at me as I closed the door. The way he slumped…it made me pause. What weighed on his mind to sit so statuesque? Both hands between his knees as he stared straight ahead? I walked toward him, each step sounding a hollow thud on the wood planks of the porch. There, I sat next to him, where I drew my knees into my chest.

"Tyler said you were at the hospital last night. Everything okay?"

"Oh, yeah. Just a little scare. They didn't find anything wrong."

Just three demons attached to me.

"Don't suppose you'd like a ride?" he offered, still without looking at me.

"You know Jansen is taking me. We talked things out.

Everything's back to normal."

God, I had a hard time believing that myself.

"Is it? Back to normal? Did he ever apologize?"

"Yes, he did. He treated me badly, and he's sorry."

"All is forgiven? Just like that?"

"I don't know what else you want to hear."

He jerked to face away. "I don't want to hear anything. I want to know what he offers you. Even when he's with you, he doesn't seem to give you what you need… What you deserve."

"What do you think I need? Or deserve?"

I wouldn't find out because Jansen's car pulled up. Before he got out, a chilled burst of air blasted through me that made me shiver and Andrew gasp. He inhaled as if to breathe in the cold, rolled his shoulders back, and cracked his knuckles. Cracked his neck to the right and then left.

Finally, he turned his gaze on me. I saw him as if for the first time, and I got caught up in the striking blue of his eyes, marveling at how the irises sat on black onyx backdrops. Funny how I'd never noticed that before. He lifted my hand and held it to his lips, a thing that made me feel giddy and lightheaded. A silly girl in a bad romance novel.

"Goodbye, Gabriella." His voice sounded melodic, and I wanted to hear him say my name again.

He descended the steps with a casual ease, offering a curt nod to Jansen as he left.

"Oh." His hand was already at the car door. "I'll wait for you after choir. You know, in case you want a ride…or something." The door closed, and the car sped off, tires squealing.

I pressed my hands tight against my burning cheeks and watched his car fishtail around the corner.

"What was that all about?" Jansen's voice startled me. How had I forgotten he stood there?

"I honestly don't know." The rhythm of my heart slowed. "He wanted to know if I wanted a ride to school."

"You could have gone."

"Jansen! I don't want to go with him."

"You could have fooled me."

My mouth opened to protest, but I didn't know what to say.

He snatched my backpack. "Come on then. We need to get going."

"About last night—"

"Yeah, Charlie filled me in. I hadn't realized you'd take to the plan quite so easily. Just get in the car."

"Great class today." Mrs. Harding lowered her baton and set it on the music stand in front of her. "You've all matured in sound beyond what most teachers ever see."

If she hadn't been staring at Jansen, we might've thought she meant the whole choir.

He'd been quiet all day. He met me at our usual haunts, walked me to classes, was generally courteous…but bothered. I wanted to know what Charlie had told him, but I didn't get a chance to talk to either of them. Jansen ensured we were always with other students, and wasn't talking in my head today. Neither was Charlie.

After class, Jansen met me and took my backpack. As we both turned to leave the choir room, I ran into Andrew, stepped on his toe, and mashed my nose into his chest.

"Whoa, didn't see you there," I said apologetically.

"My apologies." Was he getting a cold? It wasn't allergy season, but his voice flowed like silk.

I wanted him to say my name again in that liquid, dark timbre. When he held his arm out, without thinking, I took it.

"Now, Gabriella, how about that ride home?"

"You're unbelievable." Jansen pulled himself up to his full height. "Hell will freeze before I ever let her get in your car again."

"Interesting choice of words," Andrew hissed.

With unexpected force, Jansen grabbed my hand and

yanked me down the hall. I had to run to keep up.

The crowded hallway filled with kids who packed their bags, stooped to get books, and leaned against lockers, all of them parting in the middle as he stormed through the center. I tripped over one student's bag and tried to pull myself from his grasp, but he held me too tight.

"Jansen!"

"What?" His stride lengthened.

"You're hurting me!"

He stopped so fast my forehead hit his elbow. Even though it was *my* head he'd rammed into, he winced like he had hurt his own and held his fingers lightly over my throbbing skull. It was a cool touch, and I had to remind myself to be mad.

With a sharp swipe at his hand, I said, "Stop it! What was all that about?"

"It was nothing."

"It wasn't nothing."

"I shouldn't have to explain every time I get edgy," he said.

"He only offered me a ride."

"He was doing more than that." He outlined the space around him.

"His aura?"

"Brilliant red, and not just his."

"What the hell does that mean? He has a little crush on me, I know that. He's being kind, that's all. Besides, what difference does it make to you? It's not like you're ever going to…"

My words caught in my throat, but I'd said enough. I wished them back, but that's the trouble with words. They can't be erased.

"You should ride home with him." He handed me my pack.

"Jansen, wait."

As he walked backward, he shrugged apologetically. "You're right. I'm not ever going to. You're far too important to me."

I turned around and found Andrew leaning against the lockers ten feet away.

On the way home, Andrew skipped the small talk and landed on the topic of Jansen right off the bat. First, I'd had to deal with Jansen's jealousy, an emotion that made my head spin. He'd become the king of mixed messages lately. Now, I had to deal with Andrew, too.

All the while, constantly aware that a misty Charlie hovered in the backseat.

I told Andrew I had no desire to talk about Jansen, and he seemed oddly pleased to hear that.

When he pulled up to the curb in front of his house, he leaned across the divide. He took my hand and I fidgeted with my necklace. What would Charlie think of all this?

"We don't have to talk about Jansen. Let's talk about flying. Did you know I got my pilot's license?"

"No." I was surprised he hadn't told me. Yet, I shouldn't have been. I hadn't seen as much of him recently. Not since Jansen started taking me to and from school. "I can't believe it. That's amazing, Andrew. Really."

"I hoped you might take me up on my offer for a private flight. What do you say?" When I hesitated, he caressed my cheek with the backs of his fingers. "A little flight followed by a romantic dinner? Maybe in Georgia, hmm?"

"No," I said, leaning into the passenger door.

He looked surprised that I'd rejected him. Who was more shocked? Him at my rejection or me at his proposal?

"Andrew, I'm sorry if I ever gave you the wrong impression."

"Don't you feel anything for me?"

"I… I don't know how to answer that. You're a nice guy, a good neighbor, but…"

"But you don't feel *anything* for me?" His brow furrowed. "How very strange."

"I had hoped you were a friend."

After Jansen left me, forcing me to ride home with Andrew, I saw less of him. Charlie explained, poorly, that he tried to give me space. As if he could. Even when Jansen wasn't around, Charlie was. Despite Charlie's charm, I missed Jansen and felt bad for our spat.

Then Charlie developed an annoying habit while babysitting me at school that eluded me at first.

As I walked toward Spanish class, he projected, *"Aren't you thirsty? You seem thirsty. Maybe turn left and get a drink."*

The power of suggestion alone made me parched. I turned down the hallway and bent over the drinking fountain, flipping my hair over my shoulder. There stood Andrew at his locker, collecting his books.

He sauntered over, leaned in, and said close to my ear, "Hello, Gabriella." Then he was gone, up the hall toward fourth bell, taking the fluttering in my heart with him.

Another time, Charlie projected I'd forgotten something in my locker, which sent me back to it in a panic. Sure enough, there was Andrew, who smiled and waved on his way to class. He gave me a friendly pat on the arm, which sparked electricity through my body; sparks that left me feeling giddy, but it made no sense.

Also, it kind of pissed me off.

"You are so stubborn," Charlie said. *"Your aura clearly likes him."* Then, after Andrew had passed by, *"Well, you did like him. That is really weird."*

I tore off a sheet of paper and scribbled in horrible handwriting:

"I know. You're like…the perfect girlfriend."

CHAPTER TWENTY-ONE

The weeks passed slowly. Andrew pursued me more persistently, mostly at school. It so obviously irritated Jansen, but he never said anything. Even now, I could hear Andrew's muffled laughter through the bathroom I shared with Tyler, his bedroom being on the other side.

Our trio had played several convoluted rounds of three-handed Euchre with rules that made no sense. I swore they'd invented them up as they went along. Andrew used every opportunity he could find to touch me in some way. Sometimes he grazed my hand, or he'd "accidentally" fall, catching himself on my shoulder. Once, he'd even brushed a bug from my forehead, holding my gaze for an uncomfortable second too long.

Strange, too. I didn't hate it when we were near one another. Like he had some bubble around him. I became a giddy, goose-pimply mess if I moved into the bubble, but outside of that dome, my head cleared, and all interest melted away.

Jansen turned a shade less frigid and behaved cordially again. Thank goodness for that. Sure, we were supposed to focus on our friendship. Trouble was, his version of "just friends" wasn't quite as intimate as I'd been used to our entire lives. His personal space grew exponentially as he retreated every time I stepped into it. He touched me only when necessary. He even kept his sunglasses on when alone with me.

How was it so easy for him to keep his distance?

Most nights, I couldn't sleep for thinking about it. I glanced at the clock on my bedside table. Ten o'clock. I'd tried to finish a reading assignment for the better part of the past hour, but my thoughts wandered to other things. Things like the touch of Jansen's hand, the way he smiled crookedly, his chiseled arms, and how his scent stirred me.

Even after my conversation with Charlie about the vision, what good could possibly come from being apart?

I couldn't risk him finding out about the demon child, and I couldn't stop thinking about it, either. There I'd be, picturing my body against Jansen's in the pool, remembering the touch of his bare skin on mine, when—even in my daydreams—I'd turn around to face him and he'd morph into that hideous ghoul. It always brought about a cold sweat.

A tree limb flogged its wet leaves against my bedroom window, which captured my attention. The night was especially dark, and rain had been tapping on the pane for the past half hour. The wind picked up, suggesting an imminent downpour.

There had been a time when, if something stirred in my room, I'd have thought the heater kicked on. That was before I knew demons existed. Worse, that was before I knew invisible demons prowled my bedroom at night, either guarding me or there to kill me. If it was the latter, I half wished he'd get it over with.

It was hard to see, but black fog in the form of a human wrapped in cerulean, star-speckled mist hovered in the corner. Definitely Jansen. Even in that hazy state, his muscles were well-defined, and he was the only one who ever appeared slightly blue.

"We're alone. You don't have to lurk."

He materialized, looking sheepish.

Good. He should be embarrassed, always lurking. "What are you doing here?"

"You're never alone now. You know that. Charlie and I are

always hanging around somewhere."

"Maybe that's the problem!" I slammed closed the book I'd been reading. Something about the whoosh of air and the loud crack satisfied my rage.

"That's why we've been invisible. Maybe you'd forget we were here."

"Forget? Like I could forget two demons hang out in my bedroom all night. Do you think I'm insane?"

He hung his head, and I regretted the words that brought us back to days when I'd really thought I lost my mind. When I didn't yet know their secret. It had hurt him to have to keep it from me, and I hadn't meant to rub salt in the wound. But I didn't say any of that, and let him stew, instead.

"You're angry with me," he said.

Yes. Mad and hurt and frustrated and confused. Just touch me. Kiss me. Or leave me the hell alone.

As I processed this, his gaze focused on me. He didn't take his eyes from mine, and I knew the rainbow of mingled colors within the black onyx reflected his soul, which melted my cold heart. Briefly, I had a glimpse of the boy who'd been my friend all my life. Suddenly, it was just us again. I took a deep breath and sighed, defeated.

"Ellie, I wish you'd tell me what you're thinking right now."

"There's nothing worth knowing."

"I doubt that."

He walked over and sat on my bed, so I pulled my legs in pretzel-style and took his hand in mine. For once, I expected he'd pull away and clamped down at the first twitch.

He let out a resigned sigh, almost a chuckle, and he didn't retract. "I miss this."

"Me too."

"I think I know what you're angry about. You wish you had more privacy."

Is that what he thought? He didn't realize how much I still ached for him? Okay, I could go along with that.

"Privacy, yeah. How can I get some of that?"

"I'm not sure. Wish I knew. We'll figure something out,

though. Charlie and I have been talking about this, and it's unusual for a demon to attach himself to a human. It's like he's playing a game. Testing the energy between us. Charlie says Cronus thinks he orchestrated our friendship. The reason we were such good friends."

Were. Such a tiny word, but it stabbed all the same. Made me clutch my stomach and wince. We'd never be the way we were. He wouldn't let us. A tearing sensation returned, wrenching my soul from me, a horrible physical pain.

"What is it?" My friend looked concerned.

"It's nothing," I lied, trying to compose myself, trying to quell the ache.

"That's not true. What is it?"

"Cramps," I lied again.

He didn't shy away as I expected. Didn't even flinch. He pressed his lips together, furrowed his brow, and leaned in close so we were eye to eye. To my surprise, I didn't shy away either, but met him straight on.

"I feel everything you feel. You've never felt cramps in your life because I've always been there to relieve the pain."

Whoa. He was right. All those times he'd healed me, and I never knew. With a bit of extra dramatic flair, perhaps, I fell back on the bed, arms spread wide.

"Ellie, why won't you talk? I could take this pain away, but you won't let me. Come on, now, I don't think I can stand this."

"I love you!"

I dashed from the room. Dashed down the stairs and out the front door, not bothering to shut it. Rain fell in torrents, but I didn't care. It could drench my hair, my clothes. Cold, swollen drops punished my face, and I deserved it.

Before my feet hit the yard, he riddled in front of me. As if I hadn't seen that coming. Had never in my life been able to escape him. Hadn't ever really wanted to.

"I love you!" I screamed over the heavy rain and pounded my fists against his chest. "But you don't want to hear that. You want me to be your friend. Well, I don't think I can do that. I hurt inside all the time! When you're away from me, it's like you've taken a piece of me with you."

He let me beat my fists on him until they ached, as water droplets sprayed in bursts at each smack. Once I'd spent all my energy, I pulled my arms into myself, both fists clenched tight beneath my quivering chin. He folded me into his muscled chest and rested his chin on the top of my head. My body shuddered as gentle sobs erupted from my breast.

The night sky reflected black and moonless. Starless. As though all the eyes of the world had closed to give us this moment, crying for us. The rain drummed with increased intensity, but we were already soaked. It didn't matter.

Nothing mattered.

He spoke softly, but I heard his voice hum from his chest where he'd pressed my ear. Heard his rich baritone even over the pounding rain. "Do you think I don't feel the same way you do? You have no idea the strength it takes to turn you away. My feelings for you…your feelings for me… I won't put you in that kind of danger."

His finger touched under my chin as he guided me to look at him. The rain trickled off his hair and reflected the streetlight as tiny diamond droplets. All around us, it rushed down in a torrent and *tinked, tinked, tinked* on the driveway, the roof, and the leaves. The gutter roared with the flow of too much rain.

Our breaths came heavily, white puffs that arose and combined into one cloud. While my focus remained steadfastly on him, his scanned my aura. Whatever he saw, he fought back a smile as his gaze locked onto mine.

I don't think he intended to kiss me, as hellbent as he was on distancing himself. Yet, in his eyes, pure anguish mirrored mine. Our combined despair swirled in them as the brilliant sapphire haze wrapped around it with love and trust and hope. All of it an effort to smother our pain. I knew then. That connection… I felt it in my soul.

He felt it, too.

When his face drew nearer, his breath quickened. Mine hitched, like tiny hiccups, the nearer he got, and heat radiated from his skin.

Trembles rippled their way through my limbs in deliciously violent waves. With parted lips, I tried to catch my breath.

Closer. So close. His lips, soft and loose, grazed mine.

My heart tumbled.

Then Charlie appeared from nowhere, head lowered, and the fluttering wings within my chest gripped my lungs and twisted them instead. I wanted to kill him. Wanted to drown him in rain and dark and night.

At least he had the decency to look apologetic. All the trembling energy in my limbs could have strung him up by his toes, all nearly seven feet of him. Even his enormous strength couldn't match my ire.

Jansen pressed his forehead into mine and then pulled away a mere inch, leaving me aching with want. With need and a burning thirst. Pain and sorrow lodged inside his eyes, his chest heaving.

Charlie's hand clapped Jansen on the back. "Dude, I sensed the fireworks all the way at our place." All the cheerful playfulness I loved about Charlie evaporated. Though his words were light, his voice exposed a mournful heart. "Leave this shift to me. Go home and take a cold shower or something. Jansen, I am sorry."

With a sigh of resignation, Jansen bit his lip. I felt the sigh on my lips and inhaled it. His breath mixed with mine, and I shuddered to know it coated my lungs. Defeated, he released his grip around me and took a step back.

Unbelievable! I breathed heavily and stared at both of them. So much frustration had pent itself up I thought I might explode. Jansen drifted away, his palms facing me, and he bowed as if in surrender.

Then he disappeared in a wrinkle of darkness.

"Let's get out of this rain!" Charlie had to shout over the continuous pounding. "What do you say, El Girl?"

"No!"

His jaw fell, helpless. This giant of a guy, so accustomed to getting his way, stymied by a sixteen-year-old girl. It had to be frustrating, vexing even, to be told "no" and, for the first time, have no means to project. Sure, there'd probably been times he'd have been told "no," but he'd have had a choice. Accept the "no" or project. Here, he had no choice.

"Come on, kid. What are you going to accomplish standing out here in the rain?"

"No!" I stamped my foot and glared at him, daring him to steal what little independence I had left. "I ran out here to get away from all this!"

He stood dumbfounded, and if I weren't so bullheaded, I might have felt sorry for him. Poor Charlie. He had next to no experience with the human emotions of teenage girls, him being barely human, and all.

So we stared at each other. Him in confused desperation and me full of stubborn pride. The rain fell in buckets, drenching us through to the bone until there wasn't a dry spot on either of us. My hair hung in dripping strands around my face as water droplets tickled my lips, but I was too willful to scratch them. I focused all my energy on glaring at Charlie.

The heat of the denied kiss, the one that played out in my fantasy as passionate and world-altering, ebbed as the rain punished him because of me. I was more annoyed than anything, that I had to be out here at all. And I blamed Jansen for that. Yet that didn't seem fair, either. He didn't torture me. No. He just wanted me safe.

Okay, so maybe it was funny, us standing in the rain, but I wasn't about to admit it.

He fought to contain a grin.

"What?" I asked, forcing anger, attempting to keep up the façade.

"Nothing." He grinned.

"What?"

"You can't play games with me, El. I can read you, remember? You're not mad anymore, but you're stubborn and trying to hide it. Problem is, you can't."

He extended his hand again, and this time, exasperated and defeated, I took it.

CHAPTER TWENTY-TWO

When Charlie pulled me into his embrace, I felt so small. Jansen had some height, but Charlie was ridiculous, and pure muscle, too. I'd never found myself in his arms this way before, and his sheer strength filled me with awe. Like being strapped into a roller coaster car, and it felt safe, even as I anticipated the coming breathless tickle of the riddle.

Suddenly, we stood in my bedroom, where Charlie kissed the top of my wet crown. "Go get dry. I'll be right here."

I walked into the bathroom to change my clothes, but grabbed two towels instead, taking one to Charlie. He'd already peeled his wet T-shirt off over his head, so I threw the towel at him, trying not to stare at the muscles rippling on his chest and abs. He thanked me, and I turned to go back into the bathroom.

When I came out again with towel-dried hair and warm flannel pajamas, I'd had time to cool off. My mind cleared, but my mood hadn't improved much.

I took a seat beside him on the bed, where he sat still half naked. Shouldn't that bother me? I got the sense that if he wanted to charm, he could, but Charlie was safe. I recognized his beauty, but never responded to it.

"I don't have any T-shirts made to fit Thor," I said.

He winked and grabbed his soaked shirt off the bed, wadded it into a ball, then held it between his large hands. They glowed a dull sheen, like a warming bulb. "Built-in dryer."

"How? Won't it burst into flames or something?"

"Nah. I have perfect control of it."

With a movement so fast I barely saw it, he flipped his right palm up where a fireball erupted. The shirt disappeared. I flinched and thumped my heart.

"Oh, man." He snapped two fingers. "There I go again. And that was my favorite shirt, too."

I took his hand and flipped it one way, then the other, inspecting it. Gee, I hadn't meant to make him destroy his favorite shirt.

Guilt drove me to retrieve a tee from… I didn't know where. Even my dad's shirts were too small. Maybe— "I can turn up the heat."

Then the buffoon pulled his left fist out from behind his back, revealing a wadded-up, perfectly dry Charlie-sized T-shirt. What the heck!

"Just kidding?" His voice rose at the end, and his chest shook at his own very bad joke. He patted his thighs. "Now, about these wet pants…"

He wasn't seriously thinking about taking those off? The thought of him in nothing but his underwear… My cheeks burned. I remembered he could detect not only the scarlet on my skin, but also whatever color that made my aura.

His reaction wasn't at all what I expected. "I see it," he said, more to himself. He studied me with a misplaced look of admiration before placing a warm hand over mine. "I'm kidding, of course, no worries. I'll be good now."

"Charlie?"

"Yeah?"

"What is it you see?"

"Oh." He chuckled and scratched behind his ears. "Your colors. They're unusually pure. Most people's swirl with a mixture of emotions." He tugged his shirt over his head to cover his naked torso. "But you? When you're happy, there's not a trace of sadness. You're quick to anger and quick to forgive. And when you love… You don't know what you do to my brother."

"What I do to him?" I pulled the sheets down and avoided looking directly at him as I crawled beneath them. I scoffed with a huff that started in my toes.

"You two have a connection neither of you understands. It's a bond you're not built for as a human."

His pause led me to ask, "What aren't you telling me?"

"Jansen would kill me, that's what I'm not telling you. It's not possible, anyway. Not for a human."

"Charlie."

He hesitated, fussing with the towel between his knees, as he thought. "Kate told us ages ago that one day Cronus would try to kidnap you."

A kick to my heart released the hatch in the pit of my stomach, releasing a flood of ice. "Kidnap—!"

Charlie popped a hand over my mouth and his eyes darted side to side as he listened. "Hush now, or I'll have to get Jansen back here with his magic hand. Yes, kidnap. But you knew that."

I licked his finger and he released me quick. "Does this look like the face of someone who knew that!"

"Why do you think we're here all the time?" He wiped his hand on his jeans, a smile playing on his lips at what I'd done. "He can't get you, though. I mean, he could, but not with us around. He's not a physical being, remember? All he can do is mess with you. We expected to see a change in you, but it didn't happen."

"What kind of change?"

"Honestly, Jansen and I always downplayed it. Thought Kate was a little psycho. She vaguely remembered some plan our father had involving Cronus. Now *that* demon, our father? He's one of hell's most powerful demons. A legend amongst fiends. Fortunately, this Cronus guy never came for you, until…"

"My pool?"

"Yeah. That was the first we saw something unique in you. Maybe the thing he seeks." With a heavy sigh and a raise of one eyebrow, he said, "Then there's that vision you had. Seems it fits that plan. It's another layer. Another reason for you and Jansen to sever that tie. We have to make sure no demon child can come of this."

My hands trembled, and my cheeks didn't just burn. They preheated, baked, and broiled. "Oh my gosh. Worst sex talk ever. Are you seriously telling me if he kisses me, I'll get pregnant?"

He was so taken aback that he snorted. "No, that's not what I'm saying! I *am* saying that until we find out what the vision means, you two have to tone down the fireworks. You heard me say I sensed you both from our house, right? Demons can sense intense feelings, and you guys are unbelievable." He rolled his eyes and the corners of his mouth turned up in a half-grin.

"You sensed our…?" So weird.

Fortunately, he didn't make me finish my thought. "Yes, but it's much more than that. Jansen and I have a unique perspective. Since we can read emotions so clearly, we also pick up raging hormones." When I grimaced, he pinched his nose and continued. "You're wrong. I can tell what you're thinking."

"You can't read minds!"

"No, but I know you." He popped his fist playfully on my head.

Ouch! Jeez, that was hard, so I rubbed the spot.

"You are difficult, aren't you?" he said with a softer, apologetic nudge to my shoulder.

"Why can't you just be honest?"

He straightened his back. "I have been! What more would you like to know?"

"Explain what I see in his eyes."

"I told you that. You're seeing his soul."

"But what does that mean?" I stretched the last word in frustration. I grasped my decorative pillow and stuffed my face into it, then peeked over it to gauge his reaction.

He hummed a soft groan and rubbed his eyelids, trying to rub me and my female hormones from them. "The human spirit creates a glow around each person, an aura. It changes color depending on what you're feeling."

I waited for more, but he gave me nothing.

"Is that all?" I finally asked.

"Pretty much, yeah."

"What does red mean?"

"Oh, now see, that I'm not supposed to tell you. He made me swear I wouldn't."

"Blue?" I tried again.

"Definitely not. I swore I wouldn't."

I wasn't one to be defeated, so investigated for myself, bringing my face closer to exchange gazes. As our personal space diminished, he retreated with a gulp. His eyes were the same rich onyx black I'd always known.

"There's nothing there," I said.

"Gee, thanks."

I huffed at him and backed away. "I don't see your soul. Why?"

"We don't know. It's another example of the bond you two still have."

The word "still" didn't escape my attentive ears. "He still feels that way about me?"

"Oh, Ellie, do you have to ask? It torments him. I might as well use my power of torture on him. It would be kinder."

"Power of what now?"

"Yeah." Charlie looked ashamed. "My brother got the power to heal, and I got stuck with torture. Cell ripping, flesh burning, lung filling torture. Guess I've had to learn to control my temper."

It wasn't something I could believe from him. Not Charlie, who was always so gentle—or tried to be—and easy-natured. Could his jovial personality be a vast cover designed to keep his rage in check?

"So here's the whole thing," he said. "You feel pain because of that connection you two have which can't happen between species. So, he had to sever that tie. One option was to move, but that left the door open for Cronus. The other option was to make you hate him. That's what led him to be friendlier to Clara."

I scoffed. "That was friendlier? He was horrible! The only

thing that changed was he let her be near him. Did he ever even kiss her?"

The words were out of my mouth, and I wished I could suck them back in. Charlie's silence made me hopeful that maybe he wouldn't answer what I hadn't meant to ask.

Too bad the silence didn't last. He untied his boots slowly, focused all his attention on the laces, and avoided looking at me. "Yes."

It didn't matter, is what I told myself. It had taken me by surprise, that's all. My heart beat low in my chest, and an icy warmth spread from it to my arms and exited with tiny pin pricks through my fingertips. Why did it hurt so much to know that? He dated her for several months. Of course, he kissed her, but it hurt to hear all the same.

He removed his boots and set them on the floor. "He's not exactly the best actor. I encouraged him to kiss her."

"Why would you do that?"

"I made him if you want to know the truth. Aw, honey, if you'd been there, your face wouldn't look like that right now. The way he describes it, it was pretty funny, really. He was losing her, and we had to ensure he stayed in that relationship to help keep the pressure off the connection to you. You know, something to distract or confuse Cronus. So, I made him kiss her. His lips wouldn't stop twitching. It was as if his lips tried to fly off his face! I'm telling you, the way he tells it, it was very funny."

"I guess it makes sense. No one understood why she stayed with him."

"Well, she had no choice."

I stared at him in disbelief.

"Whoops." His eyes rolled up toward the ceiling. "There I go again."

"What are you talking about?"

He riddled across the room and grabbed a book off my bookshelf. "So, what's this one about?"

"Charlie."

"Charlie, huh? Must be a romance."

"Charlie!"

"He's going to kill me."

"What do you mean, she had no choice?"

"You'll be down one demon friend tomorrow."

I stood and pulled myself up to my full five-and-a-half feet, but it didn't have quite the desired effect.

"Fine, but my death will be on your head. You can't say you weren't warned. Relax, I'll talk. Not just your shoulders. Go on. Let all the tension out." He crossed the room and loomed over me, his hands on either side of my face, clumsily massaging my cheeks toward my ears. "Relax your face. Come on now. There you go. That's my girl."

He tweaked my nose, sat on the bed, and patted the spot beside him. "Okay, here goes nothing. Demons are predators. You know that. They read human emotions and find victims where they may, blah, blah, blah, so on and so forth. When they're interested in a victim, they lure them in, like a spider, to her web. They use feelings to do it. Demons aren't all the big bad Cronus-type. They're everywhere, all the time. You know, that voice that nags inside your head? The one that tells you you've left the oven on when you're certain you didn't or makes you believe you're the worst singer ever."

That seemed oddly specific.

"The quickest and easiest emotion to reel a victim in is lust. A human will do almost anything when lust is the driving force. Makes a man leave his wife, spend money he doesn't have, or follow a woman off a cliff if he feels that particular way about her. Don't confuse it with love. They aren't the same thing, though they're closely related. Romance doesn't exist without a little lust." He paused and cocked an ear to his shoulder, like studying me. "Except for you. It's that purity of color you have."

He shook his head to clear it. "No, no, never mind that. Romance does not exist without lust, but lust can exist without love. Think about the attraction one feels for someone they've never met. That's not love, right? Well, a demon possesses all the qualities that flip on the lust switch in humans. We have an exterior that's pleasing to the eye, an arousing aroma, and we're able to exude charm, you might say. Jansen used that talent on Clara."

That was a horrifying bit of news.

"It's not like he had to try very hard," Charlie said. "I'm not sure he really tried at all, honestly. She was an easy target, and if you think about it, you knew that. You saw the way she looked at him, flirted with him, pursued him. When she was nearby, she felt such strong feelings she'd follow him to the ends of the earth. Then, when they weren't close, those feelings waned, which is why you'd occasionally hear from others that she wasn't happy and wanted to leave him."

"So when people said she wanted to leave him, but couldn't…"

"She meant that literally, yeah. Because he only had to turn on his charm talent, and that powerful lust response reignited. He became, essentially, her drug."

When he tapped his fingers together between his knees, I knew something rolled around in his brain, trying to work its way out. He pinched the bridge of his nose. "She's not so bad, not really. That exterior of hers? Don't believe it."

"You said he used that talent on her. It isn't a talent if it's just who he is. How did he turn it on?"

"It's another weapon in our arsenal. People are naturally attracted to us, but we can crank it up when we want to. Make ourselves literally irresistible."

"And he used that on Clara?"

He was silent for a tick too long. "Once," he breathed. "She'd had it and was going to leave him. It was a mistake."

Little puzzle pieces snapped into place in my brain. A red aura must be lust. No wonder all the girls ogled Jansen, but could that also mean my feelings for him weren't real? Was I merely responding to some stupid demonic charm?

"Oh boy." He tapped his index fingers together. "What mess are the wheels in your head cranking out?"

"I've felt so silly these past few months."

"Silly? Angry, frustrated, confused… These I get, but silly?"

"It bothers me when the other girls are such idiots around him."

"Sure, sure. It bothers him, too. Who wants that?"

"But listen. Does he use charms on me?"

"Well, yeah. Wait, what on earth! What is the matter with you? He's a guy, Ellie. Of course, he uses his charms on you! Oh." His meaning dawned on him. "Yeah, no. That's another thing that makes you so damn cool. Like I said, we kind of radiate lust around as if it's pixie dust or something. So, everywhere we go—and I mean *everywhere* we go—the women fall all over us."

"Poor you."

"Yes, poor me! You have no idea! It's not a compliment. It's how Jansen feels about his voice. He *hates* compliments, right? Me? I can handle an accolade or two, but Jansen? He really hates it because he isn't trying. His voice is just that alluring to humans. It's the same with lust. Because we so freely send it out there into the universe, true desire never comes back our way. Those girls who fall at his feet? That's not love. But you? All he has to do is look at you, and your colors reflect back nothing but pure adoration. You are genuinely attracted to him, with all of his flaws, his ill temper, his brooding ways, his—"

"Yeah, yeah, I get it."

"His fancy speeches, his need to be right—"

"I get it."

"His—" He caught the pillow I was about to lob at him before it left my hand. "You're the only girl either of us has seen with pure sapphire-like energy. He finds it exceptionally attractive."

"I love *you*, too, ya know."

Charlie blushed crimson, which spread from his cheeks to his neck. "You sweet, sweet girl. I know you do. I see it. There are different shades of blue." He winked. "You save a special shade for me."

"So, where does that leave us now?"

He inhaled. "I'm not sure anything has changed. Instead of severing the bond between you, it has strengthened. I think if he'd kissed you, Cronus would've been there instantly. It's rather surprising he wasn't. It's the change he expected to see in you all along. That, my dear, is why I worry about the vision… At least until we can figure out what it means."

"What if he's here now?"

He bit his lip and looked away. "That's become a problem. I want to say, impossible. That we'd know. There's something about you we can't quite put our finger on. Jansen's arranged to go out of town soon to see if he can track anything down about why you distort our ability to sense other demons."

"Won't that be dangerous for him."

He waved me off as he moved himself to my recliner. "You worry too much."

CHAPTER TWENTY-THREE

With a soggy pencil eraser between my teeth, I opened my math book. Between the hours spent communing with demons and all the class periods where Charlie overran my brain, I'd turned in more than a few poorly written reports and homework assignments lately. Books and papers lay spread across our kitchen bar, but studying wasn't happening. Every time I tried to write a coherent sentence for an English report, I wrote what was in my mind. No one needed to know demons visited me at night. Or that they spoke all languages, had photographic memories, and really nobody should ever know Jansen liked it when my aura shone crystalline.

After making a pan of brownies, I switched to math because at least math maintained order. Made it less likely the word "demon" ended up scrawled on the paper where I'd meant to write "seven."

Despite protests laid on deaf ears, Charlie acted as my designated babysitter. He'd gone upstairs with Tyler, to work on homework, but I suspected they either played on the computer or talked about Amelia. Probably both, but I doubted much studying happened because noises echoed overhead. Besides, Charlie couldn't pull out his assignments in front of Tyler. How would Charlie explain his French coursework?

Jansen was out of the country, part of his plan with

Charlie to sever our tie. It didn't work, but I wasn't about to tell them that. My body ached with him so far away. Sometimes, I tried picturing him in a different part of the world, and sometimes, as I hit on a particular region, the ache would lessen, and I'd wondered if that meant I'd found him, in a way.

Always so secretive, he and Charlie wouldn't say much, but Jansen was off somewhere to dig up information about Cronus. Charlie stayed behind to chaperone, though he'd used the word "guard." Any fussing from me fell on deaf ears, but while he never complained, Charlie clearly felt he missed out on the action. Plus, I didn't like that Jansen left without any help if he ran into trouble.

No, I needed to stop thinking about that, and settle into my homework. Problem one: Where was it on this page? Come on, focus.

From the little I had learned about demons outside of the myths I'd been fed since childhood, Jansen and Charlie were young ones. I wasn't confident they knew what they were doing. So much of all they'd shared centered on on suspicions and theories. They hadn't exactly been raised as Satan's minions, but as loving and gentle boys. Also, Charlie kept assuring me they had superhuman strength, and reminded me of all the times he had tossed me in the pool. He made sure I knew he could throw me farther if he wanted to.

Still, he proved the stronger of the two and had more life experience, being nearly three years older. I didn't wish Charlie ill, but I wished he'd been the one to go.

The oven timer buzzed, which startled me. Had it been fifty minutes already? I pulled the brownies out and inhaled the homey scent of baked chocolate. Now, maybe I could focus on homework, so I set the pan on a soft kitchen towel at the edge of the bar and sat down to my task.

I'd just dug into my work when a hand fell on my shoulder, and I jumped out of my skin.

Amelia hooked her thumbs through her overalls and snickered. "Looks like you're not getting much done."

Indeed. I'd have said she was perceptive, but her ball cap could have figured that out. I slumped over my paper and groaned. "I didn't realize you were even here. This is awful. I can't seem to concentrate today."

She sat beside me and spread her books on the bar. "You were in another world when I came in earlier. It's no wonder you didn't notice. I went up to visit Tyler, but Charlie's here, and they're not exactly studying. Seemed like maybe you're at least trying. Mind if I join you?"

"Not at all."

Maybe Amelia's presence would inspire me to get through some of this. I'd done little more than scrawl the first digit of problem one on my paper, and as I looked closer, it wasn't even problem one. What had I written? Some sort of symbol? Frustrated, I turned my pencil over to scrub at the paper.

"Mind if I have a brownie?" She eyed the untouched pan.

"Yeah, sure." I brushed away the eraser bits. "They're still hot. I think all the butter knives are dirty. Just grab a sharp one from the corner over there."

"Do you want one?"

After a sip of ice water, I gurgled out the word, "Sure."

She rummaged around for the knife. "What are you thinking about?"

"Nothing."

"That's not a very kind thing to call Jansen." When I looked up, taken aback, she had a twinkle in her eye and a knowing smile. "Mm-hmm, I thought so."

Surely, her next statement would be the adolescent "do-you-like-him" question. I dreaded that one. Do I like him? No, my soul belongs to him. Thankfully, she didn't ask.

Instead, she disarmed me. "You feel electricity with him, don't you?"

"Yes," I whispered.

She grabbed two plates from overhead. "He does, too."

"Yes." Holy crap, this girl had insight. Could I trust her? I hoped so, because if she kept going, I might blurt out everything.

She struggled to lift out a brownie using the knife.

"There's a spatula to your left," I said.

"Oh, that's okay. This works fine."

She used the knife to deliver one brownie and then the other to their plates, both brownies landing with a distinct *clink*. Guess I left them in too long.

Knife still in her grip, she set a plate before me and slid the other in front of her barstool. "You two aren't willing to cross that line, huh?"

"Is it that obvious?"

She licked the thumb that wrapped around the knife and placed it between us. "No, not to others, but Ellie"—she squeezed my hand—"your aura sparkles." She wrinkled her nose, and I was pretty sure she'd just shared an enormous secret. "Oh, don't look at me like that. I thought you'd understand."

I swallowed to close my gaping mouth. "I do, only… I didn't know you could see auras."

Her nose wrinkled again. "Well, now you do."

"Everyone's?"

She ate a bite of her brownie and nodded. "Don't you?"

No. How to form the words? "Only one."

"Oh, wow. Now, that's something special. You're that in tune to him."

"It's complicated."

"It's not Andrew complicating things, is it?"

"No. What makes you ask?"

"Charlie, actually. He wants me to encourage you to spend more time with him, and I think he'd like you to go on a date."

That figured. Charlie would do almost anything to break the connection, but I'd rather be alone than with anyone else.

"Andrew's a nice guy," I said, "but I'm not interested in dating him."

"He's been acting a bit off. Have you noticed?"

"Just that he seems to seek me out at every turn. Why? What are you noticing?"

"I don't know. He's edgier, somehow. Withdrawn. Grouchy, maybe. He used to wave at me between classes or flag me down to ask if I had any notes to pass to Tyler. Lately, though, he's kind of stiff and cold. Yesterday, I tried to give him a book of piano exercises he'd shown interest in a while ago. He acted as if he had no idea what I was talking about. Wouldn't even take it. Just walked away."

That didn't seem like him. Was it possible I had hurt him that much when I turned down his offer to go flying? I'd practically promised I would when he was ready. Now that he was…

At a strange crunching sound, I looked up to see Amelia making a funny face.

She reached for a napkin and spit into it. "Eggshell surprise?"

"You can taste them? I didn't think anyone would notice."

That made her snicker a little, and she placed the wadded-up napkin on her plate. "Next time try dragon eggs. They're rare, but their shells are softer and known to possess magical energy." Before I could respond to whatever that was, she waved her hand in the air, a gesture to say, *"But enough of that."* "Anyway, I told you I hoped to accomplish some work, and I meant it."

Amelia wasn't a big talker, especially when she dug into her work. She worked hard for good grades, as unfocused as she so often was, and succeeded despite herself. Her quiet efforts inspired me to do the same.

Halfway through my second page of problems, her mood shifted. At first, I just noticed that she rubbed her temples more frequently.

"Do you need some Tylenol?" I asked.

She shook her head and picked up a pencil, then tapped it on her paper.

With nothing helpful to do, I tried returning to my work, but could feel her gaze. A predator on its prey. Her pupils seemed too big, as though she saw right through me. Clearly, she was getting sick.

"Amelia, are you okay?"

"I'm fine." She dragged her stare from me to her paper, but I was pretty sure she looked at nothing. More like through everything. She had a smooth, glassy look in her eyes; vacant and far away, as if hypnotized.

Her palm twitched on the table. Sometimes it jerked, often fluttering. Enough to snag my attention. She flinched, almost as if to grab something, but pulled back and rubbed one hand with the other tightly. As if to restrain it. Then she did it again.

And again.

With a rumbling growl, she pushed herself away from the bar and hopped a few times. Shook out her arms. Cracked her neck. Finally, she returned to her seat.

I peered over her notebook to see what caused all this nervous energy, but her assignment just involved writing out definitions.

Tap, tap, tap, her pencil bounced on her paper. Like she couldn't sit still.

Her hand, the one closest to me, curled in a tight ball. Tendons popped, looking like raised vines beneath the skin.

She shook with the intensity of that fist, and her veins throbbed as if she tried to release the hold. As though bound by invisible chains, sweat beaded down the taut wrist. Her fingers splayed and curled in spasms.

Unnatural. That's what it was. Her movements, the tension, the way she seemed to fight herself.

It was on the tip of my tongue to call for Charlie, but I couldn't. Couldn't form the word. Couldn't suck enough air to voice it.

Her head whipped back, and she grabbed the knife. Tossed it from left to right. She tore from her seat and glared, the weapon poised to stab.

I froze. Limbs, muscles, blood, breath. All of me, frozen.

Wild hair framed her blanched face. The pulse of her neck throbbed as if with a living, breathing creature. It pulsated and pumped down her throat, engorged from her blood as it feasted off her fears.

And her eyes. So strange. Though usually rich, dark-chocolate brown, they were now entirely white. Her lips pulled back in a menacing grimace, baring prominent teeth.

The four pendant lights in the kitchen hummed. They thrummed and prickled inside my ear with an incessant buzz. It droned on and on, buzzing and humming, louder and louder…

…and louder.

It grew brighter.

At first, it glowed a dull amber, but transitioned to white. A blinding, bleached color so bright I thought it would burst, but instead, it grew. Its current amped up and spread from light to light.

Though impossible, without batteries or power, lamps grew brighter until they should all explode. They buzzed and hummed and dazzled with so much light that they challenged the sun.

This was a nightmare. The kind that paralyzes. The ones where you see and feel and hear but cannot move. The nightmares where you want to scream. Can feel yourself shriek, can taste it, hear it even. It builds in the depths of you and echoes through your brain. But you can't release it.

Amelia stood in one spot and rocked from side to side.

Footsteps sounded from behind, but I didn't dare turn around. Footsteps that clacked and clomped alternately. *Clack-clomp, clack-clomp.* Footsteps that hobbled in place, never closer, never farther.

Still, she rocked, and her pace matched the invisible feet. She rocked and rocked. Right foot, left foot. She sneered, and she rocked.

Always the lights buzzed, progressively brighter. Continuously louder.

Something in the walls—a creature, a monster?—sounded in the kitchen.

Clink…wheeze.

Once. Twice. Three times. What was it?

It breathed. It burrowed, and it dug through the wall. Yet I had no voice.

Amelia tossed the knife from right to left. Looked up into

her brain. Up toward the madness of her mind, where she saw things I couldn't see. Where she heeded orders from some other realm. Only the whites of her eyes were visible, where tiny tendrils of blood-red vessels crept around.

The weapon shook, poised with menace. It lifted…rose above her head. Her hand clutched. It gripped the handle and her thumb flexed over white, corpse-like fingers.

In bursts of vapor, as if we were outside, her breathing labored.

It *was* cold. Unnaturally so. The kind that makes your breath visible. The kind that fogs the windows and turns to ice. The kind that spreads and crackles and frosts the skin, freezes the eyes—the tiny hairs in the nose. So frigid that icicles formed in my blood. In my bones.

Amelia took a step forward. Just one.

Like she gave me that moment to scream. She paused. Wavered. I knew I should scream. Opened my mouth to do it, but something gagged me. What was it? Something gripped my throat, clenched it tight. Kept me without a voice —trapped in a nightmare.

She took another step forward, the monster in the wall matching her stride. Though she obviously resisted, she moved toward me, lifting each foot as if they were lead. As if she fought something.

That something refused to lose.

In one mighty charge, she lunged with the knife as every picture on the wall popped off one by one. *Pop, pop, pop!*

I flung myself to the side, away from her, to escape the weapon. Rammed my hip into the bar and tumbled over the stools, crashing to the ground, tangled in its legs.

But Amelia? She recovered with an unnatural force not her own. She attacked again and lunged, thrusting the tip within inches of my chest.

I grabbed her arm, and though she had other-worldly might, tried to hold her off. If only I could. My strength couldn't last.

She inched the blade closer and closer. If I let go, if my muscles gave out, it would plunge into my heart. A kill stab.

Lower and lower.

I couldn't…

hold her off.

The point punctured my skin. My heart banged in my ears and for a moment, everything vanished. But only for a moment. She sank the blade between my breasts, slipping through ligaments and muscle. My strength failed and Amelia—not Amelia, a demon—slashed a gash across my collarbone.

She jerked her hand above her head and thrust it into my chest.

My blood spilled. It sprayed her crisp white shirt. Splattered crimson drops onto her neckline, her shoulder, her overalls. Beneath her lashes, a glob of red formed a tear and the taste of iron coated my tongue.

Heavy footsteps pounded the stairs. *Clomp! Clomp!* They thundered through the room, so loud the vibration coursed through my body.

The humming, buzzing, too-white lights burst with glass that exploded and rained down.

Amelia's hand raised again, poised and ready for another stab, even as she resisted. But the monster she battled was herself.

Charlie leapt over the banister, landing on his feet and hands. In one swift movement, he pounced on Amelia. Encircled her in his arms, where she fought him. Where she twisted and turned. She elbowed him in the gut with such unnatural strength that he doubled over, briefly stunned. But he never let go of the knife.

Her screams became shrieks, her lips parted, her exposed throat writhed with that throbbing, pulsating monster inside. She blinked, and where the eyes had been only white, now they were black. Black like Charlie's. Black like Jansen's. The eyes of a demon.

And she focused them on Charlie.

Unseen talons etched jagged lines across the walls with shrill shrieks—fork tines on a dinner plate. Down and over, they tore at the wall.

Tyler gaped at the growing claw marks, then at Amelia. At me. Around and around he stared before kneeling. Afraid to touch me. Terrified not to.

Blood pooled around me as it spilled from my chest. As it flowed from my shoulder, the warmth saturated my clothes.

Charlie threw his cell phone. Though it hit Tyler in the jaw, he didn't even flinch.

"Tyler, call Jansen now!"

He squatted to pick up the phone and stared with unseeing eyes. "Call Jansen, call Jansen." Over and over, he repeated the mantra.

Charlie held Amelia at his front. One hand gripped the back of her neck while the other struggled to control the knife.

Within her, the demon fought. Her fingers trembled, her knuckles clenched so tight I thought they might tear, as she readied the blade to plunge into him.

He held her off with an effort that made his biceps strain against the supernatural force. Finally, he wrenched the weapon from her and launched it across the room, where it clattered along the linoleum floor. His free hand raised above her throat and chest, where he focused his intense stare. Eyes narrowed, brow furrowed, heat radiated from him to her. With flexed fingers, Charlie appeared as though he gripped something. As if he pulled the demon out of her, ripping him and torturing him.

"Damn you!" he bellowed.

Amelia's tormented frame twitched. She writhed and convulsed. Mouth open wide, her head snapped back. Her tongue flicked in and out. Serpent-like, it licked at his cheek.

Gruff male screams erupted from her, bellows from chasms within. Shrieks of the damned, from those who rotted in Hell's fires, resounded from somewhere inside her. Back and forth, her neck turned. It whipped as she edged away from the pain Charlie inflicted, unable to escape it. From her mouth spoke an unknown language. "Nim eeb lash losehr!"

Charlie growled right back. "Dimitte eam. Redire ad

inferos!" The words bent her backward at the waist, so he moved his hand to her spine. Supported her weight as her eyes rolled up into her brain. "Monster! Let her go and return to hell!"

Tyler held the phone at his ear. "Call Jansen, call Jansen."

A black shroud surrounded her and rose from her body as dense as smoke, but black—blacker than black. Like if all light extinguished, We'd still see the black. It hovered around her, a horrible halo of darkness.

Charlie's glare intensified, his eyes as dark as the smoke. Impassioned with the fury of a demon. His hand shook from his power, his fingers contorted. They bent at every knuckle as he strained to pull the demon out of her. Veins bulged against the skin, taut ropes of blue algae, thick and sinuous.

He concentrated over her until the screaming grew and filled the room with a shriek so intense glass shelves shattered. Books, teacups, and picture frames crashed to the ground.

Higher, the voice rang, so high we couldn't hear it except as an echo in the tender center of the ear.

At last, Tyler's efforts prevailed, and Jansen appeared from nowhere. Ready for battle, he looked from me to Amelia and back.

"I've got this!" Charlie roared. He gathered his voice from the deepest recesses of his chest. "Go to her!"

The black smoke billowed from Amelia to engulf Charlie and her. He belted the roar of a demon. Expelled the last of all his strength, then manipulated the substance into a ball over her mouth, his palm facing it. Without touching it, he launched it. The smoke thrust forward an escaped through the solid wall of the house.

I watched as that beast of a man with godlike power collapsed to his knees, exhausted. His chest rose and fell in labored, raspy breaths, bobbing Amelia's head on each quick intake of air.

With a confident stab, Jansen pressed his finger into my neck. "Breathe, Ellie," he said.

My body registered nothing. How was it possible to feel

nothing?

He commanded me to breathe, which brought on panicked gasps as I jolted back to life from the shocked state of apathy that had allowed me to witness all that. Now, with him there, holding me, I felt the sting and the pool of blood that my labored breathing made worse.

"I've got you." He inserted his finger harder, farther in, like he tried to block an artery.

Warm healing traveled from my neck into my veins to cover pain receptors with its magic until I felt nothing again, and he could work on my injuries.

"It's not so bad," he said. "Deep but concentrated. It shouldn't take long to fuse the wounds. You've lost so much blood, though. I don't know how you're still awake."

His lips attempted a shallow smile. The false kind. The kind that said, *"This is bad, very, very bad, but I'm going to make you think everything's fine."*

Amelia lie limp in Charlie's arms. As he recovered himself, he pulled her into his him and embraced her, nestling his nose in her hair. With a pained expression, he supported her head, and his chest and shoulders shook.

"Is she okay?" Jansen had a slight edge to his voice.

Charlie sniffed and wiped a tear away on his shoulder. "She'll be okay. She's unconscious, but breathing."

"And you?"

To that, Charlie snorted. "Hardest damn thing I've ever done, but yeah."

Carefully, he laid her on the sofa, her eyes shut, mouth hinged open. He closed it gently with a finger beneath her chin, then held her wrist, assuring himself of a pulse. She mirrored a corpse laid out on the couch, the late morning sun highlighting the blond streaks of her auburn tresses. The deathly effect was complete when he placed her hand over her chest. He smoothed her hair behind her ears, like arranging her in a coffin.

As if he didn't want us to see, he swiped at his eyes before joining us. "How's Ellie?"

"Alive. What the hell happened? Where were you?"

"I don't know. I swear, I don't know."

My attention flickered toward the soft moans by the stairs. Tyler lay curled up in the fetal position a few feet away, the phone at his ear as he muttered to call Jansen.

I moved to point at him but found I couldn't.

"Lie still." Jansen placed his middle finger on my hairline.

I intended to block him, not wanting him to heal my mind, keeping me in a fog, and I would have, too. If only I could raise my arm one inch off the ground.

"That's not what I was doing." But he gave a soft smile before he completed the endearing gesture without the healing touch. He lingered long over my lips. "I thought there for a moment I might never get to do this again. I've almost healed you. How do you feel?"

"Fine." Ugh. My mouth was so parched.

"Liar." Yet he smiled. "There, you're finished. No, don't get up. I can't replace your blood. You'll be weak for a while. Charlie, are you strong enough? Can you get her some orange juice?"

Charlie disappeared, and I heard him rummaging around in the kitchen on the other side of the bar. When he riddled back, he handed a washcloth to Jansen and knelt beside me with a glass of water in hand. "They're out of juice."

The sneer Jansen returned said there were other methods of getting juice if he thought about it for more than half a second.

It made Charlie flush, a rose color that so rarely touched his cheeks. "Fully capable demon. Right. I'll be back."

After Jansen wiped away some of the blood, he easily pulled me into him as if I was a child. He rested my head on the expanse of his chest, tucking my arms in, as I was too weak to move them myself.

In less than a minute's time, Charlie returned with a carton of juice. He picked up my glass, still topped with water, shrugged, and tossed the contents straight onto the floor. Mystified, Jansen stared at him. Blankly.

Not to be deterred, Charlie shrugged. "What? There's already blood everywhere. Does it matter?"

He filled the cup so quickly that he spilled some on my shirt and dabbed at my breast with his palm. Just used his hand as a napkin. As if I were male. This resulted in a slapping tussle between the brothers.

"Sorry!" Charlie barked, ending it. "I don't know what's wrong with me."

"You're a bungling buffoon. Get yourself together!"

Charlie patted my shoulder awkwardly. "Sorry, but dang!" He sank backward and cradled his head in his hands. "That flat wore me out. Mia was possessed. I had to torture him out of her, and he didn't go easily. My God, I only hope she didn't feel it. I didn't know—" His voice broke. "Didn't know what to do."

"You did what you had to," Jansen said. "He would have killed her. You know that."

Charlie brought the cup to my lips, and I sipped the sweet liquid.

"Thank you." It came out with little energy. "Maybe you should drink some."

He smiled and refilled the cup. "Couldn't hurt." I had the sense he humored me, but he downed the eight ounces in two gulps.

Once he'd refilled it, he set the juice beside me and retreated toward Amelia. He picked her up with unusual care and cradled her in one arm, surprising after what she'd done.

When he got to Tyler, he did the same, minus the tenderness, and Tyler was not quite unconscious. As Charlie walked away, he projected, *"Stop calling Jansen. Sleep now and dream heroic dreams."*

"Don't mind him," Jansen said. "You scared him, and that's saying something. That and I've never seen him this exhausted."

When Charlie returned, Jansen asked if he thought he could transfer me upstairs. Without hesitation, he lifted me from Jansen's arms. Very un-Charlie-like.

"No riddling," Jansen said. "She's queasy enough."

"Didn't plan to." Charlie sauntered toward the stairs, then ascended with such an easy gait, it felt as though he walked up a ramp.

I nestled my head into his shoulder. "I'm making your shirt a mess."

"Like I care, girlie." He deposited me in my bed and sat sideways in the ugly yellow recliner, his legs draped over the armrests.

A few minutes later, Jansen joined us, dressed in clean clothes. "When will your parents be home?"

"They went to some college reunion thing for my dad at a park in Cincinnati. It depends, but probably after eight o'clock tonight."

"Good. Charlie, we can handle a lot of the glass down there and clean up the blood, but we'll need to get Damon to help with the scratches on the wall."

"I can help, too." That earned rumbles of light-hearted disbelief from my two demonic friends.

"Not you," Jansen said. "Your job is to make fresh blood. We'll take care of the spilled variety." He pulled the caramel throw over me and tucked it around my body, cocooning me in its warmth. "Charlie, what happened?"

Caught off guard, he blinked hard. "I swear I don't know. Tyler and I were upstairs with his music too loud when we heard a crash. Thought Ellie had dropped something. I clued in before Tyler did and got there as soon as I knew what happened."

Jansen turned the wand on the blinds, blocking the late morning sun. "Ellie, when did you realize she was possessed? What happened?"

I told them it was like that time Clara had pulled a cockroach from my ear, the first day Charlie had projected to me in class. After she'd been so mad at Jansen for breaking up with her. Gosh, I'd pretty much forgotten about it and hadn't said anything to either of them. Typically, Jansen was mad that I didn't mention it sooner. I could tell by the throbbing vein in his neck, though he didn't say a word. Then, his mood shifted to something close to fear.

"What is it?" I asked.

"It's nothing." He plopped beside me on the bed and

threw an arm around me, not taking his eyes off Charlie.

"Right." How naïve did they think I was? "And here I thought demons were excellent liars."

Jansen pinched the bridge of his nose as if it was a balloon, and all the air tried to escape. If he squeezed hard enough, maybe the frustration wouldn't seep out.

"We need to know. You went there so we would."

Charlie kicked one boot off. The second cartwheeled across the floor when he lost control of it. "She has a right, Jansen."

"Fine." The way his fingers dug into my upper arms, I knew it was anything but.

"There's something about you that allows demons to sneak up on us when you're around. We can't distinguish the difference between you and other demons."

"Jansen, when you helped Ellie with Tim, could you sense Cronus then?"

Jansen's face filled with anguish. "No. She distorts the signal with a hostile energy." He looked at Charlie then. "I wasn't able to find a way around that."

"Wait, are you saying I have demonic energy?" I asked.

"Not demonic, no. It's difficult to explain. The trouble is, Charlie and I can't find any other instance of it ever happening before with a human. Seems the idea is appealing to Cronus. He's figuring out how you work, and developing a way in."

"I had a thought." Charlie inspected his socked toes, rolling his ankles inward, then out. "It's pretty risky."

We both looked at him, waiting for him to continue. The way he paused made it seem he envisioned a plan we couldn't see.

"We're guessing Ellie is demonically charged, right? We can't actually see it. Can't see her soul the way we can that of a demon's."

"Right… As it should be," Jansen said.

"But what if we could? What if *you* could?"

"How would I see her soul?"

"You could…possess her."

"Yeah, right… Wait… You're serious. You're serious? Charlie, listen to yourself!"

"You can be gentle. You could distract her with one of your memories. While you're in there, maybe have a look around."

"No. Absolutely not! That's out of the question."

As far as I was concerned, I'd discovered my best friend was a super-powered demon who could heal me, and a powerful demon desired me to bring forth some demonic creature. What was a little demonic possession?

"Do it," I said.

CHAPTER TWENTY-FOUR

The heater kicked on in my bedroom, fluttering the curtains like ghostly gowns, and I jolted. The room had gone quiet, both brothers intent on me.

I swept my hair behind my shoulders and nestled down low on the pillow. "Do it. Possess me."

"It won't hurt," Charlie said.

Jansen threw my stuffed hippo at him. "You don't know that!"

"Nah, it won't hurt."

Jansen riddled and reappeared in the corner of the room, hidden, in part, by a fake tree. After riddling again, he stood by the closet.

"He does this when he's angry." Charlie turned over his shoulder to wink at me. "He'll be fine in a minute."

Jansen riddled around the bedroom, from the cushioned window seat, cluttered with pillows and animals, to the faux-wood door, cracked on the outside where Tyler rammed into it for no other reason than to "see if he could break it down."

"Show her the day you two met." Charlie headed toward the hallway, where Jansen had been seconds before, tripping over his own boot along the way. "That was a great memory."

"I can't..." He sat on the arm of the recliner Charlie had just vacated. "...believe..." He stood at the foot of the bed. "...you want..." He stood—actually stood—on my desk. Finally, he riddled to hover over me. He braced himself on his forearms and hovered so close that his nose brushed mine. "How can you want me to do this?"

I laid flat on my back and waited. My heart raced but didn't rise into my throat like fear usually caused. I should be scared. Should be terrified. Why wasn't I? Instead, I was paralyzed by the heat between his body and mine. Lost entirely in our shared breaths, willing my hips not to lift to meet his.

"I don't have to do this." His sweet breath fell over my face. I breathed him in, and it felt as if he was already inside me, tickling my lungs.

"I want you to," I whispered back.

"Good. Because your soul is too alluring to resist." He closed his eyes and shivered, his voice hushed. When he opened them again, he looked deep into mine. "I don't think I can stop."

His human form quivered before he transitioned into a soft glowing light, the colors of twilight and the tranquil sea. Had I blinked, I might not have seen him at all, but with my gaze locked on him, I saw his soul.

Anticipation churned. I knew what he was about to do but had no idea what it would feel like. Would it hurt? Would I remember?

The wait was brief. His spirit covered mine, and swaddled me in a tingling mist of wonder and starlight, of love and of him. I felt him move through my body. Felt him rest himself in my core, connecting us in a way not humanly possible. With Jansen inside me, I felt a missing part of myself become restored.

I was vaguely aware of Charlie's hand on my shoulder or that he spoke to me. But I couldn't spare him any attention. My focus was on Jansen's spirit within me.

A mental movie started; a memory I had lived. Through his eyes, I saw a room decorated in pastel shades of the sea, and it smelled of powder and the soft scent of baby shampoo.

I watched as my mom entered the nursery, holding me as an infant, looking younger than I'd ever seen her. There, she laid me in Jansen's crib, the two of us side by side.

With a mother's care, Miss Kate bent over us and covered me with a hand-knitted lace blanket. Her necklace dangled over my face, catching my eye. Through his eyes, I watched myself follow it as it swayed on her neck, back and forth, catching the light so that it winked like a cat's eye.

The memory ended, and I sensed him inside of me again. He lifted out gently, but it felt as though a part of me left with him.

Empty of his spirit, I shuddered, and the sadness passed. I thought I should be scared, but that wasn't possible. Not with all the energy and pure sensation that barreled up and down my spine. Those rich, black eyes of his focused on me. His brow knitted together and his beautiful, soft lips formed an "O." A halo of colors surrounded his face, and it made my breath quiver as I realized what it was. With him so close, one quick intake of air whisked his scent through me, inciting new tremors.

"Ellie, what have I done?" His words were a melodic baritone, his eyes wide.

I managed a giggle, but couldn't speak. Gradually, the convulsions muted to a pulsing wave, and I reached a hand toward his face. I tried to touch his aura, but he was no more than translucent light. Yet, he shivered as though he felt me. When I brushed my hand from his forehead to his chin, I hoped he understood his own gesture.

Perhaps he did, as he loosed a heavy breath, the tiniest of chortles. "You're fine, aren't you?"

I tried to say, "Uh-huh," but it came out all bumpy.

While waiting for me to settle down, he rocked me until a few shivers tickled the length of my spine. His colorful lights faded as the delicious tremors subsided, and I couldn't see it anymore.

"Wow."

Jansen kissed the crown of my head. "I'll say."

"I saw your colors."

"You? Saw mine?"

"Your aura."

A smile played at the corner of his lips as he understood. He brushed my face with his fingertips. "No wonder I felt your touch around me. Like a whisper."

Then I was free from his effects and sat cross-legged beside him.

He gave my shoulders a squeeze. "Are you okay now?"

"I was never *not* okay. That was…intense."

Charlie winked at me, amusement evident in his smile, and he stroked his chin. "Jansen, did you see anything?"

"You could say that. She has luminary points that mirror mine."

Charlie's head ticked back, and Jansen scrubbed both his eyes.

Surely there was more to that. Between Charlie's what-the-hell-are-you-talking-about expression and the fact Jansen's cheeks flushed… "What does that mean?"

"Oh, just that—" but Charlie stopped at Jansen's persistent head shakes.

Jansen grimaced. "It's not a big deal—"

"I beg to differ." Charlie had picked up a pair of my ear buds and spun them around his fingers first one way, then the other, obviously amused.

"All she needs to know right now is that it isn't a big deal. It has nothing to do with the present situation at all."

"You're wrong. Don't you get it? *That's* precisely what Cronus is looking for. Humans don't have luminary points."

"Are you saying I'm a demon?"

"No," the brothers said together emphatically.

"Then what are luminary points?"

Jansen pressed his lips with his fingertips, and I got the distinct impression he chose his words carefully. "You have to understand, we only have a bunch of theories. We haven't exactly had a mentor through any of this. Luminary points are outlets of light located on our souls. Usually, a demon's are black. Charlie's are."

"And yours?"

"No, not mine. Mine are white. We don't exactly know what they're for."

Charlie snorted. "Ha. Maybe you don't."

While Jansen growled low, he otherwise ignored his brother. "Our luminary points have reversed themselves, somehow."

"Luminary points can be magnetic." Charlie set the earbuds back on my desk and turned to face me. "When you two are apart, it acts as a knife, slicing through your souls, almost literally."

Then that's what caused the pain Charlie told me about. That blanket wrapped around my bones? It was my soul.

"I think you activated the magnets that day in the pool." Jansen's nose rested right next to mine.

My heart thrummed a fast and steady cadence.

Charlie stood, hands on his hips. "*This* is exactly what attracts Cronus." He gripped both our shoulders, gently pulling us apart. "Highly magnetized points attract demons. I'm sure he finds them very attractive on you."

Jansen's thumb caressed my arm in long, lazy circles. "We're going to have to be extra vigilant of her now. Her magnetic pull is strong. If this is the change he sought, he won't stop until he has her."

Seated in the recliner again, in Charlie-like fashion, he nudged my knee with his toe. "Ellie, that vision."

I shot him a threatening look, but too late.

"What vision?" Jansen asked.

I shook my head and glared with an intense warning at Charlie. "We have to kill him."

The brothers exchanged a pained expression.

I'd said it as more of a subject change than anything, and their reaction was unexpected. So I narrowed my focus back and forth between them. "What? What aren't you telling me?"

Charlie rubbed his eyes and then focused his gaze on me. "We don't know how to do it, El. Cronus is about a thousand years old, give or take a year. A full demon, not half, like Jansen and me. More of a phantom, and we don't think he can be killed."

"Hit him with a fireball."

Charlie made a sound that said, *"Shows how much you*

know." "That would only make him stagger, and it wears us out."

"Throw him far away. You did that downstairs."

"He would just riddle back."

"But he didn't."

"Because we were both here." Jansen rubbed his temples in exasperation. "Look. He only attacks when you're vulnerable, when one of us isn't around. If he wanted you dead, he could do that easily. We think he wants you somewhere between life and death, though it's not clear why."

Charlie snapped the lid onto his Chapstick with a *click* and stuffed it into his pocket. "We don't see how to get rid of him."

"We'll come up with something." Jansen glared at Charlie. "It isn't anything you need to worry about."

"How do you figure that? A demon wants me, and you can't kill him. He's already projected thoughts on one of my friends and possessed another. What's next?"

Again, they exchanged worried looks.

"He only partially possessed Amelia," Jansen said.

"Oh, well, let me express my great relief!" I sulked into his shirt.

"He partially possessed her the same way I possessed you. You came out unharmed, and so did she. If a demon fully possesses a human, he takes over the body. Two spirits can't exist together for long."

"Jansen, did you find anything useful in your search?" Charlie asked.

Jansen opened his mouth to speak, but after glancing in my direction, closed it again. Then he decided to go ahead. "No. I thought I might have when Tyler called. That was an interesting phone call, by the way."

Charlie nodded. "What did he say?"

"'Call Jansen.' That's it. Just 'Call Jansen' again and again."

Charlie's nose twitched, and he got a tissue from my desk. "I think he was in shock. I didn't have time to help him through it."

"Well, it worked. I got the message. Before that, though,

there was something about angels. I certainly don't know how to contact them. You might imagine I didn't want to bring about any suspicions by asking."

My ears perked up. "Can angels kill Cronus?"

"Love how you just jumped right on board with the whole angels-are-real thing," Charlie said, blowing his nose.

Jansen pulled my hair behind my shoulders and arranged it, sparking goosebumps. "That was the idea, but how many angels have you run into lately?"

The ordeal caught up with me, and I yawned. "He…" It's all I got out before a second yawn took over.

Charlie stretched, arching his back. "We need to let her sleep."

"I don't need—"

Only Charlie interrupted. "Cut us a break. You need rest to recover. See, we're demons. Demons don't typically care much what happens to humans, but we care about you. I figure we've invested our entire allotment of love in you, so you owe it to us to take care of yourself. Think of what it would do to us if anything happened to you."

I turned toward Jansen, but Charlie took my chin and made me face him. "You're going to sleep."

No, not covered in blood, I wasn't. So I peeled the blood-covered blanket away. "I need a shower."

"Are you strong enough?" Jansen asked. "I can get Amelia to help."

"No, I think I'm good. I can manage a shower."

Jansen scowled. "I'm not going anywhere. I'll be right out here if you need me. If I hear anything, and I mean *anything*, I'm riddling in there. Do you understand?"

"Wear a bathing suit." I swung my legs off the bed. "Got it."

As I closed the door, I thought I heard him mutter under his breath, "I didn't say that." It made me smile to know maybe, just maybe, he desired me more than he'd let on.

I glanced back, hoping to catch a twinkle in his eye, but he no longer paid me any attention. He looked off into the distance, tracing a star over his chest.

CHAPTER TWENTY-FIVE

I slept so hard. Could Jansen have put me in a bit of a stupor after my shower? While lathering up, I half-remembered having an epiphany, but I'd forgotten what it was by the time I had crawled into bed. The next thing I knew, the sun streamed through my window, and my head nestled into my pillow. How long had I slept?

Unable to find yesterday's pair, I put on fresh jeans. In fact, all my clothes from yesterday were missing. Probably burned by demons. I chuckled to myself at the thought because it was likely true, hiding all evidence of blood.

While leaning over in search of my sneakers, I remembered what the shower epiphany had been about.

"Where's your mother?" I demanded of the empty air occupied by a soft gray mist. Charlie appeared. "Where is she?" I asked again.

"Ellie, what's the matter? What is it?"

I checked under the bed for my shoes. "I need to talk to her."

"Okay, I can take you over there. How are you?"

Unable to find them, I stood, fists clenched at my side. "Now!"

"All right, all right. Come here."

I turned my back into Charlie's chest and waited for him to crush me to him. When he didn't, I craned my neck as far as it would go to look up at him.

With both hands on his hips, he stared me down. "You gonna tell me what this is about?"

I grabbed his arm and wrapped it around me like a giant seat belt.

"Well, alrighty then," he said, just before I felt the now familiar pull into a new place.

My toes landed on his family room's plush rug, where Jansen glanced up from a file he sat reading. He yanked himself to his feet. "Ellie, how are—"

"Your mom. Where is she?"

"I'm not sure. She—"

"Kate!" I rushed into the kitchen. "Kate! Where is she?"

Charlie and Jansen strode after me. The morning light streaming through the east-facing window illuminated Jansen's face, more angel than demon.

With a smack to Charlie's arm, Jansen gained his attention. "What's the matter?"

I grabbed the kitchen phone, knocking over one of the many little herb pots on the tile counter, and handed it to Jansen. "Call her."

"What's this about?"

"Call her!"

He hesitated, but took the phone and dialed while I tapped my foot and waited, listening to the ticking clock.

Charlie swept the spilled dirt back into its container and set it under the window.

"She doesn't answer," Jansen said. "Maybe if we knew what this was about."

"No. This is between her and me." I poked a finger at Charlie's chest. "You find her."

"We're not good at tracking, Ellie, especially humans."

"You track me. Every second of every day!"

"No, we just already know where you are. We don't know where she went."

Jansen said, "Charlie, riddle around town a bit. See if you can find her." Once Charlie left, Jansen took my hand and led me to the soft, gray upholstered couch. Miss Kate's conservatory of varying-sized plants and potted trees nearly swallowed it. A giant, sun-seeking leaf imposed itself on my ear.

He angled himself to face me. "Now, tell me what this is about."

I unclasped the necklace that hid my birthmark, but before I could answer, Charlie reappeared with his mom, a brown paper grocery bag in her arms.

"Ellie, what is it?" Seeing me sitting on the couch with the necklace wrapped around my fingers, her breath caught in her throat.

"Recognize this?"

Miss Kate bit her lip and handed the bag to Charlie.

"Do you know where it came from?"

Still, she said nothing.

"You should." I threw the pendant, hitting her squarely on the shoulder. "You have one just like it. It even winks like mine." She let it drop to the ground, discarded.

Her hand fluttered to her neck.

Jansen's tone emerged low and rough. "You have one of these? You? Why didn't you tell us?"

"Yes," Miss Kate said, her voice flat. "But let me explain."

"By all means." Jansen snarled and collapsed onto the couch, crossing one leg over his knee.

"You have to understand. This all started before I knew Ellie's family. Before I became a mom. Had I known then…" Tears glistened in the corners of her eyes. "I was young and stupid. Back in high school, I'd discovered that I could talk to ghosts. If I kept myself quiet enough, I could hear their energy. At first, I was terrified. Tried to stop listening, but couldn't. Then, in college, I met a girl who said she was a witch. She took me to a meeting. It was just a bunch of silly girls. Half of them were leftover flower children who tried to connect with nature, harmless enough. The others tried to break into witchcraft. Only none of them knew what they were doing, not really.

"I remember the first séance they held. It was late, near midnight. They'd formed a circle around this field using candles and lit each one."

Her fingers massaged her temples, and her eyes scrunched closed. As if remembering something, she ran to her bedroom.

"She isn't going to riddle out of here, is she?" I asked.

Charlie snorted. "No, she's not…one of us. Jansen, have you ever heard this story?"

Jansen shook his head as Miss Kate entered the room with a photo album in her arms.

"I have a picture in here somewhere," she said. "Yes, here it is, there." She pointed to an old photograph of a cemetery.

The lighting was bad, a tad over-exposed, but there seemed to be an enormously wide tree trunk at the far end. Perhaps a small one behind that. The candles were all laid out in a circle on the ground, a few sat on headstones, some of which appeared to be covered in blankets of moss, adding to the ghostly effect.

"We held hands and chanted, asking the spirits to be with us. I heard them, but the other girls didn't. It was like the sound a television makes when it's turned on, but the volume is all the way down. That obnoxious humming. It was louder than I'd known it before. Then I clearly caught my name spoken. It made me jump and break the chain. A few of the girls peered at me. I could tell they thought I was faking.

"Breaking the chain should have ended the voices, but it didn't. Hundreds of voices hung in the air, speaking in high-frequency tones. Later, I found I could hear them stronger if I meditated. Soon, one energy force came to me more than any other, and I started speaking with him. I had read enough to know this was no ordinary spirit. That I'd been summoning some sort of demon."

"You knew!" Jansen shouted.

"Of course, I knew! I never hid that from you."

"You've never used the word 'summoned' before. I think I might remember that!"

She slammed the photo album shut. "I tried to stop. Once I saw what he was, I didn't have to *summon* him." She grit her teeth at her son. "He just came."

This couldn't be good. I had a bad feeling about the direction of this story. Unless I was mistaken, it sounded like she had been the one who invited demons into her life, not so much the innocent victim we'd been led to believe.

"One night, he came to me so violently, my bed vibrated. The feet rattled on the floor. My light got so bright I thought it would pop, and my room became a foul-smelling ice box." She put her hand over her chest. "A pressure fell over my heart. His energy was intense, like a first kiss. Exhilarating."

"Kiss?" Charlie hissed. "A demon enters your dorm room complete with all his nasty tricks, and you liken it to a kiss!"

She took a few shallow breaths, her fingers fidgeting at her neckline. "The demon… I guess we've established that, asked me why I called him. Somehow, I couldn't explain. Didn't really think I had. Maybe I'd been dreaming. That was certainly possible. He told me he didn't bother with humans, and his presence pressed against my lungs. I thought he'd smother me. Then he stopped. 'Your mother was a witch,' he said, but it wasn't true."

Her hand trembled. Her lips pulled back in a straight line, and she cast her eyes down, away from the three of us. It felt like an end, but she had yet to mention that necklace.

"Go on," Jansen said.

"Wait, hang on." She left again and returned carrying an antique wooden box intricately carved with ornate vines and flowers that wove in and encircled themselves. It looked like the kind of box that might break apart if handled. It carried with it a palpable sense of age, whispering secrets from centuries ago.

She opened the box. "I inherited this, mother to mother, for as long as we could trace it back, somewhere around 1650. There are family stories about us being descended from witches."

With alarming speed, Jansen stood. "Did you never think that bit of information might pertain to us a little?"

"I never believed the stories! Nobody did. They were just stories about one of our foremothers, Eva Wolff."

Until she said that, I'd forgotten their last name hadn't

been passed down in the usual way, from father to son. Theirs had passed from mother to daughter, so that even if Miss Kate had married, Jansen and Charlie would still have her surname.

Miss Kate fingered the delicate design etched into the wood. "We know they tried and burned her as a witch, but that was common then. There are no such things as witches. Right?"

No, Jansen's angry eyes and cocked head said otherwise.

Kate laid her palm against her son's cheek, but he wrenched away like her hand was a branding iron.

"Yes, the demon confirmed it that night, but you must have guessed."

Jansen's head flew back. "How would I ever guess"—his voice grew louder with every word—"that my mother"—until he shouted—"is a witch!"

"I am not a witch. I am descended from witches."

"Ah, well!"

"It's probably why you have the power to heal. It isn't exactly a demonic trait, now, is it?"

Jansen seethed with such ferocity that I thought he might choke his mother. "No! And we've been to hell, Mother, searching for why!"

I had never seen him that mad, and I'd seen him mad, many, many times. Just how literally had he meant "hell?" A feeling of dread fell over me. Charlie must have been watching because he grimaced and crooked his finger, beckoning me to him. So, I slinked to his end of the L-shaped couch and nestled into his side, his giant arm slung its weight across my shoulder.

"What could I do? You were demons, both of you. I told you that. Was it so important that someone in my bloodline was considered a witch?"

Jansen turned his back on his mother and stared out the sliding glass patio door. "The necklace…Mother."

With a large intake of air, Miss Kate said, "This demon terrified me. I tried to block out everything, but it kept coming."

"The necklace!" Jansen bellowed.

"I'm getting to that!" Miss Kate's voice broke, and her breathing labored. "I told him to stop. Begged him to. Pleaded. Nothing worked. So, I changed tactics and thanked him instead, heaping praise on him. Anything to avoid his wrath. At least that way, when I behaved," she said darkly, "the beatings stopped."

"Beatings," I said.

Charlie smashed my head into his chest. His too-large-hand covered my ear, so I peeled his fingers back to hear.

Miss Kate's gray eyes zoned in on mine. "Oh, yes. You've only known good demons, Ellie. Demons without bodies? It's unfathomable, but they pinch, poke, prod, punch. Though unseen, somehow, they leave bruises. They take what they want. But if I was good…"

She trailed off. Briefly. In a throaty voice, imitating that of another, she said darkly, "'She'll serve a purpose.'"

The hairs on the back of my neck stood. Her eyes narrowed, her words shooting through my core, aimed at me. There was no other way to interpret it. I knew it, and Charlie tightened his grip. Because he knew it, too.

The vision of the demon child.

Jansen looked between Charlie and me. "What?"

Unaware of the looks we exchanged, Kate closed her eyes. "That's what he said. 'There is to be a child in the next generation who will cross the bridge between our world and yours. Our seers have foretold of him. He will be a powerful demon.'"

Charlie's hand slid from my face to his lap with a heavy thud. "Oh, Kate. You didn't."

"Charlie, wait. I'm afraid it gets worse. The demon set me up in a new dorm room, one he'd chosen specifically. My neighbor, of course, was Marie. The demon instructed me to befriend her."

"My mom?" I didn't know my voice could reach such a high pitch.

With a dropped chin, she looked for all the world like she'd be sick. I lacked all capacity to feel anything for her.

The enormity of what unfolded pressed in on me the way steam builds in a kettle. I collapsed into Charlie.

"Continue," Charlie said.

"The demon said to drop all the witchcraft nonsense. Said none of it was more than hocus-pocus, anyway. He commanded me to befriend her, but I didn't expect to love her. The demon said Marie's first child would be a girl, but then Tyler was born—"

Charlie thumped his chest. "Seems to me you're leaving something out."

"Oh, Charlie."

"You've never told me where I came from. This seems like a good time."

"You never asked."

"Is it related to this? If not, move on. But if it is…"

"I don't know."

"You don't know?" Jansen sneered.

"Then, by all means…" Charlie said.

Kate hung her head, her crimped waves flowing forward as a blond fringe curtain. "The truth is, I have no idea how you got here. All I know is that this demon liked to torment me. He visited me in the night with vivid hallucinations. Usually, they were lewd and fulfilled a primal need for him, not for me. Occasionally, his hallucinations took me on trips to other places. It always felt so real. I could never be sure."

Her voice caught in her throat, and her hand flew to her mouth. She heaved as the brothers exchanged glances, and I thought I understood; they'd never seen her like this. I knew I never had.

"He played a masterpiece of a vision the night I got Charlie. I won't tell you the gory details. In short, he made me a spectator at a birth. I don't know why. Some kind of illusion. Had to be. I can't usually see the spirits, but on that evening, my eyes were wide open. The demon, this gray and black monster, pressed himself over a woman who writhed in agony. I watched her take her last breath. Watched her spirit leave as an evil entity took her. Then, this hideous beast shrouded in torn shadowy shreds ripped a baby from her lifeless body, and left it on her stomach to die. The demon evaporated. Dissolved. I have no idea. He melted away from my vision, and she lay dead in an alley, her child on her stomach."

"Charlie?" I asked in a hushed whisper.

She turned toward me with such vacant eyes, I wasn't sure if she knew where she was. "I waited for the nightmare to end. Must have stood there for an hour, and in all that time, the infant never cried. Eventually, I thought maybe I was supposed to do something in order to be released, but I didn't know what. So, I picked the baby up. He was warm in my arms and so tiny. Perfect little fingers. Ten toes, all curling then stretching out long. I used my nightgown to clean him off, and he looked up at me with inhuman black eyes."

She crossed the room to stand in front of her oldest son and kissed the top of his head. "I named him Charlie."

Unasked questions hung in the air.

Eventually, Miss Kate said, "So that's it. If I got you some other way, I'm not aware of it. You are all, forever and always, part of my never-ending hallucination. You were supposed to desensitized Marie's baby girl to demons. Since that child was Tyler, that demon wasn't done with me. He came in the night. Wanted to repeat some of his old pleasure dreams. I fought him. I'm proud of that. Strange though, he kept saying, 'She'll serve a purpose. She'll serve a purpose.' Oh, Jansen," she said. "I tried to stop the plan, but you wouldn't be here if he hadn't had his way."

"You knew!" Jansen growled. "All this time, we've chased theories! What's so different about Ellie? Is it because we've been friends our entire lives? We're so close I've rubbed off on her? And here you've known all along it was part of a demonic plan."

"What was the purpose?" I asked.

"You have to believe I didn't know," she said. "I didn't understand what he was, not at the beginning. He spoke so softly, with hope and love in my head. He projected thoughts, I'm sure of it. After that, it was too late."

"The purpose, Mother!" Charlie's voice raged.

"To bridge the gap," she spat. "Demons can't access our plane unless they're half-human, like the two of you. You're neither fully human nor demon. Hell's army doesn't exist as anything more than energy forces in this world. This evil creature wanted to enter the earth as a physical being."

"How?" Charlie asked.

"Once he knew Marie was pregnant with a girl, he possessed her to implant a stolen soul."

My hollowed out stomached iced over. The chill stopped my heart and swept up my arms and neck to turn my tongue to dust. Whose soul? Who was I supposed to be and why did I have no memory of this? Did this make me someone else? Like who-the-heck even was I?

"She's ready now, and he wants her back."

For what? To return me? Where? To who?

Could my heart beat any faster because right now it seemed to have run out of its entire lifetime's allotment of beats?

Jansen, Charlie, and Kate all talked over each other, but I remembered what Clara had said in Mrs. Fushi's class. "When the time is right, he will reclaim what is his."

Could this be what she had been talking about? Was this the child in the vision? My evil soul was destined to produce a demon more horrific than any ever known.

Miss Kate's voice rose above those of her sons, in pitch, if not in volume. "It was supposed to be an honor." Her eyes found mine and her boys paused their arguments, mouths agape. "Demons would revere you among women as the mother of the redeemer, the one who would bring us out of darkness."

We all sat and stared at her. If they felt as I did, it was because all three of us were in shock.

"Then I watched you grow, showing no signs of anything but human. You and Jansen adored each other. I grew to love you, all three of you, in ways only a mother can understand. I learned to close my mind to the demon and raised two little half-demons to be good boys."

Kate held up a picture of herself wearing a Chrysoberyl

like mine. "It came from this box. I found it before I headed off to college."

Jansen looked ready to pounce, but Kate pulled out an ancient manuscript. "That's not all. Her birthmark appears in this diary." She turned its delicate pages, landing on the sketch of a young man who had a distinctive birthmark on his chest. One exactly like mine. It was hard to tell from a pencil drawing, but it seemed like the artist conveyed that it glowed.

My fingers flitted instinctively to my chest.

"The demon said you'd be marked with a star." She held a hand up to her sons, both of whom had risen to stand half-crouched. "You weren't though! That's new, isn't it? It wasn't a star until your sixteenth birthday. I expected to find it on your skin the first day Marie brought you to see us, but the mark wasn't there. Nothing changed about you and Cronus didn't come—"

"Didn't change! She has luminary points!" Jansen seethed. "Luminary points! We…are destined…to connect! Do you understand that? Do you comprehend the level of pain we will both endure because we can never complete it? She's human, Mother. She can't do it!"

Miss Kate's voice chilled with an icy effect as she turned her eyes on me. "Then you went and gave her that Chrysoberyl. Ellie, he didn't know what it meant."

"What did it mean?" Charlie shoved a chair from his path as he walked toward his mother. She didn't answer. "What did it mean? *I* found that necklace, Mother. What did it mean?"

"You?" I said. "I thought Uncle Fred—"

"There is no 'Uncle Fred!'" he and Jansen spat at the same time, Charlie inches from his mother's face. "*I* found that necklace, and *I* told Jansen it was perfect for Ellie's birthday. Now you tell me… What did the necklace I found do to her?"

Miss Kate took a deep breath and swallowed hard. "I'm sorry," she said. "I tried to get her to…at the party…I tried…"

Could Charlie ever strangle his mother? To distract him, I picked the necklace up from the floor, worked to relax his tight fist, and stuffed it into his hand. His eyes never left his mother's, but his fingers fiddled with the pendant.

"We don't care about what you *tried* to do," he said through gritted teeth.

"That necklace was mine, the same one I took from this box all those years ago."

"How can you possibly know that?"

"Because when I held it the day Jansen gave it to her, it changed color at my touch. I got rid of it probably ten years ago, now. But it knows the bloodline. This chrysoberyl was rumored to have signified a pact between the witches and demons. The demon recognized it from ancient days and said it awakens a sleeping soul. Damn it, Charlie, the necklace you gave her opened her senses to you two. I think that's why she hears your projections and it's probably why the monster came back."

Jansen walked with heavy feet to the window and asked, "Who was the demon?"

CHAPTER TWENTY-SIX

A hush fell over the room. The curtain whispered across Jansen's foot as the heater kicked on with a soft whir. His breath formed a circle of white on the window.

"The demon, *Mother*," he spat at the glass pane.

She covered her face with her hands and moaned into her palms.

Jansen vanished and reappeared in front of her, grasped her wrist and yanked it from her face. Unable to bear looking at him, she turned away.

"The demon!" Jansen snarled.

So softly I hardly believed I'd heard correctly, she said, "Cronus."

"Cronus! One of hell's most powerful demons? That's our father?" He fell to his knees and raked his fingers down his face. "That's who wants Ellie's soul?"

"Jansen, my son." His mother bent over him.

Then he was gone. Miss Kate wept and grasped at the air where her son had vanished.

With what should have been a mere glance at Charlie, our eyes slammed together.

"Where is he?" My voice drowned in the warm, wet tears within my throat. "Charlie, where did he go?"

He shook his head slowly.

"We have to find him." I marched up to him and tugged on his shirt. "Now, Charlie. We have to go after him."

"I can't track him."

My heart contracted forcefully. It thumped so hard I felt it in my bones. I stumbled backward until held up by the door. My hand found its knob and twisted. I stumbled again, but onto the stoop, reminding me my feet were bare when they landed on frigid concrete.

I turned and ran.

Charlie riddled in front of me so suddenly I hit him, landing me flat on my rear.

Every time! Why could I never get away from them? He dropped the shoes he held in his hand, my sneakers, and reached to help me up.

No, no, no. Do not stop me. It wasn't fair. I couldn't be alone to do what I wanted when I needed to. Didn't ask for his help. The thought of his helping me up, comforting me, pulling me close, and taking me wherever he pleased to take me made me want to vomit. I was done being the pet.

My entire life had been an orchestrated scheme, with me nothing more than a puppet. A pawn in the devil's game.

So I grabbed my shoes, scrambled to my feet, and ran in the opposite direction. I could never outrun him. Were he human, I couldn't do that. Still, I *could* get away.

"Ellie, wait," he said, jogging to keep up with my full-on sprint. "Come on, let me help."

I didn't answer, but kept a steady pace.

Houses sped by. Trees creaked in the wind. A pebble on the sidewalk found my heel, and I roared from the pain in my heart as much as from the gravel. I had to stop to brush it off and inspect my foot.

"There now." He came up beside me. "Come on, sit and put those on. Didn't anyone ever tell you it's winter out here?"

Rage has a way of building fire in the bones, so most of me wasn't exactly cold. My feet, on the other hand, were so icy they bordered on numb. The painful, pin-prickling kind. I sat and pulled the balled-up socks out of the toe of one shoe.

"Did you know?" I panted.

"Which part? That my mother's a witch? Strike that. That my mother isn't my mother at all? Did I know I'm a freaking hallucination, whatever that means? Did I know that my father…" his words trailed off.

"That your father was Cronus? That your mom knew? That she did it on purpose, Charlie. That our births…all of our births…were part of a monster's master plan!"

He sat beside me, his knees pulled under his elbows, bowing his head. His fingers made trenches through his tight curls, massaging his scalp. Guttural murmurs resonated in his chest. "I knew I was half demon. How exactly that came to be, I didn't like to ask. Kate was always so open about everything. We didn't suspect she kept a secret. The way she talked, we assumed she was under duress. Probably raped. She got so upset when we asked how we got here that we stopped asking. I never imagined she'd invited him in."

My shoes laced, I stood and began walking again with him at my heels.

"Where are you going?" he asked. "I can get you there much quicker."

I'd arrived at my destination. Guess he wasn't quite right about that.

So I reached around his waist and embraced him. His arms were slow to find me, shocked by the unexpected affection. When he did fold me into him, he covered me in warmth, and his hands engulfed me so completely that slipping his cell phone from his back pocket felt all the more devious.

I turned and entered the new section of the cemetery.

"Ellie, no, wait!" he called out.

"I'm sorry." I couldn't turn around.

"I can't follow you. I'm too angry! They won't let me pass."

I walked farther along the path and reveled in my successful effort to deceive him. It wasn't a very happy celebration, though, because behind me, he moaned. The way he strained over the shrieks and screams I couldn't hear tugged at my heart.

Go back, I thought, trying in vain to project human thoughts to my demon friend. *Go back, Charlie, and don't follow me. I have to do this.*

What was I thinking? Why was I here, traipsing through the graveyard, running away from Charlie?

All I knew was I needed to be alone to process all that had been revealed without any demonic influence, no matter how friendly the demons were.

When I got to the edge of the new section, I sank behind a black granite headstone, careful not to walk over the body. There were so many of them. I crouched low to check if Charlie followed. If he were anywhere, he'd be near the entrance, and I could just make it out from here.

When I didn't see him, I pulled out his cell phone—the one I'd swiped—and dialed home.

"Tyler? Hey, I need a ride. Can you come get me?"

"What? No. Where are you?"

"At the cemetery."

"What on earth are you doing there?" Then he spoke off to the side. "She's at the cemetery."

"Who's that?" I hoped it wasn't our mom.

"Andrew. See, I do have better things to do—"

"Just come get me, please. Bring a coat. I don't have one."

"What—"

"Just come, please, Tyler, to the gates off Market Street. I'll explain when you get here. Please hurry. It's freezing out here."

I hung up before he could protest further.

With about ten minutes to kill, I made my way toward the entrance and paused behind a headstone until Charlie popped into view. I heard every gust of wind, each twig snap, and the swish of the squirrels' tails, but I studied his pattern while I waited. By the time my brother pulled up in our mom's car, if I hurried, I could get there before Charlie reappeared. When the opportunity came, I dashed to my mom's Mazda and slid into the passenger's seat. Panting, I took the coat from Tyler and wrapped myself in it.

"Everything okay?" he asked.

The voice made me jump. It wasn't Tyler, but Andrew behind the steering wheel, in his bomber jacket, his hair disheveled, and his eyes… What was different about them?

"Andrew!" I gasped. "What—? I thought Tyler…"

"Tyler wasn't too keen on coming, as you can imagine." He threw the car into drive and sped off toward home. Did I scare you?"

"No, but…" I couldn't tell him how very much I didn't want to see him just then. "I'm sorry. I just expected Tyler. That's all.

"That's okay. I have no place to be. In fact…" He pulled the car over in front of the park where the dog had attacked me. "Can I interest you in a walk?"

I took him in. Studied him. Behind his blue eyes lay something similar to a black onyx stone. It had been an observation I'd made on my front porch the morning after the hospital. That day seemed ages ago. I leaned in closer to examine them, but he shifted his gaze and stepped out of the car, walked around it, and opened my door. What else could I do? Maybe decompressing with Andrew wasn't the worst thing in the world.

"So, what brings me here?" he asked. "Why were you at the cemetery?"

"Not sure. I was sort of looking for something."

"What kind of something?"

A Jansen kind of something. I wasn't even sure where to start. He was probably home now or, more likely, standing guard at one of the cemetery entrances where I'd left Charlie.

No, he didn't need to know any of that. "You wouldn't understand."

"I know, Ellie."

His response, laden beneath a voice too silky, too sweet, spoke of a deeper knowledge he couldn't have and my foot froze midair. It then fell as if magnetized to the path where it stuck, too heavy to lift. He didn't press me. Didn't ask further questions or protest that my words were a brush-off.

His voice dropped an octave and rumbled within his chest. "It's alright. I know."

Gradually, I turned around to face him. "What do you think you know?"

"About Charlie and about Jansen. I know they're not human."

He took a step closer, so we stood shoulder to shoulder. I flinched as he bent and whispered into my ear, "They're demons."

CHAPTER TWENTY-SEVEN

My hand at my throat, I flinched, and I understood.

This wasn't Andrew. The veil lifted, and inky black shadows seemed to leak out of him.

Sinister laughter rang in my head, the same haunting sound that had plagued me so many times before. "That's right. At last, I claim what is mine. Rather poetic, don't you think? I couldn't have planned it better myself."

With inhuman speed, he encased himself around me and swiped his hands down my face. I gasped when I smelled him: musk and earth and rot.

When he removed his hand, we stood in a cemetery. I had the disconcerting feeling I'd been here before, but couldn't quite place it. My heart pounded as the sky threatened rain with ominous gray clouds billowing overhead. An eerily quiet air settled around us, stirred only by the wind whistling through long blades of stiff, dead grass. A naked oak tree stood proudly on its massive trunk, all its leaves scattered beneath it, because there was nobody to rake them. No one ever came here.

But a cemetery? "This is just another trick. You can do nothing here. You're powerless against the spirits."

The maniacal laughter that so often embedded itself inside my head now prickled the air around us, too. "Think, Gabriella. You know this place."

It hit me then, like a memory framed by flames and witches and fear. The giant oak tree, the moss-covered headstones. All it lacked were the candles from the photo of Miss Kate's séance.

"You think my sons are the only two ever to befriend the friendless? Here, they do not fight me. No. Here they join me."

My knees buckled, and Cronus in Andrew's body tightened his hold.

My world transformed. Became a demon's reality. Day changed to night. The massive oak, winter-bare, was now full of leaves, coal-black in the dim light, its braided roots exposed. Single candles flickered on every headstone, and candelabras outlined a circle, and we were at the center.

He turned me so I faced the pond where candlelit lanterns on its glassy surface cast a soft shimmer. It glistened in the moon's pure reflection of white. "My gift to you." We stood beneath a wedding arbor fashioned of driftwood, draped with pearly satin and roses.

Most inappropriately, I didn't cry as water lapped at the pond's edge. Didn't recoil as the candle's warm glow touched my skin. I didn't even consider myself psychologically damaged when the sweet-smelling flowers promised to cover us in matrimonial bliss.

No, confronted with a wedding ceremony—my wedding —I threw my head back and laughed.

Cronus took that as desire and kissed me full on the lips. My mind rejected him, but my body responded with fire. The beat of my heart pounded so fast, so furious, he must have felt it. He groaned, a scavenger, enjoying his catch.

And I knew then what the demon's power of lust felt like. Knew he used it on me. Because although my arms didn't push him away and though I did not kick him in the crotch, I wanted to. My innermost self saw the game for what it was, this physical lust.

A flood of emotions rushed over me, a wave I had no control over. Jansen's name reverberated in my head, his face before me, the most vivid image I'd ever conjured as a thought. My body, my heart, it felt as if they ripped in two. Frantic now, my soul wiggled and tugged away from whatever attached it to me, ripping and tearing at my core.

Still, at the first swipe of his tongue between my lips, my mouth opened to him, although I wanted to bite down on it and sever it. I clung to him, even as I wished my clinging fingers gripped his throat instead. *Disgusting!* Yet, I couldn't stop. Couldn't make my limbs obey or stop myself from kissing that serpent's maw. Couldn't stop my hands from groping.

My spirit grew angry. I could feel her rock and fight and shriek with inaudible screams.

Dark power roiled in Cronus' veins, rendering me impotent. Dusk and shadow rolled off of him as though he sank claws into my mind, and those claws dragged me from myself. They pulled the essence of me to one side and left the other exposed for him to do as he pleased.

From nowhere, Jansen stepped out of his midnight shroud and materialized as the living embodiment of unleashed power.

With power I'd not yet witnessed, he wrenched Andrew from me, severing the lust charm, and hurled him at a headstone with a force so strong his body smashed the stone to rubble. The sounds of crumbling rock and breaking bones were indistinguishable. Jansen stood in a wide stance before the wreckage, his eyes a dull, charcoal black. His nostrils flared as he crouched, his jaw clenched, ready to destroy his father.

His opponent wasn't Cronus alone.

It was Andrew, wearing the brown leather bomber jacket he took such pride in. Had I ever told him how handsome he looked in it? I'd meant to. His hair lay disheveled, and he'd never let it get that way. Always styling it just-so. It made me think how I should have known it wasn't him. All that time.

His lids were closed, but I didn't have to look. I knew those blue eyes, so similar to the sea. Knew that stubbled chin. No, that wasn't right either. Why hadn't I noticed that before? Andrew never left the house unshaven.

I scrambled to my feet, stumbling, my singular thought on him. His head poked out from the rubble, one hand angled askew beside it. I needed to fix his hair. He'd never wear it like that. Before I could steady myself, Jansen grabbed me around the waist, pulling me back.

No! I clawed at his fingers and fought to free myself. "Help him!" I cried. I kicked. I pushed. I smacked and jabbed, but Jansen had unyielding strength. "Don't you see him? He needs me!"

The rubble moved.

Jansen set me on my feet as he projected for me to stay, but my legs had never stopped running. Still in motion, I rushed to Andrew, but Jansen caught my hand, whipping me around. He grasped my face between his hands.

Damn it! Let me go. How dare he? I was no rabbit to be caged. Andrew needed me. His hair stuck out, and those fingers, the ones that flew over the piano? No! He was hurt... needed help.

Then the ruins of the headstone clattered.

"Ellie!" Jansen shouted.

No, I wouldn't listen. Couldn't listen. I swung my arms, but he didn't feel it. Didn't react as I swung, punched, kicked —

"Ellie!"

I couldn't ignore that. The projection stilled my body.

"Leave. Run." The rubble over Andrew clicked and rattled. *"Now!"*

Pebbles at the top of the heap rolled in rapid succession, and Andrew moved beneath them. It happened so fast I didn't have time to react.

Like an explosion, the stones burst into the air. Rocks pelted my face. Instinctively, I ducked and covered my head, as I braced for impact.

Jansen flung himself over me, his chest heavy on my back as he forced me forward. Together, we hit a patch of ice, and I threw my hands out to brace myself, garnering shards of ice and pebbles under my skin. We skidded into a nearby headstone and my body encircled the hard slab as it imprinted itself on my ribs and knocked the wind from me. Jansen curled around me, both of us facing Andrew.

Andrew, who stood tall, as if born again from the exploded pile of stones.

But, oh. The bone at his elbow. Visibly broken, shards stuck through fleshy tears of skin. His neck hung unnaturally to the side, his long, piano-playing fingers bent at obscene angles. Dark blood streamed down his torn pant leg to pool crimson at his feet.

"Friend of the bride?" Cronus sneered through Andrew's eerie smile, crooked on his broken face. "Rather rude of you, really. I dislike uninvited guests."

Then, inky mist poured from Andrew. It was the kind of black that would stand out as even blacker than the pitch of a lightless underground cave, and I could see Cronus. Not as a misty blob. Instead, he had a defined head and flowing, beastly tentacles. Red orbs set where the eyes should have been.

Andrew's body fell to the ground with a horrible thud, where he splashed in his own blood. I should have looked away. Only he couldn't be dead.

I slumped into a heap. "Help him!"

"Now look." Cronus' voice oozed sarcasm. "You've gone and frightened my bride. She's mine, Jansen. You've lost."

"You're wrong!" The familiar ring of Charlie's timbre comforted. A safe embrace. With both brothers, I had hope. "This is no wedding! I'll speak now and never hold my peace."

I crawled through the snow and had to remind myself to move my arms and feet. The earth cut into my hands, but I didn't mind. I sobbed and choked, moving as though a thousand chains weighed me down.

Andrew's once-skilled fingers were all gnarled now. And his nails were too long. He'd never have let them grow like that, not when he played the piano.

Cronus' laughter reverberated. "I've already won. The girl rather transparently wants me."

Andrew's hair didn't lay down straight, so I licked my

fingers the way I'd seen my mom do, and smoothed it down in places. Tucked my hand under his head, where warm, sticky mud surprised me. Strange to find mud on the frozen earth, but it had to be that. Because the truth—what I knew deep down—was too awful to process.

A tear formed under his eye. For a moment, I didn't realize it was mine.

"Tell me, Jansen," Cronus said. "Did you know when she kisses, she purrs? Have you any idea how ripe—"

The sky lit in a fiery shade of bright light as Cronus exploded into black particles of dust. The wedding hallucination, with its candles and satin arbor, disintegrated. All of it. The sweet-smelling roses and floating lanterns disappeared, and the midnight sky brightened to blue, while the moon transformed into the sun.

They'd said they couldn't kill him. Thought they weren't powerful enough, thought him far stronger. I'd never been happier to find them wrong.

But then…shit! The faintest shadow of mist swirled. It grew in blackness as the monster reformed.

"Oh, did I touch a nerve?" After the briefest of pauses, Cronus said, "Gabriella, come!"

Horrified, I peeled my eyes from Andrew and stared at the black shabby-robed beast. He called me as if I was a dog. Like I would obey.

Reality pressed in hard. Andrew lay dead. Nothing could be done for him now. Cronus, however, was very much alive.

Survival instinct kicked in. I needed to do what Jansen had projected I should do.

I needed to run.

Like a crab, I crawled backward on my hands and feet, kicking up dust from the gravel path.

"Gabriella!" Cronus barked. "Come! Stand with me."

The nerve of him, thinking I'd heel to a vile, soulless beast. A blight against all that was good.

Jansen grinned and obviously struggled to keep it small. Then he glowered at Cronus. Could he make him explode with just his eyes?

Cronus growled from the bowels of the abyss inside of him, a growing rumble that shook the earth. "She was ready. She is mine!"

Lightning from Cronus' tentacles struck the oak and exploded into flames, splitting it in two with a *crack!* Tree limbs crashed, severed from their trunk, and a puff of white smoke burst into the air.

I covered both my ears and cowered.

"Her soul is ready!" he bellowed into the thunder. "It seeks the demon."

"Perhaps," Jansen said smugly. "But not you."

The creature grew, and its tattered, shadowy cloak flapped behind him as he shot into the sky. It rose and gained momentum, faster and smaller.

"Run!"

It arched toward Earth, and I knew then Cronus would have me.

Without thinking, I got up to flee.

Too late. He settled over me. His scent, the one that had been as sweet as Jansen's, now reeked of rotting death. Somehow, this demonic, formless entity pulled me to it.

I sensed the riddle as Cronus encased me in his icy, fingerless grip. He wrapped me in tendrils of frost. Tendrils that wove together soulless wraiths that bound us together. Helpless, I could only sink into the hollow rift where time stretched. Like if this were hell, I'd already endured a century of its shadows and misery.

He would riddle me to God knew where, and I could do nothing to save myself. A wave of dread crashed over me and my body lurched into that void.

Something stopped us, a thing that made me wish Cronus had taken me instead. Every cell of my skin burned from Charlie's power of torture. All the water in my brain dried up and shrank. It pulled away from my skull, and all I could hear was tearing flesh.

Charlie's torment forced Cronus to drop me, but the damage was done.

While the demon howled from Charlie's power, the

always formidable Jansen struggled to breathe. The energy that usually crackled around him now barely hummed. Like he'd spent everything to free me from that time warp.

Charlie held strong, and Cronus trembled from his might. He writhed and contorted, bearing pain I now understood.

Though weak, Cronus aimed lightning at Charlie's shoulder, but it severed the power. Charlie bellowed and grasped the wound.

"He's more of a phantom." Isn't that what he'd said? "We don't think we can kill him."

The moment Charlie's power failed, Jansen reentered the fight. Emboldened, Charlie threw off his shoulder wound to join his brother as they fought to weaken the might of their father. Balls of fire spiraled across the field. Lightning cracked the earth, dividing trees down their centers and splitting me in two with razor sharp fear.

This battle may end, but would the result be Cronus' death? Or would it be the brothers? How many of us must die?

Sweat trickled down my back even as my lungs ached from the arctic air. Doubt surged through me, a searing dread about how this would end. Could they slay Cronus? Or was this where hell and earth met?

While I feared the end of civilization, the demons charged one another, tearing at the fabric between worlds. They defended innocence with each slash through rock. Preserved hope every time they exploded a tree. And though they destroyed this sacred ground, they honored their agreement to humanity.

But it couldn't go on forever. Their strength waned, each working hard just to move. The faint hum of their powers ebbed and left both heaving.

Not Cronus, though. They couldn't defeat him. It might as well have been written in the sky; had never been more plain as the scrunch of rock against rock, the boom of fireballs, and the roar of their might pierced winter's cold embrace.

Then Charlie, that guy with otherworldly strength, struggled to stay on his feet. He doubled over, his hands on both knees as he recovered.

Shadows moved, absent of sun and wind, and I realized the fight wasn't two against one after all. It was an army of evil against my friends, who suddenly appeared very, very small.

Unearthly gusts swirled overhead. It lifted my hair and took my breath. It reached into my lungs and stole every last bit of air to offer as a sacrifice to the fiends of Hell.

"El—"

Jansen's riddle swallowed my name. He reappeared and snatched me between worlds before I could take a breath, leaving me dizzy and constricting my throat. It drove out a cough and made me wheeze.

But where were we?

CHAPTER TWENTY-EIGHT

I glanced around at the table and chairs on an ugly linoleum floor. At the yellow cupboards that framed the darkened room. Noted the sweet silence. No sound but our rapid breathing and the ticking of the clock on the wall.

Though I didn't know where we were, I had faith Jansen had taken us somewhere warm and safe.

He flipped the kitchen table on its side with a thud that rattled the floor and shoved it up against the wall. "Get behind it and don't move."

That's when I knew round two would erupt, and soon. Full demons could track their prey, and Cronus wouldn't stop.

"How are you holding up?" he asked.

Before I could answer, Cronus found us. Charlie arrived in close pursuit. Cronus' demon form was larger than I'd realized. It filled the space with dark power. His tattered cloak spread out wide, as if draped over his wingspan, and it took up the entire living area wall.

They fought to push Cronus across the room, away from me. Because he'd recovered a bit, Jansen battered him with flame after flame. Charlie threw mere warning shots, and it took a massive effort. He threw and threw and threw, but sank to his knees, each throw weaker than the one before, each fireball a little duller, until barely a candle flicker appeared in the palm of his hand.

He pounded the floor with his fist, but I didn't hear its impact over the whiz-flash of Jansen's persistent fire.

"Join me, boy!" Cronus roared at Jansen, his voice reverberating off the walls, shaking the windows and cupboard doors. "You have untapped might. I can feel it! Together, we can shatter the divide."

"Never!"

"If you knew the pleasure of the power we wield, the control we could have. We can reside in both worlds, son. She is the portal."

"Go back to Hell!"

A hand of bone and shadow slithered from Cronus' sleeve and gripped Jansen's wrist. "Listen to me. She is nothing! A blip in time. She'll die before a quarter of your life is over. Join me, and you live forever."

Then a ring of fire burst around me. Everything in its circle blazed: the wall behind me and the table in front of me. The electrical outlet sparked with the flares, its heat burning my skin as they shot within inches of the ceiling.

I was too tired to battle the delusions he wove and had to remind myself they were imaginary. He was so good that I smelled sulfur when the flames licked my hair.

This was more realistic than previous hallucinations. Though I knew it wasn't real—had experienced them before—my efforts to fight off the fear dimmed.

I tried to get up, to run away, but couldn't. My arms wouldn't move, or my legs either. Even my mouth refused to ask Jansen if he saw it, too.

It didn't matter if it was real, if it wasn't real, because I felt the searing heat along the red welts on my skin. Unable to stand it, I screamed in agony.

Cronus, with ringing laughter, bellowed in his leisurely drawl, "Illa in inferno ardebit. She'll burn in Hell. Watch the fire blaze!"

"It's not real." Jansen said. *"Listen! It's not there."*

A lion's head roared out of the flames, and wild shrieks exploded from my throat. It gnashed its sharp teeth inches from my neck as the world faded in and out of view. A viper slithered from the lion's maw and its tongue flicked my eye. Unhinging its jaw, fangs flipped out like a switchblade and sank into my cheek. I thought my chest would explode with fear. Venom burned through my veins.

"Stay with me, Ellie! There's nothing there."

No. He didn't see what I saw. Didn't feel what I felt. Cronus must be playing tricks on him. Because the acidic venom burned as the flame devoured me.

Unbelievably, the devil rode in on the wings of a gargoyle. When his sinewy arms reached, I knew it was to carry me into the fire. Cronus' plan wasn't to enter the world through me, but for me to join him. To become the portal to hell.

Images grew fuzzy, and all sounds dulled. The dark tunnel coaxed me away…farther and farther.

"Ellie! No!" Jansen bellowed the words, not in my head, but gutturally. Their sound rumbled over the ceiling and through the floor, a taser pulsating through the cotton in my ears.

Then, something happened. That sheath over my bones that sometimes ached? It quivered and twisted. From the center of my body, a magnetic force pulled me from the depths of unconsciousness.

Suddenly my vision cleared, and I focused solely on him. I emerged refreshed. Hell's fire extinguished, and the beasts and the devil vanished.

I soared, and my sight set on Jansen.

Jansen glanced in my direction, slumped, and stopped fighting. His shoulders folded in on themselves, his head dipped low. He looked utterly defeated.

Between us was Cronus, with flapping, black tentacles.

"You can't die." Jansen pleaded, his voice desolate.

No, I wasn't dead. Couldn't he see me? I shivered, unfettered from the living world. The pull I often felt from him stretched like fingers that beckoned my spirit forward, closer to him.

He felt it, too. I know he did because I watched his body transition. Intent on me, he abandoned feet and limbs and hands to exist as colors of light swirling around a velvety-black core, the image of the soul behind his eyes.

His being shook. I felt every shimmer of it because the pull made me tremble, too. Why did he resist? *How* did he resist?

I didn't.

I drove to him. It felt so right as the pain in my heart melted away.

In my haste, I didn't realize that I was all spirit or that I'd left my body. Didn't know I swirled as lights and energy.

Cronus hung between us, a soulless black wraith. My focus was so narrow, I saw past his darkness to Jansen's light.

"Do you feel it, Jansen?" Cronus roared. "Her power? She's ready. Gabriella, come to me. I am reborn!"

My head charged at him first, piercing his silhouette with an explosion of light. Though I passed through quickly, I knew the moment I hit because hatred and loathing spread through me with the agony of all the lost souls he'd stolen. His doomed spirit stripped me of hope. In him, there would never again be happiness. Only darkness and despair.

I broke through the other side, and Jansen melded back to his human self.

Shouting got my attention as a violent energy behind me rose to a feverish pitch. The demon convulsed, suspended in a dome of celestial lights. Like the blended hues of glacial streams and summer skies, and bright colored fireworks dazzled.

"Whoa," Charlie said.

"How's that feel?" Jansen shouted over the screams. "You lost!"

"This isn't possible. She's mine!" Cronus thundered between spasms. "I earned her soul. She was supposed to soar to the most powerful demon!"

"Thank you." Though his shoulders squared and his nose twitched, a faint glint of triumph lit Jansen's eyes. "You created her, alright. Yes. You created the perfect mate… just not for you!"

"No! Our seers foretold of a powerful demon. I am the

one! With her, I am lauded, our power magnified. I leave behind this spirit form as lord of the human plane!" Cronus drew a shrouded tentacle as if to throw fire, but nothing appeared. "What's happened?"

The brothers each produced fireballs, one in each hand—energized, basketball-sized spheres of flickering flame.

Jansen hauled his arm back. "You didn't create the mother of your evil plan. You created a weapon!"

Light flooded the monster's eye sockets. It penetrated his lifeless existence with its unknown power. The tattered shroud of him broke apart in granules, like dust off a grave.

Cronus bellowed in agony. "No!"

His shrieks permeated the room.

Cronus' sons hurled flaming weapons that penetrated the dome. He crumbled to sand and his bleak spirit rose in the sphere. As the shimmery light grew brighter, it crisscrossed in and around him. His blacker-than-black self intermingled with the glow from the light I'd left behind.

Transcendent colors exploded as the blackened specter transformed into a thick cloud of particles. The dome released its energy, and a rainbow of lights pulled what remained of him through the window and toward the earth below.

Traffic sounded outside; horns honked, tires swished on the asphalt. Somewhere, a train blared its horn, one long blow, then two short. Water gushed from the sink where multiple fireballs had detonated. Shattered glass littered the floor, and a small fire flickered in the trash can. Chaos, yes, but non-threatening. Calm.

Together, the brothers stood dazed, unable to speak. They heaved and their chests rose and fell sporadically.

Charlie cuffed the back of Jansen's neck as if to say "Attaboy." He then looked toward me. "Way to go, El," he said in whispered admiration.

Not Jansen, though. He took no time to elate in our victory as he transitioned into his form of mist and haze. *"Ellie, what have you done?"*

I didn't know and had rather hoped he would, but I

found I couldn't speak as a spirit.

"You're so beautiful…always… But like this…"

Our spirits drove closer to one another in a way I couldn't control. Color leaked from his soul. Light and power stretched across the divide, leaving a residual and salacious ache. I trembled to obey whatever instinct this was.

Charlie, with a force I'd never heard out of him, yelled, *"Jansen! Transition now!"*

Jansen obeyed. His spirit snapped itself together, and its tentacles of colorful lights retracted. He stood below, where he ran his fingers through his raven-black hair.

With his head inclined toward me, Charlie rubbed at his neck. "El Girl, you've got to get into that body of yours. I'm not sure how long you can be out of it. Do you know how?"

How had I even gotten out? No. I didn't see how I'd ever get back in.

"Get up close to your body, and when you do, you'll feel a strong magnetic pull…kinda like the one with you and Jansen a bit ago. Just let it happen. Don't fight it."

As I approached my body, my sense of self grew dim, and as Charlie said, a force pulled me in. The sensation alarmed me. As though I'd been sleepwalking, something shook me awake, or a vacuum sucked my soul into its shell with a jolt. I gasped as if I hadn't taken a breath in all the time I was out. The world around me spun, leaving me dizzy.

Before the earth stopped spinning, I watched as Charlie's spirit riddled away.

I scrambled to stand and faced Jansen, who stood a few feet from me. "Is it over? Is he gone?"

"He's dead. Don't you remember?"

"Yes. Only I can't believe it. What did I do?"

He took one step to close the distance between us, and our eyes collided mid-stride.

And the look on his face? What was it?

An intense silence fell, where my traitorous heart twisted, because it didn't know what I knew. That his was the look of fierce intensity, still hellbent on keeping us apart. It had to be, or he'd have me in his arms, because the tension in the room was all-consuming. Sure, Cronus was dead, but we were still different species. Isn't that what he'd said?

Then his hands were in my hair. His mouth slammed into mine, at last. He devoured it and my heart spiraled up and up and up.

Every memory of all the birthdays, every sunset, every laugh, all the secrets shared beneath the stars entwined to form this moment; charging the air with bubbles and sparkles and heat.

And that kiss—the one that fulfilled my fantasy. The kind I'd gone to bed envisioning. One that curled the toes, clenched my lungs, erased time and space and everything that wasn't his rough skin, his thumping heart, his roaming hands. A soul-ejecting crushing of lips. The epic kind that made me think—

"Finally." He groaned my exact thought into my mouth, growling the word like a long endured need. A vow. Like a promise.

It caused my neck to fall limp, and I tilted my head back to allow him to go deeper and claim more of me. When he did, I unraveled. My body trembled, my legs became liquid. I pressed into him, unable to get close enough. After so many months, I grasped at his shirt. I clutched it and never wanted the moment to end.

His responding moan rippled from his chest to mine, a tingle that ran all the way from my head down to my toes. The sound of pure desire, and—oh my God! Just knowing the rumble came from something I did to him.

My soul wiggled and began to float. Before I understood what had happened, Jansen eased himself away, and kissed the palms of my hands. Jeez, what was that and why did he stop it? I sank back into my body, but that had felt like he'd stopped my spirit from doing something called upon to do. And I didn't much want to stop.

His chest rose and fell as he grazed my forehead with his fingertips. Each of my freckles fell under his touch as he studied all of me, not just the space around me. "Are you okay?"

"Very." I took in his tattered shirt, the torn knees of his jeans, and the smudges of dirt, ash, and blood on his face. A slash on his forehead and another below his chin were yet unhealed. "Are you okay?"

A smile played around his lips. "Very. Ellie, what happened up there, what you did…" His words trailed off as he pressed my palm to his heart. "You separated. Do you know what that means?"

Assuming it a rhetorical question, I didn't even bother to shake my head.

Jansen nodded his understanding and repeatedly tapped a finger over my knuckles. "You've proven some of our theories correct. Your soul rose from your body to meet mine. Except humans can't do that and live. Not like that. I thought you were dead. Your aura faded" —he traced slow, lazy circles over the back of my hand, barely touching it— "to nothing. When Charlie stepped in… Well, I need to explain that, too."

I gazed down as Jansen's finger teased my skin. Tingles blazed a trail all the way to my fluttering heart.

He touched a fingertip to my chin, guiding me to focus on him. I had a hard time dragging my eyes up past his lips, puffy from our kiss. "Some demons, precious few, really, but some are monogamous creatures. They mate for life. Demon souls are magnetic, a thing that helps them align their powers. Stronger couples rise through the ranks to build status and power in the demon community. If a demon finds a mate, then his spirit intermingles with hers like one woven soul. Together, they become mightier as their powers combine."

His long lashes blinked a few times, as he seemed to decipher my thoughts. What he said was beautiful, but I was all sensation from the touch of his skin and his breath on my face and from the way he smelled of home. I really just wished he'd lean an inch closer, maybe brush his lips against mine.

As he chuckled softly, he caressed the space between my eyes with those lips, slightly rough where one had split. "I have found that love."

My mouth opened to form the word, "Oh," but nothing quite came out. I didn't dare to think I'd understood correctly.

"Charlie and I have theorized that you may share some of our powers, but the only thing we'd seen was that you could hear our projections and see our spirits. The simple truth is, we don't know what a demon and a human union would do. Humans can't mate with a demon. It's impossible, see, because her spirit isn't built for it. When choosing a life partner, demons stick to supernatural entities. Non-humans."

His nose brushed mine, and the backs of my fingers fell naturally over his cheek. The warmth of his skin spread through my arm and made my heart flip. He hummed a sort of moan, and my limbs dissolved. Boneless. The low bass tingled over my whole body, resulting in a convulsive shiver.

"But not you?" I asked.

"No." He cradled my cheek in his palm and met my gaze. Noticeably, he did not blink. "No, Ellie, definitely not me."

His breath entered my mouth, and I inhaled it. Trapped it in my lungs and let it nourish my soul. Hungry for more, I breathed him in again, arching into him. He caught me with an arm around my back, anchoring me to him, hip to hip. I gasped, offering him the length of my throat, and he took it. He set tiny flames along my neck with tender kisses.

"Are you sure you're okay?" He kissed behind my ear, then nibbled its ultra-sensitive shell.

"Yes." I squeezed my legs together to quell an ache.

He pulled away, gauging my reaction. "I've waited all my life."

His words—like he etched the poetry of desire over my jumping heart. He enfolded me near his chest, crushed his lips into mine, and flicked his tongue across the seam where they came together.

A wicked shiver traveled up my spine, a tiny jolt of electricity. Could he feel the tremor I couldn't control? I grew dizzy and my soul wiggled around my bones. Like before, it longed to be free. Tiny sparks danced along my skin. Then I floated, as if gravity lost its hold on me, suspended between two worlds.

A soft chuckle from Jansen zapped me back, making me whole again.

With one final breath, setting my spirit right within myself, I asked, "What makes me do that?"

He gave me a puzzled look. "I think your sweet soul desires mine. You separated from your body and rose to meet my spirit. When two people are in love, and I mean humans, we talk about them becoming one. Their spirits join. Except for them, it's a metaphor.

"What happened to you usually happens when souls make love to one another. Yours wants to join with mine." He whispered the words with reverence, as if afraid to speak them.

"That's beautiful," I said.

"It is beautiful. And apparently, you're quite good at it."

"Am I?"

"Yes, quite. But Ellie… if we met that way, we would be joined. It's a marriage of souls, the kind of act a powerful demon would want to do with an equally powerful partner."

"You don't want to do that with me because I'm not a powerful demon?" I did try to edit the despair out of my voice, but I failed.

"You are impossible." He laughed, pulling me in close. "I don't want to meet you in that way now. Not now. It would seem your soul is eager for it. I'd like that to happen at a particular time."

Comprehension came slowly. I almost got what he said, but not quite.

"I'd like to wait." He kissed the extra sensitive skin behind my ear. "I'd very much like us to become one…literally and metaphorically."

Heat started in my chest and spread to the roots of my hair, as I understood.

"Charlie knows this?"

Jansen rolled his eyes, and I pressed my lips into a firm pout as he shook the slightest bit with silent laughter.

"Yes, Charlie knows this. It's kind of why he intervened up there, and it's why he's left us alone. Your new power… well, it's kinda hot."

CHAPTER TWENTY-NINE

"Everybody decent?" Charlie riddled into the warehouse with one hand over his eyes.

I flew at him rather than answer, encircling his waist, about as high as I could reach.

Without peeking from behind his hand, he said, "Is there a ghost in the room? There's the tiniest pressure just around my waist?"

I squeezed harder, so hard any normal human wouldn't have been able to breathe.

After removing his hand, he said, "Oh, it's an Ellie hug! I should've known."

"Are you feeling better?"

"Me?"

"Well, yeah. I've never seen you two work that hard."

"Oh." Charlie gave a dismissive wave. "That. Yeah, I can't lie. Jansen, we may need to start hitting the gym. Seriously though, it just depleted our energy. It's temporary. We recharge pretty quick. And you, little missy. I have a bit of a bone to pick with you."

"Me?"

"Don't look so cute and innocent. Yes, you. Don't you ever—and I mean never—don't ever do that again. Don't even think about it. I don't want to see you even think about thinking about ever doing that again."

I needed a little help with the translation and looked to

Jansen for that.

"I think he's referring to the way you dodged him. That was a wickedly stupid thing to do."

"Oh, that." Guilt tinged my voice as I remembered how I'd evaded him back home at the cemetery.

Charlie twisted his lips up on one side, drilling me with a stern look, showing me he was quite serious. Yikes. What consequences might he dole out? His face scolded so believably. "You stole my phone! From a demon!"

"I didn't mean to."

"You absolutely meant to!" He dragged both his hands down his cheeks. "I had to riddle home and borrow Kate's so I could call Jansen. And that's another thing." He turned his ire on his brother. "Answer your damn phone!"

"I did!"

"Yeah, after the tenth try." Charlie picked a leaf out of Jansen's hair. "How did you find her?"

"My soul knew," he scoffed, sounding embarrassed. "Can you believe that?"

"With you? Yeah."

"It was like playing a game of hot and cold. I riddled within a hundred-mile radius. Sometimes my soul ached. Sometimes it lessened. I listened to the ache and found her."

There were so many things to talk about. Questions in need of answers. We talked at length about Andrew. At first, I was mad that they hadn't protected him. Why not, when they always protected me using their supernatural powers? Jansen healed my fatal wounds, but both of them failed Andrew. Why should they save me and not him?

When I brought up my arguments, I noticed how affected both were. Jansen couldn't get out more than a few words without his voice cracking, and Charlie kept swiping at his eyes. It was a grief we all shared, and I came to see they'd have done anything to help him had they known.

Charlie reminded me that when a demon possesses a person the way he had Andrew, the possessed dies. "Two spirits can't exist in one body for long."

With his arm slung behind me on the couch, Jansen

pulled me close. His voice had a controlled shake. "That wasn't Andrew I threw into the stone, but a shell. Andrew's been gone a while, now. I don't know how we missed it."

Charlie kicked out the foot of the recliner. "I should have seen it. I'm the one who stayed with her all the time… Who led her right to him. The signs were all there. Those were Cronus' eyes behind Andrew's. His demeanor changed. He became more confident. We were so stupid."

Though nothing was there, Jansen picked invisible fuzz off his knee. "I think Andrew was gone shortly after Cronus entered him. Usually, a demon possesses a person off and on over a long period. Partial possessions, like what happened with Amelia, or when I possessed Ellie. The body builds a tolerance to it. Cronus just sort of took up residence and evicted Andrew."

I didn't want to ask how long he might have survived. Given the way Jansen wouldn't meet my eyes, I felt the term "shortly" was used to lessen the impact.

Outside, a truck rumbled low. Its brakes squealed and its load clacked. Somewhere an engine revved.

I pressed my fingers to my temples. "Where are we, anyway?"

Jansen's arm tensed. "A friend's house. He won't be happy. We've kind of destroyed it."

Charlie kicked a foot over his knee and leaned back with his hands behind his head, elbows wide. "Damon's never happy, and he won't mind. But, yeah. Why here?"

"In hopes he'd be here, I guess. We needed help."

"Oh, man! We musta been in worse shape than I thought if you were willing to expose her to him."

"Regardless, we should get her home. I'll explain this mess to Damon later. El, your place or ours?"

"Yours." I wasn't okay enough to see my parents yet.

As a way to show he understood, he kissed the top of my head. Then, he wrapped me in his vast embrace, and the next thing I knew, I sat on the familiar gray couch of his family room, aglow with Miss Kate's candles.

"You're back!" She wiped her hands on a dish towel and

sprang at us from the kitchen. "Are you all okay?"

Jansen rested a hand on my knee as though he could make up for all the times he'd wanted to touch me but couldn't. "Yeah, Kate. It's all over now."

"All over? Did I hear you right?"

"You did. Come, have a seat with us. We've kind of already debriefed about it. We'll catch you up later."

A wide, prideful grin tugged at Charlie's mouth, the corners nearly touching his eyes. "Ellie killed him."

"Not completely." I felt the need to set the record straight. "You two blew him up."

Charlie kicked his feet out in front of himself, ankles crossed, reclining and taking me in. "Is that what you think? No. You did kill him. Kate, she separated and soared right through him like a dagger."

Hand at her chest, Kate plopped onto the couch, lurching it back an inch. "She did *what*? That's impossible."

Charlie shook his head. "You keep using that word wrong. She separated, so not impossible. We'll fill you in later. Cronus was dying a slow, agonizing death, and while that was okay with us, he spewed nonsense, and we weren't sure how long Ellie could be out of her body."

No, Kate wasn't buying it. Her head shook back and forth, disbelief etched on her face. "Her soul left her body. But that means—"

Jansen cut her off. "Eventually. Maybe let us figure that out? That's not the point right now."

Whatever the point was, Charlie inhaled, whistling through his teeth. "Anyway, Jansen and I finished him off, but she's the one who did it. We couldn't have done it without whatever it was she did."

Jansen gave my knee a squeeze. "I think perhaps it's because her spirit is pure, you know, not demonic. It pierced him like a weapon."

Miss Kate sat up straighter. "Well, I'm glad to hear it's over. I'm terribly sorry for my role in all this."

"Mom," Charlie said, and I believe it was the first time I'd ever heard him call her that. "Mother," yes, but never,

"Mom." "What you did was stupid beyond comprehension. You set all our lives on a collision course."

Jansen leaned forward with both elbows on his knees, casting his eyes low. "Possibly the lives of the whole world."

Charlie patted Kate's hand. "In the end, you did the right thing in all the best possible ways."

"How's that?" she asked, a tear streaming down her cheek.

"You raised two moral demons and gave us one powerful Ellie."

Monday came, and it felt like the first day of school again. Like the first day of my life. It was mid-January, and the sky wore its usual winter gray with low, fast-moving wisps of ashen clouds. The grass lay dormant, a kind of green-peppered, sandy carpet under the sepia and russet brown leaves that had fallen from the trees. Even the evergreens had dropped most of their needles, and those that remained were a dessert yellow, bordering on brown. The world outside reflected nothing but umber, beige, tan, and sepia-colored.

When I walked out the front door, I saw brilliant color. The average person may have seen brown, but I noticed the few green needles nestled within the evergreens and the sparse, but present, tufts of green grass scattered around the yard. Noticed the bright winter berries against Otis' fence. Noticed the vivid red cardinal sitting against the backdrop of a brown bush.

Most beautiful, though, Jansen leaned against his shiny black car. Had he waxed it? Or was it just that the entire world looked freshly waxed? He greeted me with open arms and pulled me into the warmth of his chest, where I breathed him in. He breathed in deeply as well.

"You smell so good," he said into my hair, his words filling me with joy. How often had I thought the same of him but kept it to myself these past long months? I belonged here, and as if he read my mind, he said, "You belong right here in my arms." His finger lifted my chin to his awaiting lips, and I collapsed, weak-kneed, into him. He chuckled and walked me to the passenger door, which he held open.

As he closed my door, I watched him. Tracked him as he strolled around the front, grinned as he smiled awkwardly, and didn't take my eyes off of him as he opened his door and slid into the driver's seat. He leaned between the seats, flashed his teeth, and drawing out the word, said, "Yes?"

"I'm sorry." I stared at my interlaced fingers.

He took my chin so I would look at him again. "Never apologize for loving me, please."

It was so easy to be with him. Nothing and everything had changed. "I'm sorry," I said again, an automatic response to which he gave me a disgruntled half-grin. "It's just… it's you… and it's me… and it's you *and* me. Aren't you nervous?"

"El, in my mind, it's been you and me since we were small. The difference," he said with a smile that widened as he paused, "is now I get to do this"—he leaned in and kissed my forehead—"and this"—he kissed my nose—"and this." He kissed my right eyelid. His lips grazed mine but didn't linger. I inhaled, anticipating the kiss, and felt disappointed when I didn't get it. "And this." He chuckled darkly as his lips found my neck, then my earlobe, then came within inches of my lips again. His eyes were pools of black, deep and rippling with sapphire lights.

I wanted him to kiss me full on the lips, but he tortured me. When I couldn't stand it any longer, I yanked his mouth to mine.

"You are impossible," I said into his mouth.

He groaned, a soft, rumbling sound, and took advantage of my parted lips. He brushed my tongue and claimed me with his. His kiss was hot cocoa and peppermint, and it heated the marrow of my bones. A shimmery power radiated from him, an energy I hadn't felt before.

When he broke away, I asked if he'd used that extra talent on me, the one involving lust.

His eyes twinkled. "No, and I never will. I love how you respond to me. Just me. That's all I need."

He started the car and pulled onto the road. It wasn't long before he interlaced his fingers with mine, and I realized this was the first time he held my hand this way. Not as the boy who led the girl, not to protect me, but to touch me. So, I caressed the wiry hairs on his hand, which caused a wicked shiver to run down his arm, to my amusement.

His skin felt deliciously warm when I kissed it. "I didn't know I had that effect on you."

"Oh, Ellie. I'm just glad I don't have to hide it anymore." He cleared his throat.

"Hey, what happened with your friend's place?"

"What, Damon? It's covered. That's all I'm telling you."

I'd been trying to get details about the elusive Damon, but with no luck. Damon was a demon, too. Or a half-demon, anyway. Of course he was. The brothers flat-out refused to let me meet him. Jansen just said, "We don't feel the need to expand your circle of demons." That had been that.

At a red light, he lurched into traffic. "I'm not at all looking forward to this morning."

My heart plunged. "Do you want to keep us a secret?"

Surprised, his head ticked back. "What? No!" His brow furrowed, and he gave my hand a gentle squeeze. "No, *that* I've been excited about our whole lives. Sharing what we have… Well, I did little last night but dream about parading you around on my arm. No, the thing I was talking about is that you and I have no classes together in the morning."

It seemed such a long time since we'd had classes together, I'd forgotten the routine. He would usually walk me to science, but then leave me until lunch.

After he pulled into a parking spot, he leaned over the seat divide. "One more thing before we go in. Damon made sure authorities discovered Andrew's body last night."

My breath caught in my throat.

He took my hand. "I wanted it to be fast so his parents wouldn't be in limbo. So they would know. The funeral will be on Thursday."

"How can you know that already?"

He hung his head and refused to look at me. So I pulled his chin up and made him meet my eyes. "Damon is taking care of the details. I asked him to ensure Andrew's family is cared for."

"But how?"

"Demon tricks. Tricks done for a good purpose, but demon tricks all the same. Doesn't bother him. It's handy having him around sometimes because he doesn't exactly mind manipulating situations. Charlie and I were raised to hide our powers. Damon, not so much. All you need to know is the funeral is Thursday, but as far as all our friends are concerned, we don't know anything yet. Not where he is or why he's not in school today. Think you can stick to that?"

I nodded, tears springing forward. "What will the story be? How will they say he died?"

"That's part of the demon manipulation. Charlie and I brought his body back and Damon moved Andrew's car into the river right here at home. Damon will convince the authorities who handle the case that he slid on a patch of ice and drove his car off the Market Street bridge. They'll tell his parents he died instantly." He placed his fingertips at my hairline, his hand glowing the subtlest shade of blue. "May I take care of that for you?"

I shook my head, but offered him a smile.

He completed the gesture anyway, first extinguishing the blue. "Ellie, we gave him a pseudo burial at the river. I want you to know that. Charlie and I said goodbye to him the best we knew how. We also removed his bomber jacket and placed it in his bedroom for his parents to find. I know it meant a lot to him."

"Thank you," I said, heaving in a gulp of air.

Jansen kissed each of my fingertips. "Are you okay to go inside?"

"Yes."

He angled closer for one last kiss before he eased away to whisper, "Don't move." With a slight tremble marring his usual confidence, he exited and raced around to my side. There he opened the door and beamed. "I'm enjoying these boyfriend things." He extended his hand. "Indulge me, won't you? It feels so very…"

"Human?"

"Yes. So very human."

I placed my hand in his and the warmth of it embraced me even before he folded me into a hug. "It feels so good to have you right here where you belong." The words were his, but I could have uttered them myself.

We walked hand in hand, me half a pace at his rear, hiding behind his shoulder. Not him, of course. He stood proud and carried a definite bounce in his step. This was perhaps the most striking difference, obvious to everyone we passed, that Jansen overflowed with delight. My cheeks burned from the attention as everybody around did double takes.

At first glance, we were just Jansen and Ellie, together as always, holding hands. A familiar sight. Only Jansen had never bounced or intertwined our fingers.

Then, quite without warning, a snarl built in his chest and his face fell. *"I hate reading their emotions sometimes."*

"What is it?"

"It appears they're misinterpreting my smile. I'm so sorry, El."

My cheeks burned hot. Is this what it was like for him, always seeing humans' reactions with alarming accuracy? Ah, the devious minds of teenagers.

In that moment, I knew I had a choice. I could hang my head in shame, which frankly would have confirmed their suspicions. Or I could play along.

Contrary to my usual self, I chose the latter and emerged from behind, no longer his shadow. I did a little dance around his steady, self-confident frame. I traced a line across his shoulder and over his chest, touching each separate inch of him. I made sure every eye followed my finger with envy as I circled. Then I halted in front of him, gave him my best sultry smile, and a beckoning finger-wiggle. He bowed low. Crushed his lips into mine. Then, hand in hand, the two of us strutted into the building.

"You realize your reputation is officially shot."

"The devil may care"—I poked a fingertip into his chest —"but *I* do not."

A groan rumbled in my head. Oh, wow. Projected groans ignited shivers down the entire length of my spine.

"This devil *does* care," he said, "but I'm elated that you do not."

Our hallway was already filled with choir friends. Mark rested cozily up against Gretta, Tyler close to Amelia. What was Aaron doing? He seemed busy making spit wads or something of the sort, and Tim carefully tied Aaron's shoelaces together without his noticing. Even Clara sat there, sulking and glaring.

Jansen took a seat on the ground and positioned himself cross-legged before he placed his hands on my hips and pulled me into his lap. There, he wrapped his arms around me in a tight, couples-embrace. It made me laugh, this sudden display of affection. His good humor met with stares and gawks, everyone probably wondering why the change. My head fell back on his shoulder, and he kissed my neck.

Gretta peered over large-rimmed glasses. "Did something happen with you two?"

Her question made Jansen grin. He actually grinned. "I couldn't stay away from Ellie another day. You all know I've loved her my entire life, and I thought it was time she knew about it." It was as good as a diatribe coming from him. They usually heard little more than "no" out of him.

Smacking Mark's shoulder, Gretta said, "I knew it! No two 'friends' are as close as the two of you were. God, Ellie, you were so clueless."

Jansen gave me a gentle squeeze. "It did take her a while to come around, I must say."

One Saturday afternoon a few weeks later, I plucked strings on my guitar while Charlie and Jansen invented silly duets to sing along to whatever melody fell from my fingers. After a particularly playful tune that reached a nonsensical climax about blazing popcorn, they tossed dull fireballs back and forth with an effect that made it look like juggling.

Their lighthearted banter reminded me of the change between Jansen and our friends at school, so I asked him about it.

"Oh, Ellie, you can't guess?"

"I really can't." I leaned over my guitar, sipping the water beside me.

With a blush, he snorted. "We've already established that I've loved you my entire life, right?"

"Yes," I said.

"And that I can read emotions quite well."

"Right."

"High school is rough. It seems everybody is lusting after, well, everyone quite frankly, but it's bothersome when directed at either of us. You have no idea what it's like to see everyone's desires, knowing what the guys feel, dream…and scheme about you. Knowing also that you weren't ready for any of it. You turned everyone down."

"Not everyone," I said sheepishly.

"No." He smirked. "Not everyone. When you *were* dating, well, that was pure hell. Guys have one thing on their minds. Remember your pool party when I dove at Tim? When he wouldn't let you go? He glowed red with your skin up against his, and I couldn't take it anymore. There was a reason I asked you to put that cover-up on. The backyard blazed red."

"Lust?"

"That's right. It's the color that dominates when physical cravings are present. If red is prominent, there isn't any love."

"Okay, but it didn't mean anything. No love, right?"

"Right, but…" Jansen sighed. "I don't deal with it well."

Charlie clapped him on the shoulder. "It makes him a bit green."

Jansen hooked his thumbs in his pockets. "I have to either put up with lust directed at me, or—"

"Poor baby," I said and received another wicked grin, this time from Jansen.

"Or I have to endure lust toward you, and let me tell you

something. The emotions that emit from men are rather more elaborate and far more frequent."

I cleared my throat, still recovering from the water that had gone down the wrong pipe. "So, you didn't like them thinking about us that way."

"It wasn't so much that. The girls I could handle. I didn't care what they thought. It's just that each time a guy looked at you, it made me insanely jealous, always on my guard, wondering which of them would steal you away from me next. And nothing could be done about it. I'd have to grin and endure another one of your boyfriends."

"That explains your ire toward the guys, but what about the girls?"

"Am I that unpleasant?"

Charlie whistled a long, descending arch.

It made me have to suppress a smile. "You could be kinder. Maybe converse a bit more than you do."

"What can I say? You've seen it. I take no joy in the way they ogle me."

"You always seemed to like Amelia well enough."

"Mia is a special girl." Charlie winked.

"A while back, before she stabbed me—boy, there's a sentence starter." I sipped my water and started again. "Anyway, Amelia said my aura glistened. Did you know she could see auras?"

Charlie looked shocked.

I shrugged. "She told me she can."

"No. I mean, I did know that, yes. We've talked. I'm surprised she told you."

"She isn't like you two, is she?"

"Amelia?" he asked. "No. She's not supernatural or anything. She has a quiet spirit. Feels things deeply. She's one of the precious few who looks into a man's mind, into his soul, before deciding if she's interested in him. Only then does she notice his physique. She's never had more than a mild red glow toward anyone, including Tyler. Even her blue is tentative. I enjoy watching her aura quite a bit."

A few days later, I found Charlie gazing out my bedroom window with the same expression Amelia had captured in her pencil sketch of Jansen as he gazed at me. That same look of utter contentment in Charlie's eyes. I glanced out the neighboring window to see what caught his attention.

A girl with sun-bronzed hair walked toward her car wearing all black, from her oversized button-down tunic to her ankle boots fitted snugly over her skinny jeans. On her head, she wore a Fedora.

Acknowledgements

Thank you so much for reading Woven Souls!
Jansen and Ellie's story continues in Rapt Souls - Book II

Please consider leaving a review of Woven Souls at Amazon.com and Goodreads.com. Reviews mean everything to authors. Your efforts are appreciated!

A very special thanks to the humans in my life who made this dream a reality.

Kelli, my Beta reader, my unofficial developmental editor, my cover-designer. My friend. Your honest feedback makes me a better writer.

Mary, who encourages me to be my best self and without whose help I wouldn't have this updated version—I can't thank you enough.

My husband for being my original inspiration.

My niece, who first encouraged me to publish.

My superfans: Aundria, Carrie, Jennifer, and Laura. You guys keep me going.

If you'd like to learn more about my upcoming work, please follow me on:
Kris Leigh - Facebook
Kris Leigh's Wordcraft Whispers - WWW.krisleigh.com

Biography

KRIS LEIGH is a full-time Speech Language Pathologist from Troy, Ohio, who currently lives in the Cincinnati area with her high school sweetheart, whom she later married. When she isn't writing, she enjoys spending time with her two adult sons, knitting, crocheting, or curled up with a good book, her dog, and a warm blanket. Woven Souls is her first novel.